D0394988

THE DRAGONS OF WINTER

THE CHRONICLES OF THE IMAGINARIUM GEOGRAPHICA

THE DRAGONS OF WINTER

Written and illustrated by

James A. Owen

SIMON & SCHUSTER BFYR

NEW YORK LONDON TORONTO SYDNEY NEW DELHI

For John Munden

SIMON & SCHUSTER BFYR

An imprint of Simon & Schuster Children's Publishing Division

1230 Avenue of the Americas, New York, New York 10020

SIMON & SCHUSTER BFYR is a trademark of Simon & Schuster, Inc.

For information about special discounts for bulk purchases, please contact Simon & Schuster
Special Sales at 1-866-506-1949 or business@simonandschuster.com.

The Simon & Schuster Speakers Bureau can bring authors to your live event.

For more information or to book an event, contact the Simon & Schuster Speakers Bureau
at 1-866-248-3049 or visit our website at www.simonspeakers.com.

Book design by Christopher Grassi and James A. Owen

The text for this book is set in Adobe Jenson Pro.

Manufactured in the United States of America

2 4 6 8 10 9 7 5 3 1

Library of Congress Cataloging-in-Publication Data

Owen, James A.

The dragons of winter / written and illustrated by James A. Owen. — 1st ed.

p. cm. — (The chronicles of the Imaginarium Geographica ; [6])

Summary: With the Archipelago of Dreams in the hands of the Echthroi and the link to the
Summer Country lost, the Grail Child, Rose Dyson; the new Cartographer, Edmund McGee;
and the Caretakers Emeritus seek to rebuild the Keep of Time, but face a terrible new enemy
who was once an ally.

ISBN 978-1-4424-1223-1 (hardcover)

[1. Time travel—Fiction. 2. Characters in literature—Fiction. 3. Fantasy.] I. Title.

PZ7.O97124Ds 2012

[Fic]—dc23

2011034891

ISBN 978-1-4424-1225-5 (eBook)

FIRST EDITION

Contents

List of Illustrations

Acknowledgments

Every successful creative venture is in some way a collaboration, and that's more true of books than almost anything else I can think of (with the possible exception of big-budget films). I could produce a book entirely on my own, and the result would probably be pretty good—but to produce a work of great quality requires the help of many hands and the labor of many minds, and without all of the people who have helped me with this book it would be a far lesser work of quality than it is.

Valerie Shea, our intrepid copyeditor, never fails to astonish me with her efforts on these books. I quite honestly do not understand how her mind works in the way it does. By the time the manuscript gets to her, my editors and I have gone through the pages several times—yet she always, *always* manages to find a hundred ways to improve the clarity and intent of my writing. On a technical level she's flawless and, frankly, a bit intimidating. But at the end of the process, I find I am grateful for her and her work, and I'm very glad she is as good at her job as she is.

Jeremy Owen is my alpha beta reader. He is the first person to see every drawing as I sketch it, and the first person to listen as I work out difficult scenes. Because he manages the Coppervale

Studio, he's always present as I create the books—but he also has a more active hand in how the work is developed than anyone else. Visually, he is responsible for the clarity and authenticity of almost everything in the illustrations. He finds all of the reference I ask for, pencils in details, and often revises layouts to help make sure they come out just as we intended. He also takes care of the myriad little details of operating the studio, which allows me to focus on the work itself. I literally could not create these books without him.

Navah Wolfe remains my best reader. Her suggestions have more than once transformed the nature of an entire book, the direction of a storyline, and the choices of the characters—and in doing so she has reshaped the series itself, for which I am very, very thankful. David Gale remains the driving force behind our efforts. He is my ideal editor, and I consider his insightful decision to take on this series as the best thing that has happened in my career.

Jenica Nasworthy, Laurent Linn, Paul Crichton, and Siena Koncsol have been invaluable in making sure this book reads well and looks even better, and that people know where to get it. I work better because I know they have my back. Jon Anderson and Justin Chanda have been incredibly supportive on the publishing end, and I sleep better because I know they have my back too.

My attorney, Craig Emanuel, is, in a word, steadfast. He and my manager, Julie Kane-Ritsch at the Gotham Group, have consistently looked after the business end of things with heart and dedication. My friends Brett, Daanon, and Shannon have looked out for me personally in ways large and small, and sometimes in ways I didn't know I needed until they were there, offering to help, to support, or just to listen. And my family, Cindy, Sophie, and Nathaniel, are the reasons I do what I do—but without all of these people, I would not do it nearly as well. I am grateful for them all.

Prologue

Pulling his trench coat tighter against the cold drizzle of the Northampton rain, the Zen Detective sighed and checked his watch. His appointment was late, as usual. He wondered how people who seemed to spend half their lives consulting their watches could ever be late for anything.

Their watches were not like his, which was a Swiss-made, gold-plated chronograph with a pleasant little chime that played Rachmaninoff on the hour and half hour. The watches carried by his clients were less like watches and more like magic devices that could do anything asked of them. He had witnessed the watches being spoken to, as if they operated as a sort of two-way radio. Once, he saw a watch actually project an image of a creature that was all but tangible. And then there seemed to be their most frequent use, which was enabling the bearer to disappear into thin air. All of which shouldn't have detracted from their ability to keep good time, which was why he wondered how his clients always seemed to be running late.

He was still wondering when the trio of gentlemen appeared behind him, silent as a whisper. "Hello, Aristophanes," one of them said softly. "Well met."

"Hades!" the detective exclaimed under his breath, half in shock and half in relief. "I hate when you do that. And I told you—I'd prefer to be called Steve, if you don't mind."

The three men ignored his remark and simply stood there, waiting. It was annoying, the way they played these childish games that seemed to do little more than test his patience. Still, he could ill afford to lose their business. Work in his profession was scarce enough to come by as it was, never mind the fact that his being just a shade lighter than purple, as well as being a Homo sapiens unicorn, always complicated client relations. Even when he wore a trench coat with his collar up and kept the horn on his forehead filed down, just taking a meeting was risky.

Finally the Zen Detective broke the silence. "Well?" he said gruffly. "You wanted to hire me?"

"Yes," one of the men said. "You know of the Caretakers, correct?"

The detective nodded. "They're the ones with that book," he said. "That bloody big atlas, or whatever it is."

"Indeed," said the speaker. "You've worked for them before, I believe."

"Just the Frenchman, and only now and again," came the reply. "Why?"

"They're going to want to hire you again," the second man said. "They will want you to find something . . . special. We simply want you to take the job. And to succeed."

The Zen Detective peered at them. Easy job requests got his hackles up, as well as his radar for a scam. "Is that it? Just take someone else's job? That's all you want me to do?"

"There is one other matter we'd like you to deal with, Aristophanes," the second speaker said. He moved closer to the Zen Detective and spoke softly into the other's ear. The detective's eyes grew wide, and against his will his mouth flew open as he uttered a loud, particularly vulgar curse.

"You can't be serious!" he said in disbelief, stepping back and looking at each of the three men in turn.

As before, none of the men replied, but simply stared impassively back at him.

Each time the three men had hired the Zen Detective, he always had the unnerving impression that they were not the same three men as the time before, even though they appeared to look almost alike.

No, he thought—exactly alike.

"There are only eleven personages still walking the Earth who knew, firsthand, those who were driven from Eden," the first speaker finally said. "Only thirteen more who were alive before the Flood, and fewer than a hundred who have memories of the Inversion that occurred when the Erl-King was born in Bethlehem.

"You live among a very privileged group, Aristophanes," he continued, and the tone made the statement more a threat than a compliment. "Don't give anyone cause to lessen that number. You are too valuable to lose."

The Zen Detective looked up sharply. "Better men, and greater beasts, than you have tried. Killing me is harder than you think, and if you doubt my words, you're welcome to try."

"I didn't say we'd try to kill you," the speaker replied, "I said you were too valuable to lose. And you should know that death is always preferable to exile."

Aristophanes held the speaker's gaze for a long moment, then dropped his eyes and nodded once, then again. "Immortality," he muttered, more to himself than the others. "It's a mug's game."

"No one lives forever, Aristophanes," the shadowy figure said as he twirled the dials on his black watch and disappeared. "Not even Caretakers of the Imaginarium Geographica."

PART ONE

The War of the Caretakers

The girls were evenly matched, and fought to a draw . . .

CHAPTER ONE
The Mission

✦

"*It's amazing how productive* dead writers can be," John commented to Jack as he scanned the shelves in the great library at Tamerlane House. "Some of our colleagues have been more productive after their natural lives than they were beforehand."

"I would chance a guess that having died brings a lot of focus and clarity to one's goals," Jack ventured. "Not that I'm planning on testing that myself any time soon."

"Take a look at this," John said, removing a fat volume bound in bright red leather and handing it to his friend. "It's Hawthorne's book *Septimius Felton*. I never realized he'd finished it."

"Finished it, and written a sequel," a familiar voice answered. The two men turned to see their friend Charles at the door, nodding enthusiastically as he strode into the room, arms outstretched. "He's having a bit of trouble with the third one, though. Twain and I are helping him work through it."

John's self-control was such that he managed to bite his tongue before blurting out what he wanted to say, but Jack was startled enough by Charles's appearance that he actually dropped the book he was holding.

"Charles!" Jack sputtered. "Your hair . . . it's—it's—"

"Purple," said John.

"Burgundy, actually," Charles said, preening slightly. "Rose helped me color it. Isn't it striking?"

"It's purple," Jack said, still staring openmouthed as he bent to pick up the book. "Whatever possessed you, Charles? That's hardly a becoming color for an editor."

"Possibly," said Charles, "but it's also the exact shade of burgundy as Queen Victoria's throne. I have it on good authority. And besides, I'm not really just an editor anymore, am I? More of a soldier of fortune."

Jack and John traded disbelieving glances, and the latter asked, "So, ah, who told you that was the color of Victoria's throne?"

"Geoffrey Chaucer."

"Mmm," John hummed. "I see."

It was traditional, in the old-fraternal-order sort of way, for the Caretakers Emeriti to prank the newer members of their secret society. The problem was that every time John, Jack, and Charles had been present at Tamerlane House, it had been in a crisis situation, and there was no time or inclination for tomfoolery. But now that Charles was a full-time resident, John suspected that the Elder Caretakers—specifically Chaucer—were having a bit of fun.

"Rose helped me do it," Charles said again as he ran a hand through his full head of hair. "She changes hers on a weekly basis."

"I'd noticed," said John, "but she's still a teenager, and you're . . ."

"Dead," Charles said. "But still optimistic about the future."

Jack laughed, and both he and John shook Charles's hands. "Fair enough," John said. "We're always happy to see you, old fellow."

The friends had gotten accustomed to having easy access to

Tamerlane House through the use of Shakespeare's Bridge in the garden at the Kilns. Despite the pain they all still felt over the loss of the Archipelago, it was a comfort to be able to simply cross over and be in the company of the other Caretakers, and thus remind themselves of the value of the work they had done—and the work they still had to do.

Jack was busying himself with preparations for the eventual establishment of a reborn Imperial Cartological Society, including Apprentice and Associate Caretaker programs. It would have to remain an underground project until the Caretakers were truly ready to make it more public, but he and John had already begun actively recruiting the next generations of Caretakers, and were deliberately making it more of a global endeavor than it had been under Verne.

"I see you've found Nathaniel's book," a voice whined from the doorway. It was Lord Byron, a disgraced Caretaker who was tolerated only reluctantly by the rest of them because of Poe's insistence that he be included. "It isn't as good as he thinks it is, you know. It was better when it was unfinished."

"Say, George," Jack said, turning to address Byron, whose real name was George Gordon. "I noticed that there's nothing new in your section of the library. Has inspiration finally failed you?"

"Hardly," Byron sniffed. "I have more inspiration in my little toe than you have in your whole body. I don't need to write to demonstrate that—my life is my art."

"You're dead, you idiot," said Sir James Barrie as he entered the room, accompanied by Charles's apprentice Caretaker, the badger Fred.

"Death is but a new adventure . . . ," Byron began before the others' laughter cut him off. "What?" he said, a blush rising in his cheeks. "What's funny about that?"

"I'm sorry, George," Jack said, giving the poet's shoulder an appreciative squeeze. "All I meant was that I've often wondered why someone of your talent never applied it to some grand epic, or an ongoing work of proportions worthy of your ability. That's all."

"Oh," said Byron, who wasn't certain whether that was actually an apology. "I simply never found the right tale for that kind of treatment."

"I thought Bert might be with you," John said, shaking Barrie's hand. "Does he know we're here?"

"I couldn't say," Barrie answered. "He's been keeping to himself lately, but I'm sure he'll be along shortly. The war council was his idea."

As the Caretakers talked, Fred maintained a respectful distance and kept his opinions to himself. Technically speaking, an apprentice Caretaker had all the standing of a full Caretaker, especially among those at Tamerlane House. But Fred was still a little uncertain about his own position, considering his predecessor was technically deceased. Charles was himself still considered a Caretaker, but a Caretaker Emeritus. He was, like Verne and Kipling, a *tulpa*—a near-immortal, youthful, new body housing an old soul. And unlike the majority of the other Caretakers, who were portraits in Tamerlane, and who could leave the frames for only one week, he could go almost anywhere—as long as it wasn't somewhere he'd been known when he was alive.

To the animals, dead was dead, and while they tolerated the portraits, none of them—especially the badgers—could quite accept the tulpas. It was something about their smell, Fred once said to Jack—there was none. Tulpas gave off no odor at all. And to an animal, who determines friend or enemy, truth or lies, based on smell—that made the whole idea completely suspect.

Still, he was sworn to serve the Caretakers, as were his father and grandfather before him, and of them all, Charles had the strongest bond to the badgers. So Fred was cheerfully stoic. Mostly.

"You could do as John is doing," Jack continued, "and base a great work on stories of the Archipelago."

"I learned my lesson about that ages ago," Byron grumbled. "They set fire to me, remember? And that was just on general principles. I'd hate to see what the others would do to me if I broke one of the cardinal rules of the Archipelago."

"Others have done it before me," said John. "Most of them, actually. And as long as the stories or characters are disguised or altered, and no secrets of the Archipelago are revealed, it isn't really a problem."

"Technically speaking," said Charles, "you aren't revealing any secrets about the Archipelago, because there's nothing left to keep any secrets about."

"Believing is seeing," Fred murmured in a low voice. "Believing is seeing, Scowler . . . Charles." He twitched his whiskers as if he were about to say something more, then turned abruptly and scurried out of the room, closing the door behind him.

"Ah, me," Charles said, sighing. "I've put my foot in it again, haven't I?"

"No argument there," said Jack.

"You'd think finding his father was really alive, and not lost with the rest of the Archipelago, would have cheered him somewhat," said Barrie, "but he can't push past the loss of every-thing else, I fear."

"It was his world," said John. "And it's gone. You can't fault the little fellow for feeling as he does."

Charles sighed heavily. "No," he said. "No, we can't. But I wish it were at least easier for him to accept that I'm, well, me. Myself."

"Remember, Charles," said Barrie. "All good things happen . . . " ". . . in time."

There was a knock at the door. Percy Shelley opened it and stepped into the room. He scowled at Byron, then regained his composure and faced the other Caretakers. "Gentlemen," he said, gesturing back down the hall. "Summon the others to the meeting room, if you please. The war council will begin within the hour."

Charles led his companions to the inner courtyard of the house, where Sir Richard Burton and the Valkyrie called Laura Glue were instructing Nathaniel Hawthorne, Mark Twain, and Rose Dyson in the ancient art of the samurai sword.

Each held a *katana* about three feet long and was in a stance of readiness. The girls faced each other, while Burton faced both of the other men. He barked a command, and all of them erupted in a flurry of shouts and clashing metal.

"I never caught the knack of it," Charles said over the din. "I'd land a good blow with one of the wooden practice swords, then pause to apologize to my opponent and allow him to regain his footing. It's an honorable discipline, but it really doesn't mesh well with gentlemanly chivalry."

The girls were evenly matched, and fought to a draw—but after handily disarming Hawthorne, Burton found himself driven to his knees by Twain, who finally relented when he realized they had an audience.

The combatants turned to face their visitors, and John was struck by how Rose seemed to have changed since his last visit. There, in battle gear, with newly colored blue hair and holding a sword, she seemed to have grown older overnight, and for a moment he felt a wistfulness for the child she had been when they first met. But then again, he reminded himself, she had never truly been a child—something for which he felt honest regret.

"Uncle John! Uncle Jack! Uncle Charles!" Rose exclaimed as she tossed away her sword and jumped across the lawn to hug and kiss the three companions. "I didn't know you were here!"

Laura Glue also went to greet the Caretakers, but only after retrieving Rose's sword. "I told you," she said, glaring at the other girl as she hugged Jack, "never drop your sword. It must be a part of you."

"Something Samuel here has learned too well," Burton said as he dusted off his trousers and rose to his feet. He glowered at Twain as they greeted the others.

"He may look older than the rest of you," Burton said to John, "but he's really full of—"

"Spirit," Twain said, winking at John. "I'm full of so much spirit it just spills out of me."

"Percy asked us to fetch you," said Charles. "It's almost time for the council."

"All right," Burton said, handing his *katana* to Hawthorne. "We'll just pick up the lesson another time. Maybe next time you can fight Laura Glue, Caretaker."

"Thank you, no," said Hawthorne. "She's better than *you* are."

John pulled Twain aside as the others gathered their weapons together. "Where is Bert?" he asked, concerned. "He's usually first to greet us, and we were expecting to have seen him well before now."

A look of concern mixed with worry crossed the older Caretaker's features as he gestured at the three of them. "Come with me," he said, turning down one of the corridors. "There's something you need to see."

As the others went to the room where the war council was to be held, Twain led John, Jack, Charles, and Rose to a large screening room. It was darkened, save for the light coming from the projector in the center of the room.

"Is that . . . ?" John asked, staring at the projection in astonishment.

"Yes," Twain answered. "That's the film you brought back from the Archipelago."

The reel had been created by Bert's daughter, Aven, and left in the ruined palace on Paralon for the Caretakers to find—but neither they nor she had expected it would be two thousand years of Archipelago time before that would happen. Two millennia, during which Aven had lain in a deathless sleep. Most of those centuries were spent in a rarely interrupted hibernation inside a bed of crystal; but before that, she had ensured that there would be a way for her friends to find out what had happened, as well as a means to try to make things right, via the film Bert was now watching.

They'd been able to speak to the projected image when they found it, but now it was simply a recorded memory of the friend who never lost hope that they would come—and who paid the ultimate price to do so.

"It's a rare day that goes by," Twain said, his voice low, "that he hasn't watched it through at least once. More commonly, he watches it several times at a sitting. Then he goes back to his work as if he hadn't a trouble in the world."

Bert's daughter had been a reluctant queen of the Silver Throne of Paralon. She much preferred her life as a dashing buccaneer and captain of the *Indigo Dragon*, and after her marriage to King Artus, did her level best to maintain that life, even as she kept an eye to her responsibilities on Paralon. But then Artus was killed in the conflict with the Shadow King, and suddenly the entire Archipelago was looking toward Aven to lead. And lead she did, right up to the moment the Keep of Time fell—and then for two thousand years after.

The companions were at a loss as to what they could say to console the old Caretaker. Of all that they had lost in their many conflicts, John thought, it was their mentor who had paid the dearest price. And it was a loss that could not be mended.

Bert finally noticed the group at the door and quickly reached out to shut off the projector. The image of Aven vanished abruptly from the screen, and the room darkened to twilight. "Ah, I'm sorry," he said, wiping at the tears on his face. "I didn't realize you were there. Just, ah . . ."

"We know," John said gently. "It's all right, Bert."

"How far can I go?" Rose asked abruptly. She was looking at Bert as she spoke. "With Edmund's help, how far in time can I travel?"

The others looked confused, but Twain realized what she was asking, if not entirely why.

"It would be my wager," Twain said, puffing on his cigar, "that young Rose here, with assistance from our new Cartographer, could go anywhere—anywhen—she chose. Isn't that correct, Bert?"

"Yes," Bert replied, looking back at Rose. "At least, that is our hope. That's what we've been working toward, after all," he continued, "finding a way to go far enough back to rebuild the Keep of Time. That will be your mission, and the reason I've called the war council. It's time. And you're ready, I think."

"That may be the primary mission, but it doesn't have to be the only one," Rose said. "Before we can attempt to go back into Deep Time, we'll have to go forward into the future anyway, right?"

"Farther than *almost* anyone has ever been," Twain agreed, nodding as he ushered the others out of the room, "to one of the only zero points we have recorded that distantly in the future. About eight thousand centuries, wasn't it, Bert?"

The old man didn't answer, but his bottom lip quivered, and his eyes started to well with tears. "Rose," he began, "I've never asked you to—"

She stepped closer to him, taking his hands in hers, and shook her head. "You don't need to ask," she said, smiling. "Of course we're going to try—as I said, we have to go there anyway."

"You've lost me," said Charles, scratching his head. "Where are you going?"

"Weena," Rose answered. "We're going to go find Weena."

CHAPTER TWO
The Bungled Burglary

As the companions made their way through the labyrinth of rooms and hallways that comprised the upper floors of Tamerlane House, Bert chatted happily with Jack and Charles, as if nothing significant had just taken place. But John knew that Rose's suggestion was incredibly significant—and that she must have been thinking about it for a very long time.

It was an open secret among the Caretakers that Bert himself was the very time traveler he had written about in *The Time Machine*, and that the woman he met there, called Weena, bore him their daughter, Aven. But what was not discussed so openly was the fact that after Bert returned to visit the Summer Country in his own time, to show his daughter the world he had come from, he had never found a way to get back to the future. Weena had been lost to him—and not even Poe himself had conceived of a way to go back to the far future. But Rose and Edmund, together, could do just that.

"Can she really do it?" John whispered to Twain, out of earshot of the others. "Do you really believe it's possible?"

"Bert thinks she is ready," Twain answered. "And I believe our war council will concur. Rose is, for all her unique experiences,

He was hooded, but his face was clearly visible . . .

still a youth. And she's made her share of youthful mistakes. But she has learned from them, John. And she would not have said what she did to Bert if there were a doubt in her head that she and Edmund could do this."

As he spoke, they rounded a corner to the Cartographer's Lair that had been set up by young Edmund McGee. There were maps and diagrams scattered around the main room, which was decorated in accordance with Edmund's late-eighteenth-century upbringing, but the space was dominated by a large construct that stood in the center of the room. The Cartographer was standing amid the tangle of rods and wires, making some sort of adjustment to the mechanism, when he looked up and saw his visitors.

"It's a tesseract," he said, answering the question that was on all their minds. "Diagramming the different trips through time and space that Rose and I have been experimenting with on paper was becoming too tedious, so I thought I'd try to build a working model of it all instead."

"Impressive," said Jack. "How's it coming?"

"It's been a struggle, I'll admit," Edmund said as he stepped gingerly out of the tesseract, "but a few of the new apprentice Caretakers—especially the young woman, Madeleine—have been very helpful."

He shook hands with each of the Caretakers in turn. "I take it you've come because of the burglary?"

"Burglary?" John said, surprised. "I hadn't been told anything about a burglary. We were summoned to a council of war."

"It's all part and parcel of the same thing," Edmund said as they stepped out of his lair and back into the corridor. "A number of things at Tamerlane House have come up missing—and my great-grandfather's maps were almost among them."

He pointed at the door as he closed it behind them. The handles were tied together with string, and the locks had been pried out entirely.

"Nothing else was touched," he explained, "but the maps were scattered around on the floor. If Archimedes hadn't been rooting around in the rafters where he could hear the intruder, they might have gotten them, too."

"Hmm," said John. "That's quite unthinkable, to invade Tamerlane House! Those maps must be more important to someone than we realized."

"They are important to me," said Edmund, "and they have some historical significance, I suppose, since they were drawn by my great-grandfather. But I don't know what use they'd be to anyone else—not so as to make them worth stealing."

"I agree," said John. "If anything, I would have thought it was all your own more recent maps that were most valuable."

"That's true," Twain said. "They probably are more valuable—but only to those who can use them. And as far as we know, there are only two groups on Earth who have the ability to travel in time."

John sighed heavily and nodded in agreement. When the Keep of Time fell completely, the connection between Chronos time, which was real, day-to-day clock time, and Kairos time, which was pure, almost imaginary time, was completely severed. This had several effects on both the Archipelago and the Caretakers. In the Archipelago, time fell out of sync with the Summer Country, and it began to speed up until thousands of years had passed, destroying anything familiar that was left there. It was only because of Aven's sacrifice, and her willingness to stay behind, that the Caretakers learned that somehow, the great Dragon Samaranth had taken the rest of the Archipelago someplace beyond the world itself. Someplace where it could be safe, until the Caretakers figured out how to restore the proper flow of time.

Unfortunately, the fall of the keep had also handicapped the Caretakers, rendering their Anabasis Machines, their time-traveling watches, almost useless. The doors of the keep had created focal points, called zero points by the Caretakers, that allowed them to align and utilize their watches. But when the keep was lost, so were all the reference points—and one of their own, a Messenger named Hank Morgan, paid the ultimate price to learn the truth.

It was only with the discovery of the McGee family, and particularly young Edmund, that the Caretakers found that time could be mapped; new zero points could be created. And with the help of Rose, Edmund could reestablish the Caretakers' ability to traverse time at will. But according to Edmund, none of those maps, which he kept in a book he called the *Imaginarium Chronographica*, had been touched. Only the maps made by his great-grandfather, Elijah McGee, had been disturbed, and those only depicted a handful of places in the Summer Country.

"I guess we'll find out soon enough," Twain said as he threw open the doors to the great hall where the war council was to take place. "It's time."

In the year since the fall of the Archipelago, the last vestiges of World War II had drawn to a close—but the War of the Caretakers had barely begun. It was a passive war, fought in small skirmishes on the outskirts of history, but that fact made it no less a war, nor its effects any less potent.

It was a war of ideas, and the battlefields were the smoke-filled taverns, and libraries, and stages, where stories were whispered with an urgency that gave them the ring of truth. Stories that were believed more and more as time passed. And that belief was what allowed the darkness in the shadowed corners to creep closer and closer, crowding out the light.

For many years the Caretakers had believed their greatest enemy was the one called the Winter King, and more than once they fought and defeated aspects of him. But his rise to prominence had been fostered by a coalition of rogue Caretakers who formed the original Imperial Cartological Society, which had even darker goals than establishing the Winter King. Many members of the Society, including Richard Burton, Harry Houdini, and Arthur Conan Doyle, realized that a greater evil had permeated their group, and so they left, defecting back to the Caretakers. But that evil, which had formerly operated in secret, was now becoming bolder and bolder. And in the last year, the Caretakers were finally able to give it a name: Echthroi—the primordial Shadows. The original Darkness. And through the Lloigor, corrupted agents recruited by the Echthroi, they had taken over the Archipelago—and now threatened the Summer Country.

A war of stories was still a war—even if the only ones who knew it was being fought were a group of storytellers, gathered together in the house of Edgar Allan Poe.

The Caretakers took their customary seats around the great table. At the head sat Geoffrey Chaucer, who, as an Elder Caretaker, often presided over their meetings. The other Elders, including Edmund Spenser and Leonardo da Vinci, took their seats to his left and right, with the younger Caretakers seated at the far end. The other guests of the house who were not Caretakers, such as Edmund McGee, Laura Glue, Rose, and the clockwork owl Archimedes, took up positions along the walls where they could watch and, when invited, participate.

Rudyard Kipling, away on assignment for Jules Verne, attended the council via trump, as he usually did. Being one of the only other Caretakers who was actually a tulpa gave him exceptional freedom to travel with none of the constraints the others had, and so he was their de facto eyes and ears in the world.

Burton leaned close to John. "What happened to Charles's head?" he whispered. "He looks as if he's been dipped in a boudoir."

"He colored it burgundy," John whispered back, "because Chaucer told him that was the exact color of Queen Victoria's throne."

Burton's brow furrowed in puzzlement. "But it wasn't . . . Ah," he said, as the realization dawned and a smile spread across his face. "Geoff's having a bit of fun, I think."

"Probably," said John.

Chaucer saw the two men conversing, and sussed out what subject they were discussing from their covert glances at Charles. He gave them a quick wink and a grin before shifting his expression to a solemn one and rapping on the table to bring the meeting to order.

"As the current Caretakers have joined us," Chaucer said with a nod to John, Jack, and Fred, which thrilled the little badger immeasurably, "we may now begin this council of war." He paused and looked around the table—one seat at the opposite end was empty. "Where is the Prime Caretaker?"

"He's, ah, indisposed at the moment," Bert said suddenly. "I'm sure Jules will be here as quickly as he can manage."

"Ah," Chaucer said in understanding. "He's with his goats again, isn't he?"

"This is behavior unbecoming of a Caretaker," da Vinci sniffed. "Especially for the Prime Caretaker."

"Oh, be quiet," Charles Dickens said, scowling at da Vinci. "This has been a difficult time for all of us, and each of us needs a way to blow off some steam before our boilers explode. Give the man his goats."

"I agree," said Spenser. "After all, Samuel there has his butter-fly collection, and Dumas loves to cook."

"True," said Alexandre Dumas. "And Tycho over there steals things."

"I do not!" said Tycho Brahe. "You can't prove that I do!"

"Tycho, my young moron," said Twain. "We live on an island. Everyone knows you stash the evidence of your crimes in the north boathouse. Nathaniel gathers it all up and replaces every-thing each Thursday."

"Oh," Brahe said, crestfallen. "Uh, thanks for that, Nathaniel."

"My pleasure," said Hawthorne. "It's easier than cleaning up after the things George Gordon, our Lord Byron, does to de-stress."

"I resent that," said Byron.

John, Jack, and Charles had long become accustomed to the fact that a meeting of the Caretakers Emeriti never went straight to the business at hand. There was always a breaking-in period when the various personalities traded brickbats with one another until things finally settled down enough to discuss the real issues.

"Who is the fellow in the west alcove?" Jack whispered to Charles as the other Caretakers continued to argue. "I don't recognize him. Is he one of Burton's people?"

Charles and John glanced up to where Jack was looking. There, some ways back in the alcove, but still near enough to comfortably observe the whole room, was a man in a sand-colored cloak. He was hooded, but his face was clearly visible, and he had taken note of the fact he was being observed.

"Well, don't look right at him!" Jack said, blushing.

"It's all right," Charles said, grinning. "He isn't one of Burton's. He's one of Verne's. That's one of the Messengers—Dr. Raven, I believe."

"A Messenger," Jack said, now glancing back up against his own will. "Interesting. I thought Jules usually had them traipsing about on errands."

"Apparently he thought this was worth sitting in on," said Charles, "although I must admit, it is a bit unusual."

"Unusual?" John said. "I should say so. This is the Caretakers' war council. Outside of Laura Glue, Edmund, Rose, Archimedes, and maybe Houdini and Conan Doyle, I wouldn't have thought anyone else would be allowed."

"You trusted Ransom and Morgan, correct?" Charles asked. "He's no different. We just know him less well."

"I don't know . . . ," Jack said doubtfully. "What do you think, John?"

Before the Caveo Principia could reply, Chaucer rapped on the table again to try to bring the meeting to order. But John had noticed that the whole time they were discussing the Messenger, Dr. Raven had not been watching the other Caretakers. . . .

He'd been watching *John*.

"There has been a burglary at Tamerlane House," Chaucer said somberly. "Verily, we have been burgled. The Cabal has brought the war to our very doorstep."

"The Cabal!" Jack said, shocked. "Are you certain?"

"As certain as we can be," Dickens said in answer. "The Echthroi themselves have no need of common burglary, so it can only be their agents who have done this."

"John Dee may have been a renegade Caretaker," Burton said gruffly, "and the other members of the ICS might have disagreed with your beliefs about the Archipelago, but I hardly think that means they're Lloigor."

"They may not know whose cause they serve, Richard," said Chaucer. "You yourself know that better than any else here."

"Harrumph," Burton growled in response. "Still, how would they have even found Tamerlane House?"

"The bridge," Jack said simply. "Shakespeare's Bridge, which connects the house to the Kilns. We've trusted that secrecy has been enough—but the location, and where it leads to, could be found out, I suppose."

"Yes," Chaucer agreed, "the way is open. And we do not know enough about our enemies' capabilities to rule out some sort of espionage effort to find and use it."

"It would seem to me," Twain said, lighting another cigar, "that the *what* of it is no longer in question, because it has already taken place. The *how* of it is, and may remain, a mystery. But what concerns me at the moment is the *why* of the thing. Why was it necessary to burgle our abode?"

"Edmund said that they tried—and failed—to steal old Elijah's maps," said John, "but if that was a failure, then what was taken?"

"A portrait," a loud voice boomed from the entry doors. "A few trinkets, a few baubles, and one of Basil's portraits. That's what was taken—and that's how we know, without doubt, that Dee's Cabal is responsible."

Jules Verne strode into the room and took his seat at the head of the table opposite Chaucer.

"How?" John exclaimed, too surprised to even offer a greeting to the Prime Caretaker. "Which portrait?"

"The only one," Verne replied, "dangerous enough to be sealed up behind a brick wall."

"Oh, dear," said Jack. "You mean . . ."

"Daniel Defoe has escaped," said Chaucer, "and to where, we have no idea."

"We had opened up the wall," Chaucer explained, "in order to interrogate Defoe about the lost prince—but he was reluctant to offer any information that could be deemed as helpful, even under extreme coercion."

"What he means," said Burton, "is that we tried our level best to torture it out of him, even to the point of setting fire to the portrait. But he held his tongue. Apparently, he's made of sterner stuff than others among us."

"Rude," Byron sniffed.

"We know that whoever broke out Defoe's portrait also wanted Elijah McGee's maps," said Chaucer, "although they failed to claim those."

"So other than Defoe, what was stolen?" asked John.

"A key, which was important but not irreplaceable," said Verne, "a statue of Jason's wife, Medea, which is irreplaceable but not important, and," he added with a slightly puzzled look on his face, "every pair of eyeglasses in Tamerlane House."

"That's a very strange laundry list for a burglar," said Jack. "Any idea why those things were taken?"

"Not particularly," Verne said, giving Bert an odd look, "but it's the escape of Defoe that we've focused on—because it's the only theft that includes a timetable."

"How do you mean?" asked John.

"Defoe's a portrait," said Verne. "He can leave the frame outside of Tamerlane House, but only for seven days."

"Yes," Bert said, nodding. "And we believe that the Cabal is planning some sort of initiative in that time, which is why I called for this council. We have spent a year reestablishing the zero points in time to allow our watches to function, but if we are truly to be able to defeat our enemies, we must resolve once and for all the question of how to rebuild the Keep of Time. And we must do it now."

"I understood that such a leap in time as that would require is not yet possible," said da Vinci.

"Rose believes that it is," Bert said, gesturing to the girl, "and I believe her. She *is* ready. It's time."

"It's time to pursue your personal agenda, you mean," said Burton. "Going to the past means going to the future first. And only an idiot couldn't guess when you want to go to, and why."

"It's not just for personal interests of my own that we're doing this," Bert shot back. "Ask Poe. He knows."

The reclusive leader of the Caretakers Emeriti nodded impassively from his post at the landing high above the room. "He is correct. In order to attempt a crossing of Deep Time into the past, to discover the identity of the Architect of the keep, a journey into the future must be made. It is the only way to balance out the chronal energies. And to go to a point that has been traveled to before only increases the odds that it will become a zero point. What Bert suggests is the only wise course of action."

"Crossing back to the present from eighteenth-century London is one thing," said Jack. "This seems like it will take more than a map and a piece of string."

"Machines have always been required to go into the future," said Verne. "That was one aspect of the Keep of Time that we realized from the start: It was recording time as much as anything else. The fact that it continued to grow, but somehow also continued to keep its connections to the past, was forever a mystery to us. As a means of travel into the past, however, it was both consistent and reliable. That ended once it fell."

"It had its own link to the future, though," said Charles. "The last door, up at the top."

"The door the stairs couldn't reach," said Bert, "but it did exist. The future was tangible, behind that door. That's how we knew traveling to it was possible."

"Anything within recorded history was reachable," said Verne, "through the means we developed here at Tamerlane House. Backward and forward within around twenty-five hundred years could be done with reasonable fidelity and accuracy. But that was when the tower still stood, and the doorway to the future still existed."

"Hah!" Burton laughed. "If we'd thought about this sooner, perhaps we could have salvaged that door. But it's a little late for that now. All the doors are gone."

"It wasn't the doors that were important," said one of the other Caretakers, who had been silent until now. "It was the *stone*."

William Shakespeare rose to his feet and continued. "If we can't yet rebuild the keep of the past, we might still be able to build a gate to the future," he said placidly. "If the council would just permit me—"

"And the time may yet come to put your plans into motion, Master Shaksberd," Chaucer said, dismissing the Bard's request with a wave, "but now is not that, uh, time." He turned to Edmund. "What does our young Cartographer say? Can you truly do this?"

Edmund swallowed hard and stood. "I believe we can, sir," he said, glancing at Rose. "It will take me most of the day to prepare the chronal map, but once that's done, we can go as soon as you give the word."

Chaucer glanced at the other Caretakers, then at Verne, who nodded, and Poe, who simply arched an eyebrow. "The word is given," Chaucer said finally. "May the light be with us all."

CHAPTER THREE
The Rings of Jules Verne

✦

The next order of business was the security of Tamerlane House, to prevent any further intrusions while Edmund prepared the new map. Shakespeare's Bridge was the only substantial access point from the Summer Country, and Hawthorne and Laura Glue were both stationed there as guards, rotating in shifts with Byron and Washington Irving. There were others among the Caretakers who were willing to serve as guards—but who hadn't the physical prowess or inclination to really be any good at it. However, there were other means of entry, and those were not so easily guarded against. The most obvious were the trumps—the illustrated cards carried by Verne's Messengers and several of the Caretakers, which allowed them to communicate with one another, and to travel between places depicted on the cards.

"There's no way of knowing what trumps the Cabal has use of," Verne said once the Caretakers had reassembled in the meeting hall, "so we must be prepared for any eventuality."

"They couldn't come here anyway," John said pointedly, "since except for the one Kipling uses, there aren't any trumps that lead directly to the Nameless Isles or to Tamerlane."

"None they'd have had access to, anyway," Verne said,

. . . *the vehicle roared away, scattering gravel as the tires spun.*

frowning. "But they might have access soon. Dee knows the process, and Defoe spent a lot of time here. So the whole place could be an entry point, if they create a new trump for it."

"How do we defend against that?" asked Charles. "If they can make a card for any spot Defoe's seen?"

"With these," said Verne. He took a small pouch from his vest pocket and emptied the contents onto the table. A scattering of silver rings spread across the surface, glittering in the light.

Charles picked up one of the small circlets and examined it. "Rings?" he said curiously. "How will these help protect Tamerlane House?"

"Hold it close to the candle flame," Verne instructed. Charles did so, and as the silver touched the flame, runes began to appear on the surface of the ring.

"Deep Magic," said Chaucer. "We had them made by the Watchmaker, after the method he used for the watches. But the runes are linked to those carved on standing stones, which Shakespeare is placing around the perimeter of the main island, and on either side of the bridge."

He pointed to the *Imaginarium Geographica*, which sat on a pedestal where it had rested, unused, since the fall of the Archipelago. "There is an incantation in the earliest pages, which will activate the stones, and the rings. And when it is spoken, no one without a ring can set foot on this island."

"How many rings are there?" asked John. "Enough for all of us?"

Verne nodded. "They were modeled after the one that Poe wears," he said, tipping his head up at the alcove above. "There are rings for everyone at Tamerlane, and all our apprentices and associates in the world beyond these doors, some of whom already have theirs. In short, there will be a ring for every agent of the Caretakers, given by my own hand. That's how we'll know who is to be trusted, and who isn't."

"It sounds complicated," Jack murmured. "How do you make sure all our allies are given rings? Can more be made if we need them? And if so, what's to stop the Cabal from having their own rings made?"

"Hell's bells, Jack," Verne snorted. "To be frank, I really can't answer most of that. I'm making this up as I go along, and just trying to do the best I can to serve the needs of whatever crisis is before us. Some of my Messengers, like the knight and his squire, have them already. Others are waiting. But in any case, I don't think it's wise to have an excess over what we actually need, and the fewer people who have access to Tamerlane House, the better."

"So this was your idea, Jules?" John asked.

"Mine, actually," a voice purred above John's right shoulder. He turned his head just in time to see the Cheshire smile appear, followed by the eyes and whiskers of his cat, Grimalkin. "Easier to say who can come and go, if those coming and going have a Binding to protect them."

"So will th' Caretakers still need th' watches, then?" Fred said glumly, looking down at his own watch. "I haven't even had mine all that long!"

"The pocket watches have long been the sole means of identifying fellow Caretakers and our agents, but in truth, they had never been intended as such," said Chaucer. "It was more in the spirit of camaraderie to approach one of our number and realize, with both joy and no small relief, that he carried a watch. He was of one's tribe."

"The rings just mark someone as an ally," Charles said to his apprentice, "but the watch still says you're a Caretaker. And you are, Fred," he added. "One of us."

"As a covert identifying marker, however," said Verne, "the method was far from infallible and had been subverted more than once." He gestured at the half-formed cat wrapped around John's shoulders. "And Grimalkin is correct," he said. "To accept a ring is to accept the Binding that comes with it. And once accepted, it cannot be taken from you, and can only be given if offered freely, and accepted on the same terms. And those are terms," he finished, "we know the Cabal will never accept. Not while they serve the Echthroi."

"Why not?" asked Jack.

"Because," said Verne, "the Binding invokes Deep Magic, which can only be used by one of noble worth, in a cause of selfless intent—and the Echthroi have only ever served themselves."

"Enough speechifying, Jules," said Bert. "Let's just get on with this, shall we?"

One by one, each of those gathered at Tamerlane House accepted a silver ring from Verne. When they had all been given out, Rose read the passage in the *Geographica* that Chaucer indicated. As she spoke the last word, a wave of energy swept over the entire island.

"Well," said Verne. "That's it and done. Unless someone has one of these rings, or is already here, they're not setting foot in the Nameless Isles."

"Amen," said Grimalkin.

After the ceremony of the rings, the Caretakers separated briefly to reflect on the events of the day and plan their next strategies.

John, Jack, and Charles, however, held back, and indicated for Twain to do the same. After a few minutes, the room had cleared, and they were alone except for a few of the Elder Caretakers who were still talking at the far end.

"What can I do for you boys?" asked Twain.

"Bert has been very, ah, anxious this entire time," said Jack, "no pun intended. I've seen him under stress before, and it's always been like water off a duck's back. It never sinks in with him. So why is he so testy now? It can't just be because he wants to go find Weena."

"It isn't," Twain said, drawing them away from the others into the corridor so he could speak to the three friends in complete privacy. "Our friend is operating under a severe time constraint. And he's aware of every tick of the clock."

"What kind of constraint?" asked John. "Is he ill?"

"Nothing like that," Twain replied. "You know that he is an anomaly, that he has a temporal near-twin, correct?"

"Sure," said John. "Herb—the real H. G. Wells, or at least, the one Verne started with."

"Precisely," said Twain. "And you know that our Bert has aged a great deal more than Herb, due in large part to all his wandering around time and space."

All three companions nodded, afraid to speak of what they feared was coming.

"Bert is," Twain said softly, "the only non-tulpa time traveler, but he is still bound by the rules of Chronos time, or real time, here in the Summer Country. And the person he was, the person he may still have a connection to, is about to kick the bucket."

"Oh dear," John said, closing his eyes.

"What?" Charles said, looking at Jack. "I don't . . ."

"What I mean to be clear about, and apparently failed at," said Twain, "is to tell you that in seven days, H. G. Wells is going to die. And that means Bert may too. So he has just one week left in which to go find his ladylove."

The statement hit the three companions like a thunderclap, shaking them so badly that for a moment, none of them was able to speak.

"Like Ransom, when Charles . . . ," John said finally, swallowing hard. "Like that."

"Yes," said Twain. "That's exactly what we expect to happen."

"That's awful, of course," said Charles, "but if I can offer my own very informed opinion, I died, and I got over it. Won't Bert? I mean, after the fact, he'll still be a Caretaker. And we have ways of dealing with these things."

"Yes," Twain agreed, "except you chose to become a tulpa, whereas Bert has never strayed from the plan that when he eventually perished, he would join the rest of us here in the portrait gallery. We've tried to convince him to do otherwise, but he simply won't be swayed. His will to do what he believes is best is simply too strong."

Finally it dawned on Charles what the real urgency was. If Bert became a portrait, he might never be able to travel through time again—and certainly not into the far future or the deep past. There was simply too great a risk that he would not make it back to Tamerlane House in the allotted week. And then . . .

"What happened to Stellan could happen to him," Jack said, completing Charles's thought. "No wonder he's so stressed."

"Indeed," said Twain as he began to guide them back into the room where the other Caretakers had started to gather again. "So, best efforts, eh, boys? For Bert, if for no other reason."

"That," John said, "is more than reason enough. And all the reason we'd ever need."

The Caretakers were gathering again in the meeting hall because there had been a crossing over Shakespeare's Bridge. Two of Verne's most trusted agents had just returned, and just in time—because they would be needed to fulfill the next part in his battle plan.

"Well met," Don Quixote said, bowing deeply as he entered the meeting hall. "Greetings, Caretakers."

John and Jack both stood to take the knight's hand—which John noticed already bore one of Verne's silver rings—and Rose gave him a hug and a kiss on the cheek, which made him blush. It was a deserved warm welcome—but it was nothing compared to the response his squire Uncas got.

Every time Uncas visited Tamerlane House, with or without the old knight, there was the equivalent of a hero's reception and parade held in the library. The library of Tamerlane House had been all but taken over by two dozen foxes and hedgehogs, all Paralon-trained librarians and archivists, who were led by the new head librarian—a fox called Myrret. And to these animals, Uncas was not merely a knight's squire or an associate of the Caretakers—he was a legendary badger.

"Since I became Don Quixote's squire," Uncas had explained to the starstruck animals, "I hadn't had as much time as I'd liked to visit back t' th' Archipelago. It was only luck that we wuz doing a secret errand for Scowler Jules that spared us bein' lost with everyone an' everything else."

"Your name was well known to all the Children of the Earth," Myrret said admiringly. "The son of the great badger Tummeler, who saved the Scholar Charles in the battle with th' Winter King . . ."

"'Saved'?" asked Charles.

"Poetic license," said Jack, "I'm sure."

". . . and the father of the Caretaker Fred," Myrret went on, "you deserved the honors given to you and monuments named for you—even if you did not perish so long ago, as we once believed."

"How many badgers can there be with the name Charles Montgolfier Hargreaves-Heald?" asked Charles.

"In point of fact," said Myrret, "there were eleven. Not counting juniors and thirds."

"All right then," said Charles. "I'm so glad I asked."

"I have another mission for you," Verne explained to Quixote and Uncas as he handed them a slender, cream-colored envelope. "Your instructions are there, as per usual. And yes," he added, with a wry look at Uncas, "you get to use the Duesenberg."

"Hot potatoes!" Uncas said, jumping onto his chair. "Let's get going!"

Several of the Caretakers accompanied the knight and his squire back to the bridge and over it, to the Kilns. Charles relished each opportunity to return to the Summer Country, given that he could only do so occasionally since he'd become a tulpa. To Jack it was simply going home. And for John, it was a chance to keep the world he lived in connected to the one he'd become responsible for. At times, long years passed between visits to the Archipelago—and it sometimes seemed as if that other world was only a dream. But now that it was gone, John thought wistfully, it seemed more real than ever. And he missed it.

"We no longer have the resources of the Archipelago to draw upon," Verne was saying, "but that does not mean we are wholly without resources—however questionable some of them may be."

"What's that supposed to mean?" asked Jack.

"That we use what resources we have," Verne said as he opened the door to the 1935 Duesenberg that sat alongside the house, "and we call in the favors that we can, from those who are able to grant them."

Uncas gleefully took the wheel as Quixote bent his lanky frame in the seat beside the badger. "We'll be back soon, Scowler Jules," Uncas said as the engine growled to life. "You c'n count on us."

"I know," Verne said, almost inaudibly. "I know we can, little fellow."

"Is it really prudent to just let them go driving around in the Duesenberg like that?" John asked as the vehicle roared away, scattering gravel as the tires spun.

"It's not really a problem," Verne replied. "Everyone in England drives like that. No one will notice one more insane driver."

"That's not what I meant," John persisted. "Quixote may be able to pass, but isn't it a little irresponsible of us to let a talking badger go driving around out in the open? In the old days, that would have gotten us in a lot of trouble."

"Ah, but it isn't the old days anymore, is it, young John?" said Verne. "The world is turning its attention away from certain things, and the loss of the Archipelago has made this even more pronounced. No one sees . . .

". . . because no one is looking. Not anymore."

"That's terrible, Jules," said John. "Someone should look. Or at least, remember."

"That's a large part of the reason it's our practice to recruit writers as Caretakers," Verne replied, looking intensely at his protégé. "It's part of your job to write down the stories so the world doesn't forget.

"So no one ever forgets."

Verne held John's eyes a moment, then wheeled about, waving to the others. "Come on, then," he called out over his shoulder as he strode back to the bridge. "We've done what we can do for now. It's up to Uncas and Quixote to see where we'll go next."

He didn't rise to greet them, but waved them over . . .

Chapter Four
The Ruby Armor of T'ai Shan

Following the directions in the cream-colored envelope, Quixote and Uncas drove northward from the Kilns and Oxford, to the gray, industrial town of Northampton. It took more than two hours to make the trip, and another two once they'd gotten there to find the address they were seeking. At first they had argued a bit as to whether they were reading the map properly—but when they found the actual building, both realized that they would have been hard-pressed to find it even if they'd been there a hundred times before.

It was a low, sloping edifice, which was tucked away on an alley off a side street near a seldom-used thoroughfare, and it looked as if it had been built at least three centuries earlier, and had not been repaired since just after that.

A dimly lit speakeasy was housed on the ground floor, and none of the windows on the two floors above showed any evidence of occupancy. Quixote was about to declare the whole adventure a misfire when Uncas tugged on his sleeve and pointed at the narrow stairs leading down to an apartment below street level.

"There," the badger said softly. "I think that's where we're supposed t' go."

Cautiously they made their way down the steps and were debating using the half-attached door knocker when a gruff, scratchy voice within called out, "Well, come on in! No sense standing out there waiting for the plaster to peel."

The knight and the badger entered the apartment, which was one large room, divided only by the struts and braces that supported the structure above. On the far side were greasy windows, framed with ramshackle blinds that let in bands of light from the street outside.

There were filing cabinets of various sizes scattered around the room, which formed rough, concentric circles around the gravity of a massive, dark desk, at which was seated a large, heavy-set man who wore a hat and a tattered trench coat. He didn't rise to greet them, but waved them over to stand in front of the desk.

"I'm Steve, the Zen Detective," the man said without offering his hand or asking his visitors to sit. "But if you knew how to find me, then you probably already knew that."

"Zen Detective?" asked Uncas. "What do you detect?"

"I help people to find themselves, among other services," the detective replied, giving no sign that he cared that the question was asked by a badger, "although most don't actually like what I find, so I've learned the hard way to ask for my fee up front, cash on the barrel."

"How do you lose yourself?" Uncas asked, patting himself on his stomach. "I'd a' thunk that'd be hard t' do."

"It's easier than you think," said the detective. "Mostly it happens through inattention, but sometimes it's deliberate." He snorted. "Those are always the ones who have the most urgent need, and are always just as reluctant to pay."

"Hmm," Uncas mused, looking around at the shabby office. "Do you really make a living doing this, uh, 'Zen detecting,' um . . . Steve?"

"His name," said Quixote, "is Aristophanes."

"I prefer Steve," the detective replied, sniffing, "but yes, you speak the truth."

"That's awfully familiar to me," said Uncas. "How is it that I would know you?"

"Well," the detective replied, "I was once a noted philosopher. Perhaps you read—"

"Naw," said Uncas. "I'm not a big reader—you're thinking of my son. Say," he added, leaning closer. "Are you, uh, purple?"

"It's a birthmark," the detective replied testily.

"Over your whole body?" said Uncas.

"Don't you have any birthmarks?" Aristophanes shot back. "Or doesn't your species have such a thing?"

"Of course we do!" said Uncas. "In fact, I myself have a birthmark around a mole on my—"

"Decorum, Uncas," Quixote interrupted, waggling a finger. "Decorum."

"Heh." Aristophanes chuckled. "A badger with a mole. That's funny."

"How does a philosopher end up becoming a detective?" asked Uncas. "That seems like two very opposite perfessions."

"All philosophical inquiry," said the detective, "can be boiled down into just two questions. The first"—he counted off on his fingers—"is 'Am I Important?' And the second is 'Can I Survive?' There's nothing in philosophy that isn't somehow covered by those questions. And every case I take as a detective ends up asking them as well."

"Hmm," Uncas said, tugging on his ear and squinting. "I don't recognize it. It is from Aristotle?"

"No, it isn't from Aristotle!" the detective shot back. "It's from one of my own teachers, who was relatively unknown, but a great philosopher still."

"What was his name?" asked Quixote.

"He didn't have one," Aristophanes replied. "He preferred to be known by an unpronounceable symbol, so most of his less imaginative students just called him 'the Philosopher.' That's part of how Johnny-come-latelies like Aristotle got credit for some of the stuff he actually thought of."

"What did *you* call him?" asked Uncas.

"He started all his dialogues by making this glottal sound with his throat," said Aristophanes, "so I called him 'Larynx.'"

"A great Greek philosopher named, erm, *Larry*?" Quixote asked, confused. "That sounds very, ah, improbable."

Uncas shrugged. "Detectives named Steve could have teachers named Larry," he theorized. "It could happen."

"Not Larry, *Larynx*!" Aristophanes retorted angrily. "And it was only a nickname, anyway. Besides, it doesn't matter what he was called—the quality of the thinking is what is important to a philosopher. The rest is just advertising."

"And yet you became a detective," said Quixote. "Interesting."

Steve scowled. This wasn't going the way it was supposed to have gone. He had assumed that a lanky, out-of-sorts knight and a talking badger would be pushovers, but somehow, this unlikely duo had managed to get him talking about himself—which simply wouldn't do. Not at all.

"So," Aristophanes said gruffly, tapping the desk. "Enough talk. Time is money. Let's see your dough, and then we'll find your Zen, or whatever."

"Is this really the right feller?" Uncas asked behind his paw. "He seems a little . . . off t' me."

"He's the right fellow, all right," Quixote said as he rummaged around in his duffel. "I know I had it here somewhere . . . ," he muttered.

"Aha!" Quixote finally exclaimed as he found what he'd been searching for. "Here you go," he said, dropping a small drawstring bag on the detective's desk. "Thirty pieces of silver—your traditional price for this kind of job."

The Zen detective made no move to retrieve the bag, but simply sat, staring at it with a passive expression on his face. At length, he inhaled deeply, then exhaled the air in a long, melancholy sigh. "Silver," he said at last, eyeing Quixote. "Verne sent you, didn't he?"

The knight nodded. "He did, yes."

"And whom is it you would like me to find?"

"It in't a whom, it's a what," said Uncas.

"We've been instructed," Quixote said with all the formality of an official request, "to ask you to locate the Ruby Opera Glasses."

Aristophanes fell backward over his chair and crashed to the floor. He rose in an instant, cursing under his breath, then more loudly as he set his chair back on its legs and took his seat.

"You don't ask for much, do you?" he said, squinting suspiciously at the knight and the badger. "Why not ask for the Cloak of the Paladin, or a shard of the true cross, or the Spear of Destiny while you're at it?"

"Actually," Uncas said, brightening, "what happened with the spear was this, see. . . ."

"Never mind that," Quixote said as he scowled at the badger. "We really do just need the Ruby Opera Glasses."

"If I *could* locate them," said the detective, "I would require an additional fee. And then there might be an additional cost to acquire them. How much is Master Verne . . ."

In response to the unfinished question, Quixote reached back into his duffel and removed a second bag of silver. Then a third. And a fourth.

Uncas let out a slow whistle of appreciation. "That's a lotta nuts," he said, looking from Quixote to the detective and back again. "What's so special about these glasses anyhoo?"

"The glasses are the only object in all of the Summer Country that can detect the presence of an Echthroi," said Aristophanes.

"Is this sufficient?" Quixote asked, indicating the bags on the desk. "I'm not authorized to pay more, but I could ask if needed."

"To locate them, yes. But it won't be nearly enough," the detective answered, "for what we're actually going to propose to the Frenchman."

"And what is that?"

"The rest of the armor," Aristophanes said simply. "It still exists. And what's more, I know where to find it."

It was a credit to Quixote's self-control that he did not react to this news, but kept his expression steady; and it was a credit to Uncas's self-control that all he did was whoop with excitement.

"Th' scowlers will be so excited to know that!" Uncas exclaimed. "Th' rest of the armor! Imagine that!"

"Do you even know what the armor is?" asked the detective.

"Not at all!" Uncas admitted. "But it sounds right stellar!"

"What do you ask of us?" said Quixote.

"Simple," Aristophanes replied as he leaned back in his chair and crossed his feet on top of his desk. "I want to be dealt back in."

The old knight looked confused. "Dealt back in? You want to play cards?"

Aristophanes groaned. "No, you idiot. Dealt back into the *game*. The Great Game. I want my seat at the table. I want to rejoin the flow of the world."

"That's for the Prime Caretaker to decide," Quixote said after a moment, "and I daren't even consult him with such a request, when we don't even know if you're capable . . ."

Aristophanes ignored the knight's comments and opened up a drawer on the left side of his desk. He reached in, removed an object, and placed it on the desktop.

"There," he said. "The Ruby Opera Glasses. That alone should convince Master Verne that I can find the rest of the armor."

The knight and the badger peered curiously at the glasses, which, other than the thick red lenses, looked like any other pair of antique opera glasses. "Tell us about this armor," Quixote said, gingerly touching the glasses. "To whom did it belong?"

"A great warrior named T'ai Shan," Aristophanes answered, "who lived many, many thousands of years ago. She was the Imago of this world, which made her the mistress of time and space, and she was respected and feared by all. Even," he added darkly, "the Echthroi."

Uncas frowned. "So this, Inag . . . Imuh . . . This person lived thousands of years ago, did she?" he said as he examined the opera glasses. "Beggin' y'r pardon, but these seem t' be a bit too muchly on th' contemporary side t' be real."

"Master, uh, mistress of time and space, remember?" said Quixote. "Perhaps she acquired them during the dispatching of her duties as Imago—whatever those entailed."

"She disappeared long ago, even before the Archipelago of Dreams was created," said the detective, "and the armor was thought to be lost. But it was found again during the Bronze Age, by those who knew of its power and sought to use it.

"The helmet, breastplate, and gauntlets are still intact," Aristophanes continued, "but the leggings were dismantled so that the ruby could be used in the creation of five other objects of power."

"Like the opera glasses," Uncas said. "I get it."

"The light dawns," said Aristophanes. "As I told you, the glasses can be used to detect the presence of the Echthroi, and also their servants, the Lloigor. The second object that was created is a brooch, which does exactly the opposite: It can hide someone from being seen by an Echthros or a Lloigor.

"The third object, which has been missing for several centuries, is a comb. That's the one I really wish I could find," he added ruefully. "Using it banishes an Echthroi Shadow from its host.

"The fourth object is almost as useful—a Ruby Dagger, which can actually cut an Echthros, even those who have bonded themselves to a mortal. Although," Aristophanes said, "the damage to the Shadow is mirrored in damage to the host. So it's a weapon of last resort, unless you really don't care about the host."

"I suppose that would depend," said Uncas, "on who th' host was."

"A pragmatic attitude," the detective philosopher replied with a surprised expression on his face. "Very wise."

Uncas shrugged. "Animal logic. What's the last object?"

"Objects, not object, actually. A pair," Aristophanes corrected. "Ruby shoes. They allow the wearer to instantly transport to anywhere they wish, simply by fixing the location in their mind, then tapping the heels together."

"What of the intact armor pieces?" asked Quixote.

"Of those, the helmet may be the hardest to find," said the Zen Detective, "which is ironic, because it enables the wearer to find their way between any two places. Someone wearing the Ruby Helm cannot get lost.

"The breastplate has been the object most sought after through the centuries, because the general perception was that it was the most powerful. He who wears the Ruby Breastplate is invulnerable in battle against any mortal foe," Aristophanes said, with a slight emphasis on "mortal."

"And against, say, the Echthroi?" asked Quixote.

The Zen Detective shook his head. "Against them, not so much. It's still very powerful, but without the comb and the brooch, no defense against an Echthros."

"And the gauntlets?" asked Uncas. "What about them?"

"Strength," Aristophanes said. "The more opposition, the stronger the wearer becomes, with," he added, "one proviso. They don't give you strength, they just allow you to draw more of the strength you already possess. So if they are used for too long in battle, you could conceivably win . . ."

"And still lose your life," Quixote finished. "Worth noting, I think."

"You really know where all these things is? Uh, are?" asked Uncas.

"I do," Aristophanes said. "They are secreted away, in the corners of the world where magic is real and still worth looking for."

"Alas, but those lands are gone now," said Quixote. "The Archipelago of Dreams—"

"There was a lot of magic in the lands of the Archipelago, that's true," the detective interrupted, nodding. "But they were not all the magic places there are."

"And you can find these places then?" asked Quixote. "We've already paid a considerable fee just to find the glasses—which you already had in your possession. So for the rest . . ."

"I'm not bartering with you here," Aristophanes said gruffly. "This is an all-or-nothing deal. If you take me with you and Verne agrees to my request, then I'll help you find the rest of the objects. If you decline to do even that much, then I swear on all the gods of Olympus that you will never see me again."

Quixote sighed heavily, and with a nod of assent from Uncas, held out his hand. "Your word?"

Aristophanes paused long enough that Quixote dropped his hand, then the detective nodded sharply. "For whatever it's worth, you have it," he said brusquely. "Give me just a moment, and then we can go."

He took the bags of silver and locked them all in a heavy safe set within one of the filing cabinets. Then he opened another and removed a large black case, which he handled very carefully.

"This should be all we'll need," he said, looking at the two companions. "Let's go find your armor."

It was perhaps the most unusual group to ever arrive at the Kilns, Warnie decided, and after the last several years, that was not an easy benchmark to clear. He had procured the 1935 Duesenberg specifically for the Caretakers to modify for Quixote and Uncas's use—mostly because of the small windows, which made it harder to see the badger. Unless, he noted ruefully, Uncas was driving, which happened more frequently than not. Quixote complained that he simply hadn't the temperament for dealing with a horse-less carriage, and so was perfectly content to let the badger drive. This was again the case as the battered old vehicle came skidding into the drive next to the cottage.

"Almost like driving one of th' old principles back home," Uncas chortled as he clambered from the driver's seat. "'Cept it smells. Steam and ecstatic lectricity is so much cleaner."

A stout man with an unusually dark complexion stepped from the seat behind the driver. "You mean static electricity," he said brusquely. "There's no such thing as 'ecstatic lectricity.'"

"That's a very skeptical outlook," Quixote said as he unfolded himself from the passenger seat and stretched out his cramped frame in the sunlight. "Especially coming from a two-thousand-year-old philosopher unicorn detective."

Before any of them could comment further, a delegation of Caretakers emerged from behind the house. Jack and John led the way, followed by Charles and Byron, Bert and Verne, and behind them, Dickens and Burton, with Twain and Hawthorne, both of whom carried samurai swords, bringing up the rear.

"You come bearing arms, Caretakers?" asked Aristophanes. "A strange way to greet your guests."

"You're a contractor, not a guest," Verne said without bothering to make introductions. He turned to Quixote and Uncas. "What's the meaning of this?"

"We did as you requested, Master Verne," Quixote said. "The price was acceptable, and he located the Ruby Opera Glasses right away." This last was said with a wink at the detective—the old knight's effort at camaraderie. "As to the cost for acquiring them, he has a proposal he'd like to make. I think you should give him a hearing."

"Why did you bring the detective with you? For all we know, you've just brought the serpent into the heart of the garden, so to speak."

"I'm not *that* old," Aristophanes snorted.

"It is my understanding," said Quixote, "that this fellow excels in finding things that are hidden, and he already knows a great deal about the Caretakers. So we trusted him the full mile—but only because of what else he has to offer."

Verne and the others looked at the detective expectantly. "Well?" asked Verne.

"The Ruby Armor of T'ai Shan," Aristophanes replied. "I know where it is. All of it. And if you bring me into the inner circle, I'll lead you to it all."

Quixote and Uncas briefly recounted the Zen Detective's proposal, along with the description of the armor and what it could do. When they finished, John and Verne both asked if they could look at the glasses, and after a moment's reluctance, Aristophanes handed them to the two Caretakers.

"You didn't say anything about these, Jules," John murmured as he peered into the ruby lenses. "Why? Especially if they'd be so useful against the Echthroi."

"I didn't know if they could be found," Verne admitted, "so I didn't want to get anyone's hopes up. But now," he added, taking back the glasses and returning them to the detective, "it seems they may have led us to an even greater treasure—if we can afford the price."

The detective nodded. "I think you can."

"Well, possibly," John said. He turned to Aristophanes. "I'm sorry, but I know nothing of you. And I'm not that prepared to trust you. The fact that Verne could not bring you in openly, as one of his Messengers, gives me pause. And if he does not trust you fully, then I don't believe the rest of us can either. Revealing the secrets of the Caretakers is too high a price to pay for this armor, or whatever it is."

"Speaking as one who has been on both sides of this debate," said Burton, "I have to agree."

John turned to Bert and Verne. "This deal is suspect. I don't trust his motives."

"My motives?" Aristophanes exclaimed. "My motive is the one you can depend on most—self-preservation. If that is a man's true motive, then all his other causes may lay exposed to the world, naked as a babe. Because you can always determine the truth of his words, by simply asking whether he benefits from his choices."

"I hate to be the bearer of bad tidings," said Charles, "but we have a *lot* of enemies, and their number seems to be growing almost daily. How exactly is it an act of self-preservation to plant your flag on Caretaker Hill?"

"You're not a fool," the detective replied, eyeing Charles's pocket watch. "Men are judged by the quality of their enemies, and that makes you powerful indeed. And I know"—he glanced at Verne—"who it is that runs the secret machineries of the world."

"Your benefit is obvious," said John, "but ours is not."

"If this armor is that important," Jack suggested, "can't the Messengers find it?"

"They're engaged in other work," Verne replied. "And there aren't as many of them as there used to be."

"The truth of it is that you need me," said Aristophanes. "That swings the weight to my side of the scale."

"You're not as indispensable as you think," said Verne. "We have maps of all the places the armor may be hidden—finding it is just a matter of time."

"Maybe you do," the detective said quickly, "but you are unable to make good use of them—or you wouldn't really need me at all. And after the recent burglary at Poe's house, you almost didn't have *those*."

Verne turned and raised an eyebrow at Uncas.

The badger squirmed. "Uh, was I not s'pposed t' tell him about that?" he asked apologetically.

"Well, since we already have the glasses . . . ," Verne murmured. "But on the rest of the matter, we seem to be at an impasse."

"In point of fact," Aristophanes said, raising a finger, "you paid me to locate the glasses, not give them up. I think I'll hold on to them, for now. And it's you who are at an impasse, not me.

"I've named my price, Frenchman," the detective continued, feeling his boldness grow in the opportunity of the moment. "The whole package—you hire me to find and acquire all of the Ruby Armor, and I will deliver it to you complete—including the glasses. If you decline, then I go, and the glasses go with me."

John looked at Jack, Charles, and Bert, who all nodded. "The glasses alone seem invaluable," said Jack, "and it seems he *can* deliver what he's asked to find. So I think it's worth risking."

The Caveo Principia held the detective in his regard a few moments longer, then nodded his assent to Verne.

"All or nothing, is it? Then it seems we have no choice but to trust you," Verne said heavily. "We have our agreement, detective."

"Excellent. Shake on it?" Aristophanes said, sticking out his hand and laughing as Verne recoiled. "Sorry. Just a little joke."

"Very little," said Verne.

Warnie bid his brother and friends good-bye, making certain to give Charles an especially warm handshake, before going inside to put on a pot of tea. Verne excused himself to retrieve Elijah McGee's maps from Tamerlane House—taking great care not to allow Aristophanes to see the bridge—leaving the other Caretakers to keep an eye on the Zen Detective.

"I like your hair, Caretaker," Aristophanes said to Charles. "It's very distinguished."

"Thank you," Charles said, beaming. He gave a look of *I told you so* to his friends. "It's the exact shade of Queen Victoria's throne, you know."

Aristophanes looked puzzled. "No, it isn't. Her throne was black—black velvet."

Charles looked flustered. "But—but—" he stammered. "Chaucer said—"

"Chaucer?" Aristophanes exclaimed. "*Geoffrey Chaucer?* He wouldn't know the truth if it bit him in the—"

"Hang on there, detective," Twain said, swinging his *katana* up under the other's nose. "Let's not be maligning senior staff now, hey?"

"Whatever," Aristophanes said, holding up his hands. "I think all you people are crazy." He chuckled grimly. "I must be crazy myself to want to side with you."

"You're probably right on both counts," Twain said as he twirled the sword in the air, "and don't you forget it."

The detective grunted in response as Verne crossed back over the lawn and handed Uncas a leather folder.

"Here they are," he said to the badger. "The maps of Elijah McGee. They should be everything the Zen Detective needs to find the armor, and I am entrusting them to your care, Uncas."

The badger's eyes widened, and he gulped as he accepted the parcel of maps, but he nodded in understanding and gave the Prime Caretaker a dignified salute. "You can count on me, Scowler Jules," he said. "I mean, uh, on us. Except for Aristophanes, I mean."

"By Zeus's knickers!" the detective exclaimed as he climbed into the passenger seat of the Duesenberg. "I told you—call me Steve."

"We'll keep an eye on him, too," said Quixote. "Never fear," he added as he lowered himself into the rear seat. "We'll see this through."

"We have no doubt," Jack said as the automobile roared to life. "Do we, fellows?"

But none of the men answered. John was looking at the vehicle as it sped off into the distance, and Verne . . .

. . . was looking at John. His brow creased with worry for the young Caretaker and what was to come, but only for a moment.

His face broke into his customary smile, and when John turned, Verne winked at him.

After a moment, the sounds of the Duesenberg faded, and without speaking further, the Caretakers crossed back over the bridge.

PART TWO

The Chronic Argonauts

"So," said Twain . . . "who's up for an adventure?"

CHAPTER FIVE
Days of Future Past

❖

The Chronographer of Lost Times stood at the tall windows in his athenaeum and considered the small stoppered flask he held in his hand.

Inside, a wisp of smoke curled against the glass in a slow, almost deliberate motion. In the right light, it sometimes seemed to coalesce into a face, and the expression it wore was one of confusion.

The Chronographer smiled grimly. Confusion was acceptable, but fear would have been better. It would come in time, however. Everything comes in time.

"Dr. Dee," someone called out to the Chronographer from the doorway. "I trust it's as you hoped?"

"It was nearly too late," Dee snapped back before composing himself. "You took too long, and we nearly lost our opportunity."

Tesla clenched his jaw, then strode into the room to stand next to the other man. Tesla was tall and fit, and his features were handsome, although he often wore a cold, clinical expression, which ensured that no one looked at him for long, or twice. "We nearly lost Crowley in acquiring it as it was," he said, his voice clipped and precise. "The Caretaker's brother returned to the cottage as he was leaving, and that would have undone us all."

Dee scowled. "He wasn't supposed to be near the house at all!" he snapped. "It was too great a risk."

"It was a necessary one," Tesla replied soothingly. No point in irritating Dee for nothing. "He couldn't risk transporting from the Caretakers' fortress itself—we still don't even know if it exists in real space or not. Better to have risked exposure than to lose them both. It was difficult enough just to get across the bridge."

Dee eyed the flask. "Yes—yes, you're correct. I had just assumed that more precautions would be taken."

Tesla shrugged. "The cat was watching out for any interlopers and could have dealt with them accordingly. And Lovecraft and I were waiting here on our side should he need any intervention in Oxford. Really, it went about as well as it could go. And now," he said, pointing at the flask, "we have it."

"Indeed," said Dee. He handed the flask to the scientist and noticed a marked increase in the motion of the smoke inside. "You know what to do. Is the other one ready?"

"Quite nearly," Tesla replied as he turned on his heel and began to walk out of the room. "I'll give you a further report later today."

"And our Archimago project?" Dee added. "How goes that, Nikola?"

The scientist stopped, and paused for a moment before answering. "It goes . . . according to plan," he said, measuring his words carefully. "Complete isolation, as you'd instructed. He will have grown to adulthood without having the slightest idea of who he really is."

Dee turned to look at his colleague. "You still disapprove, I take it?"

Tesla ran his hand through his hair and looked at the floor. "Blake believes—"

"Blake is not the Chronographer!" Dee shouted. "He is an adept, but he is not irreplaceable. No one is, except for the boy. The girl whom they believe is the Imago was raised to believe she had a great destiny, and that makes her unpredictable. So the only way to control the Archimago was to make sure he believed he had no destiny at all."

Tesla looked up. "If he is what we believe, then he won't believe that for long, once we bring him back. And once he realizes what he can do . . ."

"He will already be sworn to serve our ends," said Dee. "And if for some reason he chooses not to, we'll just cast him back into the future. Irreplaceable does not mean necessary," he added, look-ing at the flask in the scientist's fingers. "The girl is Shadowed, remember. And if we can't use him, then perhaps we'll still be able to turn her. Either way," he finished, eyes glittering, "we win."

Tesla seemed to want to say something further, but instead pocketed the flask and walked out, shutting the door harder than necessary.

"Excellent," the Chronographer murmured to himself when he was alone once more. "All things pass, in time. And soon enough, they will. And then . . . at last . . . I will truly be the Master of the World."

Almost as if responding to his words, the long shadows in the room rose from the floor and swirled about until the entire athenaeum was cloaked in darkness.

◆ ◆ ◆

The returning Caretakers were greeted on the East Lawn of Tamerlane House by Fred, who rushed to embrace Uncas; Laura Glue, who was still brandishing her own *katana*, and upset that she hadn't been allowed to go with the others to the Kilns; and Edmund and Rose.

"I'm one of the best fighters at Tamerlane," Laura Glue pouted. "I should have been with you, even if you didn't really need me."

"There will be a much more important mission at hand for you, little Valkyrie," Verne chided gently as they walked to the house, "and against much more dangerous adversaries than old Aristophanes."

"She ought to go with Rose and Edmund, then," Byron offered, trying to lighten the mood. "Not much point to saving the world if you can't save your woman, too, eh, Bert?"

"Shut up, George," said Hawthorne.

"What?" said Byron. "I was being sincere! How can I ever participate if you try to shut me up whenever I say anything at all?"

"You can't," said Hawthorne. "And just so you know, I'm not agreeing with you here."

"Well," Byron grumbled, "I'm just saying I think Bert's reason for going is better than everyone else's."

"Mmm, thank you, George," said Bert. "But it really is more important to repair the Keep of Time. Anything else must be secondary to that goal—however much I would want it to happen."

"Whoever else goes with Rose and Edmund," said Verne, "you'll be among them. You've earned that, Bert."

"If push came to shove, I suppose *you* could always have just tried taking the machine in the basement yourself, Jules," Bert replied, not entirely with conviction. "After all, we know it worked at least *once*."

Verne started, then shifted in his chair, as if the suggestion was an uncomfortable one. "I . . . appreciate that, Bert," he said with a bit too much joviality, "but the machine wouldn't work for me. Not again, at any rate."

Bert looked at his associate, puzzled. "You've taken it out? And come safely back? I wasn't aware of that."

Verne waved off the remark. "Yes, yes. It went . . . well. But it's not important now. Our concern is how to get you to the future and back safely, so we can finally go about this business of rebuilding the Keep of Time."

"I meant to ask," Jack said to Verne, "what's this about goats in the Himalayas?"

"It's a lake in Mongolia, actually," Verne said. "Not many people know about it. I keep the herd in the ruins of an old castle there."

Jack suppressed a grin. "I, ah, never took you for a goatherd, Master Verne."

Verne drew himself up and frowned. "I don't spend all my, ah, time traipsing around in history," he huffed. "I have to have a way to vent my stresses. Everyone does, or they turn into Byron."

"Hey, now," said Byron.

"Interesting," said Charles. "What do you call your herd?"

"The Post-Jurassic Lower Mongolian Capra Hircus Horde," Verne said with such obvious pride that Rose feared he might actually pop a vest button or two. "I'm raising two of them in particular to be show goats," he went on. "Elly Mae and Coraline. Fine, fine stock. Took first and third in their classes at the Navajo County Fair last year."

"Erm, Navajo County Fair?" Charles asked.

"Arizona," Verne answered. "No one knows livestock better than the Navajo, except for perhaps the Lower Mongolians. They appreciate the exotic lineage of my goats in ways the European cultures cannot."

It was John's turn to suppress a grin. "And what lineage would that be?"

Verne's eyes narrowed and he pursed his lips, unsure if he was about to be made the fool, but he explained anyway. "My goats," he said, resuming his prideful tone, "are descended from the stock of Genghis Khan himself, and were brought into the West by Marco Polo. Some mingled with the lesser stock of the northern Europeans, but Elly Mae's line bred true, and Coraline's almost as much."

"Hmm," said Charles. "I take it that's where the third-place award came from?"

"The judge cheated," Verne replied. "He put a foot out of place when I wasn't looking."

Jack looked at John and shrugged. "Jules Verne showing goats descended from the herds of Genghis Khan in a county fair in an Indian nation in America," he said. "Now I think I *have* heard everything."

"I would have thought you would raise goats from the Archipelago," said Charles, "if you really wanted to make a showing, that is."

"Considered it," said Verne, "but for one thing, they're harder to breed, and for another, they kept insisting on driving the car themselves."

"And," Byron added, "there is no Archipelago anymore. It's all Shadow."

Hawthorne cuffed Byron across the back of his head. "You see?" he huffed. "This is why we don't take you anywhere."

More quickly than any of them had expected, including himself, Edmund finished the chronal map. It was almost three feet across, mostly to allow for the symbols that ringed its border, which were necessary to accurately pinpoint the date to which they would travel.

In celebration, the Elder Caretakers called for a dinner in honor of the mission. John and Jack exchanged silent glances of frustration with Twain, knowing that every second that passed was another one lost to Bert, but nothing could be done. To the Caretakers Emeriti, who were largely confined to Tamerlane House, ceremony was everything. In the dining hall, Alexandre Dumas and the Feast Beasts quickly put together what Dumas referred to as "a light dinner," which nevertheless consisted of enough food to have stocked the Kilns for a year.

"So," said Twain when they had all eaten their fill, "who's up for an adventure?"

Burton let out a loud belch. "What you're really asking is, 'Who gets to go?'"

The Caretakers and their associates all looked up from their plates. It was not an academic question—the group selected to go on the mission had to be carefully chosen, if for no other reason than if they ran into trouble, they would not be able to draw on the Caretakers' resources for help. Those chosen would be on their own.

"Rose and Edmund, as per usual," said Verne. "And of course, Bert will go," he added, clapping his colleague on the shoulder.

"Th' three Scowlers should go," said Fred. "For something this important, *they* should make the trip, if anyone."

Verne hesitated and looked at the other Caretakers. Until this moment, none of them had considered whether—or if—they wanted to actually make this trip. But now, faced with the possibility, they realized that all of them wanted to, badly.

"I'm sorry," Verne said before any of them could volunteer, "but of the three of you, only Charles should be allowed to go."

John and Jack were immediately crestfallen—but they also understood right away what Verne meant. They were still living Caretakers, in the Prime Time of their actual life spans—but Charles was a tulpa, like Verne, Kipling, and a few others. He could withstand stresses and injuries that they could not—but more importantly, if he were lost, it would not affect the natural timeline.

"But Scowler Verne," Fred started to protest, clutching his paws in sympathetic anguish. "Scowler John an' Scowler Jack . . ."

"No, no, it's all right," John said, chuckling softly. He bowed his head for a moment, then looked up at his friends. His eyes were shining with tears. "I suppose in a way, I was looking forward to one last, great adventure, just like we had when all this began. That's how we all met, remember? When Bert came to the club at Baker Street?"

"Impossible to forget it, old friend," Charles said, giving in to his impulses and hugging his friend. "I'm, ah, sorry you're still alive and can't come along."

"I've had my adventures," Jack said, putting his arms around both Edmund and Rose. "It's time for a younger generation to earn their teeth."

"To, uh, *what?*" asked Edmund.

"It's a rite of passage," Jack replied, "for every crewman aboard a Dragonship."

"Do you remember, Jack?" Bert asked. "Do you remember the day you earned your dragon's tooth from Aven?"

Involuntarily Jack put a hand to his chest and felt the small bump where the tooth hung around his neck underneath his shirt. "I remember," he said, smiling wistfully. "I've never taken it off."

During their first adventure together, when a younger Jack was infatuated with the older captain of the *Indigo Dragon*, he had performed many feats of bravery, and more than once had saved the ship and its crew. And so during a quieter moment, she had presented him with a dragon's tooth—the mark that he had earned his place among the crew. It was more than decorative—it was one of the original dragon's teeth sown by Jason of the *Argo*, in his quest for the Golden Fleece, and thus it had several magical properties that came in handy onboard a ship. It could be turned into a stave for fighting, or a grappling hook. But mostly it was a symbol to other sailors—a statement that his place among them had been earned, not given.

Later, after having made some terrible mistakes, Jack had tried to give it back, but Aven refused. "No," she had told him firmly, "it's not an honor you lose. You earned this. But you're learning some hard lessons—and that's part of the deal too." So he kept it. And in that moment at Tamerlane House, he was glad he had. It was one of the connections he had had with Aven that neither of his friends had been given, and for that reason, he treasured the memories it brought.

"Yes," Bert said as he looked at Jack and wiped away the tears that were welling in his eyes at the memory of his daughter. "I can see that you do."

None of the Caretakers Emeriti could go, because of the limitations of the portraits—they could survive for one week outside the bounds of Tamerlane House, and no more. This was a guideline that had been underscored by the terrible loss of John's mentor, Professor Sigurdsson.

For the same reasons that John and Jack couldn't go, a petulant Laura Glue was also denied the chance to join the others, as was Fred. Burton, however, insisted on going, and stated it flatly, as if the matter was not open to debate.

"Technically speaking," he said, "I still represent what's left of the official ICS, and I'm not really a Caretaker. So I have a right to go. Also," he added, "like our friend Charles, I'm a tulpa, so there will be less risk."

"We don't have other tulpas who can go?" Jack asked Verne. "Like Kipling? Or maybe . . ." He stopped and looked around at the gathering. "Where are Houdini and Conan Doyle, anyway, Jules?"

"Er, ah," Verne sputtered, caught off guard by the question. "Kipling is on other business, and Houdini and Conan Doyle are, ah . . ."

"Tell them," said Dickens.

"They're tending my goats," Verne admitted sheepishly. "I've taken them on as apprentice shepherds."

"Good Lord," Burton said, slapping his forehead. "I weep for this and all future generations."

+ + +

The discussion continued as the Caretakers left the banquet hall and repaired to the lawn outside, where Shakespeare had constructed a simple stone platform to mark the point where the company of travelers would cross into the future.

"It's cavorite," he explained to the others. "Edmund and I realized it would give him and Rose a stronger point to link to for the return trip."

"Brilliant," said Jack. "Marlowe would never have come close to anything this clever."

Shakespeare tried not to beam with pleasure at the compliment, but failed miserably. "My thanks, Jack."

Fred was quite put out at not being allowed to accompany his friends on their journey into the future, particularly since Charles was going.

"It's my job," the little badger protested. "I'm the fourth Caretaker, after you, an' I should be going along to watch your back."

"I understand," Charles said with sincere sympathy, "but it's precisely because of that that I need you to stay here at Tamerlane House. John and Jack are going to need you here— no one else is as skilled a researcher as you are, Fred. That's part of your job too."

The little badger tried not to pout, but wasn't very successful. "Th' *bird* is going, though."

"Archie is the best reconnaissance agent we have," Bert said, winking at the clockwork owl perched on Rose's shoulder. "Taking him along is a safety precaution."

"Also," Burton interjected, "there's very little danger of the Morlocks accidentally eating the bird."

"Well, all right," Fred said with obvious reluctance. "But at least take along my copy of the Little Whatsit. I won't need it here, since I'll have th' whole library at my disposal. But you never know when it might just save your lives with some tidbit or another you didn't know you needed to know until you needed to know it."

Charles took the book and scratched Fred's head. "Of course, my friend. Thank you." He stored the book in his duffel alongside the *Imaginarium Geographica* and a few of the Histories that Verne and Bert had selected.

"Humph," Byron snorted. "He scratches the badger and the animal preens, but I try to do it as a friendly gesture, and the little beast bites me."

"Badgers are excellent judges of character," said Twain.

"Oh—right," said Byron.

Charles shouldered the duffel bag and moved to stand alongside Bert, Rose, Burton, and Edmund. Archie hopped to Charles's shoulder and beamed at Fred, as Rose tucked her sword, Caliburn, under one arm.

"We have our company then," said Bert, "and all of you have my gratitude."

"Close your eyes and think of Weena," Rose whispered, taking Bert by the hand. "You're going to see her, very soon."

Edmund and Rose held the map in front of them and concentrated on it. Instantly it began to glow, then expand, and in seconds was large enough to cross through. It was dark on the other side, but the sun was setting behind Tamerlane House as well, so that meant little.

"Farewell, my friends," said Verne, "and safe return."

The Chronic Argonauts, as Archie had dubbed them, in honor of one of Bert's stories, stepped through the portal and into darkness.

*. . . a hunched, shabby-looking man was muttering
to himself and cradling a rock . . .*

Chapter Six
The Anachronic Man

It was definitely not the world they came from, or at least, it was obvious that it was a different time. The air smelled different, and there was a startling sort of energy that vibrated through the gloomy twilight.

As soon as they were through, the portal closed, becoming a map once more, and where there had been the images of all those they had left behind at the Nameless Isles, there was now only more of that penetrating darkness that surrounded them.

"We were right," Rose said in both delight and relief as she turned to Charles and embraced him. "We did it!"

"Well done, both of you!" Charles said, returning Rose's hug and clapping Edmund on the back. "I daresay you're getting better at these jaunts all the time."

"Quiet, all of you!" Burton snapped. He was looking at Bert, who had already walked several paces away from the others. "Something's wrong."

The other companions moved to stand with Bert, so they could have a better look at where and when they'd actually come to. Charles and Burton removed two electronic flashlights from Charles's duffel, so they could illuminate the area and get their bearings.

The portal had opened onto a small plaza, which was paved with some form of concrete. It was seamless, and nearly smooth, and it spread outward in geometric patterns from where they stood on Shakespeare's platform all the way to the buildings that formed yet more geometric patterns in the distance. Beyond those, they could see the shapes of great, dark pyramids, which rose above the rest of the city like silent guardians.

Charles whistled. "Impressive," he said, looking at Bert. "You never mentioned the city in your book."

Bert looked back at the taller man, his brow furrowed with worry. "That's because there *wasn't* one—not one like this, at any rate. There was no London, no Oxford. No cities of any kind. None of this should be here, Charles."

"I read it too," Rose said, pointing up at the sky, "and I don't remember any mention of those, either."

Higher in the sky, above the spires of the city and obscured by the clouds, were the faint outlines of massive structures that arced across the sky from horizon to horizon. The companions all gasped in shock at the immensity of what they now realized were all-too-familiar shapes.

They were *chains*.

Unimaginably massive, each link was larger than the tallest building before them, and there were at least seven chains that they could see crisscrossing in the atmosphere.

"No," Bert breathed when he could find his voice again. "Those were definitely not here."

"Who could have built such incredible chains?" said Edmund, clearly overwhelmed with the concept. "And raised them so high into the air?"

"I'd be more concerned with why," Burton said as Charles nodded in agreement. "Chains are made to keep something out, or . . ."

"To keep something in," Charles finished.

"I think," Bert said, his voice trembling, "that we are in trouble. This is not my future," he continued, the trepidation and fear rising in his voice as he spoke. "Not the future I came to before."

Charles checked the date on his watch. "No," he said, trying to sound reassuring even as he fought his own rising panic at Bert's words. "It's the correct time. Ransom and Will calculated it from the point you left the first time, plus almost four years, so that we would arrive almost exactly after you and Aven left. This should be exactly the right place, exactly the right time."

Bert looked at Charles, then opened his own Anabasis device. "Eight hundred thousand years?"

"And a pinch more," said Charles. "It should be the year 802,704 AD, and a few months."

"Something *has* changed," Bert said, the anguish in his voice tearing at their hearts. "Something happened, and the future changed . . . and Weena is not here."

"Wouldn't the Histories of the future give us some clue?" asked Rose. "Surely there would be some sort of pattern to them that can be traced, to see if we miscalculated."

"Not over eight hundred thousand years," said Burton. "Not over that long a time. Too many things may have changed for the same lives he remembers to have been lived. He's right—she's gone. She's not here, and she never was."

Bert turned to the Barbarian and swung his fist, connecting hard with the other man's chin.

Burton staggered backward and rubbed his jaw. "I'm getting very tired of being struck by Caretakers."

"You aren't that stupid, Richard," a glowering Bert said, almost breathless with anger. "You understand better than most how this all is supposed to work. If something's gone wrong, it can still be fixed. If reality has been changed, then it can be changed *back*."

"If it's a reality that no longer exists in this time, Bert," Charles said gently, "then why do you believe it can still be put right?"

"Because," Bert said, opening his hand to show them what he kept in his inner pocket, "I still have Weena's petals."

Charles whistled, then reached out and gently stroked the fragile wisps of color in Bert's hand. "The flower she gave you before you left," he said admiringly. "You've kept them all this time?"

"I have," Bert said as he replaced the petals inside the jacket pocket, "to remember. And now I keep them to believe," he added, jabbing a finger at Burton. "She existed. She exists. And somehow, I will find my way back to her."

"Fair enough," Charles said, realizing that his largest role in this expedition might be that of peacemaker. "So let's start by finding out what's happened to the world in the last eight thousand centuries."

The companions walked slowly along the paved pathways, being cautious about their surroundings. At Rose's behest, Archie took flight to better scan the area, but on Bert's advice never flew higher than twenty or thirty feet. Something about the great chains in the atmosphere made him wary of intruding into the airspace of this world any more than absolutely necessary.

"Is this anything like the Winterland?" Burton asked Charles. "That alternate reality we, ah, accidentally caused with the Dyson incident?"

"I wasn't there," Charles said, looking a bit crestfallen. "I'm sorry. Whatever aspects of Chaz I may have don't include his memories of that time—so I have no idea if this is a similar situation or not."

Bert was paying less attention to the men conversing than he was to Rose and Edmund, who were trying to work out something that seemed troubling to them both.

"It's Ariadne's Thread," Rose explained when Bert inquired as to what was the matter. "I can't manage to connect it to Edmund's map. If it won't connect, we can't establish a zero point here, and the Caretakers will have no idea of when we really are. And," she added, "we might have a really difficult time getting *home*."

Ariadne's Thread was the magical cord given to Rose by the Morgaine—the three near-eternal goddesses also called the Fates. The thread was what allowed Rose to connect the maps of time made by Edmund to other zero points.

"It's always worked before," said Edmund, "ever since that first time, in London. There's no place in real time we *haven't* been able to connect to."

Bert smacked a fist into his other hand. "By the cat's pajamas," he exclaimed. "I knew it! This is a might-have-been, not the real reality. Otherwise, Edmund would be able to connect Rose's thread to his map. It won't connect because this is only an imaginary land. Which means," he added with a note of hopefulness that matched the expression on his face, "we can go back and try it again. And this time, I know we'll succeed."

Hastened by their shared desire to leave the dismal Night Land and return as quickly as possible to Tamerlane House and the Kilns, the companions made their way back to the plaza much more quickly than they'd anticipated. And so it was still only twilight when they finally reached the platform.

Edmund opened his *Chronographica*, where all his maps were stored, and retrieved the one that would take them back to Tamerlane House in 1946. Together he and Rose concentrated on the map, but nothing happened.

"That's odd," said Edmund.

"Worse than odd," Rose said. "Ariadne's Thread isn't connected to this one either—and it's a confirmed zero point."

They tried several other maps, but to no avail. None of them were working, or connected by Ariadne's Thread.

"Oh dear," Bert said weakly. "I think that we are in trouble."

"The usual kind?" Charles said.

"No," Bert replied. "The special kind. With nuts and caramel sauce. And a cherry. A great big, red, flaming cherry on top of a huge, delicious pile of nut-and-caramel-coated, special-delivery, once-in-a-lifetime trouble. That kind."

"It's this might-have-been business, isn't it?" Charles asked, rattled by the realization of what was happening. "That's the problem."

"Going from a place that exists to a place that doesn't exist is easy," Bert lamented, nodding. "But going from a place that doesn't exist to a place that does . . . not so much."

Rose gasped. Edmund scowled. And Burton uttered a string of curse words that had not been spoken aloud by a human more than twice since the fall of Babylon, just as a large stone came flying through the air, striking him viciously in the face.

The companions spun about to look in the direction from which the rock had come, expecting to see some fearsome enemy, or a clutch of Morlocks. That wasn't what they saw.

To one side of the plaza, a hunched, shabby-looking man was muttering to himself and cradling a rock in his hands as if preparing for another throw.

Shouting, Burton and Charles rushed forward and grabbed the man's arms, throwing him down and pinning him to the pavement.

Burton, who was bleeding profusely from the wound along his left cheekbone, removed the second rock from the wailing man's hand, and was not gentle about it. There was a snapping sound as the man's wrist broke, which only caused him to howl all the louder.

"Stop that infernal screeching!" Burton bellowed, "or I'll really give you something to howl about!"

"Oh," Bert said. He'd suddenly gone pale, as all the blood drained out of his face.

Rose recognized the expression on her teacher's face. "What is it?" she asked as she looked from Bert to the strange man and back again. "Do you know him? Is he one of Weena's people? One of the Eloi?"

Bert shook his head. "Not one of the Eloi, no," he said, his voice trembling with emotion. "One of us."

Charles blanched as he and Burton lifted the man roughly to his feet. "What? He's a Caretaker?"

"Not a Caretaker," Bert answered. "A Messenger, and the only time traveler to become so completely lost that no trace could be found to even hint as to where he went. Jules called him the Anachronic Man—the man lost in time."

At the mention of Verne's name the man took a breath to start howling again, but a stern look from Burton silenced him, and he simply swallowed hard, then looked at Bert with wide, frightened eyes. "Far Traveler?" he said meekly. "Is that you? Have you come to rescue me at last?"

"Rescue?" Burton said in surprise. "Who is this, Bert?"

Bert sighed heavily before answering. "Rose, gentle sentients," he said with a tight grin, "I'd like you to meet Arthur Gordon Pym."

"Had to do it," Pym said once he'd calmed down and gathered his wits. Rose and Charles were using bandages from the kit Bert always carried to bind up his broken wrist as he spoke. "No telling whose side you were on," Pym went on. "Can't leave one's enemies just strolling about."

"But," said Edmund, "we aren't your enemies at all. We didn't come to rescue you, but you've just attacked your friends."

"The irony is delicious to me," said Pym.

"He's an idiot," said Burton, who was gingerly touching his own bandaged face as the others tended to the injured Messenger. "We didn't have any idea you'd be here."

"Oh," said Pym. "Did you come here for the others, then?"

That stopped everyone in their tracks.

"What others?" Charles asked carefully, fully aware that the Messenger might still be speaking stuff and nonsense. "Other Caretakers?"

Pym seemed about to answer when his eyes widened in

shock as Archie circled low enough to join in the conversation.

"If he's a friend, I fear to see our enemies in this place," the mechanical bird said, "but I suppose there's no accounting for taste."

"It . . . it isn't real!" an astonished Pym stammered.

"No, he's real, all right," Burton said wryly. "Nothing imaginary could be so irritating."

"What do you think, Archie?" Edmund called to the bird circling overhead. "Are you real, or aren't you?"

"All of you sound smarter," the bird replied, sneering at Burton's feigned respect, "when you aren't trying to sound like philosophers."

"So speaketh the adding machine," said Burton. "I can barely hear you over the sound of your gears."

"That's why I keep a small oilcan in my pack," Edmund said, glancing at the dark clouds. "In foul weather, Archimedes tends to, um, squeak."

"I do not!" Archie squawked in indignation. "I emit nothing but the sounds of my proper functioning. To squeak would be uncouth."

"You squeak," Rose said, nodding and holding up her hands in resignation. "Sorry. Edmund is right."

Suddenly, without warning, Pym's right arm shot up in a curving arc, launching a large, jagged rock high into the air . . .

. . . where it struck the hovering Archimedes with a terrible, grinding crunch.

"Spies," Pym said, panting. "His spies are *everywhere.*"

Edmund and Rose cried out and rushed to where the damaged bird had fallen. Edmund reached Archie first, and he cradled the bird in his arms.

"Are you *insane?*" Charles exclaimed, shaking the hapless Pym by the shoulders. "No wonder Verne stopped looking for you! You're worse than Magwich!"

The stone had struck the bird with such force that it tore a gash in Archie's torso from just above his right leg to his neck. Only luck or the bird's quick reflexes had allowed him to tip his chin back at the last instant and avoid having his head torn off his neck.

As it was, the damage was bad enough. Gears and wires were spilling out of his chest and onto the ground, where a tearful Rose was attempting frantically to gather them up and stuff them back in.

"Oh, my Archie!" Rose cried. "You've killed him!"

"He's a clockwork, Rose," Bert explained gently. "He can be repaired back at Tamerlane. We have Roger Bacon's books, and Shakespeare has become quite adept at working with delicate machinery. We'll fix him, I promise."

Pym seemed to have already forgotten the entire incident and had gone back to muttering to himself. Charles and Burton joined the others and circled around Edmund and the damaged bird.

Edmund seemed almost numb with shock. He knew, intellectually, that his recently acquired companion was a mechanical bird—but it was a different thing to have that point clarified in such a violent manner.

"Well," said Charles, "Messenger or not, when we get back to Tamerlane House, there's going to be an—" He stopped and looked around, groaning. "Drat! Where's Pym gotten off to?"

"I couldn't say, since I didn't see him go," Burton said, his voice low but steady. "I did, however, see the new arrival, who is watching us now."

He tipped his head to the north, and the others turned to see a man calmly watching them from about twenty paces off.

The man was pale—no, more than that, Rose realized. He was an albino. His skin was almost entirely free of pigmentation. He wore something that resembled sunglasses over his eyes, and was dressed simply, in a tunic and breeches made of the same unbleached fabric.

On his forehead was a strange marker, or perhaps a tattoo: a circle, surrounded by four diamonds.

"I don't recognize the symbol," Burton murmured to Charles. "Do you?"

"Not at all," Charles concurred, "but it's been such a long time, who knows what is meaningful, and in what ways? We might have to resort to using sign language, just to be understood."

"Greetings," the strange man said in perfect, unaccented English, "and salutations. May I be of assistance?"

Bert gave a gasp and dashed forward, almost grasping at the strange man. The old Caretaker seemed to have difficulty finding the right words to say, and it also appeared to the others that this was more than an overture to a stranger—this was recognition of . . .

. . . a friend?

"Is it you?" Bert said, his voice faint in his breathlessness. "Nebogipfel?"

"He was my sire," the pale man replied. "You may call me Vanamonde."

"Nebogipfel?" Charles asked. "You know this man's father, Bert?"

"Dr. Moses Nebogipfel," Bert said, relieved to have another

touch point of familiarity in that dark place. "He is a Welsh inventor, who had developed some remarkable theories about time travel."

He strode over to Vanamonde and extended his hand. After a moment's hesitation, the pale man shook it, bowing slightly.

"I knew your father well, Vanamonde," said Bert. "How is he?"

"He died many years ago," Vanamonde replied with no obvious emotion, and enough finality that Bert knew not to ask further. "Your mek," he said, gesturing at Archie. "It has been damaged. We have the means to repair it, if you like."

"That's very kind of you," Rose said, before the others could answer. "Yes. Help him, please."

A look passed between Charles and Burton that expressed the same thought—caution was necessary, but there was no reason not to agree.

"Here," Vanamonde said, turning toward the towers of the city. "Follow me, if you please."

The companions fell into step behind the mysterious man as he began to walk. In a few minutes, it was obvious that their destination was the largest, tallest, darkest tower on the skyline.

"Heh." Charles chuckled and gestured at Rose. "'Child Rowland to the dark tower came,'" he said jovially. "She is our Child Rowland."

"Child?" asked Edmund.

"Childe, with an *e*," said Charles. "It means an untested knight."

"Hmm," said Bert. "Are you quoting Browning?"

"Shakespeare," said Charles. "*King Lear.*"

"Oh dear," said Bert. "You couldn't have quoted from one of the happy ones, could you?"

"Hey," Charles said, shrugging. "At least it's not *Macbeth.*"

+   +   +

As they walked toward the dark tower, Bert was unable to contain himself and continued to pepper Vanamonde with questions,
which the albino answered patiently.

"The city is called Dys," he said without taking his eyes from
the path. "It has always been called Dys, since the earliest days of
the master's reign."

"And how long is that?" asked Bert.

"Since the beginning of time."

"You mean since the beginning of Dys," Burton corrected.

"What," Vanamonde asked without turning around, "is the
difference?"

Occasionally, the companions would pass other people,
some nearby, some in the distance. All were dressed similarly to
Nebogipfel's son, but only a few bore the same markings on their
forehead.

Charles asked if the markings had some sort of meaning, and
Vanamonde bowed his head. "They do," he said. "They signify
that one is a Dragon."

The pale man did not see the others' reactions to this remark.
They were intrigued, to say the least. And more than a little surprised.

"You know, Vanamonde," Burton suggested, "some might say
that it takes more than a tattoo to signify that one is a Dragon.
What do you think of that?"

Vanamonde's eyes flashed briefly to Burton's forehead, but he
kept walking and chose not to answer.

"What of the others?" Bert pressed, intent on finding out
something about what had befallen Weena's people, the Eloi. "If

they are not, ah, Dragons, what is it they're called?"

At this, Vanamonde merely shrugged, as if the question was of no importance. Before Bert could ask him anything further, they reached the base of the tower.

Vanamonde pressed a panel on the wall and a door irised open, revealing a staircase. Motioning for the others to follow, Vanamonde started walking up the stairs.

After climbing for what seemed an eternity in the deep, windowless stairwell, Vanamonde led the companions to a landing where there was a door with a traditional handle and lock.

"Here," he said, opening the door and gesturing inside. "You may wait here as our guests while I see to the repairs on your mek and inform my master of your arrival. He will want to meet you. Of that I'm certain."

The companions filed into the room, which was simply furnished, but expansive, and more comfortable than anything they had seen on the outside.

Rose and Edmund gently handed Archimedes over to Vanamonde, who cradled the mechanical owl in his arms and, with no further comment, turned to leave.

"Vanamonde, wait!" Bert implored. "You said that you are a Dragon, is that right?"

Vanamonde did not speak, but answered with a single nod.

"All right," said Bert, "then tell us this. Is everyone here a Dragon? Everyone on Earth? You never answered me when I asked you earlier."

A light of realization went on in Vanamonde's eyes. "No," he said. "Dragon is an office of high regard. Only a few are Dragons here."

"Then the rest," Bert pressed. "The other people. Are they Eloi, or Morlocks?"

Their host furrowed his brow, as if trying to comprehend the question. "Eloi and Morlocks . . . ," he said slowly. "These are not ranks, like Dragon?"

"No, you idiot," said Burton. "We aren't asking what people do, we're asking what they are. The others here—people like us."

"Ah," Vanamonde said as he stepped back onto the landing outside the door and grasped the handle. "But there are no others like you. All are like me."

"Eloi?" asked Bert. "Or Morlock?"

"No Eloi," Vanamonde said, "no Morlocks. Only us," he finished as the door closed. "Only Lloigor."

The Cheshire cat began to slowly appear a piece at a time . . .

CHAPTER SEVEN
The Messenger

❖

"So," said Byron. "Did it work?"

"Of course it worked, you biscuit," Twain snorted. "The minute they stepped through, they vanished, just as they have with every other trip. I'd say the mission is off to a rousing start."

Dickens moved closer to the platform and tapped the cavorite with his shoe. "I wonder, Jules . . . wouldn't they be able to return almost the instant they left? I mean, wouldn't they have the capability to do that?"

"Could, but shouldn't," Shakespeare said quickly. "That would involve reworking the markings on the maps, because the time differential would change."

"That's why it's actually safer to allow them to explore in real time," Verne said. "It keeps the maps synchronized between the two times—the time they left and the time they arrived both move forward in Chronos time, so that nothing needs to be redrawn. Otherwise, a whole new set of calculations would have to be made. Rose might be able to do it, but it's going to be far easier for them to simply reverse the procedure when they've done all that they need to do."

"So an hour here is an hour there, and vice versa," Jack said, rubbing his chin. "Exquisite."

"How long are they expected to be gone, then?" asked John.

"They need to spend at least one full day there, in order to bank a chronal reserve of time for the trip into the past," Verne explained, "which gives them plenty of time to make their way to London."

John nodded in understanding. The site formerly known as London in the future time was the region where Weena would most likely be found.

"We allotted up to one day there, and one day back," Verne continued. "If all goes well, they should be coming back on Thursday, midday."

"Will they be bringing Weena with them?"

Verne paused and looked at John and Jack. "If at all possible, I'm sure that they will," he said, not entirely convincingly. "Chronal altruism aside, that is, after all, the reason that Bert went to begin with."

"An hour here is an hour there, and vice versa," Twain murmured, echoing Jack's earlier words. "And a day there is a day here. And a week there . . ." He let the words trail off as he looked up at the other Caretakers, who all understood what he was getting at. Bert's last clock had started—and every tick that did not see his return was another tick closer to the possibility that he might not return at all.

With that sobering thought heavy on their minds, the Caretakers and their friends left the platform and went back into Tamerlane House.

❖   ❖   ❖

"Do we need to return to your office first," Don Quixote asked the Zen Detective, "or do you have what you need to find the Ruby Armor in that box you placed in the boot of the car?"

"I may have been exaggerating just slightly," Aristophanes admitted as the Duesenberg sped away from the Kilns. Uncas was driving erratically, as usual, which hadn't unnerved the detective the first time, but was a little more troubling now that he'd agreed to an extended trip. "What I really meant is that I know how to find the people who know how to find the armor."

"That in't what you told us," Uncas said without taking his eyes off the road, "or the Scowlers."

"I find it difficult to condemn a man for the same moral failings I myself have grappled with time and again," said Quixote, "and besides, the truth of things now will be borne out upon the success of our quest later."

"That's a very pragmatic attitude," Aristophanes said admiringly. "You'd have made an excellent philosopher, Don Quixote."

"I couldn't have afforded it," Quixote said. "That's one profession that pays even less than being a questing knight. And then there are the occasional missteps—one irritated audience, one awkward philosophical comment, and then someone starts talking about hemlock, and that's about the point you wish you'd listened to your mother and just become a fisherman."

"Does he always take compliments that poorly?" Aristophanes asked the badger.

"You have no idea," said Uncas. "I am surprised, though, that no one kept better track o' this armor, if it's as important as all that."

"The pieces could not be kept in the Archipelago, and neither were they safe in the Summer Country," said the detective, "and so the only way they could be kept completely safe was to hide them in the Soft Places—the places that aren't there."

"And no one kept a ledger?" Uncas said. "Impractical."

"Whose job is it to keep track of the places that aren't there?" Aristophanes asked. "Yours?" He pointed at the badger next to him. "Or his?" he said, hooking his thumb over his shoulder at Quixote. "The Caretakers cared only about the real places of consequence—those in the Archipelago of Dreams. But the rest were just overlooked, or," he added with a touch of rancor, "exiled.

"Only someone like Elijah McGee had the skill to set down maps of the unknown places, and only his children had the presence of mind to preserve them. That the Caretakers have them now for us to use is—"

"Zen?" offered Quixote.

Aristophanes started to scowl, then lowered his head and smiled before turning to look at the knight in the backseat. "I was going to say 'luck,' but Zen will have to do. That's how we're going to find the places we need to find. With a little Zen, and a little luck. And hopefully, the world won't end before we've done it."

"Someone's world is always ending," said Quixote.

"And I care less about that," said Aristophanes, "than I care about making sure the world that does end isn't mine."

Quixote sat back and sighed. "You'd have made a terrible knight."

"I know," Aristophanes replied, turning to face the front again. "That's why I became a philosopher."

◆　　◆　　◆

"Our first destination should be no trouble to get to," said Aristophanes. "But we'll need to arrange passage to all the rest."

"Not necessary," the badger replied. "Not when we've got old Betsy here." He patted the dashboard.

"No, you don't understand," said the detective, irritated. "I'm talking about places that are thousands of miles away, so we've got to—"

"No problem," Uncas said, "as long as you know precisely where you want to go. Pick anyplace in th' world, an ol' Betsy can take us there."

Aristophanes blinked. "How about Madagascar?"

Quixote opened up a large compartment in the dashboard, which was filled with rows and rows of photographic slides, all ordered alphabetically. "Ah!" the knight finally exclaimed. "Here it is. I had it in Mauritania's slot. Took a minute to find."

He removed the slide and inserted it into a device on the dash that resembled a radio but had an external motor and some sort of arrangement of lenses.

"It's Scowler Jules's latest innovation," Uncas said proudly. "It projects an image through a special lamp on the bumper, like . . . *so*," he said, switching on the device. Immediately a large projection of the image on the slide appeared on the wall of fog in front of them, and Uncas gunned the engine.

"It works best with brick walls," said the badger, "but fog works pretty well too."

Before the detective could vocalize his astonishment, the Duesenberg had barreled through the projection, bouncing jarringly from the country road in England and onto a nicely paved cobblestone road in a hilly area that was clear of fog. Palm trees lined the streets, and the smell of seawater was strong in the air.

"I'm impressed," said the detective.

"So," Uncas said. "Where to first?"

"I'm almost afraid to say," said Aristophanes, "but you're going to need to turn around."

As the rest of the Caretakers converged in the portrait gallery to discuss the recent events, Jules Verne quietly pulled John down the adjacent hallway and closed the door behind them. "I need to take you with me to consult some of our allies in the war," Verne said, his voice quiet until they were a safe distance away from other ears, "and I don't want anyone else to know we're going—not yet."

"Isn't that a bit chancy?" John asked, glancing around. "We ought to—"

"Poe knows," Verne said, interrupting, "and Kipling. And for now, that must be sufficient."

He chuckled to himself, then looked at John. "You'll never believe that the pun wasn't intentional, but I told Poe we're going to see the Raven. Dr. Raven, to be precise."

"The Messenger?"

Verne nodded. "The only one among them who is still wholly mobile, and therefore wholly useful," he explained, "and that in itself brings some degree of risk, because he is also the most unknown."

"How so?"

"He's the only one we didn't actively recruit," said Verne. "Bert and I were taking a breakfast meeting in Prague in the late eighteenth century, and we observed that we were being observed ourselves. We took no notice of him, but quickly made our departure so as not to attract more attention—but then he turned up again at a café in Amsterdam."

"You have refined tastes," John said. "Perhaps he was simply running in similar epicurean circles."

"Ahh, that explanation may have sufficed," offered Verne, "if our lunch in Amsterdam had not been a century later."

John stopped in his tracks, blinking in amazement. "He was a time traveler?"

Verne nodded. "All the Messengers are, of course—but he was doing it before he became a Messenger, and," he added, with just a hint of menace in his voice, "he already had an Anabasis Machine."

John removed his watch from his pocket and examined it carefully. His was identical to the one Verne himself carried: a silver case, emblazoned with a red dragon. "How is that possible? I thought only the Caretakers possessed the watches."

"The Watchmaker gives them to us to use," said Verne, "but we may not be the only ones he has made them for. I've never been able to wheedle a straight answer out of him regarding that particular question. But in any regard, Dr. Raven, as he introduced himself, has never been anything but faithful to our goals. We asked him to join us, and he has made himself available at each point where he's been needed. As far as I know, he keeps rooms in Tamerlane, but as to the rest of his life, he is still a mystery."

"He sounds more like a secret," John said as he pocketed his watch.

"Secrets and mysteries, mysteries and secrets," a voice purred from somewhere above their heads. "Answer one and win, answer the other and lose. But who can tell which one is which? And which of you shall choose?"

John glanced above his left shoulder and smiled. "Hello, Grimalkin."

The Cheshire cat began to slowly appear a piece at a time as the men made turn after turn down the seemingly endless corridors. He had once been Jacob Grimm's familiar, but he seemed to have bonded himself to John. He was, however, still a cat, and he came and went as he chose.

"So," Grimalkin said as his hindquarters appeared, "you're going to see the Raven, are you?"

"We are," said John.

"Mmmmrrrr," the cat growled. "We do not like him. He has no place."

"What do you mean?" John asked, puzzled. "Jules said he has a room here."

"Not room, *place*," the cat spat back, clearly irritated. "The Raven has no place. He is here, but not here. It's very confusing, and it vexes us."

"What the Cheshire is trying to explain," said Verne, "is that Dr. Raven is unique among the Messengers, and even among the Caretakers, in that he has no trumps."

Again John stopped and looked at the older man. "He doesn't travel by trump? So how does he get to where you need him to be?"

Verne shrugged. "We aren't really sure. He just . . . goes to wherever he is needed. We tried to press him about it once, and he vanished for six months. When he returned, he acted as if nothing had happened, so we never addressed it again."

"No place," the cat repeated as it started to vanish again. "We will be watching, Caretakers."

"Can we really trust him then, Jules?" John said as Verne indicated a rather plain green door at the end of the last hallway. "He sounds more like someone we should be worried about than entrusting with our future."

"The best assessment we were able to make is that he is a fiction, like Herman Melville, or Hank Morgan," said Verne. "Or possibly an anomaly, like Bert himself. But he has never acted against us, and in this war, we may be less able to choose our friends than we are our enemies."

He rapped sharply on the door, which swung open immediately. The room was small, obviously an antechamber to a larger warren of living spaces, but it was utilized fully. There were desks and shelves filled with antiquities and relics of the distant past—and, John observed, some from possible futures. Toward the right side, sitting in a tall, straight-backed chair, was a slender, slightly hawkish man who immediately rose to greet them.

"You assess correctly, Caveo Principia," Dr. Raven said, noting John's interest in the items of the collection that were not antiques. "We once kept most of these items at the Cartographer's room in Solitude, but for obvious reasons, they had to be relocated."

John gave a slightly formal nod and handshake to the other, still chewing over what Verne had been telling him in the hallways. "I recognize a few things," he said, moving over to a shelf filled with record albums. "Merlin was very fond of his Marx Brothers collection."

"He also enjoyed the films of Clint Eastwood," said Dr. Raven, "although you'd never have gotten him to admit it." He spoke in a friendly and courteous manner, but his eyes never left John's face, and John had also noticed that Dr. Raven addressed him using his most formal title.

The Messenger was hooded, but enough of his face was visible that John could see the honest smile of greeting, and the well-earned wrinkles at the corners of his eyes. The other Messengers had been roughly John's contemporaries, but this Dr. Raven was somewhat older, perhaps closer to Bert in age. Regardless, John understood some of what Verne saw in the man—he seemed immediately trustworthy, which bothered John, because nothing else he knew about him was.

"So," Dr. Raven said, rubbing his hands together. "What may I do for the Caveo Principia?"

"Harrumph." Verne cleared his throat and stepped slightly in front of John. He was used to being deferred to, and Dr. Raven's seeming interest in John was off-putting. "We need you to be a chaperone, basically. No time travel will be involved, simply spatial travel—to the Soft Places."

"Ah," Dr. Raven said, as if he understood more than Verne was saying aloud. "The badger and the knight. You've sent them on another quest, I take it? Are they after another Sphinx?"

"Not quite," said Verne. "They're looking for the Ruby Armor. And Aristophanes is guiding them."

For the briefest instant, John thought he saw the Messenger's expression darken, as if this was a disturbing surprise.

"The Zen Detective," said Dr. Raven. "I see. And that's all you need? For them to be chaperoned?"

"Shadowed," Verne corrected. "No assistance, unless their lives are in imminent danger. If they succeed, we'll have won a major victory against the enemy. But if they fail, then the armor remains out of reach to our enemy as well."

"Understood." The Messenger bowed to Verne, but he kept his eyes firmly locked on John, as if they shared some sort of secret. "I serve at the will of the Caretakers. It shall be done."

"Thank you, Doctor," Verne said as he opened the door and ushered John outside. "We'll expect a report soon, then." He closed the door, and the Messenger was alone.

The room shimmered, as if it were slightly out of focus with the rest of the world; then it clarified again, and the room was just as it had been—with one exception. Dr. Raven was younger. The wrinkles at his eyes were fewer, and he stood just a bit straighter, with just a little more vigor. It was as if several years of his life had suddenly fallen away.

"Be seeing you," Dr. Raven said to no one in particular, before he removed the watch from his pocket, twirled the dials, and disappeared.

. . . in the middle sat a beautiful woman in a blue silk dress . . .

CHAPTER EIGHT
The Last Caretaker

✥

Vanamonde's last word hung in the air and echoed in the companions' minds so strongly that it took a few seconds for them to realize that they might actually be prisoners, and not merely guests.

Burton got to the door first. It was locked.

"Fools," he muttered, eyes downcast. "We are all fools. Especially"—he turned, pointing at Bert—"*you.*"

"We were all taken in," Charles said mildly. "We can't blame Bert for trusting in a familiar face."

"We all chose to follow him," said Edmund, "and he did offer to help Archie."

"It isn't that stout a door," Burton said, flexing his muscles. "I think I can take it down." He threw his weight against the door—which didn't move. Charles joined him, but even together, they couldn't budge the door.

"This door has a Binding," Bert mused, rubbing his chin. "Rose, try using Caliburn."

As her mentor suggested, Rose swung the great sword at the door. It struck with an explosion of sparks—but made no mark at all where the sword hit.

"Deep Magic, then," said Bert. "We're in this room until Vanamonde—or his Master—say otherwise."

There was nothing the companions could do but wait for Vanamonde to return and hope for the best. But hope was in short supply, after the reversals they'd experienced in the last few hours. They paired off into different corners of the room, to commiserate, and try to rest, and prepare themselves for whatever might come next.

"All Lloigor," Charles said bleakly. "That's a bad, bad circumstance, I think."

"Not all," Burton corrected. "Pym certainly was no Lloigor—I think."

"Perhaps, but then again, he's the one who attacked you and nearly demolished poor Archie," Charles replied. "At this point, I'm feeling less threatened by the Lloigor than by Verne's own lieutenant."

"Been there, done that," said Burton.

Across the room in the far corner, Rose and Edmund were sprawled out on their coats, using their duffels for pillows and trying to rest. Sleep was unlikely, but Burton had taught them both how to meditate, so they decided it was as good a time as any to balance their minds. Mostly, though, they were just talking about the friends they'd left behind at Tamerlane—particularly Laura Glue.

There had been a curious sort of dance among the three of them, since Rose and Laura Glue first met Edmund in Revolutionary War–era London. There had been flirtations— after all, Edmund was the only available male at Tamerlane House who was not a portrait, tulpa, or small forest creature—but Rose, for the most part, kept a discreet distance whenever an opportunity arose to be alone with the young Cartographer. An innocent romance had developed between Edmund and Laura Glue, and she didn't know whether—or if—she should complicate several friendships by seeing if there was anything deeper between herself and Edmund.

In terms of education, all three were equally balanced, with expertise in different areas—but in terms of life experience, Edmund and Laura Glue were closer. Rose simply had been through too many experiences that they could not relate to for them to be true equals. So, while the interest had been there, she had never so much as flirted with Edmund.

But now, in impossible circumstances, and facing the very real possibility that they had been caught in an Echthroi trap, she wasn't thinking about anything except the handsome young man drifting in and out of a meditative trance, who lay just inches away from her.

He was, she thought as her shadow curled up and around her like a scarf, right next to her.

And Laura Glue was very, very far away.

"Do you ever regret coming back with us from London?" she asked abruptly, taking him out of his trance.

Edmund blinked as he thought about the question and wondered what kind of an answer she was asking for. Sure, there were times when he missed his father, and the life he had led as a student of Dr. Franklin's. But there had always been that deeper yearning, the inner conviction that he was destined for greater things. Of course, that could also be his pirate blood speaking to him—not that that would be such a bad thing.

"Regret, no," he said finally, taking her hand in his as he spoke. "But there are days when I do wonder if I was crazy to have followed you."

"I don't think we could have gotten back without your help," said Rose.

Edmund smiled. "Yes, you could have. Once I made the chronal trump, you just needed to step through. And the connection was yours, anyroad."

"If you hadn't come back with us then, you wouldn't be stuck here with me now."

He sat up so that he could look at her more directly, and he squeezed her hand just a bit more tightly.

"I'm happy that I did follow you, though, whatever else may come, Rose. I am. Even ending up here has already turned into an adventure. Traveling with you is just too much fun to be had."

Her eyes flashed with anger for just a moment, until she realized that he was teasing her, and she moved closer to him and lifted her chin. "I'm glad you came with us too. Whatever may come."

He smiled at her briefly, but with an expression in his eyes that said he was worried. And afraid. So she clutched his hand a little more tightly against the darkness, and they were afraid together. And that made it more bearable. A little, at least.

From the other side of the chamber Charles watched the shadows shift and move where Rose sat with the young Cartographer. Bert moved alongside him, where he could speak without being overheard by the others.

"They're a good team," the Far Traveler said softly. "She complements him, and he, her."

"I know," Charles agreed. "His abilities to make maps may actually rival Merlin's, although I'd never have confessed that to him. And combined with her understanding of time . . . Well. It's an impressive combination, even if it did result in our getting stuck here in the far future."

Suddenly the room was shaken by a loud rumbling from outside—a tremendous noise that made the tower sway to and fro as if it were caught up in an earthquake. The sound and motion brought everyone to their feet, concerned that something awful was happening.

Bert took Charles by the arm. "That was no earthquake," he said, a spark of fear in his eyes. "I've felt that before, in another tower."

"The Keep of Time," Charles said flatly. "When it grew."

"Shades," muttered Burton. "That would explain the Deep Magic that's sealed us here in the room, too."

"It isn't a Keep of Time, though," said Rose. "Otherwise I'd feel it. This is simply a tower."

"But a living one, like the keep," said Bert, "which makes me very curious who Vanamonde's Master is."

"Begging your pardon, sir," said Edmund, "but maybe it's an enemy we already know.

"I've read about the, ah, Dyson incident," he went on, casting a sidelong glance at Rose, who pursed her lips in return. "It created the Winterland because of what Hugo Dyson changed in the past, but the Caretakers were able to largely restore everything by going into the past themselves, and fixing what Dyson set into motion. So might that not be the case here as well?"

"Not quite," Charles said, shaking his head. "The Winterland was an altered present, because of changes made in the past. But here we're in the future. Things aren't as they are because of something we've done that has to be undone," he explained. "The world has become this . . . this terrible place because of something we haven't done *yet*."

"Speaking as one who was largely responsible for initiating the, ah, 'incident,'" said Burton, "I have to say that it may also have been inevitable. There were events that we caused that had already happened in the past—such as the Winterland's version of Charles, Chaz, going back in time to become the first Green Knight."

"As awful as it is to admit, what *has* happened had to happen," said Bert. "Circumstances were thrust upon us like a football thrown to a one-legged player, and we simply played through as best we could. That it turned out that the plays we made had already been scumbled in some sort of cosmic playbook was neither to our credit nor our blame. The important fact here is that we never asked for the ball."

"So what do we do?" asked Edmund.

Bert squeezed the young Cartographer's shoulder. "Rest. Try to regain some strength. And then be prepared for anything."

The shadows that enveloped the city were not static: They were living things that flowed like the tides, overlapping one another and blocking all but the faintest of twilit gloom from reaching the surface. But every so often, they would shift in such a way that a small, insignificant corner of sky was left exposed. And it was through just such an opening that the Lady sent her moonbeam to wake the sleeping Grail Child.

The light that awakened Rose wasn't terribly bright, but it was soft, and tinged with blue. It seeped underneath the doorway and through the lock—which, with a gentle clicking, disengaged, slowly swinging the door open.

Curiosity won out over caution, and Rose got up to investigate. She was careful not to disturb any of her slumbering friends—somehow she understood that they would not wake, were not meant to wake, to see this light. It was sent to awaken only her, and as it retreated down the long hallways outside the door, she felt compelled to follow it.

The light led her to a door several landings above the room where they'd been imprisoned. The door was slightly ajar, and the light was emanating from within. Slowly Rose pushed it open and entered.

In the center of the room were three chairs. The first was occupied by a corpse wearing a dress of fine red silk, embroidered with pearls. The third chair was empty. And in the middle sat a beautiful woman in a blue silk dress, who gestured for Rose to come closer.

"Hello, daughter," the woman said. "Please, come in. Sit. We have much to tell you, and only these few moments in which to do it."

"Are you Mother Night?" Rose asked as she moved closer.

"We are," the woman said, "but before that I was Lachesis, and I am the only one who may speak to you here. Clotho is no more, and Atropos is no longer permitted on this world."

"What is it?" asked Rose. "What has happened? I tried using Ariadne's Thread, but—"

"It will not work, not in this place," Lachesis confirmed. "This is now a fully Shadowed world. Its connections have been severed. But there is still a chance for you to change what has happened."

Lachesis reached out her hand and gave something to Rose. It was a small, multifaceted mirror. "Use this only when you must. Solve the riddle of the last Dragon. And you may yet claim your destiny as protector of this world, before it is too late."

Before Rose could ask any questions, Lachesis suddenly turned her head in alarm. "Oh!" she exclaimed. "Something fell."

Then she disappeared, along with the corpse of her sister and the empty chair. And Rose woke up, still sleeping next to Edmund.

She almost imagined that it had been a dream—but in her hand was the mirror.

Rose was about to rouse the others to tell them what had happened when they were all brought to their feet by a soft tapping at the door.

"Greetings," Vanamonde said as he entered the room. "I trust you all rested well."

Burton started to respond with a well-built-up reserve of expletives, but Vanamonde stopped him with an upraised hand. "All your questions will be answered in due time," he said placidly, "and so you are not concerned, the repairs on your mek have gone well, and he will be returned to you soon. But for now," he finished, standing to one side and bowing, "Lord Winter has requested your presence, if you will be so kind as to follow me."

At the mention of the name 'Lord Winter,' Charles scowled at Burton, whose face had gone red. But Bert put his hands on both of their shoulders and smiled broadly at Vanamonde. "Yes," he said, agreeing for all of them. "We shall."

Vanamonde led them to the stairway, where they climbed

farther than they had to reach their cell, and eventually got to the very top of the dark tower.

The stairs opened onto a broad terrace, so high that the wind should have been ferocious—but it was cold, and the air was calm. At the far end of the terrace, Vanamonde spoke to a man who had been looking out over Dys, who now turned to greet the companions.

"Welcome," he said. "I'm very pleased to see you all. It has been . . . a very long time."

Lord Winter was not terribly tall, but he had unmistakable presence. He was dressed entirely in black, in fashionable clothes that would not have been out of place in their own century. His hair was nearly as long as he was tall, and he wore the same dark spectacles as Vanamonde. He was flanked by three of his Dragons—long-robed attendants, who wore masks of stone that bore the markings of their office and that flared up and away from their faces as if they were the tails of comets falling to Earth. Behind them, floating in the sky, but considerably lower than the great chains high above, were several geometric shapes. Charles couldn't shake the feeling that these hexagons and cubes were somehow sentient, and there to observe the meeting.

"Well," he whispered to the others, "that isn't Mordred. That's something, at least. Although," he added nervously, "his voice does sound quite familiar."

"No," Bert said, a chill in his voice—and loudly enough to be heard by Lord Winter. "It isn't Mordred. But it is someone else we know."

"Ah," Lord Winter said as he suppressed a wry smile. "You've recognized me after all. I was afraid that after so many thousands of years, you might not. . . . But then again, it hasn't been quite so long for any of you, has it? By your reckoning, it's been barely a day since you last spoke to the man I once was."

"It can't be," Rose whispered. "Not here. Not like this."

"I'm sorry, child," said Burton, "but it is."

Edmund looked around, confused by the growing horror he read in his companions' faces. It was obvious that Lord Winter, this dark and terrible figure, was someone they knew well. He turned to the pale man. "Your Highness," Edmund began, only to be silenced by a crisp wave of the other's hand.

"Now, now, my young Cartographer," he said smoothly. "You needn't be so formal. We are, after all, old friends, are we not? So please," he said, his voice dropping to a soft tone that nevertheless rang clearly in their ears, "call me *Jack*."

PART THREE

The Mystorians

She raised her chin in acknowledgment of her guests . . .

CHAPTER NINE
Through the Looking-Glass

❖

The man who knelt looking at his reflection in the lake at the ends of the Earth appeared younger than he really was. Everyone in the lands where he had been born lived very, very long lives, in the manner of the first men, and so youth lasted not merely for decades, but for centuries. By the accounting of this world, he was in fact very advanced in years, even before his exile from Alexandria.

He had been compelled, by a Binding of Deep Magic, to journey to the farthest ends of the Earth—and that compulsion had brought him here, to the mountains on the far side of the Mongolian plateau. It was not the farthest place where men dwelled, but it was the farthest place that had been named.

The man was considering whether this meant he might have to travel farther still when the Dragon landed behind him, silent as a dream. He didn't turn around but merely considered the great beast's reflection, behind and beside his own.

"Greetings, Madoc, son of Odysseus," the reflection of the Dragon said. "I have been seeking you a long while."

"I'm not Madoc any longer," he replied. "I stopped being Madoc when my brother betrayed me and drove me from Alexandria.

"The people here call this place Baikal," the young man

continued, "and they call me Mordraut. Baikal refers to the lake, apparently. It means 'deepest.'"

The Dragon growled. "And Mordraut?"

The man turned and looked up at him. "Driven," he said after a moment. "They say it means driven."

"And are you driven?" the Dragon said. "You must have been, to journey so far."

Mordraut's face darkened. "The journey," he said softly, "wasn't my idea."

"Hmm," the great Dragon rumbled. "The Binding. Of course. I apologize, Ma—Mordraut."

The man considered the Dragon before deciding to ask a question—something not lightly done with Dragons.

"You are from the Archipelago, are you not?"

The Dragon did not answer, but merely met his gaze.

"Can you take me there?" Mordraut pressed. "Can you take me home?"

The Dragon shook his head. "I'm sorry," he said, "but I cannot. Not bound, as you are now. But perhaps . . . there might be a way. It is why I have come to find you."

The man Mordraut had listened only to the first part of the Dragon's response and was already deflating when the second part registered on his consciousness. "You came here for me?" he asked, more earnest now. "Why? And how can that get me back?"

"My brethren and I guard the barrier that separates the Archipelago from this, the Summer Country," the Dragon said, "but we only guard, we do not govern.

"Long ago," he continued, "it was decided that a king from this world should be chosen to rule over both. But the one chosen was betrayed and *fell from grace. There has been none who could replace him, until now.*

"There is to be a competition, judged by the bloodline of the first king, to choose who will sit on the Silver Throne of the Archipelago. If you would become my apprentice, I will prepare you to sit on that throne and rule. But you must first win, and there will be many vying for the honor. You will have to defeat them all."

Mordraut shook his head. "I'm not interested in defeating anyone," he said brusquely. "And I'm no fighter."

"These people here can train you to fight," said the Dragon, "and I can prepare you to rule. But I think you will find the drive to win on your own."

"Why?"

"Because," the Dragon rumbled, "if you choose not to compete, the first king of the Archipelago will be the strongest contender—your brother, Myrddyn."

There was no way to parse the complex mix of emotions that passed across the man's face as the Dragon spoke the name of the brother who had bound him, and betrayed him, and it took several moments for Mordraut to regain his self-control. When he finally did, he looked up again.

"What are you called, Dragon?"

The great beast raised an eyebrow. "You, youngling, may call me Samaranth."

Mordraut nodded and turned back to the lake.

"Yes, Samaranth," he said finally. "I shall become your apprentice."

"Good," the Dragon replied. "Then let us begin."

John and Verne's journey back to the main wings of the house took considerably less time, due in large part to a more direct route, but also, John was certain, to Tamerlane House's penchant for moving the rooms around when the Caretakers weren't looking.

As opposed to Dr. Raven's quarters, which occupied the lowest level above the basements, and which were therefore windowless, the part of the house Verne was leading John to was in the upper floors, as evidenced by the scatterings of windows and skylights that began appearing in hallways and over stairwells.

"There are eleven arboreta in Tamerlane House . . . that I know of," Verne said as they reached the end of one of the uppermost corridors, "but this one can only be unlocked with one of three keys: mine, Poe's, and the occupant's."

He spun a large key ring out of his pocket and twirled through several brilliant gold and silver keys before choosing a rather ordinary-looking iron key, which he inserted into the lock. Verne turned the key once, then again, and with a click, the door swung open into an enormous room, which was dimly lit despite the expanse of windows in the walls and the ceiling.

The air was cloyingly thick with the scent of pollen and decay. Along the walls—which, except for the one where the door was located, were all glass—were wooden tables lined with flowerpots and trays bearing an amazing array of plants. Some were flowering, punctuating the swaths of green with bursts of magenta, orange, and turquoise. Others were climbers, and had escaped the confines of the trays to spread along the walls, nearly obscuring the glass with their leafy expanses.

On the floor, loam was scattered freely over the Oriental carpets, a clear indication of the priorities of the occupant. The room was there to house the flora, and housekeeping was a distant second.

"Step where I step," said Verne, "and don't touch anything."

"All right," said John.

As John and Verne crossed the threshold, the room's occupant, a disarmingly attractive young woman, rose from between two of the planter boxes and drew a soiled arm across a forehead damp with sweat.

She raised her chin in acknowledgment of her guests, and Verne stepped forward.

"John," he said, gesturing at the young woman, "I believe you know Beatrice—Dr. Rappaccini's daughter."

She was one of the Messengers—Verne's special envoys who traveled by use of the trumps, and each of whom had a special affinity for matters of time and space. The first of them, Hank Morgan, had recently perished during the events that had separated Tamerlane House from the Archipelago. Soon after, the second Messenger, Alvin Ransom, also died when his dimensional counterpart, Charles, reached the end of his chronal lifespan—but unlike Charles, who'd been revived as an unaging tulpa, Ransom joined the other Caretakers in the portrait gallery, and could only leave Tamerlane House for seven days. The third Messenger, Arthur Pym, had been on a mission when he became lost in time. Beatrice was the fourth, and the one least known to the other Caretakers. Except to go on missions for Verne, she seldom left her own quarters, and when she did, she spoke even less frequently. They all knew of her, of course, but this was the first time Verne had ever deigned to make a formal introduction.

"I'm pleased to meet you," John said pleasantly, offering his hand. "I'm John."

"Don't touch her!" Verne shouted as he struck the younger

man's hand, pushing him away. "Forgive me," he said, more to the girl than to his fellow Caretaker. "I should have cautioned him beforehand."

"It's all right," John said as he rubbed the top of his hand. "I meant no harm."

Verne shook his head. "Nor would you have caused any," he said, his voice softer now. "When I said 'Don't touch anything,' what I really meant was, you can't touch everything. Including the lady Beatrice.

"Some stories are true," Verne added. "Hers is one of them. Her father's experiments made her a mistress of toxins—and unable to touch anyone else. Anyone living, that is. Even her voice can be deadly to others, so she seldom uses it."

"Point taken," said John, who bowed to Beatrice before Verne guided him across the room.

In the far corner stood three massive mirrors. They were each fully six feet tall, and almost four feet wide. They hung inside frames carved from a dark wood that seemed to absorb the dim light in Beatrice's arboretum. Moving closer, John could see that there were hundreds of intricate figures carved into the frames with such detail he could almost make out the expressions on their faces.

"They were patterned after a Brueghel," Verne said, noticing John's admiration of the frames, "but the mirrors are far, far older. Walk around to the other side and take a look."

John did as he was instructed and was startled to get to the back of the mirrors and see Verne's smiling face grinning at him from the other side.

"Are they transparent?" John asked. "An invisible backing of some kind?"

"Not transparent, nonexistent," said Verne. "Go ahead, try to touch them. It's safe enough from that side."

John put out his hand to touch the center mirror, and to his astonishment it went through where the mirror was supposed to be, right through the frame.

"They're literally one-way mirrors," Verne said as John came around to the front. "There are no backs to them, only a front. Poe told me about them, although I don't think even he knows who made them."

"Astonishing," said John. "Where did you get them?"

"Aristophanes found them for me," Verne answered. "He's been useful in that way. They actually belonged to one of the fellows you're going to meet."

"So what are we supposed to do with them?"

"Do?" said Verne. "Why, go through one of them, of course. "Lots of interesting things can happen when you go through a looking-glass."

"One of them?" John asked. "They don't all work in the same way?"

"Oh, they all work," said Verne, "but only one goes to the place we need it to. The other two are, shall we say, the last line of defense—here within the house proper, that is."

"Where do they go?"

"No place you want to be," said Verne, "unless you feel like you missed something in life by not being at Pompeii."

"The other two lead to the volcano?" John exclaimed. "But isn't it dormant now?"

"The top of it is." Verne chuckled. "Look at the frame, and follow what you see."

John examined the figures along the frames and noticed that they were all similar in one regard: Each had a bas-relief carving of the Minotaur at the top, and all the figures were facing right.

"Just like in the labyrinth, then," said John.

"Take the right-hand side," Verne said, nodding, "or, as our Minotaur friend would say, the right-hand right-hand right-hand side."

Chuckling at his own joke, he turned and offered a courtly bow to Beatrice, who nodded her head in return. Then, with no further commentary, Verne stepped into the glass to the right, pulling John along with him.

The sensation was not unlike moving through water—water with the consistency of molasses. It was not at all as natural as using one of the trumps. Still, it took only a few seconds to go through, and they found themselves in an alleyway facing a broad cobblestone street. The sun was high and bright, and the air was crisp, with a cold bite to it.

"Are we in one of the Soft Places?" John asked, pulling his collar closed. "One of those in-between places that's neither here nor there?"

"You might say that, John," said Verne. "Welcome to Switzerland."

"The mirror," John exclaimed, turning about. "It's gone?"

Verne smiled wanly. "It's a one-way mirror, young John," he said. "We can't be having people just popping through to Tamerlane House now, can we?"

"I wanted to ask but didn't want to offend Beatrice," John said, biting his lip. "You said Dr. Raven is the only Messenger who remains wholly mobile. Is she ill, or has she been hurt in some way, that she can no longer travel for you?"

Verne shook his head. "It's the end progression of her father's meddling in nature, I'm afraid," he said with sincere regret. "Her toxic nature makes her the ideal guardian of the mirror, but she's no longer just exuding the essences of the plants she cares for—she's starting to become one. She's taking root. And in time, she'll have to leave Tamerlane and join others of her kind in the jungles of the South American continent, along the River Tefé."

"How can there be others of her kind?" John asked. "Are you talking about living plants? Plants that were once human?"

"Something like that," said Verne. "More like living tree-creatures . . . Guardians of the Green. As we look after the world of men, so they look after the flora."

John scowled. "They aren't like Magwich, are they? That would be . . . well, Charles wouldn't be happy, knowing there's a grove of Magwiches in the world."

Verne laughed. "Not quite, but that really should be looked into. We ought to ask Bea about your little shrub when we return. She can consult with the grove about him."

"Will I ever meet them?"

"Perhaps," said Verne, "but trust me—once you do, you'll never feel the same about pruning your roses."

Verne led John out of the alley and onto a busy street. As they walked, he explained that they were in the canton of Fribourg, which was near Lake Neuchâtel, but that their specific destination was a small, well-appointed hotel a few blocks away.

"Not that I doubt the precision of your planning," John said as he threw a backward glance at the alleyway where they had come through the looking-glass, "but if it's a one-way portal, how are you planning to get us back?"

In reply Verne flashed open his jacket. There, in the inner breast pocket, John could see one of the trumps peeking out over the top. Just enough of the card was visible for him to recognize the towers and minarets of Tamerlane House.

"You have a trump back to the Nameless Isles?" he said, more impressed than surprised. "I thought it was forbidden for anyone but Kipling to have one."

"It was," Verne replied, "by *me*. Being the Prime Caretaker does have its privileges, you know. Here," he said, pointing across the street. "We've arrived."

The hotel stood at the corner of a busy intersection—busy enough that John was nearly clipped by an automobile speeding past. He spun around and shook his fist at the rapidly receding car.

"Curse it all, Uncas!" he yelled. "Slow down!"

Suddenly he realized what he'd just shouted, and he turned crimson from the neck up as Verne roared with laughter.

"Sorry," John said. "Force of habit."

CHAPTER TEN
The Hotel d'Ailleurs

✦

The hotel was only three stories tall, and the exterior was not especially imposing. It was a Swiss building in a Swiss town, and so it was practical, efficient, and just a little bit bland. John was about to make a comment to that effect when Verne opened the front door and ushered him inside.

To the left of the clerk's desk—which Verne bypassed with a wave of his hand—was a bar, which was to be expected, and a small kitchen from which a delicious aroma was wafting. But to the right was a great room, and suddenly John started to realize what it was about this hotel that kept Verne's attention. From Persian-rug floor to pressed-tin ceiling, the walls were covered with perhaps the greatest collection of fantastic art John had ever seen.

There were framed paintings, and etchings, and pencil drawings, and in the corners even a few sculptures—and the common theme that tied them all together was that they were based on great works of science fiction. John also noted, wryly, that a large percentage of the art was based on the work of Jules Verne.

"But of course!" Verne exclaimed when John commented on

It was appointed to resemble a private club . . .

it. "It's my hotel, so why shouldn't most of the decoration be based on my own best works?"

"I see," John said as he examined a painting based on one of Verne's earliest works, *In Search of the Castaways*. "And how many of Bert's works are represented here?"

"A goodly number," Verne replied, "at least fifteen percent."

"Fifteen percent?"

"All right, ten," Verne admitted, "but it's a really excellent ten percent."

He led John past all the paintings to a doorway located under the stairs to the rooms above. The door led down to an older structure that the hotel was built on. As they passed, John could see the notches in the walls that were meant to hold lamps before the gas lines had been installed.

Verne continued down the corridor to a cramped foyer, which was lit by a small Chinese lamp on a rather rickety oak table. Opposite the lamp were double doors, which were fitted with an elaborate lock. On the center of the right-hand door was a large knocker.

John had noticed as they walked through the hallway that in the older part of the hotel there were ancient Icelandic runes carved into every bit of exposed wood, and around these doors, they were so thick that they looked like another layer of graining in the wood.

"You know," he said as he peered more closely at the runes, "with a good magnifying lens I could probably translate these in fairly short order."

"I've no doubt you could, young John," said Verne, "but I'll save you the trouble. They basically say 'Here you leave the world of the flesh and enter the realm of the spirit,' or something like that. Shall we go in?"

"Knock, or do you have the key?"

"Both," replied Verne. "Knock to let them know we're coming, and use the key to actually get in. After the recent incidents at Tamerlane House, security is ever more on my mind."

The door knocker was an ornate carving of a face, with a kerchief tied around its jaw. "A Marley knocker," Verne said as he reached for the tappet. "Charles gave it to me as a Christmas gift some years back, and I couldn't think of anything else to do with it."

He rapped with the knocker once, then again, then a third time before inserting the key into the lock below and turning the handle.

The door opened, and John's jaw dropped as he recognized the man behind it as Benjamin Franklin.

"Why, John, my fine young fellow," Franklin said, roaring with laughter. "What's wrong? You look as if you've seen a ghost!"

"That's not funny," said Verne as they stepped across the threshold. "I haven't explained everything to him yet."

"I apologize, then," Franklin said, ushering them inside. "It's good to see you again, John."

"And you, Doctor," said John. "What is this place?"

"Some of us have taken to calling it the Wonder Cabinet," Franklin answered. "It's the place where wonderful, improbable things are kept. And also," he added, "we're in Switzerland, so, you know, of course no one knows about it who isn't supposed to."

The room was expansive, but crowded with individuals who

all stopped what they were doing to take note of their visitors. It was appointed to resemble a private club, much like the club on Baker Street in London—except that instead of being a club for gentlemen scholars, this one was more of an eclectic think tank populated by Caretaker candidates.

"John, my boy," said Verne, "meet the *Mystorians*."

He immediately recognized Charles Dodgson, also known as Lewis Carroll, sitting with George Macdonald on a riser over to the right. Christina Rossetti was arguing with the American writers Robert E. Howard and L. Frank Baum on another riser over to the left, while Arthur Machen and Hope Mirrlees were in the center, debating politely with Sir Isaac Newton and two other men whom John didn't recognize.

"This is Dr. Demetrius Doboobie, and Master Erasmus Holiday," Verne said in introduction, "both here by way of the novel *Kenilworth*."

"Sir Walter Scott's book?" John asked, scanning the room again. "Is he here?"

"Sorry," Dr. Doboobie said, standing, but not offering his hand. "He was a fiction—but luckily, we are not."

"Not as long as we're here, anyroad," said Holiday.

"Agatha Christie is also with us," said Verne, "but she's less able to travel, since on her last mission, her absence was noticed— a little too prominently, shall we say."

"When was that?"

"In 1926," said Franklin. "She was shadowing you, incidentally, John. But it turned out all right. I'd have done it myself, but"—he gestured at the room—"being dead, I was a bit more limited than she was."

It was only then that John realized that most of those in the room were actually well past their allotted time spans.

"Yes," Franklin said jovially. "We're dead—well, most of us anyway. We served as Mystorians in our own times, and now we exist here, to help those who serve during yours."

Suddenly John understood. "The runes, outside, on the walls."

"Yes," said Verne. "That's what allows these spirits to exist here, alongside the living."

"It's why I also impolitely declined to shake your hand," said Franklin. "My substance has not kept pace with my influence, it seems."

"They are present, but insubstantial," Verne explained, "so they can't touch anything. They can only advise and discuss—and they do a lot of that."

"You don't have to speak as if we're not here," sniffed Carroll.

"Sorry, Doctor," said Verne. "I apologize."

"Doctor?" asked John.

"There's no real seniority or ranking among them," said Verne, "and the living Mystorians got irritated by Franklin's insistence that he be addressed as 'Doctor,' and so at some point they all started requesting it."

"Is this hotel the only place where ghosts are actually visible to, ah, the still living?" asked John.

"Not at all," Franklin said, chuckling, "but it is the only place where ghosts are visible *by design*."

"Hmm," said John, rubbing his chin. "What do Houdini and Conan Doyle think about all this?"

"I've thought now and again about bringing them here," Verne replied, "in part because they both have an affinity for the realm of the spirit, but also because they are both brilliant minds. And then," he added ruefully, "Harry says or does something so completely irresponsible that I want to throttle him, and I think better of it."

"And Sir Arthur?"

Verne shook his head. "Tell the one, tell them both," he said dismissively. "They really are decent Caretaker material, or would be, if they weren't perpetually sixteen."

"I take offense at that," said Frank Baum, who was in a corner immersed in a stack of comic books. "Sixteen was a good year to be alive."

"All our scientific research is done here," said Verne, "away from the prying eyes of the Cabal, or traitors like Defoe."

"Forgive my ignorance," said John, "but other than Dr. Franklin and Sir Isaac, I don't see any other . . ."

"Scientists?" Carroll said, rising from his seat. "You do not look deeply enough, boy. My prime specialty is mathematics, and Frank's—"

"Ahem-hem," said Baum.

"I apologize—*Dr.* Baum is a technological genius greater than even Dr. Franklin. It's part of what makes us effective as Mystorians," he concluded. "I can tell you all the secrets of time travel in a poem. And have. It's just that no one has bothered to look to poetry for the secrets of the universe."

"I'm sorry," John said, shaking his head in disbelief, "but you make it sound as if time travel were much simpler than it really is."

"In actuality," said Carroll, "*everything* is much simpler than it appears to be. Everything."

Another young man from the back of the room stood up to meet John.

"My name is Joseph," the ghost said as he started to offer his hand to the Caretaker, then, with a wry smile, thought better of it. "I admire your work very much."

"Thank you," John replied. He looked over the young ghost, trying to ascertain where he fit among the pantheon of noted men and women in the Mystorians.

When Joseph realized why he was being scrutinized, his ghostly cheeks pinked self-consciously. "No, good sir, you do not know me," he said, answering John's unspoken question. "At least, not in this form."

"Some of the Mystorians were not so much engaged in active work on our behalf, as they were in observing and reporting on the players in the Great Game at the time they were alive," Verne explained. "Young Joseph here was just such an observer—and later in his life, he was as famous as any of those he reported on. That was his shield—he was so famous that no one noticed the activities he engaged in for himself."

Again, the young ghost's face reddened. "That's very charitable of you to say, Mr. Verne, but we both know that's not the reason no one paid attention."

He looked John squarely in the eye and smiled a sad smile, which was made more beautiful by the perfect symmetry of his features. "The reason no one gave credence to me or what I was covertly doing for the Prime Caretaker was that I was hideously deformed, and no one among the members of polite society could fathom that my mind was not similarly deformed."

John considered this for a moment, then stepped back in surprise. "Joseph . . . *Merrick?*" he said hesitantly. "You're Joseph Merrick!"

The young ghost nodded gravely. "I am. You would have known me by the appellation 'The Elephant Man.'"

John looked at Joseph, then at Verne and back again. "I'm not sure I understand," he said. "Are you a tulpa? How is it that . . . ah . . ." He stumbled over his words, unsure of what to ask without offending the young man.

Joseph smiled. "How is it that I have the appearance that I do? It's simple—this is how I really am."

"But you were so terribly deformed—," John began.

"No," Joseph said firmly, cutting him off. "My *body* was terribly deformed. I was not."

"I don't understand."

"I *am* a soul," Joseph answered. "I *had* a body."

The clarity of it suddenly flashed across John's face. "Ah," he said. "I do understand, and I apologize. My friend Jack would have seen that right away."

"Here," Verne said, drawing John to the far side of the room and pulling out two chairs so they could sit. "Let me show you what the good Doctors Baum and Carroll have been doing.

"They've been working on a theory that the trumps are actually opening something called wormholes," Verne explained, gesturing at some diagrams on Carroll's table. "The smaller ones permit communication, and the larger ones actual travel. And what Carroll here has been working on—"

"Dr. Carroll, if you please," said Carroll.

Verne sighed, then went on. "Yes—what *Dr.* Carroll has been working on is the instances where the trumps were used to traverse time."

"It was actually that Clarke fellow who thought of it,"

said Baum. "He's got a lot of good ideas, that one."

Now it was Carroll's turn to scowl. "Yes, yes he did," he said with an irritated look at Baum, "but I've been the one developing the actual science behind the theory."

"The young theoreticians have been invaluable to our processes," said Franklin. "Especially that Asimov fellow, the Russian. He's going to outshine us all, I think."

"Easy for you to say," Newton said without really joining the conversation. "It's easy to create great works when one stands on the shoulders of giants."

"He's a little sensitive," Baum whispered. "The first time Newton met Asimov, the joker offered him an apple."

"It's young Asimov's work that has allowed the Mystorians to help us calculate probabilities on the might-have-beens to come," Verne explained. "It's one reason I have the Messengers traveling so frequently gathering information. The more we know about what has happened, the better we can predict what may happen in the future. And the wonder of it all is that it's completely based in scientific principle. He calls it 'psychohistory.'"

"No offense," John said, hesitant to speak, as he fully expected he was about to offend someone, "but there's something slightly disconcerting about knowing that such intense scientific research is being carried out in a hotel in Switzerland by a group of ghosts and children's book authors."

"I should like to point out that most of your colleagues at Tamerlane House," Franklin said sternly, poking his walking stick at Verne, "including your French tour guide there, are in fact themselves deceased. So I'd like to know just what you have against ghosts."

"I'm doubly offended," said Baum, "seeing as how I'm both a ghost and a children's book author, as is Charles."

"I'm a mathematician," sniffed Carroll. "And it's Dr. Carroll, if you please."

"Really, I meant no offense," John said, holding his hands up in either supplication or surrender. "Honestly, some of my best friends write books for children."

"And you don't?" asked Baum.

"Not really, you see," John began.

"Wait a moment," said Holiday. "Didn't you write the book about the little fellow with the furry feet? And trolls? And dwarves?"

"Well, yes," John admitted, "but—"

"What do you call that, then?"

"It's actually an initial tale that I'm broadening into a much wider invented mythology for—"

"Blah, blah, blah, blah," said Baum. "Elves and dwarves and trolls. Fairy tales. You're a children's book author, John."

Before John could argue the point further, they were interrupted by another knock at the door.

"Ah," Verne said as he rose to usher in the new arrival. "Unless I miss my guess, that'll be our secret weapon coming along now."

John stood and took a place next to Verne to greet the newcomers. The first was tall, firmly built, and had a crest of white hair that gave him the appearance of a classical philosopher. His eyes flashed briefly as he noticed John's presence, but he said nothing and merely smiled as he took his companion's coat.

The second man was smaller, more slender, and noticeably older than the other. Verne stepped forward to greet him first.

"Hello," the slight gentleman said as he entered the room and removed his hat. "I apologize for being late. I had a concern I was being followed and so some extra precautions—and delays—were necessary."

John nearly fell off his feet, astonished, confused, and delighted all at once. He was so taken off guard that he forgot to offer his hand to the bemused man, who was clearly enjoying the effect his arrival had on the younger Caretaker. John looked at Verne. "Is this some sort of illusion? How is he here?"

"Not an illusion," Verne replied, smiling broadly. "A Mystorian. One our adversaries would never have suspected, never watched, because they thought that they already were watching him. It was just a *different* him."

John recovered a small degree of his composure. "So, the last person they would suspect of becoming one of your special operatives was someone who was already a Caretaker," he said, "so to speak. Ingenious." He wiped his hand on his trousers and quickly offered it to the bemused Mystorian. "It's a pleasure to be meeting you at last."

"The pleasure is all mine, I assure you," the gentleman said, taking John's proffered hand. "My name is H. G. Wells."

CHAPTER ELEVEN
Lower Oxford

✦

According to Aristophanes, the first destination they needed to travel to in their quest for the Ruby Armor was very close—practically in the neighborhood.

"Oxford?" Uncas said, surprised. "That's right under the scowlers' noses."

"Literally, in this case," said the detective. "Quite literally, in fact."

The street Aristophanes guided them to was less than two miles from the building where Jack kept his teaching rooms at the college, and it was small enough that they were able to park the Duesenberg and get out without attracting undue attention.

"Shouldn't you be wearing a hat, or a scarf, or something?" Aristophanes said to Uncas as he glanced around the street. "I know this is a university, and everyone has their nose buried in books, but some deliveryman or other passerby might take notice we're strolling along with a talking animal."

"I'll be honest," said Uncas, "it's not indifference to th' opinions of passersby that lets me walk around in th' open." He produced a small piece of parchment from his vest pocket. It was covered in runes.

. . . atop a ladder, was a woman who could only be the librarian . . .

"Ah," the detective said in understanding. "A glamour. That makes sense."

"All most people see is a short feller with hairy feet," said Uncas. "Maybe a beard."

"Well then," Aristophanes said as he led them to a nondescript door at the end of the alley, "you'll not be surprised at where we're going. Everyone there is using one glamour or another."

The door opened onto a stairwell, which dropped away several floors below ground level—much farther than any basement should have extended. It was lit with torches that were set at regular intervals, but nothing other than the granite walls of the stairwell was visible until they reached the bottom.

Aristophanes threw open the great green wooden doors at the bottom of the stairs, and revealed an enormous cavern that seemed to contain a city at least the size of Oxford above.

"Welcome," the detective said, "to Lower Oxford."

The three companions wove their way through the warren of buildings that seemed to have been cobbled together from every culture on the continent—none of which had been updated since the fifteenth century, and many of which seemed far, far older.

"These buildings seem to predate Oxford itself," commented Uncas.

"Little badger," Aristophanes said with a touch of irritation at the animal's small thinking, "most of these buildings predate *England*."

There were Moorish harems, and Byzantine bazaars; English banks and colleges; and Ottoman markets that could have been operating since the first millennium.

As they walked, Aristophanes explained that this was one of the Soft Places that were known only to the lost and disenfranchised— that it was all but lost to those who never looked, and only findable by those who were truly lost.

"The Caretakers would barely take note of such a place," he said brusquely, "although perhaps that Burton fellow might. And most other people would take no notice of it at all. In a way, what happens every day in Lower Oxford is exactly what happened long ago to the entire Archipelago."

He stopped. "They just stopped believing. Here," he said, gesturing down a crowded street. "This is the district we want."

All the buildings along the street bore Chinese markings, including the one where they stopped.

"This is one of the oldest libraries in existence," Aristophanes explained, pointing at the cracked, faded sign above the door. "It was here, in this spot, for two thousand years before I was born, and was collecting stories of the earliest cultures of the world when our ancestors were living in caves and hunting with obsidian spears."

"What does the sign say?" asked Uncas.

"You know it already," said the Zen Detective. "The statues in the window should give you a clue."

Inside the windows on either side of the door were paper lanterns, a stringer of plucked, headless ducks—which made Uncas shiver just a bit—and four soapstone statues. Each was of a different Chinese man, but all four bore attributes . . .

. . . of *Dragons*.

"Ah," Quixote said, looking up at the sign. "'Go ye no further, for here, there be Dragons.'"

Aristophanes nodded. "Or something to that effect. Those four statues represent the four great dragon kings of ancient China, and this shop is what remains of the library that began when they ruled under the Jade Empress."

Quixote wanted to ask something about who the Jade Empress might be, but the detective had already pushed open the door with a loud jangling of bells and entered the shop.

The shop that purported to be a library was tightly packed with shelves, which made passing down the aisles difficult for Quixote, and almost impossible for the stouter Aristophanes. Smoke from a brazier hung cloyingly in the air, and there were small birds in cages hung randomly throughout the clutter.

Toward the back, the aisles suddenly opened up to a wider working space that was ringed about with more shelving that reached to the ceiling ten feet above. To one side, atop a ladder, was a woman who could only be the librarian Aristophanes had told them about on the drive.

She was short and plump, and wore a tight silk dress, which was straining at the seams in a number of potentially inconvenient places. Her black hair was pinned up neatly with long sticks carved into the shape of dragons. And she was not in a very receptive mood.

"What it is, what it is?" the librarian called down from the ladder. "I cannot be bothering now. I am very busty."

Uncas turned to Quixote. "Does she mean something else?"

"Probably," the knight whispered, "but better not to ask. Just smile and nod."

Aristophanes removed his hat and spoke in a respectful

manner. "Song-Sseu," he said, hat in hand, "thank you for allowing us to enter your library. We have come to ask for your help."

At the mention of her name, the librarian stiffened, but did not turn to look at them. A long moment passed, and then she answered. "I am not who you think me to be, strange, and am to work much, too much mind, to talk. To help."

"You are the person we're looking for, Song-Sseu, to find what we're after," Aristophanes said. "If you cannot help us, then there is no one else who can. We're looking for the Ruby Armor of T'ai Shan."

She turned her head slowly and fixed the detective with a thousand-yard stare that would have driven a lesser man, or perhaps a more prudent one, right out the door. But as it was, Aristophanes held his ground, and she descended the ladder.

"Wait here," the librarian said, "and don't think to be touch anything."

She descended the ladder without actually tearing any seams, and removed herself to a room farther back. After some rattling around, followed by unintelligible cursing, she returned holding a ring of keys. "How would you know that even I know, the place of the armor?"

Aristophanes shrugged. "I didn't know. But it's apparent that you do. That's Zen for you."

"Hmm." She folded her arms and pursed her lips. "What would you know of Zen, Westerner?"

Aristophanes stiffened at that, but he kept his demeanor and voice steady. "More than you would believe, Song-Sseu," he replied. "Can you help us?"

"Help you, or help Caretakers?" she asked. "It not surprise," she added before he could react. "Who else send purple unicorn, talking rat, and crazy man to ask about T'ai Shan?"

"I'm a badger," said Uncas.

"And I'm, uh," said Quixote. "I have no defense."

"Yes, they sent us," said Aristophanes.

"You know the Archipelago, that it is gone," she said. "Something happened to it. All Shadow now. So now they Caretakers of air."

"We know," said Quixote. "That's why we need the armor—to fight the Shadows."

She looked at the three of them for a few moments—at Aristophanes for longer and more critically than the others—before she finally assented. "Yes," she said primly. "I help you. But it cost you much, I think."

"I expected it would," the detective said, rummaging around in his pockets. "Ah!" he exclaimed. "Here it is!"

It was a very old piece of parchment, covered in Arabic writing.

The librarian peered at it. "A Scheherazade story? Pfah! I have all already. All thousand and three."

"This," said Aristophanes, "is the one thousand and *fourth* tale."

Her eyes grew wide as she realized he was quite serious, and the parchment, quite authentic.

Song-Sseu snatched it out of his hand and filed the parchment in a desk drawer, which she then locked with a key. Using a second key, she opened a different drawer and took out a sheaf of paper.

"You know these not work by themselves," said Song-Sseu. "Need the Quill of Minos, or Letter-Blocks of—"

"I have an Infernal Device," Aristophanes said, giving a sideways glance at Uncas and Quixote.

"Ah," she said, as if that explained everything. "How many sheets you need?"

"Seven," said the detective. "Seven should do."

Song-Sseu's brow furrowed in puzzlement. "Seven? But there are eight pieces. . . ."

"We already got the Ruby Opera Glasses," Uncas offered, and Aristophanes's complexion turned a full shade darker, "so we don't need t' look fer them."

"You do know," she said as she counted off seven sheets and handed them to the Zen Detective, "that knowing that places exist, and be able to locate those places, are two different thing. And there be places in the world that even Caretakers know not about."

"Maybe they don't," Aristophanes said as he folded the papers and stuck them inside his coat, "but we do. We have the maps of Elijah McGee."

The expression on her face, Aristophanes thought, was worth all the grief he'd had to take just to be able to witness that moment.

"You lie," she finally said after closing her mouth and regaining her composure. "They were lost in fire, in London."

"Not all of them," Aristophanes said, "and not the important ones."

She tried to look casually uninterested, and was failing miserably. "Do you have with you?" she asked. "Could I have to look at them?"

"Maybe next time," Aristophanes said as he slowly guided Uncas and Quixote out of the shop. He bowed, then quickly closed the door before she could say anything further.

"Stupid, stupid, stupid," he muttered as they retraced their steps to the stairwell. "Never should have mentioned the maps!"

"Then, uh, why did you?" asked Uncas. "We already had what we wanted, didn't we?"

Aristophanes glowered, then nodded. "I was showing off," he said. "Wanted her to know I was in a loop she wasn't in. And now maybe I've compromised us."

"How so?" Quixote asked, looking a bit worried.

"Because," the detective said as he pushed open the great green doors, "people who are willing to sell what they know always have a price. And we just gave her something very, very valuable. And you," he growled at Uncas, "should not have told her we had the glasses, either. But what's done is done, and it's not to be helped, now.

"Come on," he finished, jumping to the stairs. "We've just sped up our timetable."

"We shouldn't discuss the details of the pieces here," Aristophanes said as they reached street level and Oxford Above, "and we sure as Hades shouldn't look at the maps anywhere in the open. Does your instant-travel-projector have a slide for someplace more private?"

"We have just th' place," said Uncas. "Hop in. We'll be there in two shakes of a fox's tail."

The three companions climbed into the Duesenberg, and Uncas pulled out the appropriate slide. Starting the motor, he wheeled the car around and, projector whirring, drove straight into—and through—a solid brick wall.

They were so intent on getting someplace more secure, where they could talk unmolested, that none of them had noticed the tall, hooded man at the end of the street, who had been observing them since they entered Lower Oxford. No one else, not even the few ragged denizens who were coming and going through the door to the stairwell, took any more notice of him. He was simply another near-invisible lost soul, minding his own business. And so no one noticed at all when he took the watch out of his pocket, twirled the dials, and vanished.

"Have you ever noticed," Uncas said conversationally, as the barmaid brought another round of drinks to their table, "that all th' so-called 'Soft Places' seem t' be centered around taverns and th' like?"

Aristophanes snorted and took a long swallow of ale.

Quixote frowned. "I'm sure I don't know what you mean," he said. "There are plenty of Soft Places with no ale whatsoever."

"Yeah?" Aristophanes replied, wiping his mouth on his sleeve. "Name *three*."

"Hmm," mused the knight. "There's, ah, Midian. And, um . . ."

"I thought so," said Uncas.

"Oh, just be quiet and drink your prune juice," said Quixote.

The Inn of the Flying Dragon was one of the Caretakers' favorite meeting places to discuss Archipelago business, and it had come as a huge relief to all of them that the loss of the Archipelago did not mean the loss of the Flying Dragon.

It was not the only Soft Place where they could drink away the night, but it was one of the few that consisted of a single edifice at a Crossroads. There were some, like Club Mephistopheles, that existed in London, for those who knew how to see them. Others, like Midian, were entire cities. Some, like Abaton, were both a city and a country, with indefinable borders.

Fortunately, according to Aristophanes, the Soft Places they would need to go to were a bit smaller in size.

"So," Quixote said, having downed his second ale, "how are we going to find the pieces, anyroad?"

"With this," Aristophanes said. He opened the box he'd taken from his office and removed a device that resembled a typewriter's larger, more complicated, slightly preindustrial brother. "It's called a Machine Cryptographique," he explained as he set up the contraption on the table. "It was invented by a printer in Marseilles in 1836, and he claimed it could write as fast as a pen."

The detective showed them how each letter had its own bar, which would rotate into place to type a letter. Uncas noticed that there were several bars that were engraved with numerals—as well as several more that bore marks he didn't recognize.

"The inventor had more than commercial uses in mind," Aristophanes was telling Quixote, "which is why he added the Hermetic markings to some of the bars. The problem was, he didn't know enough about what he was getting into, and the device became possessed by a djinn."

"By gin?" asked Uncas.

"A *djinn*," the exasperated detective said. "An imp. Something that can grant wishes, tell your fortune, and make predictions."

"That sounds like something th' Caretakers would like, all right," said Uncas.

"Actually, it was deemed too dangerous for the Caretakers," said the detective. "The power to use it came with a condition— if you died while it was in your possession, yours became the next soul that powered it. The Frenchman—Verne—acquired it in 1882 and quickly realized the danger of keeping and using it. So he sold it to someone less likely to die than even a Caretaker."

He stroked the gears and wheels of the device and grinned. "I call it Darwin, after the last supposed owner who died while he had it," Aristophanes said. "It's been very reliable. Just don't," he added, "ask it any questions about the Garden of Eden. It gets very testy when you do that."

"If you have this machine," Quixote asked, "then what did we need to acquire the parchment from Song-Sseu for?"

"The original djinn is gone," said Aristophanes, "and Darwin has no predictive powers of his own. So," he continued, as he pulled out the seven sheets of parchment, "we needed some oracular parchment to do the job instead."

"Hmm," said Uncas. "Where d'you get oracular parchment?"

"From an oracular pig."

"An oracular pig?" Uncas asked, shuddering. "D'you mean like the famous one, from the farm on Prydain?"

"The very same," said Aristophanes. "Same pig, actually."

"That's a shame," Uncas said, shaking his head. "Sacrificing an entire oracular pig just for some stupid parchment."

"Oh, I don't think they killed her," the detective said quickly. "They just used her hindquarters. A pig that valuable, you can't use all at once."

"Ewww," said Uncas.

"Well," said Quixote, "I have seen those little carts with the wheels they can attach. . . ."

"Never mind about the pig!" Aristophanes snorted. "Let's find out where we're to go first."

The Zen Detective threaded a sheet of parchment into the

machine, then slowly, deliberately, pecked out a question, which appeared in faint, reddish-gray letters.

Suddenly the machine took charge of its own operation, and more quickly than Aristophanes had typed, click-clacked out an answer one line below the question.

"There we go," Aristophanes said, whipping the parchment out of the machine and stuffing it quickly into his pocket. "We'll compare it with the maps in the morning."

"In the morning?" asked Quixote. "Why not right now?"

"Because for one, I don't think it's safe to pull out the maps in sight of others, even here," said Aristophanes. "And for another, I'm tuckered out and could use some sleep before we start off on this treasure hunt."

"Why not just take a room here?" Uncas protested as the detective boxed up his machine and rose to leave. "The rooms are very nice."

"They are," he replied in a soft, low voice, so he couldn't be overheard past their table. "It's the other clientele that I'm wary of, like the fellow in the corner—no, don't look, Uncas!—wearing the hood, who has been watching us since we got here."

Neither Uncas nor Quixote turned to look in the direction Aristophanes indicated, but simply dropped some coins on the table and followed him out the door.

The detective instructed Uncas to drive the Duesenberg back to the Summer Country, to a wooded hilltop in Wales, where he said they would camp for the night.

"This ought to be safe enough," Aristophanes said as he removed his hat and ran his fingers through his hair. "The

Welsh mind their own business, and not everyone else's."

Both Uncas and Quixote, who were taking some camping supplies out of the boot of the Duesenberg, stopped short at the sight of the hatless detective. They had both known he was a unicorn, but thus far in their acquaintanceship, he had never removed the hat.

The base of his horn spread a full five inches across his forehead, like a thick plate of cartilage, and the markings from his having filed it down were easily visible. But from the base, a wicked-looking point had begun to grow, and it was already curving upward several inches from his brow.

"I like to grow it out when I'm working," said Aristophanes. "And besides, where we're going, no one will notice anyway."

"No one noticing is pretty much why I don't wear pants," said Uncas.

"I like to sleep under the stars," Quixote complained as he and Aristophanes unfolded the seemingly endless tent. "I really don't see why we have to go to so much trouble."

The Zen Detective nodded his head to the eastern horizon. "Those clouds are why. There may be weather later, and I'd rather not spend the night in a downpour, thank you very much."

"I'd really rather have stayed at th' Flying Dragon," Uncas grumbled as he struck some flint to spark a fire.

"Not while we're being observed," said Aristophanes. "For all we know, that fellow was someone sent by Song-Sseu, to see what we're using the parchment for."

"She seemed like such a nice lady," said Uncas.

"Everyone," Aristophanes said as he handed his own knapsack

to the badger, "can be bought. Get the bedrolls set out. I have to go find a peach tree to water."

"You have a peach tree in Wales?" asked Quixote.

The detective groaned. "I have to pee, you idiot."

"Hey," Uncas whispered as the detective cursed his way to the trees. "Look at this!"

It was the Ruby Opera Glasses. They were inside the knapsack.

"Manners, my squire," Quixote scolded. "You shouldn't be looking in his bag. And besides, those won't do us much good out here, anyway."

"They might," Uncas disagreed, tipping his head at the tent flap. "Anyone can be bought, remember?"

The knight shook his head. "Being a thug for hire and giving oneself entirely to the Echthroi are different things. If he has simply been bought, the glasses wouldn't show it, would they?"

"If he's a Lloigor," the badger replied, "they will."

Quixote chewed on that thought a moment. It might be worth having a quick peek at the detective—just to be sure he was, as he claimed to be, on the side of the angels.

"What are you doing?" Aristophanes exclaimed as he suddenly entered the tent. "I told you those are only good for . . ." He made the connection and scowled, then smirked. "Oh. I see. Wanted to check out your partner, did you? You were wondering if I was an Echthros?"

"Technically, you'd be a Lloigor," Uncas said as Quixote elbowed him in the arm. "Uh, I mean, well, yes. Sorta."

"Hmph," the Zen Detective grunted as he sat next to the old knight and opened a bottle. "I suppose I can't blame you," he said as he tipped back the bottle to have a drink. "Very well, then. If it'll make you feel better, go ahead and have a look."

With a nod from Quixote, Uncas held the opera glasses up to his eyes and peered through them at the detective.

"Well?" asked Aristophanes. "Satisfied?'

Uncas nodded and handed the glasses to Quixote. "He's not one of them. Not a Lloigor."

"You just needed to ask," Aristophanes said, a genuine note of hurt in his voice. "I could have told you."

"Not to degrade our already shaky position with you," Quixote said, clearing his throat, "but couldn't you just have lied?"

"Maybe," said the detective, "but not about that. I'm a unicorn—we can't be possessed by Shadows, nor can we lose our own. It's one of our more useful features."

"Ah," exclaimed Quixote. "So that's why Verne trusts you."

"No," Aristophanes corrected. "That's why Verne uses me. He sent you two along precisely because he doesn't trust me. And, it appears, neither do you." Without waiting for a response, he got up and opened the tent flap. "I'm going to go stretch my legs. I'll be back later . . .

"*. . . partners.*"

The way he said that last word left Uncas and Quixote both flustered enough that they couldn't say anything. Worse, they realized there wasn't much they *could* say. Aristophanes was right. They didn't trust him. They hadn't trusted him from the beginning.

"But Verne didn't . . . doesn't," said Uncas. "Is it really any wiser of us if we chose to, just to avoid hurting his feelings?"

"Something I have learned in my long years as a knight," said Quixote, "is that everyone rises to the level of trust they earn. Your part in that is to simply give him a chance to rise or fall as his actions dictate."

The little mammal's whiskers twitched as he looked from the knight to outside the tent and back again. At last he smacked his badger fist into the other paw. "Then I'll do it," he declared. "I'm going to trust him."

Quixote nodded approvingly as his little companion busied himself with getting their bedrolls ready to sleep for the night—but inwardly, he felt a twinge of regret. Not that the little badger was so willing to be trusting, but because, in Quixote's experience, such trust could be easily justified . . .

. . . and just as easily betrayed.

Outside, there was a flash of light, followed by a low rumble of thunder. Moments later the first drops of rain began to speckle the ground outside.

"Looks like Steve was right about the storm," Uncas said as he rolled over to sleep. "G'night, sir."

"Good night, my little friend," Quixote replied as the rain began falling harder, and a second burst of lightning illuminated the tent.

The knight could see that outside, silhouetted against the firelight, the detective had once again donned his hat. The rain didn't seem to be bothering him, so Quixote decided that rather than press the issue, he'd just follow Uncas's example and go to sleep. The detective could do as he wished.

Quixote wondered as he blew out the light which choice Aristophanes might make, to justify or betray the trust the badger—the trust that both of them—were giving to him. And he wondered what Uncas was going to feel if they were proven wrong.

He was still wondering when, finally, he drifted off to sleep. It was still raining.

The Cabal seldom met in full quorum . . .

CHAPTER TWELVE
The Cabal

"*I hope you're ready* for another shock, young John," Verne said as he put his arm around the shoulders of the man who had entered with Wells. "This is the true leader of the Mystorians, and the one without whom the Caretakers would have been lost long ago.

"John," Verne continued in introduction, "I'd like you to meet William Blake."

Almost involuntarily, John jumped backward, ignoring the man's outstretched hand.

"*Blake?*" he exclaimed angrily. "John Dee's right-hand man? The second great betrayer of the Caretakers?"

"*My* right-hand man," said Verne, "and the one who has given us what few actual advantages we have over the Cabal."

"I understand your misgivings, John," Blake said, unruffled by the younger man's reaction, "but what I'm doing is very similar to Kipling's own covert missions among the ICS—I'm just playing a deeper game."

"It's the idea that it is a game at all that bothers me," John said testily. "Our circumstances are far more serious than that."

"It is exactly that degree of importance that makes it a game worth playing," Wells cut in. "The Little Wars, the small games of conflict, and one-upmanship, all add up into history. The timeline of the world has ever been nothing but games.

"And," he added, "as Heraclitus said, those who approach life like a child playing a game, moving and pushing pieces, possess the power of kings."

"Is that what the Mystorians are?" John asked. "Kings playing games?"

"No," Wells replied. "The Caretakers are the true kings. We're just the ones who make sure no one removes you from the board."

John sighed and turned to Verne. "I can see why he's your secret weapon. He's smarter than we are."

Verne laughed, as did Blake. Wells merely smiled and removed his coat, nodding in greeting to the other Mystorians.

"It was always my strategy to use those whom I recruited only in their own Prime Time," said Verne, "but then as events started to accelerate, I realized the value of having them available to consult with, and so in secret, we established the hotel, and this room, to better serve the cause."

"Thereby having the help of men like Dr. Franklin both in life and in death," said John. "I understand that. But why, ah, continue to work with them as ghosts, rather than create portraits, as with the Caretakers?"

"The portraits only work within the walls of Tamerlane House," said Verne. "Outside, they would only last a week. And we needed to preserve the secrecy of our operations."

John chuckled. "It almost seems like cheating," he said blithely. "To continue to draw on all these great minds, after their deaths."

"How is that any different from influencing the minds of those who read our books?" Carroll asked. "Or our overinflated autobiographies, in some cases."

"Noted," said Franklin.

"Your books are full of thoughts you've already, ah, thought," said John, "but everything you're doing here is . . ."

"New?" said Franklin. "So our influence should end, just because our earthly lives have?"

"I suppose if I really believed that," John admitted, "I wouldn't be a Caretaker."

"As I told you, our adversaries were no longer playing by the rules," Verne said, "so I started changing a few rules myself."

"How is it that they haven't suspected you before now?" John asked Blake. "Especially after the defection of Burton, Houdini, and Conan Doyle?"

"You're confusing the frosting with the cake," Blake replied, "if you think the Imperial Cartological Society had anything to do with Dee's Cabal. He founded the ICS, sure—but only as a cover for his true goals. Burton, however, really believed in what the ICS set out to do, and that made his transition back to the Caretakers much easier."

"Easier for you, maybe," said John. "He put us through a lot of grief before coming back over. He—"

John stopped, and watched, dumbfounded, as a second William Blake, and then a third, walked out of one of the back rooms and began conversing with Sir Isaac Newton.

"Blake perfected the creation of tulpas," Verne said, amused at John's shock, "and he liked himself so much, he made more."

"How many more?"

"We call them Blake's Seven," said Verne, "although in point of fact, there are now only six of you, aren't there?"

"Yes, six," Blake acknowledged as if he were tallying bags of flour instead of tulpas. "We lost the one on that ill-advised trip past the Edge of the World. From what I understand, he was turned to solid gold, or some such."

"And losing yourself doesn't, ah, bother you?" John asked. "I would think you'd be slightly more put out. If it was me, I'd be rather traumatized."

"There are no limitations on those who are serving the cause of the Echthroi," said Carroll, "so why should we have limitations on those of us who are in the service of the angels?"

"I wouldn't mind a few of the angels themselves popping in to lend a hand now and again," murmured Macdonald.

"There must be some limitations, er, ah, Doctor," said Baum, "or else what's to keep us from becoming them?"

"There are *some* limitations," said Wells. "Just enough."

"So what are the Mystorians working on?"

"The problem the Caretakers haven't yet taken the time for," said Jules. "They're trying to find Coal—the missing boy prince of Paralon who was kidnapped by Daniel Defoe."

"Where do we stand on it?" asked Verne. "Any leads?"

"A few," Wells said, "mostly by virtue of the leads Blake has given us, and with help from young Asimov's psychohistory."

"Herb is the best resource we have," Verne said, gesturing at Wells, "in part because he and I disagree about a great many things."

"How is that helpful?" John asked.

"Too often scholars limit themselves by working with what

they know they know," said Baum, "when what they really need to know is what they know they need to know but don't yet know. So we aren't bothering with looking in the places we think he might be—we're looking in all the places we would never think to look. Because otherwise, we'd have already found him."

"I'm starting to understand why you keep them sequestered in a hotel in Switzerland," John said to Verne. "He's not steering with both hands."

"It's probably true," Baum admitted cheerfully.

"All we know is that he's in the future," said Blake. "We believe that's why the Cabal broke Defoe free from Tamerlane House."

"You knew about the burglary?" John said in astonishment. "And you did nothing about it?"

"Better than that," said Verne. "He facilitated the burglary, but also prevented their success by interfering with their attempt to get the maps of Elijah McGee. And nothing else they took was of any value."

"We'll find him, Jules," Franklin said, more somber now. "If it takes an eternity yet to come, we'll find him."

"Speaking of Defoe, I need to leave," said Blake. "One of my tulpas is still helping Harry and Arthur with the goats, and three of me are expected for the meeting with the Cabal."

"Be careful," Verne said. "Call if you need us."

"I shall," said Blake. "Farewell, Caveo Principia."

"Sure," said John. "You too."

As Blake left, John turned to Wells. "So, I imagine you're aware of what our Bert is doing," he said. "Is that matter creating any anxiety for you, as it has for Bert?"

"Not if he's successful," Wells replied. "If they made the first swing of the pendulum into the future, I'm confident they'll be able to ride it back into the past."

"I meant his, uh, his other mission," said John, "and the . . . timetable, so to speak."

"Ah," Wells said, blushing slightly. "No. I never met Weena, so I never lost her. And Aven was never my child. So my path diverged dramatically from Bert's, and I have never been under the same compulsions as he to solve the riddles of time travel. I've been perfectly happy to do research for the Mystorians, and, of course, to spend my time writing more books."

He stood and offered his hand to Verne. "I'm sorry I can't stay longer," Wells said. "I needed to bring you my reports, but now I must repair. It was a pleasure, young John. A true pleasure."

"Thank you . . . Mr. Wells."

"Please—call me Herb," Wells said, with a twinkle in his eyes that very much resembled John's mentor.

"I've enjoyed your work very much, ah, Herb," John said, shaking the older man's hand. He looked askance at Verne. "Ah, does he . . . I mean . . ."

"Yes," Herb said, looking John in the eye and giving his hand another firm shake. "I know what's coming. I've known for a very long time. And I'm all right with it. I've had a very full and successful life. And I've had a number of friends who have made it rich beyond compare. So don't fret—I'm going to be fine."

Soon after, John and Verne also took their leave of the hotel so that they could return to Tamerlane House and await word from Blake.

"I'm curious," John asked as they crossed the busy street outside the hotel. "Is searching for the lost boy really a job for the Mystorians? That fellow Aristophanes certainly seems capable enough, if not entirely trustworthy. Surely he'd be your man for this, too?"

Verne shook his head. "It's a different kind of problem," he explained. "The boy was deliberately hidden from us, by those whom we know to be our enemies. They can therefore plot and counterplot against all the moves we make, which is why having Blake among them is so necessary.

"Normally," Verne continued, "this would have been a task for the Messengers. But after losing Henry Morgan, and then with Alvin Ransom's effectiveness being lessened, all I've really had to work with is Raven—and he has had no luck in finding the lost boy. So the Mystorians really are the best option, even with a Zen Detective at our disposal.

"And besides," he added ruefully, "I *don't* trust Aristophanes. I can't risk trusting him."

"And yet you sent him to search for those talismans of incredible power."

Verne shook his head again. "Not alone," he said with a wry grin. "As you already saw yourself, I made certain one of our best agents was with him and will be keeping me apprised of everything."

John furrowed his brow. "Do you really think Quixote is up to that?"

The Frenchman paused a moment, and then laughed. "Quixote? You're joking, surely. I meant Uncas."

The younger Caretaker seemed unconvinced. "He's not exactly Tummeler."

"No," Verne replied. "But he is a badger, and his heart is mighty. He won't let us down."

They walked along in silence for a few moments as they made their way back to the alleyway where they could safely activate their trump to Tamerlane House.

"There's something more you want to ask me," Verne said without taking his eyes from the path in front of them. "So ask."

"What I'm wondering about," John mused, "is that if there are so many ways for one's essence to survive death—Basil's portraits, or becoming a tulpa, or these ghosts of yours in a hotel in Switzerland—then is there really any reason to fear death at all? Doesn't all that mean that death, far from being the end, is just another state of existence?"

Verne turned to look at the younger Caretaker with an expression of delighted admiration. "John, my boy," he said, grasping the other man's arm, "if you understand even that much, then you are already a greater Caretaker than I ever dreamed you might be. And a far better man."

Before the younger man could respond, Verne activated his trump, and in a few moments it had grown large enough for them to step back through to Tamerlane House. They were both so focused on returning to the other Caretakers to report on the work of the Mystorians that they didn't notice the Shadow that slipped through underneath their feet, and that stayed behind when the portal closed.

He arrived, as usual, in a room of near-total darkness. He was John Dee's most trusted lieutenant, and one of the most powerful and influential members of the Cabal. But William Blake had never seen the exterior of the House of John Dee. None of the Cabal had.

Blake had designed the black watches the Cabal used to transport between places and times, but Dee himself had calibrated their primary orientation. Setting the dials to midnight always returned the bearer to Dee's house, but never on the outside, always to some inner chamber. So in point of fact, Blake had no earthly idea where the house was actually located in space. If he had, then perhaps the Caretakers' War could have been resolved long before then. Verne had certainly pressed him to find it often enough. But Blake had always resisted, feeling that it would be a mistake to confront the enemy on their home ground—particularly when no one knew where that home *was*.

Dee's residence had been at times referred to as the Nightmare Abbey, and sometimes as the House on the Borderlands. But mostly, it was just referred to as the House.

From Blake's limited explorations of the interior, it appeared to be an old family manse, possibly even a castellated abbey, as one of the names suggested. From the smell, Blake knew there was a moat, or, barring that, a nearby marsh. But sometimes that changed.

Blake wondered if perhaps the House moved from place to place, much in the same way the rooms at Tamerlane House often moved of their own accord. That would make it even more difficult to attack.

The house was maintained by a veritable army of young, attractive men and women, all of whom bore the name Deathshead. There were rumors among members of the Cabal that a young squire named Diggory Deathshead had once visited and made the acquaintance of the maidens in residence—leaving behind a colony of young Deathsheads. However, in all the years Blake had been visiting, none of the staff had seemed to age. He suspected it was because they were, in fact, all dead. But there were some questions he preferred to avoid asking.

He rounded a corner to the meeting hall, which was filled with a massive oak table. At the head, perched on a chair, sat an enormous crow.

"Greetings, Loki," said Blake. "How goes the effort?"

The large bird bowed in deference to a guest of the house and made a clicking noise with its tongue. Blake knew from experience that this meant the bird was irritated about something but was trying to maintain a sense of decorum. It was Dee's familiar, and always preceded his appearance.

Blake assumed the great black bird served the same purpose as Dee's shadow once did, as a sort of conscience. But it had been a long time since Dee had actually possessed a shadow, so Blake couldn't really be sure.

His second and third tulpas entered the meeting hall from the opposite corridor and nodded a brief greeting as they took their seats. Blake himself had only just sat down as Dee and the rest of the Cabal entered the room.

The Cabal seldom met in full quorum—whether this was by chance or by design, Blake could not guess. Ever since Jules Verne had convinced Richard Burton to defect to the Caretakers, and to bring Arthur Conan Doyle and Harry Houdini with him, Dee had become more and more suspicious, and kept his activities cloaked in greater and greater secrecy. Part of the reason was because the three defectors had been the primary operatives of Dee's Imperial

Cartological Society—and were therefore the most visible of John Dee's disciples. The other part was Rudyard Kipling's infiltration of the ICS, which resulted in the destruction of the Shadow that had belonged to the Winter King, and the second Keep of Time the ICS had been constructing.

Blake had to suppress a shudder at the memory of Dee's response to that fiasco—which was that it wasn't a total loss, because they'd managed to destroy all the Dragons in the process.

All but one, as far as they knew. And a second, about which the Cabal knew nothing.

But the main reason that Dee had become more secretive, even to the point of abandoning their cover of the ICS, which allowed them to operate in semi-secrecy, was that his true goals were finally coming to the fore.

It had never been about the misguided goals of the Caretakers, or the secrets of the Archipelago, or even about the injustices done to the man who became the Winter King. For Dr. Dee, it was about knowledge, and power—both of which had been promised to him by the Echthroi. They had offered to reveal the secrets of creation to Dee, and in doing so, make him Shadows' agent of hell on Earth.

If Dee's plans succeeded, the entire world would be open to the Echthroi. That could not be allowed to happen. And that reason alone had been motivation enough for Blake to continue to help Dee and the Cabal, even to the point of doing things that were reprehensible to him.

Someone once said that it was sometimes necessary to commit small acts of evil, if those acts were in the service of a greater good. Blake knew that if he didn't believe that, on some deep level, then he wouldn't be able to bear sitting at this table, among these men, putting these plans into motion.

But he also knew, with some regret, that this was a reason he was not comfortable being among the Caretakers. Perfect knights, who saw the world in terms of black and white, good and evil, right and wrong, were very difficult to argue with. But he understood that living that way to begin with made them far stronger—and far better—men than he.

Dr. Dee, as usual, took his seat at the head of the table. The three Blakes sat to his left, and the inventor Nikola Tesla sat on his right. Next to Tesla were Aleister Crowley, the occultist, and the original discoverer of the House, William Hope Hodgson.

To the Blakes' right were the writers James Branch Cabell, H. P. Lovecraft, and, three seats farther down, G. K. Chesterton, who preferred a bit more personal space than the others—perhaps because other than Blake, Chesterton was the only member of the Cabal who had retained his own shadow.

At the far end of the table sat a very fidgety and disgruntled Daniel Defoe. He had been recruited into the ICS by Burton when he was still a Caretaker—but by then, he had already performed several services for Dee. And during the battle with the Winter King's shadow, when he overstepped his mandate and tried to seize power for himself, he was captured and imprisoned by the Caretakers.

He'd been left there, mortared up behind a wall, for several years—and as far as Dee was concerned, could have been written off completely as a minor casualty in the Caretakers' War, except for one salient fact.

The boy whom Defoe had hidden in the future was not trackable by any means known to the Cabal—which meant that only Daniel Defoe knew when and where he could be retrieved. And so Defoe himself had to be retrieved from the Caretakers' fortress. Fortunately, Dee also had other reasons for ordering the burglary, so the effort, which nearly failed, was worthwhile.

"It took you long enough," Defoe complained. "Don't think I don't know that the only reason you broke me out of that dratted wall was because you need me to find the boy."

"No," Dee said coolly. "We broke you out because it was convenient. And it will be just as convenient to put you back, if you don't hold your tongue."

Defoe glowered, but wisely said nothing.

"What do you have to report?" Dee asked the Cabal.

"Aristophanes is not looking for the boy at all," said Crowley. "They approached him, just as we expected, but to ask him to find something else. Not the child."

Dee's eyes narrowed. "What, then?"

"The Ruby Opera Glasses."

A murmur of consternation rippled through the group. "If they sent him looking for the glasses," exclaimed Tesla, "it won't be long before he offers to seek out the rest of the armor for them, if he hasn't already."

"They do have someone looking for the boy," Chesterton said. "Or several someones, in point of fact. They call themselves the Mystorians."

A chill ran up Blake's spine, and it was a testament to his self-control that neither he nor his other tulpas reacted visibly to Chesterton's remark. Apparently, Verne's secrets were not as well kept as they believed.

"They have nothing," said Tesla. "Some fiction writers, a few students, a few women, Newton, and Lord Kelvin. Their technology will be not only out of date compared to ours, but functionally useless. We have nothing to fear from the Mystorians."

Dee turned to Blake. "Monitoring Verne's activities has been under your purview, William. Do you know anything about these 'Mystorians'?"

Blake wasn't sure whether he was being tested. "I do," he said finally, "but since none of them are actually Caretakers, I didn't see any import in addressing the matter. They are no threat to our plans. The Caretakers can enlist whomever they wish. But our devices, and our knowledge of how to use them, are greater. I think these Mystorians are merely a distraction."

"Indeed," said Dee. "Interesting that the Caretakers have chosen to recruit outside of their fortress in the Nameless Isles. And more interesting," he added, pointedly glancing at Blake, "that these allies, these Mystorians, are only now coming to our attention."

"We got all that we needed, even without the maps," said Tesla. "We won't need to go back."

"I beg to differ!" Defoe exclaimed, pounding his fist on the table for emphasis. "If they're watching too closely, I can't get back into Tamerlane House!"

"And this is a problem, how?" asked Tesla.

"You know good and well how it's a problem," Defoe shot back. "I'm limited to seven days without going back across that threshold."

"This would not be a problem if you hadn't gotten yourself

crushed, Daniel," said Lovecraft. "That this problem has fallen at your feet is entirely your own fault."

"Actually, you owe the Caretakers a debt of gratitude," said Crowley. "If they hadn't created a portrait of you, you'd simply be dead now."

"Yes, well," Defoe said. "You brought me back for a reason, I assume, Nikola?"

"It's time to bring the boy back into our Prime Time, Daniel," said Tesla. "We cannot wait any longer. And," he added, swallowing hard, as if reluctant to make the admission, "so far, none of us have been able to, ah, locate the precise time in which you have him hidden."

Defoe smiled and slouched in his seat. "I'm cleverer than you give me credit for," he said, preening in his rare moment of prominence. "I didn't just hide him in the *future*—I hid him in an *imaginary* one."

"A might-have-been?" Dee said slowly. So that was the reason that despite their collective skills, they had been unable to locate the boy on their own. The idiot Defoe had basically hidden him inside a living *fiction*. If the boy had Defoe's original watch, they could still possibly track him—without Daniel Defoe—but someone would have to physically retrieve him. Even with a means to do so, which the Cabal had, it was still almost impossibly dangerous and risky to even attempt.

"If you know his physical origin point," Dee said to Tesla, "could you track the boy?"

Tesla nodded. "The number of zero points Daniel had access to are limited. If we know where the boy was left, we should be able to ascertain when."

"The boy," Dee said, eyes glittering, "is in London."

Defoe sat up with a start. "Uh, how did you . . . ?"

"There's only one means of travel back from a might-have-been to the real world," said Dee, "and it's in the subbasement of the British Museum. You left him in London because you wanted easy access to your means for returning here."

Defoe swallowed hard. "There's no need to search for him," he said, a frantic tone creeping into his voice. "I can retrieve him for you, no problem."

Blake and the others watched Dee's face as he debated what to do. Finally, and to Defoe's relief, Dee nodded at him.

"Do it, then," he said. "Bring him back. Don't show your face here again until you do."

Defoe removed the ebony watch he'd been given as a replacement for his own, twirled the dials, and disappeared.

Dee looked at his own watch. "This meeting is adjourned. You all have things to be doing. Attend to them."

Without further discussion, each of the Cabal removed their own watches and disappeared. The three Blakes went last, leaving only Tesla and the black bird in the meeting hall with Dee.

"William didn't react to the mention of the Mystorians," Tesla said. "Impressive."

"Maybe," said Dee, "but we cannot let him interfere with our endgame—not until he's finished with the new tulpas."

"Do you really think he'll finish them?" Tesla asked. "At some point, he'll realize that one of them is—"

"We'll deal with that when it happens," Dee said, rising from his seat, "but for now, we must take the next step. We must close their ears and cover their eyes."

"Then the word is given?" said Tesla.

"It is," said Dee. "Destroy these Mystorians. And then, when that has been accomplished . . .

". . . we're going to cut off the head of the Dragon and kill Jules Verne."

Part Four

The Winter World

"Call me Jack."

CHAPTER THIRTEEN
The Dragons of Winter

✧

The castle that stood on the shores of Lake Baikal was as gray as the surrounding mountains, and nearly as timeless. It had been built for functionality, not vanity, and when, at long last, Mordred had been summoned to compete in the Gatherum, he had closed the castle doors with no intention of ever opening them again.

He reflected bitterly on the memory, and the second betrayal at the tourney, and the twenty lost years that only resulted in another, final betrayal, and worse, the loss of his right hand.

This, he thought coldly, was the result of believing too strongly in the nobility of men—and in the Dragon who had promised him a reward that was now as insubstantial as a dream.

The Dragon had been waiting for him when he arrived, and stoked a fire in the long-cold hearth. It had burned down to glowing embers before Samaranth chose to speak.

"Your brother has been exiled," the Dragon said.

"Exiled?" Mordred answered, a glimmer of interest rising in his eyes. "To where?"

"Solitude."

Mordred's face fell. "You mean in the Archipelago. You've let him return. . . . But not . . ." The words trailed off as the expression on his face hardened once more into an inscrutable mask. "And his son, the Arthur?"

"He is king," Samaranth answered, "and has claimed the Silver Throne."

Mordred's shoulders slumped forward, and a bit of the craziness that had possessed him when he lost his hand seemed to have returned.

"So," he said, giggling, "my brother betrayed me, more than once, and his punishment is to return home, where we have been trying to go for centuries. And his son, who betrayed me utterly, and took this," he said, waving the still-bloody stump of an arm, "is punished by being made the High King and steward of two worlds.

"And I," he continued, his bitterness adding sanity as he spoke, "have done nothing but honor my obligations, love my family, accept unjust exile, and spend my life being schooled to become the last Dragon, and for what?"

He spun around before the Dragon could answer.

"I'll tell you," Mordred said. "It's to become educated—and I have learned my lesson, oh yes, I have. And I know, Samaranth, who has betrayed me the most."

The Dragon did not answer, but merely regarded his apprentice with an expression closer to sorrow than pity.

"I'm through as your apprentice," Mordred said. "And you can leave now."

The Dragon growled in response. "You are still the apprentice," he said sternly. "And as poor a student as you have been at times, it is a calling, not a cloak to be dropped on the floor when you grow too hot. You may refuse my teaching, but you will remain a Dragon's apprentice until the end of your days."

"Then I'll be what you made of me, Samaranth," Mordred said, turning back to the fire, "and the next time I see you, we shall see if one Dragon may kill another."

He said nothing more, and after a time, the great Dragon gave a sigh, and with a stroke of his wings, lifted silently into the night.

It was not an hour later when the Scholar appeared, quietly, unobtrusively, in the corner of the room, just out of range of the firelight.

"Greetings, young Madoc," he said, his voice quiet but firm. "Well met."

"My name," Mordred spat, not bothering to turn around, "is Mordred. And you have chosen a poor time to introduce yourself, who-ever in Hades's name you are."

"Wrong twice," the Scholar said. "I have neither chosen poorly nor introduced myself."

Mordred spun about, reaching for his sword, then flushed with both anger and embarrassment when he realized he'd reached with his missing hand.

"You have been the victim of a grave injustice," the Scholar said. "I have come to right that wrong."

"I've heard that before," Mordred said, hiding his stump under his cloak as if it were naked.

"From the Elder Dragon, yes," the Scholar replied. "But his agenda is not mine. And I am not going to ask you for anything. I am merely here to serve."

"Serve?" Mordred barked. "Whom do you serve, here, in this place?"

The Scholar bowed. "A king, my lord. I serve you."

Mordred's face grew tight. "I am no king," he said brusquely. "Especially not here."

"You are a king with no country," the Scholar said, "but you remain a king, nevertheless."

Mordred hesitated—the Scholar's soothing words were doing the job they were intended to do.

"Winter is approaching," he said, turning to stoke the fire and add tinder to it. "A poor time to become a king."

"Winter's king now," the Scholar said persuasively, "and king of all else in time."

"Do not promise that which you cannot give," said Mordred.

"I never do," said the Scholar. "May we sit, and speak further . . . my lord?"

Mordred regarded the Scholar warily. His manner was not imposing, and his words dripped with honey. . . . But somehow, this strange, slight man who wore a monk's robe and called him lord understood what he needed to hear. And, Mordred realized, it had been a very, very long time since anyone had understood that, much less spoken the words.

"All right," he said, gesturing to the chair opposite his seat by the hearth. "Whom am I conversing with?"

The Scholar took a seat and extended his hand. "Dr. Dee," he said firmly. "But you can call me John."

"Call me Jack." Hearing those terrible words, spoken by this pale man who called himself Lord Winter, was like stumbling into the Styx and feeling the cold death of the water splashing against one's soul.

Lord Winter noted the companions' shocked reaction with a wry expression, then walked across the terrace to where a long table had been set up for a feast.

The geometric shapes and the attendants marked as Dragons stayed where they were, watching silently.

The settings at the table were familiar, as were the dishes the food was served on—it was patterned after the Feast Beasts' dinner table at Tamerlane House. Except none of the foods were recognizable, and the details of the plates were not quite right.

They were made of bronze rather than silver, and the designs were imprecise, as if they were being viewed through a fuzzy lens, or had been made of wax that had softened over time. Or, thought Rose, as if they had been remade from old, imperfect memories of what the real dishes looked like.

Lord Winter took his seat at the head of the table and gestured for his guests to join him—but none of them moved. A look of irritation flashed across his features, and with a gesture, he signaled to his Dragon aides to escort each of the companions to their seats around the table. Winter watched as each of his "guests" pulled out their chairs to sit, giving each one a thorough once-over, but paying particularly close attention to Rose.

When everyone was in their place, Burton broke the tension by blurting out the first question that was on all their minds: "Your servant, Vanamonde, said that everyone on this world is Lloigor. Are you also a Lloigor, 'Jack'?"

"Right to the point, eh, Sir Richard?" Lord Winter said, unruffled by the question. "The answer is yes, I am. But the larger question is, why aren't all of you?"

"Why would we be?" asked Charles. "If you were truly Jack—"

"I am," Lord Winter replied, "just as much as you are who you are, Charles."

"You haven't answered me," Charles said, his voice reflecting the misery in his face. "Why would we be Lloigor?"

"On the rare—exceedingly rare—occasions that we encounter someone who has not chosen the path," said Winter, "their shadows are severed, and they are assigned new shadows, from those of the Echthroi who are still waiting for hosts." His eyes flickered up to the geometric shapes in the air, which vibrated slightly with the attention. "It is a condition of living in Dys."

"And if they choose not to, are they permitted to leave?" asked Burton. "I only wonder this because we were called your guests—but last night, the door was locked."

"That was for security," said Winter. "I shall order it kept unlocked in the future."

The companions exchanged uneasy glances at this suggestion that their stay might be longer than they wished—whatever their choice would have been.

"Have you ever had 'guests,'" Burton pressed, "who wanted to stay in Dys but didn't want to become Lloigor?"

"A few," Winter admitted, "like Vanamonde's father—your old colleague, Bert. Moses . . . Nebogipfel, I think it was. I'll have to check the label on his skull."

"Keeping the skulls of your enemies as trophies?" Bert asked with a barely suppressed shudder. "Isn't that a bit . . ."

"Barbaric?" Lord Winter finished for him. "Perhaps. But one man's barbarism is another man's culture. Isn't that right, Sir Richard? And besides," he added with a grin at Bert, "I learned it from *you*."

Bert looked horrorstruck. "I've never taken a head from anyone in my life!" he exclaimed vehemently. "Nor would I keep the skull as a trophy!"

"Ah, not to quarrel," Charles put in, "but according to what John and, ah, Jack, told me, that isn't precisely true."

"How do you mean?" asked Bert.

"You did exactly those things in the country of the Winter King during the Dyson incident," Charles said, a pained expression on his face. He seemed to hate the appearance of supporting this Lord Winter's point of view on anything, least of all on a point regarding their mentor. But the truth was the truth.

"That wasn't me!" sputtered Bert. "That was—"

"A version of you, who had lived through some terrible tragedies," said Lord Winter, "and in the process, had to make some terrible choices. But make no mistake, Bert. It was you. I know. I remember."

"It weren't—I mean, it wasn't," Bert shot back. "I wasn't there."

"We all like to think that we will always make the choices that flow in line with our image of ourselves," Lord Winter said, turning to look out over the city, "but the truth is, we never know what we'll really do until we're already in the soup. And then, we do what we must, just as you did. It doesn't diminish the good choices you made to have chosen to do something you abhor," he continued, "but neither does it mean you suddenly changed character when you made those other choices. You are who you are."

Bert shook his head. "I would not have done those things—not if I had any choice," he added before Charles could correct him. "It just isn't in my character."

Their host spun about to face him. "Nothing we actually do," Lord Winter said, "is out of character."

He stood, and with a little encouragement from Lord Winter's

Dragons, the others rose as well. None of them had so much as touched a morsel of food.

"No one was hungry, I guess," Winter said. "Come—let me escort you back to your room. After all, traveling so many thousands of years must have made you all very tired."

The companions followed Winter and Vanamonde back down the stairs to the room where they'd spent the night. None of their belongings seemed to have been touched. Not their duffels, or their books, or . . .

. . . their *weapons*.

"Perhaps we may speak again later," Lord Winter said from the open doorway, "and I can tell you more about my decision to join the Echthroi and why"—he smiled broadly—"you will make the same choice, in the end."

Rose had already been considering a choice, and there, in that moment, as Lord Winter spoke those words, she made it.

Steeling herself to her task, she carefully, quietly removed the sword Caliburn from its sheath underneath her duffel, and before he could speak, she whirled around and rushed over to Lord Winter.

"You," she cried, "are *not* Jack!" and she buried the sword to the hilt in his chest.

It had absolutely no effect.

She stared at him, eyes wide and unblinking in disbelief.

"I was wondering why it was taking you so long to try that," Winter said, not even trying to conceal the pleasure in his voice. "I decided that you were either too timid to actually strike, or you were too overwrought with emotion for your dear uncle Jack to try it. But I'm glad to know that you weren't too weak to try. And I'm sorry that you had to fail so badly."

He gave her a shove, and she flew backward into the corner, hitting her head roughly against the wall.

"And," he said, taking little notice of the companions who had flown across the room to Rose's aid, "I'm sorry that I have to break your little toy."

He reached up and grabbed the hilt of Caliburn—and snapped it off. Then he simply pulled out the blade, which emerged clean and bloodless from his chest. He dropped it to the floor with a clatter.

"Impossible!" Burton breathed. "That sword should have defeated any Shadow!"

"Any mortal's shadow, eh, Sir Richard?" Winter said, winking. "But not primordial Shadow. Not Lloigor. Not Echthroi. And especially not while I wear this armor."

The fear in the companions' eyes was evident, and he chuckled, then held up his hands.

"It's all right," Lord Winter said. "I've no desire to harm you. Step closer, and observe."

To better facilitate their examination, Lord Winter stepped forward himself and raised his arms, turning slowly so they could see all the armor he wore.

"What is it?" asked Burton. "Where did you get it?"

"There was an old Chinese legend," Lord Winter began, "about a young girl named T'ai Shan. In the beginnings of time, there came upon the gods of the world a great drought—and I say gods, and not peoples, because in those days, all were considered as gods. They spoke with the beasts of the Earth, and lived long lives, and knew all the secrets that there were. But not the reasons for the drought.

"Crops died, livestock perished, and soon starvation followed. And all the great gods came together to try to find a solution, but none was forthcoming. No one knew what had caused the drought, and no one knew how to resolve it. But one child, a crippled girl named T'ai Shan, who lived as a beggar on the outskirts of the first city of the gods, knew what must be done.

"She recalled a story told by her grandfather, who was one of the elder gods, that when the gods needed aid, they prayed to the stars, and the stars came to Earth and aided them. So she rose on her crutch and hobbled away from the city, which was radiantly bright, into the darkness where she could see the stars, and she began to pray.

"One of the stars heard her prayer and descended to Earth to give her aid. He said that far to the west there grew a flower, a rose, which contained within it a single drop of dew. If she were to find that rose and return to the city, the drop of dew would become a torrent that would restore rain to the world and fill the oceans again.

"All he required of her was that when this was done, she give the rose to him. And T'ai Shan agreed.

"So the star took from himself scales of fire and gave them to the girl, instructing her that she should find a smithy to forge them into armor. And when she had done so, she would be able to traverse the great distance and retrieve the rose."

Lord Winter paused, as if he were struggling to remember— but after a few moments he regained his composure and continued on, his voice strong and unwavering.

"T'ai Shan found a smith, and her armor was made. And as the gods of the Earth began to die, she went on her great journey, defeating terrible beasts and overcoming immense obstacles to succeed in her quest. And succeed she did—but when at last she returned, the star declared that he wished to keep the rose, and the dewdrop, for himself, and thus force the gods to swear homage to him, that he should rule over all the Earth.

"But T'ai Shan knew that this was wrong, and she resisted. The star tried to take the rose from her, but he had given her too much of his own fire, and in the great battle that followed, he was defeated, and fell.

"T'ai Shan succeeded in bringing the water back to the world, but she could not control it, and a deluge flooded all the Earth. Only through great sacrifice were the gods able to save parts of their world—and when the waters again receded, they found that the world had changed. It was no longer theirs—T'ai Shan had given it to their children, as it should have been all along. As her grandfather, the elder god, had told her the world was meant to be. To ensure that the gods would not try to reclaim it, she left her armor to the children, so that they might defend the world themselves. And with that, she walked into the mountains and vanished forever."

Lord Winter lowered his head, and the companions looked at one another, uncertain whether he was done—and more uncertain whether they dared to say anything.

Edmund was the one who finally broke the silence. "Begging your pardon, lord," he said respectfully, "but why did you tell us that story?"

Lord Winter laughed, a short, sharp bark, and turned to face the boy. "Innocence," he said, more to himself than to any of them. "It's a refreshing thing, after so long."

"I told you that story, my young Cartographer," he said, holding Edmund by the chin so the boy was looking him in the eye, "so that you would understand—I serve the Shadows, but fire still has its uses."

"You are not wearing the Ruby Armor of T'ai Shan," Bert said firmly. "As powerful as that armor is, an Echthros would not be able to countenance its touch. And the armor forged from a star would not shatter Caliburn. Only Deep Magic could do that. So your armor is something else."

Lord Winter started to respond in anger, but caught himself and replaced the harsh words on his tongue with a sickly sweet smile. "Very good, old friend. I'm impressed."

He released Edmund's chin. "I told you the story, boy, because somewhere in time and space, the bearer of that armor still exists. And unlike this sword, he does have the ability to injure me. So I forged armor of my own."

"Armor strong enough to break the sword of Aeneas?" asked Rose. "How?"

"As useful as the Spear of Destiny once was as a weapon, I found it to be far more useful as armor," Lord Winter replied, stroking his chest. "It heals any wound, deflects any blow against me. And together with the energies of the Echthroi, makes me all but immortal. And so I have had all the time needed to create this," he continued, spreading his arms to indicate the city that stretched into the distance, "my perfect world."

As it had before, the tower began to shake with a loud rumbling, lasting longer this time.

Bert snorted. "Hardly perfect, 'Lord Winter,'" he said. "Your dark tower seems to be coming apart."

"Not coming apart," Winter replied. "On the contrary—Camazotz is *growing*."

Charles threw a surreptitious glance at Burton, who nodded almost imperceptibly. So they were right—it was like the keep, in some ways at least.

"Growing?" said Edmund. "Why?"

"It no longer matters," Winter replied, trying—and failing—not to glance at Rose. "My plans have recently undergone a change, and soon I'll no longer need the tower."

"Why?" asked Burton.

"Because," Lord Winter said as he turned to walk away, "I've realized it is a world of perfect order, just as the Echthroi have ordained it to be. Just as it was always meant to be. Just as it will always be. And soon," he added as the door closed with an almost imperceptible hiss, "just as it will have always *been*."

Again the companions were alone, and in the silence, they let the full possibility of his words sink in.

"It's us," Charles said. "We're the somethings that changed him doing whatever it is he plans to do."

"Agreed," said Burton. "What think you, Bert?"

But the Far Traveler wasn't paying any attention to the discussion. Instead he was listening at the door. Then he reached down, grasped the latch . . .

. . . and pulled it open.

"The door!" Rose exclaimed. "It's unlocked! We can leave!"

"Of course," Edmund said, still not entirely grasping whether they were supposed to be prisoners. "He did say we are his guests."

"Guests are always free to leave the party," Bert said hastily, cutting off whatever sarcastic remark Burton was about to make to the boy, "and a good guest knows when it's time to dust the crumbs off his lap and bid the host good evening."

"If it's all the same to you," Charles said as the companions headed out the door, "I think we'll pass on saying good-bye."

"Agreed," Burton and Rose said together.

"Wait!" Edmund exclaimed, stopping in the doorway. "What about Archie? We can't just leave him behind!"

Rose started to answer, but it was Bert who turned around. "That can't be helped right now," he said, sternly but also with honest regret and sympathy. "You may not realize this yet, young Edmund, but it's a miracle enough that we're leaving this room alive."

"B-But Lord Jack . . . ," Edmund stammered.

"That is *not* Jack," Rose said firmly. "I don't know who he is, but Lord Winter is not our Jack. Listen," she added, putting a comforting arm across his shoulders, "we aren't leaving him for good. We'll come back for him. But right now, we are in the heart of the enemy's stronghold—and we aren't safe. We have to find high ground, where we can make a plan. But we'll come back. I promise."

Comforted, Edmund nodded and followed her and Bert out to the corridor where the others were waiting. Swiftly, and thanks in part to Edmund's unerring sense of direction, they retraced the path that Vanamonde had used to bring them along to their room, and in short order were again outside the tower.

Keeping close to the buildings, they made their way back to the massive entry doors, trying to avoid being seen—but very quickly they noticed that no one was looking for them. The few of

Lord Winter's Dragons they passed took no notice of them. And so their escape proceeded swiftly and without event. Their flight from the tower was done in silence, each of the companions keeping their thoughts to themselves. There would be time enough to talk and commiserate later. But as they ran, all Rose could think of was whether she would be able to keep the promise she'd made to Edmund.

And whether, if they were given the chance, she would be brave enough to.

Ringed about the high canyon walls were the great, skeletal remains . . .

CHAPTER FOURTEEN
The Unforgotten

❖

"Something's gone wrong," Jack said as he and John examined the cavorite pedestal in front of Tamerlane House. "I can feel it in my spleen. Something's wrong. They should have come back before now, don't you think?"

"It's only been a couple of days," John replied as he sat on a nearby rock and started pulling at the long grass that grew in patchy clumps all over the islands. "That's the point of them staying there in real time—so that they'll have more time at the other end of the mission, in the past. And as to their other goal, well, there's no telling what's needed."

"I understand," Jack said, "but you've read the book. England isn't that big. They should have found her and returned by now. And Bert . . ."

"I know," John said irritably. They didn't speak of it much, but both men were constantly aware of the time—and how little of it Bert had left.

"At least," Jack said as he moved over to sit in the grass next to John, "when they do get back, we'll have another solid zero point connection for our *Imaginarium Chronographica*."

"That's the thing that disturbs me about our *Imaginarium*

Chronographica," John murmured. "I think our adversaries already have one, or something very much like it. And," he added, "it's better than ours."

"One of the reasons," said Verne's voice behind them, "that the Cabal's *Imaginarium Chronographica* is, well, not necessarily better . . . let us say, more complete than ours, is that not only did they have a head start in creating one, but somehow, they are adding all our zero points to their own—as we discover them."

Verne, Dickens, Twain, and Byron stepped off the porch and walked to where John and Jack were sitting. Verne lowered himself to the ground and sat with the younger men. "We do not know 'when' they have gone, but they know 'when' we have. And in that," he finished, "they have a decided advantage over us."

"But if a zero point isn't created until Rose and Edmund create it, how could they do that?" asked John.

"Bread crumbs," said Byron.

"If this is the start of a poem, I'm going to clock you," said Dickens.

"I mean, they're leaving a trail of bread crumbs," Byron said, irritated at being marginalized—again. "Rose and the Cartographer must somehow be leaving a marker that the Cabal can follow to each zero point. It's the logical explanation."

"Perhaps," Verne said, stroking his beard. "But how?"

Jack sighed. "This was all a whole lot easier when we just had to climb up some stairs and open a door in a tower someone else had already built."

"That is part of our quest," a quiet voice said. "It's part of why the travelers needed to undertake their journey—to restore what was."

The companions turned in surprise at hearing the speaker. It was Poe. Edmund Spenser was also with him.

It was surprising not that Poe had spoken, but that he had left the confines of the house. He rarely ventured outside—at most once or twice during the time that John and Jack had known him.

"That's the other thing I miss about the good old days," said Twain. "We didn't have to rely on a blasted deck of cards to go anywhere. We had the Dragonships."

"The trumps are more convenient, Samuel," said Verne, "and let us do our work more efficiently."

"But it's a device our enemies also use to go where they want to," said Dickens. "In fact, I think they've figured out some way to travel in space better than we do."

"Like the cat," Twain said, puffing thoughtfully on his cigar. "Grimalkin can appear wherever, whenever he pleases, and he does so without benefit of a trump."

"Yes," Dickens agreed, "but he is a cat, and obeys as well as the rest of his species—which is to say, not at all."

"We'll have the means ourselves soon," Verne said firmly. "Someone wearing the Ruby Shoes will be able to go anywhere they please—perhaps even into our enemy's stronghold."

"If we can acquire them," John pointed out. "Uncas and Quixote still have to find them first."

"Finding them is one thing," said Twain. "Keeping them is a horse of a different color."

"They're meant to be used by an adept, like Rose," Verne said. "Perhaps she can give them a try when they get back."

John looked at the others. "Maybe we ought to try to send someone after them with one of the devices in the basement, just in case there's been trouble," he said. "I'd certainly volunteer. Anyone else game?"

For a few long moments, none of them moved, until finally Twain reached out and squeezed the younger man's shoulder. "We are all with you, my boy. To the last man, to the last mouse. We are with you. But we cannot follow them into the future. Not until they return."

Suddenly it dawned on John why his suggestion couldn't be followed—and why it hadn't been suggested and implemented already by one of the others.

"The chronal energies," he said, crestfallen. "I'd forgotten. We can't go after them."

"Not," Verne said cautiously, "with what we now know about time travel, young John. But there are those working on . . . new ways."

"Who?" asked Jack.

"Top men," Verne answered cryptically. Which angered John, who stood up and clenched his fists.

"Your Messengers, you mean, like Dr. Raven, and the Mystorians!" John exclaimed, barely containing his frustration. "I don't care if we're meant to keep them a secret. Now is the time to play your cards, Jules!"

"The who?" said Byron.

"The thing you should know about cards, young John," Verne replied, "is never play an ace when a two will do."

"Jules learned that from the badgers," said Twain.

"How is this not the time to play all your aces, Jules?" said John. "How much larger do the stakes have to be?"

"It's not the stakes that you're misunderstanding, Caretaker,"

Edmund Spenser said, moving past the others and standing next to John, "but the size of the game."

It was an accepted tradition that due respect and deference was given to the Caretakers in accordance with their seniority. The only exceptions to this were Verne and Poe, who were accorded more because of their more prominent roles in the work of the Caretakers, and da Vinci, who was accorded less because of his arrogance among his peers. And thus Spenser or Chaucer usually presided over meetings, but less frequently got involved in the debates. So when one of them actually went out of his way to make a point, the rest of them listened. John sat back down on the rock and waited.

"All it takes for the opposition to win is to defeat us once—because the corruption that will cause can never be completely winnowed out again. And thus for us, a victory means never letting that take place. Constant, eternal vigilance—in all the times past, and all those still to come.

"So have patience, Caveo Principia," Spenser finished, holding out his hand to John. "Trust in your mentor, and the Grail Child, and the Cartographer. Trust in those you believe in. And they will find a way to come home."

John puffed his cheeks and blew out the air to calm down. "All right," he said, shaking Spenser's hand. "Let's go back into the house, shall we?" He glanced at Verne, still clearly annoyed. "All this hot air out here is giving me a headache."

As the others moved into Tamerlane House, Verne held Poe back to speak with him more privately.

"I need . . . ," Verne began. He stopped. Poe was holding a key in his outstretched hand.

"I know," the master of Tamerlane House said simply. "She is downstairs, where she has been since Quixote and the Child of the Earth retrieved her from the museum in London."

"I've prepared some memory rings," said Verne, "but if they're truly lost that far in the ancient future . . . If they indeed did just as you fear, and ended up in a might-have-been . . ."

"The Sphinx will persist, but the rings themselves may not last," Poe confirmed. "She may be the only one who can help them there, then."

It did not take Defoe long to return to the House on the Borderlands, but against Dee's express request, he returned without the boy prince.

"I have some good news and some bad news," Defoe said, slumped in his chair at the Cabal's table. He looked as if his head were splitting in two. "Which do you want to hear first?"

"I only care about why you came back without the boy," Dee replied through clenched teeth. "Tell me that before I have you drawn and quartered and fed to Loki."

Defoe glanced up at the huge black bird and gulped. "I went to find the Sphinx at the British Museum, but she's, uh, she's no longer *there*."

"Moved?" asked Tesla.

"Stolen," said Defoe. "Burgled."

"Well, there's irony for you," said Chesterton. "Can't say we didn't deserve *that*."

"Without the Sphinx, there's no way to return him from a might-have-been—," a now livid Dee started to say before Defoe interrupted him.

"That's just it," he insisted. "The boy *is* here, in the *House.* He's waiting in the next room. I just can't decide if that's the good news or the bad news."

On hearing the boy was there, Dee started to calm down, but now he stiffened up again. "How is that bad news?"

"*I* didn't bring him," Defoe said. "He found us entirely on his own."

The Chronographer's eyes narrowed, and he looked at Blake. "How is that possible?"

"Because," Blake said testily, "he's not just an heir to the powers that be. It seems he's also an adept."

Dee's eyes widened, and he leaned forward. "Explain."

"He has all the abilities we hoped he might have," Tesla said, glancing sideways at Blake, "and more, he is using them. He has learned how to activate his Anabasis Machine, and he has already been traveling in time."

Dr. Dee turned to look at Defoe, eyes blazing with anger. "You left him with a *functional* watch?"

"I had to!" Defoe exclaimed. "If he had been left in the past, no problem. We record where he is and retrieve him at our leisure. But in the future, especially in a might-have-been, we needed to leave a marker. And that meant giving him a watch and making sure it was activated."

He slumped back in his chair, pouting. "It isn't my fault, you know," he said to no one in particular. "How was I to know the boy would figure it out on his own?"

Blake knew from Dee's expression that he was considering whether to just dump Defoe in the ocean and be done with him.

"He more than 'figured it out' if he returned from a

might-have-been all on his own," Dee murmured, more to himself than to the others, "and to have found the House so easily . . ."

He looked up at Defoe. "Bring him here. Now."

Defoe leaped out of his chair and vanished through the door. He reappeared a moment later, followed closely by a young man of perhaps nineteen who stood next to him as he took his seat.

"Greetings," said Dr. Dee. "You can call me John."

"If it's all the same to you," the young man replied, "I'll call you Dr. Dee."

Dee and the others reacted in surprise. "Daniel has told you about who we are?"

"No," the young man replied, "but I learned about you and who you are from my studies. And I know you can help me. That's why I decided to find you."

Interesting, Blake thought as he observed the young man, who was unruffled and very, very self-assured. *Dee may have actually bitten off more than he can chew.* He thought they'd taken a hostage who could be converted to an acolyte. But now, Blake realized, even if the others in the Cabal did not quite yet, they might have created a predator.

"We can help you," Dee said persuasively.

"I know I have these abilities," the young man said. "I just don't know what I have them *for.*"

"I can tell you that," said Dee. "You shall use them in the service of a great cause. There are immense forces at work in the world, and I am offering you the chance to shape what the world will become. If you work with us, there is no limit to what your destiny may be. Will you accept?"

In response, the young man simply nodded, once.

"Good," said Dee. "Daniel, will you see to it our young guest is made comfortable? We'll finish our business here, and then I'll come to personally instruct him."

Defoe again rose from his seat and motioned for the young man to follow, and without another word, they left the room.

"We should simply kill him now," Tesla said flatly. "He's more dangerous than he appears, Dee. And he's too unknown a quantity."

"He's an adept!" Dee snapped. "Like Mordred before him. Only we've gotten him before he's had a chance to lose his focus."

"His focus is precisely what worries me," said Tesla. "And if he's already learned to use the watch *on his own* . . ."

"Then he'll be at least as useful as Daniel Defoe," said Dee, "and longer-lived, to boot."

"What is his name?" Chesterton asked. "No one asked him."

"What does that matter?" Dee replied. "He's here, and he's ours. The plan proceeds apace."

"Where should we go?" Charles asked the others as they hurried down one of the paved pathways amid the dark buildings. "Back to the plaza, perhaps?"

Bert shook his head. "If that's really Jack up there, that'll be the first place he comes to look for us. We should find somewhere else where we can try to plan our next move."

"I'm all for going to find that Messenger, Pym," Burton growled, "and wringing his scrawny little neck."

"In that," Charles said, "we are absolutely agreed."

As it turned out, the companions had the opportunity to do both. When they exited through one of the city gates, they also found Arthur Pym, who seemed to have been waiting for them.

The scruffy Messenger threw himself to the ground, wailing. "Please!" he howled, tears rolling down his cheeks. "Forgive! I did not realize the birdy was a hurdy-gurdy! Only Echthroi fly here! Forgive!"

"Archie isn't a hurdy-gurdy," Edmund said sternly. "He's a *Teacher.*"

"Oh, for crying out loud," Charles said, rolling his eyes. "Have a little dignity, man." He pulled the still wailing Pym to his feet and offered him a handkerchief, which the Messenger promptly covered in snot.

"You can keep that," Charles said when Pym offered it back. "I've got a perfectly good sleeve here."

"Do you think the Lloigor will be looking for us?" Rose asked the others.

"Possibly," Bert said, looking around, "but we're still in the open here. We need to find someplace safe."

"Safe haven!" Pym exclaimed, tugging on Bert's arm. "That's where the others are. Safe haven."

"You mentioned 'others' before," said Burton. "Are they Lloigor too?"

Pym shook his head. "Not Lloigor. Not Messenger, either. People of the Book."

"Librarians?" asked Bert. "Or writers?"

"A little yes, a little no," said Pym.

"Which one?" asked Rose.

"Exactly," said Pym.

"All I care about," Charles interrupted, "is if this 'safe haven' is away from the city."

Pym nodded and started walking across the pavement. "Yes," he answered over his shoulder with a loopy, triumphant grin. "Very far." He motioned for the others to follow and picked up his pace.

"That," Charles said as they all fell into line behind Pym, "sounds pretty darn good to me—at least, better than our alternative. Lead on, Arthur."

The companions, led by the Anachronic Man, Arthur Pym, followed a paved path that led due east away from Dys. They walked in relative peace—the denizens of the city apparently didn't venture beyond its gates, or so Pym told them.

The Messenger kept up a rambling travelogue about their surroundings, none of which made an impression until they came to the canyon.

"This," Pym said, his voice echoing even though he spoke barely above a whisper, "this I wanted to show you especially, Bert."

Ringed about the high canyon walls were the great, skeletal remains of several ships, which had nonetheless survived enough of the passing centuries to be easily recognizable.

"It's all the ships," Bert said breathlessly. "All the Dragonships, come together again."

"Come together in a graveyard, you mean," Charles said scornfully, giving Burton a withering glance. "They're all dead, Bert. All of them. They would have been dead, as living ships, anyway, long before he ever brought them here."

"I . . . didn't know," Burton said, looking away, unwilling to face any of the others. "I swear to Christ—I didn't know the

Dragons would be lost, when we took all their shadows."

None of them responded to Burton's apology, but Rose stepped forward, simply taking Burton's hand and squeezing it in empathy.

"I don't see the *Blue Dragon* anywhere," said Bert. "The Elves' ship."

"Nor would I expect you to," said Charles as he climbed over a protrusion of rock for a better view. "It was left behind, there on Paralon, and perished with the island when the Echthroi took over."

"But the rest of them are here," Bert said, pointing, "including the old *Black Dragon*. Which means that at some time in the past, the Archipelago was restored."

Before any of them could comment further, Pym moved farther down the path on the canyon floor, toward an old, ramshackle gate. "There's more to see," he said, beckoning for the others to follow. "Much more."

They followed him through the gate, where they saw a massive, gleaming pyramid that rose up from the ground and dominated the horizon. It was surrounded by an immense wall that was nearly twice Burton's height. "The Last Redoubt," said Pym, trying to hurry them on. His eyes kept darting from side to side on the path, as if he were waiting for some beast to leap out and attack them.

At the pyramid's base, they saw something else familiar. "These are the rune stones!" Bert exclaimed as he examined the wall around it. "The ones we set up as wards around Tamerlane House. They've been repurposed to protect the pyramid and whatever else is behind this wall."

"The entrance is here," Pym said, showing them a looming, ornate door a little farther down the slope.

"It's of Caretaker manufacture," Bert said, excitement rising in his voice. "What's inside, Arthur?"

"Don't know." Pym shrugged. "Never been inside. Can't. Have to have a watch or a silver ring to get in at all—but you need two Caretaker's watches, just to open the entrance—and Lord Winter took my watch ages ago."

That piece of information elicited a quick glance of concern between Charles and Rose, but Bert was too excited to notice.

"Tried without using a ring," Pym said plaintively. "Tried and tried and tried. Don't like it out here a'tall. But no use. I couldn't get through."

"Maybe you can't," Charles said, "but I'm betting that *we* can."

There was a protective ornamental lock that was affixed to both sides of the door, where Pym said that the watches must be inserted to allow passage. "Otherwise," he said, "can't get through, even with a ring."

"Nice," said Burton. "Good forethought. Whoever built this place wanted to make sure that at least two Caretakers or their emissaries were present for it to work. Just one wouldn't do the trick."

"No," Pym echoed. "Wouldn't."

"Arthur was lost in time before Jules conceived of the rings," said Bert, "and so of course he wouldn't have one. But," he added, "I have mine, so he can use my watch to pass through."

He handed the device to Pym and nodded at Rose. She inserted her own watch in the indentation on the left of the door, as Edmund inserted his on the right. Then she reached out her hand and pushed the door . . .

. . . which swung soundlessly open.

"There," said Bert. "We're in."

From inside the wall, they realized the pyramid was in fact still a good distance away. There were crumbling temples and fallen archways, all overgrown with foliage, lining the gentle slopes of land that led to the pyramid's base. It was an architectural and arboreal disaster area—but somehow, it all managed to look deliberate. And the atmosphere was far less oppressive than that just on the other side of the gate.

"Well enough and good," said Bert, looking around. "There are people here." He pointed to the right of the pyramid. Against the dark sky, they could see the wispy trails of smoke rising.

"Why I brought you here," said Pym. "To meet the Unforgotten."

"Who are?" asked Charles.

Before Pym could answer, a tall creature with the beaked skull of a bird and the skin and claws of a reptile stepped out of the trees just ahead of them. He was carrying a spear and was adorned with ringlets of beads and feathers.

He stood watching the companions a moment, then tipped his head back and spoke—and it was then they realized it was a man, dressed as some kind of creature.

His words were unintelligible, but he was immediately joined by several others, all dressed as similar creatures.

The tallest of them cocked his head, as if he, too, were appraising these strange visitors; then he strode forward—to *Charles*.

"It's the glasses," Bert whispered. "They give him presence."

The strange man looked Charles over, then began to recite in a surprisingly delicate and refined voice:

He that is thy friend indeed,
He will help thee in thy need:
If thou sorrow, he will weep;
If thou wake, he cannot sleep;
Thus of every grief in heart
He with thee doth bear a part.
These are certain signs to know
Faithful friend from flattering foe.

"Dear Lord," said Bert, "That's —"

"Shakespeare!" Rose exclaimed. "He's reciting Shakespeare!"

Another of the strange people, a female this time, approached Charles and examined the silver ring he wore. As one, all the companions held up their rings, and Pym held up Charles's soiled handkerchief, grinning.

The response was unexpected, to say the least.

"You are of our tribe," the tall man said in perfect, unaccented English, his face breaking into a bright, gapped smile. He turned and raised his arms in triumph. "*They are of our tribe!*" he shouted, and the others broke out into loud cheering.

They clustered around the companions and started herding them toward the smoke. "They have a village there," Pym explained. "In this good a humor, just go along."

"How did these people survive?" Burton asked as they were jostled along by the exceedingly happy bird-skull-lizard-dressed people that Pym called the Unforgotten.

"Big world," Pym said, shrugging. "Even Echthroi couldn't take it over all at once. Some parts, didn't want to take over."

"So they just ignored those parts?"

"No," said Pym. "Usually, simply obliterated whatever they couldn't possess. This place, though, think they couldn't take over."

"Because of the wards," said Bert. "The protective rune stones."

"This isn't all that far from the city, or Dys, or Camazotz, or whatever it is that he's calling that dark tower," said Charles. "I wonder where we are."

"Thought you'd know where we are," said Pym. "From what I've learned, when the world fell to the Echthroi and Lord Winter began his rise to power, was the only place of free, truth-seeking, higher learning left on Earth."

"The Last Redoubt," Bert said, echoing the Messenger's words from earlier. "The last haven."

Pym nodded, as interested in what was inside as the others. "Didn't find this place until after I'd lost my watch," he said, "or else I'd have been in here, being Unforgotten myself.

"An ironic shame," he added with a tone of sincere regret, "that it happened to be the very place your friend Jack taught . . . you know. Before."

Charles slapped his forehead and Rose suppressed a grin, while Bert rolled his eyes at both of them.

"What?" asked Edmund. "I don't get it."

"Inside joke," Bert replied, "that's either gotten funnier or lamer depending on which side you're on."

"Cambridge," Charles muttered. "My old friend Tummeler would be absolutely appalled."

CHAPTER FIFTEEN
The Sphinx

❖

The companions were led to an outdoor amphitheater that bore traces of Greek design, as well as designs of China, India, the Navajo, and other cultures that perhaps hadn't even existed yet in their own time.

When these "Unforgotten" removed the bird skulls and lizard cloaks they wore, the companions could see that they were simply men and women—and, Bert was thrilled to note, children—like those they had known in the past. And these people were far from being Lloigor. They were simple but happy, and, once they had established tribal affiliation, more than happy to receive guests.

There were homes fashioned from the fallen buildings that stood in the clear spaces between the wall and the pyramid, and more in the overgrowth of shrubbery and trees that pockmarked the area. There were cooking fires, and foods of the same sort that Lord Winter had offered—but this time the offer was combined with genuine hospitality, and the companions happily accepted.

"Have you noticed," Rose said, keeping her voice deliberately low, "that they almost all wear silver rings?"

... *these people were far from being Lloigor.*
They were simple but happy ...

"The adults do," Pym said as he bit into what appeared to be a roast hen—with six legs. "Rings are passed to the tribal elders from generation to generation. Allows the Unforgotten who wear them to pass freely into the outside. Although," he added with a shiver, "they seldom do, unless they must."

"Why are they called the Unforgotten?" Rose asked.

"Last remnants of our civilization," Pym replied, "the most important parts, some would say. Preserved that which was most important, which would otherwise not have survived so many centuries."

"Not engineering, or science," Charles said, looking around at the feather-clad children sitting nearby.

"Architecture?" Burton said, glancing at the pyramid.

"The books," said Edmund. "The stories—that's what's most important in any culture, I think."

As if that was a request, one of the group that had met them at the entrance leaped to his feet and began, in a rough American accent, to recite:

"CAMELOT—*Camelot*," said I to myself. "I don't seem to remember hearing of it before. Name of the asylum, likely."

It was a soft, reposeful summer landscape, as lovely as a dream, and as lonesome as Sunday. The air was full of the smell of flowers, and the buzzing of insects, and the twittering of birds . . .

"Dear Lord!" Bert exclaimed, nearly dropping his plate. "Those are the first lines of Samuel Clemens's book! Do you mean to tell me he's memorized the *whole book?*"

Pym nodded. "As his forefathers before him do, done, did. In fact, he *is* the book. So are they all."

The man shyly walked over to Bert and offered his hand, which the Far Traveler shook, slightly dazzled and definitely bewildered.

"This is A Connecticut Yankee in King Arthur's Court 417," Pym said by way of introduction, "although among friends and family, he's simply known as 'In.'"

"'In'?" asked Charles.

"If that whole title was your name, you'd want a short nickname too," said Pym.

"Good point," said Charles. "Who's this fellow?"

Pym put his arm around a slim, fair-haired man who appeared to be in his forties. "Treasure Island 519. And his brother, the fellow just there by the pylon—Oliver Twist 522."

"So everyone here is a living book?" Charles asked. "Amazing!"

"Not all the books that started in the beginning have survived to this day," said Pym. "There have been accidents, and natural deaths before books could be passed on in their entirety. The family line that had *Anna Karenina* lost the last chapter around ninety generations ago, and subsequent generations have decreed it to have improved the book immeasurably.

"Also," he continued, "*Silas Marner* didn't last into the fifteenth generation."

"Was that because of an accident, or a natural death?" asked Edmund.

"Neither," said Pym. "Just couldn't stand it anymore. Ended up marrying into and merging with *The Wizard of Oz*."

One youth stepped forward hesitantly, trying to decide whether he should introduce himself.

"Go ahead, lad," said Pym. "He'll be very pleased to meet you in particular."

"I am The Time Machine 43," the gangly, copper-headed youth said, unsure whether to offer a hand to Bert. "Are . . . are you really my creator?"

"*The Time Machine?*" Bert said incredulously. "I can't believe it!"

The young man was a bit flustered at this and took Bert's statement as a request for verification. So he gulped down his nervousness and began to recite: "The Time Traveller (for so it will be convenient to speak of him) was expounding a recondite matter . . ."

Bert rushed forward and embraced the startled young man before he could continue. "Oh, my stars and garters!" he exclaimed. "You know it! You do know it!"

"Of course," Pym said, a hangdog expression on his face. "Told you he did—these people are the books, Bert. And he is one of yours, as were forty-two generations before him."

"Oh, my," Bert said, unable to keep the tears from streaming down his face. "Do you know what this means, Rose, Charles?" The expression on his face was a mix of joy and pain. "It means that in a way, Weena is still here, in her future. Because I wrote her into the book, and because these people have kept it alive all these centuries, she's still here."

"I say," Charles asked, craning his neck to look at all the Unforgotten gathered around them. "Which, ah, which of these fellows or families represents *my* books?"

Pym looked at him curiously. "Sorry, Charlie, but I don't

know that any families here ever really took to any poetry."

Charles frowned. "Oh. Uh, of course not," he stammered, "but I was asking more about my novels."

"Novels?" Pym asked, scratching his head. "Thought you were an editor."

"Editors can *write!*" Charles exclaimed. "I mean, I'm a novelist, besides being an editor. And a poet." He looked crestfallen. "So—no one here memorized any of *my* books?"

"Wait a moment," one of the Unforgotten said, stepping closer to Charles. "He said you were friends with the Caveo Principia and the Caveo Secundus?"

"Yes!" Charles said. "They are my friends. My good friends. Actually," he added with a nervous glance at his companions, "I was, ah, a bit of a mentor to them, in fact."

A light came on in the Unforgotten's eyes. "Aha!" he said, turning to the others. "Yes! I do know you."

Charles exhaled. "That's quite a relief."

"You are the Third!" the man said. "This is the *Third!*" he cried to the crowd. "He *did* truly exist after all!"

"Oh for heaven's sake," Charles said, totally deflated. "Shoot me. Shoot me now."

"Is the Unforgotten all that they are called?" asked Rose. "It seems a shame that such a noble group, with such a worthy calling, is simply known as 'Unforgotten.'"

"Not only name," said Pym. "Unforgotten describes their purpose, but they have another name to describe identity. Forefathers many generations ago chose another name. Felt it did honor to the path they chose. Called themselves that ever since.

"They," Pym said, "are known as the Children of the Summer King."

After a wonderful, plentiful meal, during which they were entertained by many great and classic stories, the companions were shown to a small tumbledown building where they could rest for the night and gather their wits.

"May I bring you anything else, Third?" one of the young women asked Charles, who answered with a weary smile and a deep sigh.

"No thank you," he said. "We're all fine here. And," he added, "please, call me Charles."

"As you wish, Third," she said, bowing.

"I think he's getting really annoyed with that," Edmund said with as much sincerity as he could muster.

"He ought to be looking on the bright side," said Burton. "It's been eight thousand centuries—to even be remembered as 'Third' is quite a testament to him and his place in history."

"Easy for you to say," Charles grumbled, "seeing as *Arabian Nights* is one of the books that survived."

"That's just because it was full of all sorts of lewd, lascivious, awful things that gave people something to feel ashamed about," said Bert. "You should feel proud that your books faded into obscurity in part because they had none of those things."

"Thanks," said Charles, "but that doesn't really help, you know."

"Have you noticed," said Rose, "the longer we've been here, the more composed Arthur seems to be getting?"

"His madness does seem to be fading," Burton agreed, "a bit."

"At least he's starting to use pronouns again," said Charles. "Just listening to him talk was making me itchy."

Pym, along with the Unforgotten he called Twist, after Dickens's book, had been explaining more details about this strange world, about the Unforgotten, and especially the dark city, Dys, and Lord Winter.

"The rings they wear are the rings of the Caretakers," said Pym, "as are the rune stones in the walls. But outside of that, they know little else about how and why this place came to be. They were focused on preserving the books."

"It's interesting, don't you think?" Rose said to the others. "How the Children of the Summer King are essentially the last vestiges of civilization, of all the learning of humankind . . . and yet they live almost as savages, in the most basic ways possible. But the city dwellers, living in thrall to Lord Winter and the Echthroi, who don't know anything of their own history, live in relative luxury, in that extraordinary metropolis."

"It's the same division as the Eloi and the Morlocks," said Bert. "The Eloi were simpler, purer—but the Morlocks were the ones who retained the technological knowledge that allowed their society to function."

"So what are we to make of Lord Winter, then?" asked Edmund. "Or the fact that it is Shadow that has ruled the world for all these thousands of years?"

"I'm not sure," Bert said, frowning. "I had always believed that the Echthroi represented chaos, but that apparently isn't true. In fact, it's just the opposite—the Echthroi have imposed an incredible state of order on the whole world."

"But shouldn't that have been the goal of all humanity?"

asked Charles. "Isn't a world of perfect order something to have striven for?"

"You tell me, Caretaker," Burton said as he tore off a piece of chicken with his teeth. "You've spent time in both worlds now. Which place were you more comfortable? There in the city, or here with these wild folk?"

"If I had to choose," said Charles, "I'd take this place, no doubt. Plus indoor plumbing, if there was an extra wish in the genie bottle."

"Choice," Rose said, her voice low and cool, "is the entire point of it all. Choice is the difference. The Echthroi do not allow those whom they make Lloigor to choose to be thus. They compel it. That these people managed to preserve their ability to choose seems almost . . . accidental."

"You think all this was an accident?" Pym sputtered. "Are you serious? This was no accident—nothing Verne does is accidental. It's all part of a plan, his and Poe's. Even my being here, in this horrid place—it was a plan, I'm sure of it."

"And yet you're the one who chose to do their bidding," said Burton. "You idiot."

"I am prone to occasional lapses of judgment," Pym admitted, "but those are mostly confined to time travel, and trips to the Arctic Circle."

"There's no way to know if Verne or Poe foresaw this," said Bert. "Not unless they can send a message across eight thousand centuries."

At this, Twist brightened. "But he did, great creator," the Unforgotten said. "Follow me—I can show you."

✦　　✦　　✦

Twist led them through a warren of tunnels that wrapped around the base of the pyramid to an entrance. As with the gate, it opened for a ring bearer, and they all went inside. The narrow entry corridor opened into a large anteroom that was torch-lit, and empty save for a round, metallic table that was slightly concave. On it rested three golden rings, each about four inches in diameter.

"Oh, my stars and garters!" Bert exclaimed. "These are memory rings! Jules created them, after the ones I saw here—well, in Weena's future, anyway." He picked up one of the rings and peered through it. "Sort of a 'chicken-and-the-egg-and-the-chicken' kind of setup. I told him about the rings I'd found that recorded history, and he thought it was a capital idea and tried to duplicate them. He designed them to last for as long as ten thousand years."

"Ten?" asked Burton. So for these to have existed eighty times that long . . ."

". . . is exceptional and extraordinary," said Bert. "But they're here, nonetheless. And we may as well, ah, give them a whirl, so to speak."

Delicately, he picked up the other two rings, then set one on edge on the table and gave it a spin.

As the ring whirled about, the voice of Jules Verne suddenly echoed across the anteroom:

"No way to know which of these rings may survive into the ancient future," Verne's voice was saying. ". . . last of the Caretakers in exile after the restoration of the Archipelago . . ."

"It's fading in and out," said Edmund. "I can't hear it clearly."

"They're too old," said Burton. "It's been too long."

"Shush," said Bert. "Listen!"

". . . all the lands put in their proper place, then . . . at the waterfall . . . Lloigor . . ."

The ring slowed and clattered to a stop.

"Oh dear," Charles murmured. "Perhaps the next one will be more cheerful."

It wasn't. When Bert spun the second golden ring, it emitted nothing but hissing and scratching, then a few unintelligible words, and then . . . a scream.

"That was Laura Glue," Rose said numbly as the ring slowed and stopped. "I'm sure of it."

The third ring was shorter, but infinitely more promising—at first. ". . . not forgotten you!" were the first words, followed by ". . . given you the means to return, which only you can use . . . answer to the riddle . . . the last Dragon . . . Sphinx . . ." then static. And just as the ring began to spin down, one final, chilling hint of what befell them in the past:

"Jack . . . at the waterfall . . . Lloigor . . . and there was . . . he fell."

The ring stopped. That was all.

"So," Charles said glumly, "Lord Winter really *is* our Jack."

"He is not the Caveo Secundus!" Twist exclaimed. "He is dust! He is the smoke!"

That got Burton's attention. "Smoke?" he asked, more to his companions than to Twist. "Was Jack planning to become a tulpa?"

"As far as I know," Charles said, "Jack's plan is to follow your own course of action, Bert, and join the portrait gallery at Tamerlane House. He has never spoken to me about becoming a tulpa."

"Well, unless he changed his mind, or someone made a tulpa of Jack against his will, we may never know what really happened," said Burton.

"Oh," Charles said, as all the blood drained out of his face. "Oh dear."

"What?" asked Bert.

"I, ah, I made a tulpa of Jack, just for practice, remember? But once I knew I could, I stopped concentrating on it, and it just faded away into . . ." He swallowed hard. "A whiff of smoke."

"You infernal fool!" Burton shouted. "It takes time to dissolve a tulpa! Time! And effort! And if even the smallest whisper still existed . . ."

"Then someone could steal it, and build it up again," said Bert. "As I think the Cabal did. Yes. Exactly that."

"B-But even if they did," stammered Charles, "how would he have become Lord Winter?"

"A tulpa that you make of another person has no aiua, no soul," said Burton, "because unlike one you make and claim for yourself, it would just be a shell, a copy of someone who already *has* a soul. It would be the perfect vessel for an Echthros to possess.

"Your choices destroyed the Archipelago," he added, his face an inch from the hapless Caretaker's, "and it's your choices that may have doomed this world as well."

"Wait!" Rose exclaimed. "I'd completely forgotten!" She turned to Bert. "Can we play the rings again? Please? It's important."

Bert complied, and again they listed to the rings. When they had done so, the companions all turned expectantly to Rose.

"In all the rush to get away from Dys," she said, "I forgot to tell you what happened to me while you were sleeping. I think I know now what it all meant, and what we're supposed to do."

Quickly Rose told them of the moonbeam that led her to the Morgaine, and about the message she'd been given. They might have believed it was just a dream except for Rose's conviction that it had really happened—and the fact that she actually had the multifaceted mirror Lachesis had given her.

"Technically speaking, I think my father, as the Black Dragon, was supposed to be the last Dragon," Rose said. "And we lost him when the Archipelago fell to the Echthroi, so I'm at a loss as to what riddle she meant."

"Maybe she meant the *other* last Dragon," Twist offered helpfully. "The one in the next chamber."

The companions all turned to Twist, who returned their slack-jawed amazement with a wan smile. "I was going to mention it sooner," he said helpfully, "but I don't like to interrupt."

"Like the door in the wall outside, it takes two watches to open the inner chamber," Pym explained, "and they are greatly treasured, so they almost never take them out."

Twist and several of the other Unforgotten ceremoniously unwrapped a box of folded palm fronds, which contained their greatest treasures: two of the silver Caretaker's watches.

"So that's how they get to the outside," Burton murmured. "Verne always was the good Boy Scout."

"One is Jules's," Bert confirmed, "and the other is . . . Twain's? Or maybe Dickens's."

"The watches survived all these centuries?" Edmund exclaimed. "I've never seen a watch that could last that long."

"These aren't the silver watches the McGee family worked with," said Bert. "These are cavorite. They'll outlast pretty much everything!"

Twist fumbled with the placement of the watches into the two slots, and an exasperated Pym stepped forward to help. "Here," he said a bit gruffly. "You're getting them in backward."

When the two watches were properly in place, something in the walls shifted, and a wedge of stone slid up into the ceiling. There, in a much larger room, was what Twist had called the last Dragon—but it was not really a Dragon at all. It was a Sphinx.

It was perched atop a squarish, solid-looking structure that was approximately twenty feet wide, with a semicircular arch in front that held a metallic door. The Sphinx itself was greenish-gold, and indeed resembled a Dragon—but not a full-bodied Dragon, as they were thinking they'd see.

She had wings, and the lower body, legs, and hindquarters of a Dragon—but her torso, neck, and head were those of something much more human, and her eyes were closed. Still, she had a terrible kind of beauty, and just looking at her inspired a hushed reverence.

"Here," Twist said, pointing to a plate set in the wall of the structure. "This may be the riddle you're seeking."

It was. There were several lines of text, written not in English, but in . . .

"Elvish," said Rose. "If Jules left this here for us, and made certain only ring bearers and Caretakers could enter, then he left this riddle that could only be read by someone like John. Or," she added with a wink at Bert, "his best student."

Rose brought the torch closer and translated for the others:

Come not between the Dragon and her wrath;
But give unto her a choice;
Redeem her life, that distant past,
By easing others' strife;
Or choose again, the folly path,
In anger or in sorrow,
And once more sleep, 'gainst her will,
Till there be no tomorrows.

Naming is waking, speak loudly and clear;
Then offer the choice, and pay what is asked;
No passage is free, all prices are dear;
The heart of the Dragon belongs to the past.

"So we're to give her a choice?" asked Charles. "That's not really a riddle, is it?"

"The riddle is in naming her," said Bert. "To wake a Sphinx, you must speak its name."

"They wouldn't have left this for us without the means to solve it," said Rose. "it's probably in a book."

"The answer to the riddle is in a book?" Charles groaned, looking at Twist. "But *which* book? There are hundreds of them here, running all over the place, and it's not as if we can simply skim through them for what we want."

"Then maybe it's something we already know," said Bert. "There are surely many stories where hidden names are the solution to the problem."

"Got it!" Charles said, snapping his fingers. He stood in front of the Sphinx, taking a heroic stance—feet spread apart, hands on his hips, chin lifted in anticipation of victory.

"Rumpelstiltskin!" he declared in triumph.

In response, the Sphinx didn't even acknowledge that he had spoken, but merely continued to sleep.

Bert slapped his hand to his forehead, and Rose blushed in sympathetic embarrassment.

"What?" asked Edmund, clearly confused. "Is it working? Was that the right name?"

"No, that wasn't the right bloody name," Burton growled. He frowned at Charles. "I can't believe you thought that was worth trying, you idiot. And you call yourself a scowler!"

"Actually, I think it's pronounced 'scholar,'" Edmund said helpfully.

"Never mind," said Charles, who was now both deflated and embarrassed. "That was the best example I could think of where a name was the answer."

"Maybe that's just the wrong address on the right road," Bert said, rubbing his chin. "John was including just such a thing in that new book he's been working on, remember?"

"That's it!" Charles exclaimed. "The lock on the door to Samaranth's cave. It opened when we spoke the word 'friend' in Elvish."

"Really?" said Burton. "That's a stupid idea."

Charles smirked. "That's what he said too. At first."

"Just try it," Rose said, clambering to her feet. "Speak the word 'name' in Elvish, Uncle Charles."

He did, but to no avail. The Sphinx remained impassive, unmoved, and the eyes stayed closed up tight. Burton argued that the original riddle was too easy to break—but noted that the door was also guarded by a large dragon—Samaranth—who had no problem roasting unwelcome visitors, so any other riddle using the same premise would, by necessity, need to be more difficult. So Charles tried both "friend" and "name" in Elvish once more—just for good measure—before trying both words again in Dwarvish, Orc, Goblin, Badger, and French.

"Why French?" asked Bert after the last failed attempt.

"Because," Charles answered, "for all we know, Verne set the terms here, and not John."

"But John is the Caretaker Principia," said Edmund.

"And Jules Verne is the Prime Caretaker," Burton said, answering the young Cartographer's unspoken question, "and thus has greater latitude to muck about with history than his understudy."

"Oh," said Edmund, looking up at the Sphinx. "Maybe when we left, that was true. But we have no idea when this was put here for us to find, or who among them was still alive to leave it."

"The boy has a point," Burton admitted, "even if it's a brutal one." He turned to Twist, who was eager to help, but helpfully staying out of the way. "What about you? Do your people have a name for the Sphinx?"

"Sure," said Twist. "We call her Isis."

Charles tried that, but the results were the same—no response. "Why do you call her that, anyway?"

"It's engraved on the wall behind her," Twist said, pointing at the near-obscured letters. "There."

"Not Isis!" Charles exclaimed, crouching for a closer look. "I—C—S! The initials of the Imperial Cartological Society! Someone in the past must have just started calling the Sphinx by these letters, and eventually that's all anyone remembered."

"There's no way any of the Caretakers, or Jack's version of the ICS, could have anticipated the Unforgotten," Bert said. "How could they? None of this should have been here. So any riddle they left, they would have expected us to be able to solve with whatever we had on hand. Unfortunately, I don't think any of the books we have will be helpful."

"There's *one*!" Rose said excitedly. "The Little Whatsit. If there's only one real book left on Earth to use for solving a riddle, that would be the one I'd want. And Fred made certain that we'd bring it with us. That had to be their plan."

Burton scoffed. "The badger's book isn't going to tell us how to escape from this place," he said, scowling at her. "We need a practical solution."

"That's as practical as it gets," Bert said. "The Little Whatsit can tell us when the Sphinx was created, and the *Imaginarium Geographica* can tell us where. And between the two, we may be able to discover her name."

"There's only one problem," said Charles. "We left all our things—including the books—back in Dys, at the dark tower."

"Then we know what we have to do," said Rose. "We've got to go back."

CHAPTER SIXTEEN
The Last Dragon

✦

Pym chose to remain with the Unforgotten, which suited the companions just fine—especially Burton, whose main contribution to the group seemed to be that he was suspicious of everyone. Not that Pym didn't invite it—more than one of them noticed he knew how to open the Sphinx's chamber in the pyramid, a place he had supposedly never been.

No one the companions passed even glanced in their direction as they made their way up into the tower, to the room where they'd left their belongings. The door was open, but the room was not entirely as they'd left it.

"It's Archimedes!" Edmund exclaimed joyfully as he dashed to the far side of the room. There, perched on a beautiful mahogany stand, was the owl—whole again. The gash across his torso had been completely repaired.

Forgetting the urgency with which they'd arrived, the companions circled around Archie in grateful relief.

The bird was silent, but his head pivoted to each of the companions, observing them with an unblinking gaze. Rose almost hugged him, and for a moment, she thought Edmund actually would.

"Greetings, Moonchild," Azer said . . . "What do you desire?"

But it was Rose, the one who had known Archimedes the longest, who realized something was wrong.

"Step back," she said, gesturing for the others to move away from the still-observant bird. "Something is amiss here."

"What's wrong?" Edmund said, unwilling to move away. He stroked the owl's back and beamed. "Tell them, Archie. Tell them you're all right."

Archie looked at him, but still didn't speak.

"Archimedes," Rose said slowly, "how long is a rope?"

The workings of the bird whirred and clicked as it answered. "There is no answer to that query. It has no absolute value."

Rose frowned. "He taught me that question, when I was younger. It's a test of numbers, but also of philosophical thinking. The answer is, 'Exactly twice the length of the distance from the center to one end.' But he answered it like . . ."

"Like a machine," Vanamonde appeared at the doorway and bowed.

"We have taken the chaos from him," a chilling and familiar voice said from the corridor behind Vanamonde. "We repaired his form and cleared all the clutter from his mind. He is now a creation of perfect order."

Lord Winter stepped inside the doorway and stood next to his servant. "How, pray tell, was he broken?"

"He was . . . ah, damaged," said Edmund. "Outside the city, when we found—"

"It was an accident," Rose said, interrupting Edmund before one of the others could. He was a smart young man, but he did not have the kind of experience the rest of them had in dealing with a Shadow-possessed person—especially one he might believe he could trust. "Thank you for fixing him."

"Of course," Lord Winter said, almost dismissively. "Such repairs are a simple thing in the city of Dys."

"What clutter are you talking about?" Edmund asked. "Archie was smarter than all of us, and he never hesitated to say so."

"Indeed, and that is exactly my point," Lord Winter said as he stepped into the room and closed the door behind him. This time, the click of the lock was definite. "His brilliance was cluttered with the detritus of free will—but we removed that. And now he functions as he was meant to—as a machine."

"We're grateful that you helped Archimedes," Bert said, "but it appears that we're expected to stay here now, whether we like it or not."

"I apologize for treating guests in such a manner," Lord Winter said with a tone of sincere regret. "I had assumed that you would be unable to cause any mischief if I allowed you to wander freely. It is obvious that I was mistaken."

"What mischief?" asked Charles. "We simply went to—"

"The Renegades," Lord Winter said. "The ones who have prevented us from completing our control of this world."

"The keepers of the faith, you mean," said Bert. "The ones who preserved your own legacy . . . *Jack*."

Lord Winter tried to suppress a slight smile. "Not for much longer, I fear."

He spun about on his heel and opened the door. The corridor outside was filled with Winter Dragons—far more than the companions could evade or fight. "It is time to begin our negotiations," he said curtly, "regarding what place each of you shall have in Dys. I would speak with Charles first."

He walked out of the room, with Vanamonde close behind. It was clear they expected the Caretaker to follow.

"You aren't going to go?" Rose said, aghast.

"I must," Charles replied. "Following him, negotiating . . ." He dropped his head and gestured with his hands in frustration. "We may have nothing else left."

"Yes we do," Bert said. "We have hope. And that cannot be taken from us."

"How can you say that, Bert?" asked Charles. "You've even lost your wife. Here, in this time, she never even existed."

"She did exist," Bert said simply, his eyes brimming with tears. "She existed, and I loved her, and together we had a daughter whose name was Aven. And Aven lived a long, full life, and was brave and beautiful, and when it seemed as if all hope was lost for her, she found a way to keep it alive. And that act is what paved the way for your own redemption, Charles. To make right a mistake you have paid too dear a price for already. And you know, as much as the rest of us, that it's in the darkest moments that hope shines brightest.

"Here," he finished, pressing Weena's petals into the Caretaker's hand. "Let these guide your choices. As they have mine."

Charles gave Bert a long, appraising look before slipping the petals into a pocket and turning away. The door closed behind him with silent efficiency as he strode away from the room. He did not look back.

The Winter Dragons escorted Charles to an expansive room where Lord Winter was already waiting. He was looking out a window toward the Last Redoubt and did not turn when Charles entered.

"Once, you were my mentor," Winter said, never taking his

eyes from the window, "and now it seems I have become the teacher, and he who was once my teacher may now become my apprentice."

"You were made a similar offer long ago," Charles said softly, "by someone who also had no shadow. And as I recall, you declined the invitation."

At that, Jack lowered his head and smiled. "Not without a struggle, I assure you, old friend. I was young and far too innocent to understand what Mordred was offering me."

"As I recall," said Charles, "he also had a penchant for stabbing his teachers."

"Just the one," replied Winter. "Otherwise, he was an excellent student himself. He just had his own ideas of how to go about things. It never went well when his affairs were guided by someone else's intentions."

"As your intentions guide the choices of your Dragons, Jack?"

"They're Dragons in name only, you know," Winter said, indicating the masked servants who stood at posts around the great room. "It was my way of establishing a hierarchy among the Lloigor. But none are really Dragons. There have been none here for millennia who even knew what becoming a true Dragon meant, and then," he said, turning, "*you* came."

"The Echthroi are mighty," Charles said, "and obviously dominate this world, even if there are places left that still defy your rule. So what need have you of Dragons?"

Winter inhaled sharply, and the breath rattled in his throat. "Because," he answered, "only a Dragon can leave this world and travel to another."

All at once Charles understood. A real Dragon, who had

accepted his calling, as Madoc once had, could cross even the great wall that existed at the far edge of the Archipelago.

"Then the chains in the sky . . . ," he said.

"My fetters," Winter answered, "imposed by Shadow."

Charles started, surprised. "Your own masters imprisoned you here? Why?"

"Because of that," Winter said, gesturing to the pyramid in the distance. "Because I do not control the whole of this Earth, I am not permitted to leave. But with a Dragon as my apprentice, who could also take me as her apprentice, there will be no boundaries to stop me."

"I hate to tell you, old fellow," said Charles, "but I'm not . . ." He stopped, suddenly realizing what Winter had actually said: *her* apprentice. "You mean . . ."

"Rose," Winter said, nodding. "When Madoc became the Black Dragon, he entrusted her with his heart. That is how the mantle of responsibility is passed. She is now the Dragon's apprentice. And all she need do is choose it, and she will become a Dragon in more than name."

"And the reason you asked to speak with me first . . ."

"We are old friends, are we not?" said Winter. "Together we could convince her. The others need not be involved. Just you and I. Just like old times."

He turned and placed a hand on Charles's shoulder. "I know you," Winter said, his voice dropping to a whisper. "I know you chafed, as John and I received the recognition and the glory. But what I'm offering you now can be far greater than that, Charles. Greater than you are able to imagine."

"Yes," Charles replied. "But at what cost?"

"I paid the cost myself, long ago," said Winter. "All your friends died, long ago. Their work turned to dust, long ago. All you have to do now is say yes."

"If I agree to help you," Charles said slowly, "will you let the others go?"

"I'm sorry, but that just isn't possible," Winter said, an almost gentle tone in his voice. "They cannot remain as they are. But join me, help me convince Rose to take the mantle of Dragon, and I as her apprentice, and we will all be together forever, living lives of perfect order as servants of the Echthroi."

Charles couldn't contain his reaction, and he recoiled in horror. "You want us all to become Lloigor? Are you *insane?*"

"I understand," Winter said soothingly. "But you have no idea how free will has burdened you all. You may argue, but eventually you must agree."

Charles shook his head. "That isn't a reality I have the right to choose for my friends. And I refuse to choose it for myself."

"There *is* no other reality," Lord Winter hissed, irritated that the Caretaker was not ceding his point. "There has been no other reality for eight thousand centuries. There has been no opposition to my dominance of this world for a longer time than all of human history before it, many times over. Open your eyes, Charles, and see the world as it truly is."

Almost absentmindedly, Charles put his hand into his pocket and removed what he found there, cradling them gently in his hand.

Weena's petals.

"My eyes *are* open," said Charles, "and what I see is that you have nothing to give me that I do not already have. I decline your offer. I will not join you, nor will I help you convince Rose to do so. And that is *your* reality."

Lord Winter stared at Charles, trembling, then with a gesture had him escorted from the room.

"He wants us to *choose* to become Lloigor?" Bert exclaimed. "He *is* insane."

"It's greater than that," Charles said after he'd related the gist of the conversation with Lord Winter to his friends. "He wants our Dragon to make him her apprentice."

Rose went pale and touched the circlet that hung on the chain around her neck—the Dragon's heart her father had given her. "My apprentice?" she said in disbelief. "But that would mean . . ."

"Yes," Charles said. "When your father gave you his heart, he marked you as his apprentice. You were meant to become the next Dragon, Rose, if you chose to be—and if in turn you made Lord Winter your apprentice, then he could learn to become a Dragon too. And that's what he wants."

"I'm a little unclear on the power structure," said Burton. "He's practically the absolute ruler of the entire planet, and he has the soul of an Echthros. So what would he have to gain by becoming a Dragon?"

"The one ability that has only ever been invoked by one Dragon I know of," said Bert. "The choice that is all-encompassing, and for which an impossible price must be paid. But still the only thing a Dragon can do that an Echthros or Lloigor cannot."

"What?" asked Rose.

"Heaven," Bert said grimly. "He wants to become a Dragon so that he can storm the gates of heaven itself."

✦ ✦ ✦

Before any of them could remark on Bert's words, there was a tap-ping at the door, which opened. They all expected it to be the ever-polite Vanamonde, but it wasn't Lord Winter's chief Dragon—it was Arthur Pym.

"Oh, my stars and garters!" Bert exclaimed. "Am I ever so glad to see you, Arthur!"

"Quickly, quickly!" Arthur exclaimed, eyes darting back and forth in fear. "Distracted the guards, and there's no one in the cor-ridors! To escape, it must be now!"

Hastily the companions gathered up their belongings, includ-ing the broken sword Caliburn, and the books they'd come back to retrieve in the first place.

"That's everything," said Burton. "Let's go!"

"What about Archie?" Edmund said. "We can't just leave him here!"

"Lad," Bert said, as gently as he could manage. "That isn't the Archimedes we know. Not any longer."

The young Cartographer backed away and shook his head. "I don't believe that. They may have been able to change around some of his parts, but what made him our Archie is still in there somewhere. I know it."

Bert looked at Rose, then at Charles, who shrugged.

"I'm here now because my soul, my aiua, my . . . whatever it is that makes me *me*, didn't need my old body to go on," he said. "So I found a new one. So who am I to tell Edmund that Archie's soul isn't still there, somewhere, buried under all those cogs and wheels and wires?"

"I can carry him," Edmund said, ending the discussion. "We

won't leave him behind. Maybe Shakespeare can fix him."

"I've got him," Burton said, putting the compliant clock-work into his own bag. "We aren't leaving anyone behind. Not today."

At the gates, Pym's anxiousness eased visibly, and swiftly they made their way back through the canyon of ships and toward the entrance of the Last Redoubt.

"What is it?" Burton asked Charles, keeping his voice low so the others couldn't overhear them. "You're chewing on something, I can sense it."

Charles nodded. "It's Pym, the Messenger. Before, he wouldn't go anywhere near the doors to Dys. Was absolutely terrified just at the prospect of it. But suddenly, to rescue us . . ."

Burton tipped his head in agreement. "I see where you're going. Somehow he overcame his fear, made his way deep into a city he'd never been in before, snuck into the tower where Lord Winter lives, located us, and is now leading us to . . . safety?"

"Wherever this leads," Charles whispered, "be prepared for it to go terribly wrong."

"I hope you're wrong," Burton said, glancing ahead at where Pym was animatedly chatting with Bert and Charles.

I hope so too, Charles said silently to himself, *but I'm not.*

As they moved along the paved pathways, Rose, Bert, and Edmund were scanning through the Little Whatsit and the *Imaginarium Geographica* for clues to the riddle of the Sphinx.

"What I don't understand," Rose said, "is why Lachesis called it the last Dragon's riddle. What would the Sphinx have to do with my father?"

"Technically you're the last Dragon," said Edmund, "in waiting, as it were."

"You're letting your own notions guide you, rather than the riddle itself," said Bert. "Obviously, the Sphinx was a Dragon once. So she has to be who the Morgaine was referring to."

"I think that's what Lord Winter brought the Dragonships here to do," said Edmund. "He was trying to find a Dragon to make him its apprentice."

"And one was here, in the only place he couldn't get to," said Rose. "No wonder he wanted to get into the pyramid."

"If the Dragon's heart is what he needs," said Edmund, "why didn't he simply take it? Rose even tried to kill him and couldn't, so he obviously could have overpowered all of us anytime he chose to."

"It's a matter of free will," said Bert. "It's an office that must be conferred, then accepted—not taken by force. She had to choose it—that's why he needed Charles's help to persuade her."

"I never would have—," Charles began.

"I never doubted, Uncle Charles," Rose said, hugging him. "You'd never let me fall."

"Here," Edmund said, pointing to a map in the *Geographica*. "This looks like the Sphinx, doesn't it?"

The map was one that Bert had seen before—and he knew the drawing well. It depicted a chariot being drawn by two Dragons, one scarlet, the other the greenish-gold of the Sphinx.

"Oh my stars and garters!" Bert exclaimed. "I think I know what her name is. Rose," he said, eyes wide, "I want you to look up the Little Whatsit's entry on Samaranth."

"You think the Sphinx is Samaranth?" asked Charles, who was listening in with one ear.

"No," Bert replied, "I think the Sphinx is Samaranth's *wife*."

The companions crossed the plazas inside the wall and entered the passageway to the chamber of the Sphinx.

"I'm guessing that Jules left something inside for us," said Charles. "Maybe something we can use to reestablish a connection to another zero point."

"They wouldn't even know what had happened," Burton said, looking up at the sleeping Sphinx, "so how could they know what we needed to come home?"

"The Sphinx knows—," Pym started to say before Burton finally lost his temper and clocked the Messenger upside his head. "We know that, you cretin! That's why we have to solve the riddle!"

Pym, in a rare moment of assertion, actually shoved Burton and spun away, pressing his back to a wall. He took a deep breath. "No," he wheezed, "not 'knows.' Nose. The Sphinx *nose*. Look at the nose."

They all looked at the Sphinx. The nose, and places along the wings, were more worn than in other spots, allowing the underlying material it was made of to show through. "It needs a little plaster," said Charles. "Why is that significant?"

"Because," Bert said as the realization suddenly dawned on him, "underneath the centuries of paint, and soot, and dust, the Sphinx's nose—in fact, the entire Sphinx—is made of cavorite. Including the structure—and the arch."

Rose suddenly beamed. "They knew a machine would never

survive all those centuries," she said brightly, "but something made entirely of cavorite *would*."

"Here," Edmund said, indicating an entry in the Little Whatsit. "There's not much about Samaranth or his wife, just that they pulled a chariot for the legendary Jason, of the Argonauts. It also says that she was punished for betraying the Archipelago," he finished, "but that's about all."

"Her name is here in the *Geographica*," Bert said, handing the atlas to Rose. "It can't hurt to try."

"It will work," Rose answered. "Somehow, I know it." She looked up at the Sphinx and laid a hand on the cool stone. "Azer," she whispered, hardly daring to breathe. "You're Azer."

For a long moment, the Sphinx did not answer. Then, slowly, she opened her eyes.

"Greetings, Moonchild," Azer said in a voice that sounded of silk and ancient gardens in a long-ago place. "What do you desire?"

Before Rose could answer, there was a terrible noise outside— the sounds of combat, and screaming, and suffering.

"Oh no," Charles exclaimed. "What's happened now?"

The companions rushed out of the chamber and into the amphitheater—which was in flames. The Unforgotten were running away from the center of the chaos: a dozen masked servants of Lord Winter, who was standing at the top of the steps, where the dark geometric shapes of the Echthroi hovered in the air above him.

He was holding one of the old Caretakers' books in his hand. One of their future histories—a book that would have turned to dust long ago, were it not for the Lloigor's eldritch magicks running through it.

"This was once a prophecy," Lord Winter said, "that warned

of what might happen if the Echthroi were to finally conquer this world in full. And now I'm going to turn prophecy . . .

". . . into *history*."

The companions' minds raced to try to figure out what could be done. There were too many Lloigor to fight, and the Unforgotten were already scattered.

"I think," Bert said, mostly to buy them more time, "that you are not completely in the thrall of the Echthroi. I think you are not wholly Lloigor."

"Really," Lord Winter said with an amused smile. "Do tell."

"All this power," Bert said, gesturing widely with his arms, "and such absolute domination for so many centuries, and somehow you never managed to overcome the Unforgotten until *we* arrived?"

"Oh, on occasion I captured and killed or converted a few," Winter said. "Those who strayed too far, or for too long, from their haven. I still have the skull of The Golden Compass 519 on my wall. But," he went on, "until you came, I didn't have *this*."

He was holding Bert's watch. A terrified Arthur Pym stepped out from behind one of the servants. He looked overcome with sorrow—but he was standing behind Winter, not the Caretakers.

Charles and Burton glowered, but Rose and Edmund held them back as Bert continued to talk.

"Speaking of Pym," he said, gesturing at the terrified Messenger, "he's been here, what? A decade? And he aided us. He's been running freely around this world of yours, and yet you never managed to stop him, either. And it's not because you couldn't—I think it's because you wouldn't."

"He betrayed us, Caretaker," Burton said coldly. "It was his choice."

"No," said Pym. "It wasn't."

Trembling, he held out his arm and pulled back his sleeve. There, tattooed on his forearm, was the mark of Lord Winter—a circle, surrounded by four diamonds.

"Not useful enough to be a Dragon, I'm afraid," said Lord Winter, "but useful enough, when the time came."

"What did he promise you?" Charles asked.

"Freedom," said Pym. "I get to go home."

"And I always keep my promises," said Winter. He lowered his glasses, and dark bolts of ebony fire leaped from his eyes and in a trice had consumed the hapless man.

"Arthur!" Bert screamed. "Oh, dear me, Arthur!" He dropped to his knees, scrabbling after the drifting wisps of flame-singed cloth that were all that remained of the Anachronic Man.

"I kept him around far longer than I should have, anyway," Winter said dispassionately. "He had begun to bore me."

As one, Burton and Charles both stepped protectively in front of Rose and Edmund, who scowled and moved forward to stand shoulder to shoulder with them. Charles also kept a steadying hand on Bert, who was trembling with anger.

"Don't worry, I have no intention of destroying any of you," Winter said blithely. "You're all very interesting, and you will make excellent Lloigor."

"We'll find out how we failed, and we'll make things right," Bert said. His voice was trembling, but his face was a mask of defiance. "We'll find a way to defeat you, Lord Winter."

"Mmm, all formal now, are we, old friend?" Lord Winter said with a trace of sarcasm. "You should just call me Jack."

He shook his head. "You aren't Jack. I'm not sure who you are, but you're not him."

"I thought you wanted to become a Dragon," said Charles, "to get past your masters' chains."

"Pym told me about the Sphinx," said Winter, "and that she may, in fact, be a time travel device. And if that's true, I can use her to go back and correct my own mistakes—and I can make sure that this place," he added, gesturing at the pyramid, "will never be built, and all the books destroyed."

"What if I accept your offer?" Rose said suddenly. "What if I become a Lloigor and make you my apprentice Dragon?"

"Rose, no!" Charles cried. "Don't!"

"Hmm," said Winter. "That's an interesting proposition. I might even consider sparing your friends, just for old times' sake."

As the others cried out in protest, the Winter Dragons parted and allowed Rose to approach Lord Winter.

"Just take my hand," Winter said, "and kneel."

Instead of taking Lord Winter's outstretched hand, Rose picked a shard of flint off the ground and jabbed it into her thumb, drawing blood. She stepped to one side and spun around, too quickly for Lord Winter to respond. Rose locked her arm around Winter's neck and warned the servants to back away. Then, she reached up and swiftly marked the Lloigor's forehead with blood.

"What are you doing?" Winter screeched. "What—"

"Silence!" Rose commanded, with the full confidence and

authority of her heritage. The Lord of the Night Land went instantly quiet. "I am the Grail Child Rose Dyson, daughter to Madoc the Maker, apprentice to the Black Dragon, and I thus bind thee."

Lord Winter trembled and shuddered, but stood stock-still as Rose continued to speak:

> *By right and rule*
> *For need of might*
> *I thus bind thee*
> *I thus bind thee*
>
> *By blood bound*
> *By honor given*
> *I thus bind thee*
> *I thus bind thee*
>
> *For strength and speed and heaven's power*
> *By ancient claim in this dark hour*
> *I thus bind thee*
> *I thus bind thee*

Rose released her hold on Lord Winter, who remained frozen in place. The Winter Dragons kept a discreet distance, waiting to see how this would play out—but the shapes floating overhead were vibrating madly enough to make the air buzz with their anger.

"That won't hold him long," Rose said, panting with the effort of the binding, "but it'll hold him long enough, I think. Now," she declared to her companions, "we must run for our lives, and for the sake of the world we left, and all we hold dear. Now! Run!"

Without a backward glance, the friends gathered up their belongings and ran into the pyramid.

PART FIVE

The Corinthian Legend

... the Goblin Market was a cacophony of ornate wagons, huts, tents ...

CHAPTER SEVENTEEN
The Goblin Market

❖

Of the many notable events that marked the Victorian age, the most significant was one witnessed by only three people.

The creation of the Black Dragon was attended only by Mordred, the Winter King, who summoned the Dragon that was to become one with the ship; Argus, the shipbuilder, who was compelled by a Binding and an ancient promise to perform the task; and Mordred's mentor, Dr. John Dee, who watched from a nearby rooftop as Mordred and Argus went about their work.

It wasn't until the shipbuilder was done, and dismissed, and Mordred had sailed the newly christened Black Dragon out of the harbor on the Thames and into the open sea that the great red Dragon, Samaranth, spoke to the doctor.

"Ill met, Dee," the Dragon growled, not bothering to cover the rising anger in his tone. "You should not have done this."

"I," said Dr. Dee, "have done nothing—nothing except teach the student that you betrayed and abandoned."

"You have corrupted his spirit," the Dragon rumbled.

"His brother did that when he betrayed him," Dr. Dee spat back. "I have simply shaped what was already there." He turned and faced the great beast with no trace of fear. "You had your chance, Old Serpent,"

Dee said. "Now I am going to shape him into the great man he was always meant to be."

"He is not the Imago," Samaranth said. "Once, perhaps, he might have become such. But that time is past."

"The Imago, if he exists, will be made, not found, Dragon," said Dee. "We have differed on that point before."

"Regardless, he is not now worthy, even if he has the skill. And now you have given him a Dragonship—the means to cross through the Frontier."

"Yes. I have."

"To what end?"

"Order," said Dee. "To bring order to two worlds that have fallen into chaos under your stewardship."

"You are not seeking to create the Imago at all," the Dragon concluded, more to himself than to Dee. "This cannot be permitted to continue."

"There are many streaks of white in your beard, Dragon," said Dee. "You are getting old."

"Your services are no longer needed, Dee. There are others better suited to the task. I only hope," Samaranth said with a hiss of melancholy, "that it is not too late to undo what you have done."

"There are none qualified to replace me," said Dee. "Whom would you have, Old Dragon? Will Shaksberd? Or that old fool, Alighieri?"

"I have all of history to choose from," Samaranth replied, "and choosing wisely is the one thing that I must take the time to do, whomever it is that I choose."

He stopped and drew in a breath, as if intending to exhale on the Scholar—but stopped, as he realized Dee was completely unconcerned.

It was only then that the Dragon noticed Dee's shadow was moving about completely independently of its owner.

Samaranth took a step backward and hissed. "You have fallen," he said, his voice laced with sadness. "You have joined the enemy, John Dee. And that choice will result in nothing but suffering for your protégé."

"The Winter King may surprise you yet, Dragon," said Dr. Dee. "It took me decades to choose to give up my shadow in the cause of order. It took Mordred far less time to do the same."

The Dragon stretched out his wings and shook his head. "He will never sit on the Silver Throne," Samaranth said as he took flight. "The Caretakers will see to that. And he will never," he added as he vanished into the clouds, "be the Imago."

The Scholar watched until the Dragon disappeared from view, then took a small pocket watch out of his coat.

"Perhaps," he said to no one in particular. "But if not him," he finished as he twirled the dials on his device, "then certainly another of my choosing will."

The rain on the Welsh mountainside lasted only three-quarters of an hour and was sufficient to settle the dust, and little more. When Don Quixote and his squire, the badger Uncas, awoke during the morning's sunrise, the Zen Detective Aristophanes was already busying himself with breakfast. His bedroll seemed untouched. Quixote couldn't tell whether the detective had slept much, or at all, and decided it was the better part of knightly decorum not to ask.

After a surprisingly delicious meal, during which Quixote reversed yet another judgment he'd made about the gruff detective, the three companions set about determining their plan of action.

Uncas carefully opened the vellum folder Verne had entrusted to him and spread out the fourteen maps of Elijah McGee.

"There really aren't too many of them, you know," said Quixote. "We could practically go about locating the armor by trial and error."

Aristophanes scowled. "No, we really couldn't," he said. "There isn't time."

"I know this is important," said Uncas, "but until we met you, and asked about th' glasses, we didn't even know the armor existed. So why do we suddenly have a timer on finding it?"

"Anything to which attention is paid becomes a magnet for more attention," Aristophanes said primly. "I promise you, even if Song-Sseu has not already sold the knowledge that we are looking for the armor and in possession of the McGee maps, there will still be a dozen other denizens in every one of the Soft Places who will take note of our arrival. And once the first piece has been found, word will spread—and from that point, it will be a race. And those who would also seek the armor will think nothing of killing us to get even a single piece, much less the whole set."

"So, this quest becomes more dangerous the more successful we are," said Quixote. "That sounds like a Caretaker's mission, all right."

"Fair enough," said Uncas. "We'd better get cracking, then!"

Aristophanes unfolded the first sheet of parchment, on which he had asked the location of the Ruby Dagger, and read the name the machine had typed: "Castra Regis."

Uncas scanned the maps and quickly found the one that matched the name. "It's a close one," he said happily. "Staffordshire."

The detective's brow furrowed in puzzlement as he looked at

the map. "Castra Regis was the ancestral home of an infamous family called Caswell," he said, "but both it and the neighboring mansion, Mercy Farm, were destroyed when . . ."

He stopped and put a finger on the map. "Here," he said, voice rising with excitement. "This is the place, I'm sure of it."

The knight and the badger peered closely at the spot on the map. "Th' crossroads?" asked Uncas. "Why there?"

"All the interesting stuff happens at a crossroads," Aristophanes said, "and especially at this one. It's in a wood called Diana's Grove. And that's where we'll buy the dagger."

"Buy, and not find?" asked Quixote.

"Yes," the detective said, standing. "Diana's Grove is the site of one of the oldest Goblin Markets in the world. That's the place, I'm sure of it."

"A market!" Uncas said, brightening. "I love markets. That don't sound dangerous at all."

"I said 'interesting,' not safe," retorted the detective. "Just follow along with me and pay attention. And don't touch anything."

"I wasn't planning to," said the badger.

Aristophanes smirked and hooked his thumb at the knight. "I was talking to *him*."

"Rude," said Quixote.

The Goblin Market was not the Victorianesque tapestry the companions might have been expecting, but rather a ramshackle collection of carts, wagons, and makeshift pens for various horses and horselike creatures.

"This is, ah, quaint," said Quixote. "It seems a little horse-centric for a market. Or is it run by Houyhnhnms?"

The detective sighed and gave the knight a withering look. "This isn't the market, you idiot. This is where all the pack animals are stabled. I thought it would be better to leave the Duesenberg here than to drive up to a Seelie Court–run Goblin Market in a 1935 automobile. The market," he finished, only slightly less exasperated, "is over that rise, there."

Both Quixote and Uncas chuckled in understanding as they topped the small hill and the full wonder of the market came into view.

Sitting just beyond the crossroads indicated on the map, the Goblin Market was a cacophony of ornate wagons, huts, tents, and all other manner of temporary structures, which nevertheless looked as if they had always stood there. That was because, according to Aristophanes, they always had.

The explosions of color were scattered among and amid the trees, which themselves seemed to be first growth, and in a few places were built into the fabric of the market, lending their trunks and branches to the anchoring of the tents.

In the distance, the ruins of both Castra Regis and Mercy Farm stood over the small hollow like watchful sentries, but slightly more benignly than the real sentries, armored wraiths, who gave the companions a careful once-over as they crossed the road and entered the market.

At one of the tents, a man in a turban was selling the wind, in various gusts and gales. Each one came with a caution about when and where the bag could be opened safely, as well as a customer satisfaction guarantee that promised the wind would work—but allowed that no promise could be made about the destination to which it carried the purchaser.

At a small cart, another vendor, a stout, bespectacled shopkeeper, was demonstrating various clockwork animals, some of which were real, and some mythical. He winked at Uncas, intuiting that the badger might be an easy mark. "The windup monsters are good company for extended trips," the shopkeeper explained, "but for some real entertainment, it's hard to beat the Steam Crows." He proffered one to Uncas. "Would you like to see how it works?"

Aristophanes rather brusquely guided Uncas and Quixote away from the tempting display of toys. "Keep your eyes open and touch nothing—*nothing*," he said, waggling his finger for emphasis. "Have you ever heard the expression 'you break it, you buy it'? Well, here, just touching something can be considered an ironclad contract. It's Seelie Court law. So don't touch anything I don't tell you to touch."

One small woman was selling hand-painted calendars, which changed the seasons as the pages were turned. Patrons were looking through the various works, and as they did so, the seasons in her tent changed from summer, to fall, to winter, and back again. Summer was by far the most popular, with fall a close second, so the tent was full of gentle, warm breezes that scattered crimson and gold leaves, amid the only occasional flurry of snow. No one, it seemed, was all that interested in spring.

"Here's the fellow we want, unless I miss my guess—and I seldom do," Aristophanes said, pointing down the slope to a smithy's shop. It was set against the side of the hill so it could take advantage of the slope for the bellows on the forge.

"My name is Schmendrick," the smithy said, giving the companions the once-over. "What can I be doin' f'r y' t'day?"

"We're looking to barter," Aristophanes said with as much authority as he could muster. "We have relics from the Summer Country to trade, and"—his voice dropped to a softer tone—"even a few from the Archipelago."

"Really?" Schmendrick exclaimed. "Those be rarer and rarer these days, ever since th' Day of Charles's Lament."

"Ooh," Uncas groaned to Quixote. "We best not tell Scowler Charles there's people callin' it that."

"He shouldn't be surprised," said Quixote. "He does berate himself over the whole destruction-of-the-keep matter rather often."

"I'm working here!" Aristophanes said to the badger and the knight. "Why don't you two go browse around in the next tent? And remember . . .'"

"Don't touch anything, I know, I know," Uncas grumbled. "Come on, sir," he said to Quixote. "Let's fraternize with th' wee folk."

"Do y' have any deadly nursery rhymes?" the smithy asked. "They're really useful for takin' care of changelings, if y' know what I mean."

"No," said Aristophanes, "but I'm sure I can find something to your liking, if you have what it is we're looking for."

Schmendrick squinted up at him. "An' that is?"

"The Ruby Dagger."

The smithy's eyes widened and darted from side to side, to see if anyone was listening. "I might be able t' help you," he replied. "Come, let us discuss what you have t' offer."

As the detective and the smithy continued to speak in hushed whispers inside the shop, Uncas and Quixote browsed the wares of the tent three spaces down, in the lee of a large stone. The proprietor was a wizened old woman with a hat that resembled a tree growing from her head, on which were perched two buzzards, who seemed to be doing all the negotiating with the customers.

The goods the woman—or possibly the vultures—were selling were ornamental crystals of every color, shape, and size. Some had been set into pendants, and others, sculpted into miniature cathedrals. Some had even been set into the hilts and scabbards of weapons.

"Asking a smithy who makes weapons for a dagger that already exists isn't very Zen," Uncas said as he peered through the tiny doors of an amethyst city. "He'd be better off looking over—"

The little badger gasped, then slowly, carefully, drew a bronze-hilted ruby knife from out of the back of the display.

"Is it . . . ?" he breathed.

"I think so," said an astonished Quixote. "We should go get Steve."

"Don't worry," Uncas said smoothly. "I got this."

"Badgers?" one of the vultures squawked as Uncas examined the dagger. "We don't need no steenkin' badgers!"

"Why not?" the other vulture replied. "Iff'n his money's good."

"We can pay," said Uncas. "No fuss, no muss."

"See?" said the second vulture. "Say hello to my leetle friend."

The first vulture sighed. "All right, all right. That one ees a bad piece, anyway. Eet can only damage Shadows. No good for cutting oxen or Harpy. What you got to trade, leetle badger?"

"Hmm." Uncas thought a moment, then rummaged around in his pocket. "Y' seem t' like crystals," he said, producing a small ebony shard from his pocket. "P'rhaps you'd trade f'r this, straight across?"

Both vultures snorted in contempt, and even the old woman tsk-tsked at Uncas.

"You be crazy badger," said the first vulture, "to be thinkin' we take a sliver—"

"It's a shard, actually," Uncas corrected, "and it's from th' Nameless Isles."

That stopped both vultures cold, and the old woman's jaw dropped open. It also got the attention of several other patrons at nearby shops.

"Deal," the second vulture said, snatching up the shard before Uncas could change his mind. "A pleasure do business with you, my leetle badger friend."

With a broad smile that would light up a barn, Uncas leaped into the pathway to find the detective, who was still arguing with the smithy. "I have it!" Uncas proclaimed proudly—and loudly. "I have the Ruby Dagger!"

"Oh, fewmets," Schmendrick cursed, apparently having been close to a deal for the dagger he didn't have. "C'n I interest you in a carnelian ice pick, mebbe?"

"Never mind." Aristophanes strode out of the smithy's to meet the triumphant badger. "At last!" he exclaimed as he lunged forward—and tripped over a discarded Spanish helmet at the edge of the tent.

Aristophanes went sprawling, and his hat flew off, landing at Quixote's feet.

The smithy, the old woman with the vultures on her head, and several others circled around to look at the strange purple man who was cursing under his breath as he dusted himself off.

"A unicorn!" Schmendrick whispered in astonishment. "I haven't seen th' like! Not in a hound's age!"

"Unicorn!" the haggard old woman echoed, bellowing at the top of her lungs. "Uuuuunicooorrrnnn!!!!"

"Oh, dung," said Aristophanes. "Run."

"What?" said Quixote. "They—"

"Just shut up and run!" the Zen Detective shouted as he grabbed the knight by the arm and the badger by the collar and propelled all three of them down the pathway and out of the wood.

The news of the unicorn spread through the market like the Black Plague, but at lightning speed, and as the companions crested the hill and headed for the Duesenberg, they realized they were now being chased by quite a sizeable mob.

"Oh, my stars an' garters," Uncas exclaimed as they ran, "but I wish Sir Richard was with us!"

"Burton?" Quixote blurted out as he glanced backward at their pursuers, who were rapidly closing the distance between them. "You think he would have fared any better?"

"Not really," Uncas replied, "but he'd give them a bigger target than us."

Under the spreading branches of a chestnut tree, the Messenger watched. The sunlight that broke through the clouds above passed through the leaves to form mottled patterns of light and shadow on Dr. Raven's face, which remained impassive, observing.

"They seem to be in a bit of a pickle, neh?" a voice said from somewhere above in the branches. "We wonder why you are not helping them to evade their pursuers."

Dr. Raven didn't look up—he didn't need to, to know who was speaking. "That wasn't my responsibility. I'm to shadow them, and nothing more."

"Lies," Grimalkin purred as an upside-down smile appeared in the air next to the Messenger's face. "All lies. You are the Caretaker's errand boy, are you not? And he is nothing but wheels within wheels, and games within games. You serve a greater purpose, we think, than to simply watch."

The Doctor didn't flinch at the cat's slight insult, but turned to look at Grimalkin as the badger, the Zen Detective, and the knight disappeared over a rise in the distance. "They'll do fine without my help," he said, not caring to distinguish whether he meant the Caretakers or the hapless trio running from the irate merchants of the Goblin Market. "And as to games, methinks you would know something of those . . . *cat*," he added with emphasis. "Don't you? Or else you'd have already told Dee all about me."

"We serve our own interests, and none other," said Grimalkin, who had now begun to vanish again, starting with his half-formed head.

"Now who is lying?" Dr. Raven said, looking pointedly at the Cheshire cat's ornate collar. The runes on it glowed slightly, whether or not the rest of the cat was visible. "You serve whom you are compelled to serve, as do I."

"Well, of course," said the voice of the disembodied cat, more weakly now. It was obviously bored, and returning to wherever it spent its time in between appearances. "If we were not compelled, would we choose to serve anyone at all? Even ourselves?"

Dr. Raven wanted to ask if the cat was including him in that statement, or was still merely speaking with the royal "we" as it so often did. But by the time he opened his mouth to speak, the cat was already gone—as was, he noted with some relief, the Duesenberg. Uncas, Quixote, and the Zen Detective had evaded their pursuers and moved on to the next destination.

Looking around to ensure that no one would notice his own departure, and assuring himself that he was alone, the Messenger removed the watch from his pocket, twirled the dials, and disappeared.

If anyone had been watching, they might have noticed that there, under the shadows of the chestnut tree, the silver casing of the watch appeared darker.

In fact, it was almost black.

Shakespeare, Laura Glue, and the badger Fred closed the doors and drew curtains over the windows in the small room that was far from where the other Caretakers ventured throughout Tamerlane House.

"Have we heard anything from them?" Laura Glue asked hopefully.

"Nothing yet, it seems," Shakespeare said, dropping the last curtain. "They haven't returned. And the other Caretakers do not seem overly encouraged that they will."

"If the Scowlers are all stumped," said Fred, "then us figuring out a way t' help will be impossible."

"Nothing's impossible," Laura Glue said, folding her arms. "Nothing."

"But some things really are," Fred said sadly. "Like making crème brûlée with a kerosene torch, or teaching Byron t' fight with a *katana*."

"Everything is impossible until someone does something for the first time," said Laura Glue. "Half the time I've been here the Caretakers are usually discussing why a trump did or didn't work the way they thought it was supposed to, or how the keep really worked, or all sorts of other stuff that nobody really knows anyway. So I think if nobody really knows how anything is supposed to work, then anything is worth trying, neh?"

"Neh," said Fred, tapping her fist with his. "Our unknowledge is our only hope."

"'Our doubts are traitors, and make us lose the good we oft might win, by fearing to attempt,'" said Shakespeare.

"Ah," Fred said, nodding. "*Measure for Measure*. One of your great plays."

"Well," Shakespeare said, reddening. "Yes. But that particular line actually did come from Kit Marlowe, thrice curse his eyes. But he spake it while deep in his cups, and I wasn't going to let it go to waste.

"So," he said, wiping his hands on his trousers. "What be our plan, my children?"

"Our plan be to have their back, neh?" said Laura Glue. "Sometime soon, someone is going to have to go after them, to help them. And we're not going to let them down. We're going to find a way, even if every scholar who has ever lived and died says it's impossible. We'll find a way. And when they need us," she concluded, a determined look in her eyes, "we're going to be *ready*."

CHAPTER EIGHTEEN
The Sorceress

✦

The companions dashed through the passageways to where the Sphinx sat, silently watching.

"We aren't going to have enough time!" Charles said, panicked. "That was the bravest act I've ever witnessed—but they aren't going to be able to hold him for long."

"We won't need much time," said Rose. "We just have to let Azer make her choice."

"What choice is that, Moonchild?" Azer asked impassively.

"The one in the riddle," Rose said. "Here, on the wall. It says we're to give you a choice. So we discovered your name and woke you. Can you help us?"

"Help you?" the Sphinx said. "How?"

"Can you help us go back in time?" Charles asked, getting straight to the heart of their urgency. "Are you able to travel in time?"

The Sphinx ignored him completely. "There is a price, Moonchild, for all things. Pay the price, and you shall have what you wish."

"What do you want?"

"A Dragon's heart," she said, looking at Rose, "to restore me to what I was, long ago."

. . . a woman, tall and regal . . .
with the bearing and manner of a queen.

"To become a Dragon again?" asked Rose.

"No," said Azer, still looking at the Grail Child. "To once again ascend, and leave this world at last."

Rose removed the circlet of stone she wore around her neck, which her father had given her when he became the Black Dragon. She looked up at the others, doubtful.

"Your destiny is greater than just being a Dragon, Rose," Bert said gently, "and you don't need that circle of stone to fulfill it. In truth, I don't think you ever did."

"Then I think . . . ," Rose began—but she was interrupted by an unearthly shrieking sound coming from the passages outside the chambers.

"Lord Winter is freed," Burton said, "and this world now belongs to the Echthroi."

"Not fully," Azer said, looking at Rose. "Not if a Dragon remains. The Shadows cannot prevail against a true Dragon. You can choose to stay, or you may give the heart to another and save the world as it is. Or you may give it to me, and return to your own world as it was. The choice is yours."

"No, it isn't," Rose said in sudden understanding. "The choice is yours."

Azer stared at Rose, who held the Sphinx's gaze, unafraid. A thousand regrets passed through the eyes of the once-Dragon, as she considered the truth of Rose's words.

"He's coming!" Charles shouted. "Hurry!"

At last the Sphinx made her decision. She closed her eyes, and below where she sat, the doors set into the arch slid open. "Give the heart to another," she said, "and go to thy journey."

The companions suddenly realized what had to happen—Azer

had agreed to give them passage, but unless a Dragon stayed behind, the world would still be lost to the Echthroi.

"The world must have its defender, it seems," Rose said sadly. "Maybe this is my destiny. You should all go. I'll stay."

"No," Burton said, laying a muscular hand on Rose's shoulder. "Not this time you're not."

Rose began to protest, but the old adventurer shushed her.

"I served the man your father once was because I believed a grave injustice had been done to him," Burton said calmly, clearly, "and somehow along the way, the cause I served became as distorted as the man, and I lost my way. But I found it again. I found myself. And I lived to see him redeemed. So this is not a request— this is what I was meant to do. This is the reason I am here. And taking his daughter's place is the best way I know to honor your father's memory."

Rose nodded in understanding. She handed the stone circlet to Burton, then stood on tiptoe and kissed him on the cheek. He blushed, and pushed them all toward the open doorway, then turned to meet the Lloigor.

"I never got to see my own daughter grown and married," Burton called over his shoulder as he strode to the antechamber. "But I can do this thing for you, Rose. For Lord Mor—for Madoc."

The Scholar Barbarian stepped into the passageway. Dark Shadows were cascading up against the pyramid, swirling so thickly he could barely make out the features of Lord Winter standing just outside.

Burton turned and called back to his friends. "Bert, don't . . . don't stop looking. . . . Find him. Find our boy."

Rose lifted her head, locking eyes with Burton, and answered for all of them. "We won't, Sir Richard. None of us will stop looking. We'll find your heir, if we have to travel to the beginning of time."

He didn't reply, but gave a curt nod, then slipped the Dragon's heart around his neck and stepped out to do battle with the Lloigor.

Rose looked up at the Sphinx. "I'm ready to make my wish," she said.

"Speak."

"Take us home," Rose said. "That's all. Just take us home."

In answer, the Sphinx closed her eyes and nodded once. "It shall be as you desire."

Rose stepped inside with the others, and the door underneath the Sphinx slid closed.

"In another life, in another reality, you were a Namer, Jack," Burton said, reaching to grasp the Lloigor's arms. As he grappled with the slender man, Burton's features, his very form, began to ripple and change. "So, name me now. Name me for what it is I have become because of you."

Lord Winter glowered, and his footing slipped. He lurched to one side, and his glasses fell from his face. Where his eyes were supposed to be were orbs of impenetrable blackness. "You are Chaos," he hissed, steadying his stance and tightening his grip. "You are disorder!"

"Damn straight I am," said Burton.

The air vibrated around him, almost as if it were responding to his will and expanding his presence; and perhaps it was doing just that. He resonated with the countenance of a Dragon, a true, living Dragon—and suddenly the Echthroi that attended Lord Winter trembled themselves—and began to withdraw.

For the first time in many millennia, Lord Winter felt a thrill of fear run through him.

"No, wait!" he called out to the ascending geometric shapes. "Stop! Grimalkin! Loki! Do not abandon me!"

"What," Burton hissed, eyes narrowing, "did you just say?"

Lord Winter's only response was to howl in despair. He was losing—had lost. And he knew it, and so did his masters.

"Name me!" Burton roared. "Name me, Jack!"

"*You are Dragon!*" the Echthroi screeched, as much from the darkness that enveloped Burton as from the throat of the Lloigor Jack. "*Dragon!*"

"Yes," Burton said, almost as a whisper. "And I have made the right choice at last."

When the doors of the Sphinx closed behind them, none of the time-lost companions knew what to expect. Certainly, that they might be transported to another time, at least. Edmund and Rose were hopeful that they would end up back at Tamerlane House, although that was longer odds than they could really expect. Bert harbored a secret hope that they might actually end up in the future they were aiming for—with Weena. And Charles simply wanted to get away from Lord Winter.

"So, uh," Charles stammered. "Is it on?"

"Not yet," said Rose, who had been examining the interior, "otherwise there'd be too much risk of someone else using it." She didn't need to say more.

"This panel," said Edmund. "The symbols on it match some of those in the *Geographica!*"

"It's how we activate the Sphinx," Rose said, running her fingers across the engravings in the stone. "I'd bet my life on it."

"Actually," said Bert, "I think we have."

"Are there any, ah, instructions?" asked Charles.

"No," she replied, "just these markings." Among them was a crescent moon, set in an indentation within the panel. She pressed it, and instantly they were surrounded by a glow of radiant light.

"Excellent, Moonchild," Bert murmured. "You are less and less the student, I see."

The light lasted only a few seconds, and then as quickly as it had risen, vanished.

"Now what?" said Charles. "Is it over?"

"Only one way to find out," Edmund said. He stepped to the doors and slipped his fingers between them. Then, with a great effort, he slid them open, and at once the companions were blinded by bright, golden sunlight.

"Well, Toto," Charles said in relief, "I don't think we're in Camazotz anymore."

They stepped out onto a low, grassy hilltop that overlooked a broad, sandy beach. The structure they emerged from was the same as it had been in the future, but there was no sign of the Sphinx.

"It doesn't smell right," said Charles, sniffing. "Not like England smells. But it smells . . . familiar."

"I agree," said Rose.

"I must confess my ignorance," Edmund said, "being that my education in these things is more limited than I'd have liked it to be, but aren't those runic columns over there?"

They were—and not ancient ones, but freshly constructed, newly painted columns. And farther back, they could see larger structures.

"Greek temples?" asked Charles. "In 1946?"

"This isn't 1946," said Bert. "I think we may have overshot our mark."

"Not really," Edmund said as he consulted his chronal maps. "We did go back approximately eight hundred thousand years . . . give or take. My chronal map might have taken us back to England in 1946, but it was designed to do that. We came through a different device that couldn't be set for a specific time, because they had no way of knowing when—or if—we'd use it. And we've moved in space as well as time, so something else had to determine why we came here now."

"But then how . . . ," Bert began before the realization struck him and his face fell. "Oh . . . oh, my stars and garters."

Charles groaned and put his face in his hands. His shoulders started to shake, and for a moment the companions were concerned for him—until they realized he was laughing.

"Not determine," he said, clapping Edmund on the back. "Choose. Someone chose to bring us here. You are correct, Edmund. I don't even have to see your maps to know that."

Rose sat on a boulder, her shoulders slumping forward in misery as she realized what the others all meant. The Sphinx had done precisely as she had asked—she had taken them home. But to *her* home, her time and place—not theirs.

"Can't we simply go through it again?" the young mapmaker asked, his face eager with hope.

"Even if we could reuse the Sphinx," said Rose, "I don't know what else we'd use to barter with her for passage. We'd also be risking ending up stranded in the future again. And anyway," she added, looking around at the dunes, "she's gone."

"Look at it this way," Edmund said, "at least we're not still in that awful might-have-been future. We're much closer to home here."

"Indeed!" said Charles. "Instead of being stuck a million years from home, we may only be trapped a few thousand years from home. Luck is definitely with us."

"Have you ever noticed," Edmund said to Rose, "that these Caretakers' view of reality differs widely from pretty much everyone else's?"

"All the time," said Rose.

Edmund made a few calculations on one of his chronal maps and confirmed that they were approximately somewhere around the era of 2500 BC.

"If we're at that point in the past," Rose asked, "wouldn't the keep itself still exist? Could we use that to either go home, or maybe even go farther back to find the Architect?"

"You spent more time there than any of us, Bert," Charles said, thinking. "Would that work?"

"It doesn't have a basement, if that's what you're asking," Bert retorted. "When the Dragons created the doors, it was already standing. I don't know that there's any way to use it to go back to a point before its own making. And besides, it burned from the ground up—meaning the passages to the oldest times were lost *first*. So it may not actually be here at all anymore."

"Great," Charles groaned. "I not only botched up the future, but I've retroactively messed up the past."

"I want to go home too," said Bert, "but if we returned now, we'd simply have to come back this way again anyway. Or," he added with a bit of a catch in his voice, "someone would, at any rate."

"If we're somewhere in Greece," asked Edmund, "where would we go to find the keep if we did look?"

"In this era," Bert said, turning to look at the ocean, "it would be . . ."

His voice trailed off as his jaw dropped. The others looked out over the water and were similarly shocked by what they saw.

Far in the distance, with the bearing of thunderclouds, and the slow, steady movement of tectonic plates, giants were striding through the ocean. They were pulling islands behind them by great chains, much like the ones the companions had seen circling the Earth in the ancient future.

These were the giants of old, not the misshapen, mythological creatures. These were Titans, and they were awesome to behold.

"What are they?" Edmund asked, his voice trembling with awe.

"The Corinthian Giants, of course," a voice said as they gawped. "They are almost finished here, and will soon move on to other climes."

It was a woman, tall and regal, and speaking with the bearing and manner of a queen. She was dressed in a simple tunic, but her belt and jewelry were equal to the cost of entire cities.

She was speaking in ancient Greek, which Rose understood easily, and Charles less so. Bert and Edmund would have been completely out of luck—but somehow they understood her.

"What are they doing?" Edmund said, motioning to the giants.

She seemed taken aback by the question, as if she expected they would already know. "They are taking the rest of the lands through the Frontier and into the Archipelago, as was agreed at the—" She stopped and examined them more closely. "You are not the Watchers. And you are not of Corinth. Who are you?"

Edmund was the most startled to be spoken to in Greek and to realize he understood it completely, being the companion with the least amount of experience with magic. "How is it that I can understand your words?" he exclaimed in openmouthed astonishment. "Or that you can understand mine?"

"A minor incantation," the woman said haughtily, "and if you do not know even that much of me, then it is a waste of my time to be conversing with you at all."

"We beg your pardon," Rose said. "We are strangers to your land, and meant no offense." As she spoke, she bowed deeply and took one knee to the sand—a gesture of deference and respect. As she did so, the woman noticed Rose's bracelets, which her grandfather had given to her. They were golden, ornate, and the mark of royalty. Not something worn by someone bowing to a stranger.

The woman took a step backward. "Why are you here?" she asked. "Has my husband sent you? I have broken no laws. My children are my own, and if I choose to hide them among the islands of the Archipelago, it is my own business. He will wander an eternity before he sees them again."

"By Zeus," Bert whispered to Edmund and Charles. "She means Jason! This is Medea!"

"And the sons she is talking about are William and Hugh," Charles whispered back.

"That's terrible!" whispered Bert, remembering the wraith that Jason became after searching for his lost sons. "If there was ever a man who needed a hand, it's him."

"But we have the *Geographica*!" Charles exclaimed. "We can take him right to the island where she abandoned their sons!"

"At what risk?" Bert said with a touch of surprise. "We could irrevocably damage the future in the process."

"Haven't you already done that?" asked Edmund. "The Archipelago has already been swept away. Can anything we do here really make it worse?"

"The Archipelago is not what I'm worried about," Bert replied, casting a glance at Medea, who was still conversing with Rose. "In this time, the Summer Country is still very much connected to the Archipelago. And everything that has happened, did happen. Every moment that we spend here risks derailing that, and possibly changing our futures."

"When the rest of the islands of the Mediterranean are taken across," Medea was saying in answer to something Rose had asked, "then the Corinthian Giants will return for Autunno—this island.

"The last remnant of old Atlantis, the Silver Throne, sits in my temple," she said, "and when Autunno is taken through the Frontier, it will be the seat of power of both worlds."

Bert and Charles looked at each other, confused. The Archipelago was not built overnight—they knew that much from the old shipbuilder, Ordo Maas. It had taken centuries. But this was the first they had ever heard about Medea becoming Queen of the Silver Throne.

"Begging your pardon," said Bert, "but you *are* Queen Medea, are you not?"

She tilted her head slightly in acknowledgment. "I am. Since the death of my father, Aeetes, I have become queen of Corinth."

"And what of your husband, Jason?"

Her face darkened. "My husband is . . . occupied elsewhere. I don't expect that he shall return soon, if at all."

"A queen should not be walking thus, unattended and alone," said Rose. This was closer to her own era, Bert knew, so the mannerisms and proper courtesy to royal blood came more easily to her.

"My chariot was damaged crossing the Frontier," Medea answered. "Only one of my Dragons chose to attend me after . . . a dispute with my husband. And her strength was insufficient to weather the storms as smoothly as with both. One of my shipbuilders is down the beach," she said, pointing, "but I fear it's beyond his skill to repair.

"A shame to have to have him killed," she added. "He did build good ships."

"The chariot," Bert murmured to the others. "That's how it was done, before Ordo Maas built the Dragonships. The Dragons personally escorted Jason and Medea to the Archipelago, through the Frontier."

"I have experience at a forge," Edmund said bluntly. "I could effect the repairs your chariot requires."

Medea's eyes brightened for a moment, then dimmed in distrust. "At what cost?"

"A boon," Edmund said evenly. "I shall do you this service, and you'll owe me one in return."

She shook her head. "That's too high a price," she said haughtily, tossing her head and folding her arms. "Still . . ." She thought a moment, glancing now and again at Rose's bracelets.

"Agreed," she said finally—to Rose, not Edmund. "But if your servant is unable to fix it to my liking, then you and all your servants will stay on Autunno to serve me, until I choose to release you."

Rose bowed. "We have a bargain."

Medea turned and strode down the beach. Quickly the companions gathered their things and followed her.

"You're not offended to be called 'servants'?" Rose asked her companions, smiling.

"I've been there before," Charles replied. "I'm just happy she didn't call me 'Third.'"

The stables were well-appointed and had all the materials necessary for Edmund to reshape Medea's chariot.

"I can do this," he whispered to Rose, "but just the same, I'd give almost anything to have your father with us for the next few hours."

"You'll do fine," Rose reassured him, "and for what it's worth, so would I."

"I didn't know he'd been trained as a blacksmith," Charles remarked. "I thought he came from a line of silversmiths."

"He wasn't trained by a smithy," Rose said, grinning. "He was trained by a scientist—Dr. Franklin. That may not mean much in twentieth-century Oxford, but in ancient Greece, it makes him a Magic Man."

The young Cartographer set to work, and in short order had

restructured the chariot to be pulled by a single creature instead of two.

"You did that rather easily, and quickly," Medea said as she looked over his handiwork. "Impressive. Perhaps too impressive. I think that maybe I bargained too quickly, Master Smith."

"I said I could do it, and I have done it," he replied, wiping his brow with a cloth.

"And far more quickly than that fool Argus," she said. "If I'd left him to it, he'd have taken a week, and the wheels would still rattle."

"Your shipbuilder's name is Argus?" Edmund asked, as casually as he could manage. "As in, the man who built the *Argo* for Jason and the Argonauts?"

"Yes," she said, face darkening. "Why?"

He set the cloth aside. "That is the boon I ask. Spare his life."

"What are you doing?" Rose whispered.

"I know what she did to her sons," Edmund whispered back. "She's a really horrible person, and so I asked for the one thing I know will twist her in knots to grant me."

Rose was surprised by Edmund's request, but nonetheless nodded her agreement. "That is our request," she said to the queen. "Spare the shipbuilder Argus."

"A boon is a boon," said Medea, "but this is more. This is blood. By what right do you ask a life-boon?"

Rose glanced back at Edmund, who folded his arms defiantly. "By right of blood—blood ties of family, great-grandmother," she said softly, her voice low and cool, but with a trace of menace nonetheless. "A bond that cannot be taken, only given."

Medea did not understand what she meant by these

words—and had no way of knowing that Rose was descended from the bloodline of the Argonauts. But it was Edmund's handiwork on the chariot that gave her pause. This youth was no mere servant. He was clearly a Maker—and thus, not to be trifled with. That the young woman who bore the ornament of royalty also claimed a blood-bond told Medea she should not overplay her hand.

"Agreed," she said, and made as if to leave, but paused in the doorway of the stables.

"Interesting that this should be your request, today of all days," Medea said.

"Why is that?" asked Rose.

Medea shook her head. "Just coincidence, or perhaps . . . fate," she answered. "He was to be killed in service of another blood-debt, which is still owed. But no matter—I gave you my word. And the word of a queen of Corinth is sacrosanct.

"The regent of the Old World will be arriving soon, and I must prepare for him. The shipbuilder will be freed, as you have asked."

The queen of Corinth left the stables, and a few moments later they saw she was good to her word, as a young, rather ragged man appeared at the doorway.

He looked curiously at the strange band of travelers, then walked over to Edmund and offered his arm, in the old Greek tradition.

"I understand you are the one who is responsible for my good fortune," Argus said slowly, "and I find I have no words to . . ."

Edmund took his arm. "A boon was given for your life," he said. "Perhaps someday, you'll do the same for another."

Argus stepped back and bowed. "I will. You have my word—although my skills are rarely called upon these days. Few adventurers are bold enough to hire a shipmaker who can bind the spirit of living creatures into a vessel."

The companions all stilled at hearing this.

"Have you ever bound a Dragon to a ship?" Bert asked. "Could you, if someone wished it done?"

Argus laughed. "I have the skill, but no one will ask me to," he said. "Not while my master is still working in the trade. His are far better than mine."

"Who is your master?"

"The greatest of all shipbuilders," Argus replied. "Ordo Maas."

A bright gleam suddenly appeared in Bert's eyes. "Does anyone else have this skill other than yourself and Ordo Maas?"

Argus folded his arms and shook his head, grinning. "None living, or otherwise. Only he and I."

"That's awfully self-assured," said Charles.

"Not at all," said Argus. "Merely the truth."

"That's the boon," Bert said suddenly, glancing at Edmund, who looked startled, but nodded his assent. "Someday, perhaps many years from now, someone will ask you to build such a ship. All we ask is that you do it."

"Done and done," Argus said in surprise. "And a bargain at twice the price." He stretched his back and turned to the doorway.

"Again, you have my gratitude," he said. "I have to go find my master—but I shall always remember. Call on me if you are ever in need. And when the time comes, I'll build your ship."

With that, he trotted off down the beach.

"What was that all about?" Charles asked. "What Dragonship did you want him to build, Bert?"

"One that in our time, he's perhaps already built," Charles's mentor replied. "A ship that only Ordo Maas could have built, but didn't. A ship that no one living knows the origin of. A ship," he added, looking pointedly at Rose, "that has been at the heart of one of the great mysteries of the Archipelago."

Charles gave a low whistle. "Do you really think so, Bert?"

"I do," Bert said, nodding. "I think we've just saved the life of the man who will build the *Black Dragon*."

Before the companions could discuss this extraordinary turn of events further, another voice called out from the darkness at the far end of the stables. It sounded inebriated.

"Was that the shipbuilder, Argus?" it called out. "I was s'pposed t' kill him today. Blood-debt, you know."

Cautiously, Edmund picked up an iron bar, as did Charles, and they motioned for the others to stay back. "Who goes there?" Charles called out.

"I'd say it's the Comedian, but the Comedian is dead," said the voice. It was coming from the far stalls, away from the entrance, where the torchlight didn't reach.

"I'd say it's th' Philosopher, but the Philosopher is terrible at Philosophizing," the voice rambled on. "So I must be th' Executioner—'cept you just freed the executionee, so I think I'm out of a job again."

As he spoke, they heard another sound—rattling chains. He was not a servant of Medea, but a prisoner.

"You sound very familiar to me," Charles said. "Something in the tenor of your voice—I've heard it somewhere before. Did you say you were a philosopher?"

"I did, but I don't mind telling you again," came the answer. "I *was* a philosopher. Of some renown, I might add, although of late"—he clanked his chains for emphasis—"I seem to have fallen into disfavor with th' queen. Again."

"Ah!" Charles said as he and Edmund lowered the iron bars. Whoever this drunkard was, he was no danger to them. "A learned man, then."

"A learned man who's just been sick all over his sandals," said the voice.

"Mmm, sorry," said Charles. "I'm Charles, by the way, and these are my friends Rose, Bert, and Edmund. Despite the circumstances, we're very pleased to make your acquaintance."

"And I you," the voice replied. "My name is Aristophanes."

Standing at one of the tall windows . . .
the Chronographer of Lost Times waited . . .

CHAPTER NINETEEN
The Unicorn

❖

The flight from the Goblin Market was marked by both the speed Uncas was driving, and the nearly endless stream of curse words being generated by the Zen Detective. Apparently, he was fluent in over a dozen languages—at least, fluent enough to competently curse.

At Aristophanes's urging, Uncas flipped on the projector and drove them through a slide to an out-of-the-way spot where they could catch their collective breath and locate the next object. The badger chose a grassy field in Finland. Other than the Duesenberg, the only thing that broke the monotony of the fields was a small fishing shack that stood on the top of a cliff in the distance. "It's th' calmest place I knows of," Uncas said as they got out of the car. "Nothing exciting ever happens in Finland."

Aristophanes inserted the second parchment into the Machine Cryptographique and carefully typed in a question. As swiftly as before, the Infernal Device returned the answer: "Pohjola."

Uncas rummaged through the maps and stopped on the second to last. He stared at it with a bewildered expression and looked up at Quixote and Aristophanes. "I, uh, I have it. I think."

"So?" said the detective. "Will we be able to find it?"

Uncas nodded. "I'm pretty sure."

Aristophanes waited. "Well? Where is this 'Pohjola'?"

The little mammal pointed at his feet. "Right here. We're *standin'* on it."

"Give me that!" Aristophanes exclaimed, snatching the map out of the badger's paws. A moment later, though, his expression changed. "Well," he admitted, handing the map back to Uncas, "this might be easier than we thought."

Quixote was dumbfounded. "You mean he's right? That we just happened to pick a place to hide from that mob, and we ended up coming to the very place we needed to go next?" He shook his head. "That's just too incredible to believe."

"That's Zen for you," Aristophanes said, shrugging. "Let's go see if anyone's home."

The little old fisherman who answered their knock at the hut acted as if they were expected and invited them in. "Would you like some *sima*? Sweet mead?" he offered as they sat on the pelt-covered benches inside. "I have just made it, fresh. But," he added ruefully, "I have no lemon. It would be lemonless *sima*."

Quixote gave Aristophanes a look that said what they were both thinking—the old fisherman had spent way too long inhaling the salt air. But Uncas cheerfully accepted, and with shaking hands, the old man poured them all a drink.

"I assume," he said, sipping mead from his own cup, "that you've come to ask for the Sampo. Well, I have some bad news for you—I have no idea where it is."

"Is that some sort of, uh, magical object?" Uncas asked, winking at Aristophanes, who rolled his eyes and groaned inwardly. The badger had no sense of subterfuge whatsoever.

"It is," said the fisherman. "Everyone thinks I have it because of those cursed stories in the *Kalevala*. 'Ask Kullervo,' they say. 'Go seek Kullervo—he's bound to have it.' And on and on. As if I'd end up with a magic box that grants you all you desire. Not after the life I've had, I wouldn't. Every time something good started to happen, someone evil would turn my cows into bears, and my family would get eaten while they were tending to the milking. Very frustrating."

"Even this," he continued, standing up. He set down his mead and walked to the corner, where he lifted up a long, black sword. "I finally won something valuable—a magic sword—but every time I remove it from the sheath, it starts singing. Do you know how embarrassing it is to go into battle with a singing sword that won't shut up?"

"The sword of Turambar," the detective murmured, making a mental note to remember where it was. "Interesting."

"We're sorry to hear about your troubles," said Uncas. "We've actually come looking for a different magical object."

"Well, you won't have much luck here," said Kullervo glumly. "About the only other thing I've got is a brooch—but it's not worth very much. Would you like to see it?"

"Yes," Uncas said, and nodded. "We would, please."

The fisherman reached into a basket of straw hanging on a hook and, after rummaging around in the straw, removed a small, red brooch. "Here you go," he said, tossing it to Uncas. "If you're interested, I'll part with it for cheap."

"How cheap?" asked Aristophanes, suspicious. Easy was acceptable, once in a while. But this was going a bit too smoothly for his liking.

Kullervo shrugged. "I'd really like some fish."

Uncas blinked. "Aren't you a fisherman?"

He shrugged again. "Not a very good one, I'm afraid. And the fish aren't as plentiful here as they once were."

Aristophanes leaned over and looked at the object Uncas held. It was indeed the Ruby Brooch.

"We don't have time to go fishing," he whispered. "I think we should—"

"Don't sweat it," said Uncas. "I got this."

The badger stood up. "I got six bottles of pickled trout in my car," he said brightly. "Is it a trade?"

Kullervo thought it over. "Is trout like herring?"

"It's fish," said Uncas, "what's been pickled."

"Deal," said Kullervo. "The brooch is yours."

"Why in Hades's name," Aristophanes asked as they drove away in the Duesenberg, "would you have *six jars* of pickled trout in the boot of the car?"

"In case of a 'mergency," said Uncas. "Also, I really like pickled trout."

"Two for two," Quixote said from the rear seats. "So far, so good. And it's been Uncas who's done all the bartering!"

"Yes, well," said the detective. "As I said—we make a good team."

"Just remember you said that," Uncas chortled, "when you gets my bill."

As the car vanished into the distance, the cloaked man stepped out of the shadow of the fishing hut and walked around to the door, which was open. Kullervo was waiting.

"Did I do it right?" he asked, the tone of his voice an odd mix of both longing and resignation. "I did as you wanted—I took off the brooch so their machine would find me, and then I treated them like guests and gave them the brooch."

"Yes," the Messenger said. "You did fine, Kullervo." He looked inside the hut. "Would you like to do it now?"

"Weeelll," the fisherman replied. "I just came into some pickled trout. So I thought, if you wanted to join me, we could have a bite first?"

The man nodded. "Of course."

The trout was excellent, especially with some dark bread that was just stale enough to be really good, and when they had finished, the Messenger walked the fisherman to the edge of the cliff, where he used the long black sword to lop off the old man's head. He tossed the sword in after, then removed his watch and spun the dials.

As he disappeared, he imagined he could still hear the sword singing. It probably was.

The next piece the companions asked about was the helmet, and the machine and the map guided them to a much smaller place than a country or an island—a place even smaller than the Inn of the Flying Dragon.

"It's a shop in Vienna," Aristophanes said, "but what's inside the Abraxas House isn't quite as unusual as the building itself."

"How so?" asked Quixote.

"You'll see," the detective said.

It took several hours of driving around the twisty Austrian streets before they actually found the place they were searching for. "There!" Aristophanes exclaimed, pointing through the windshield. "That's it just up ahead."

The Abraxas House was located mid-block just past the inter-section of Laimgrubengasse and Gumpendorferstraße. The streets were lined with small cafés and pastry shops, which fronted the ground floors of stately old Viennese hotels and apartment build-ings. Thus, the Abraxas House was a bit of an anomaly—but then again, as Aristophanes explained, it was an anomaly in just about every other way as well.

The first unique characteristic was obvious—the entire build-ing was seven stories tall, but only a dozen feet wide. It was deeper than it was wide, but not by much, because it backed up to a com-mon square used by the buildings adjacent to it and on the street one block over. That was what made it unusual from the outside. What made it unusual on the inside was that it appeared to be infinitely large; room after room after high-ceilinged room stretched away past every corner they looked around. Minuscule on the outside, the Abraxas House was massive on the inside.

The shelves were primarily full of books, but there were various other artifacts scattered in and among them: ornate boxes, weapons, earthenware, and even armor.

"It's a Whatsit," Uncas said, awed by the sight. "It's just like th' Great Whatsit, on Paralon, 'cept there are pastry shops on either side. Brings a tear to one's eyes, it does."

Quixote saw an elderly gentleman with an apron moving boxes in another room, and gestured to him for service. The man nodded in acknowledgment and came toward them, wiping his hands on a cloth.

"Greetings," the white-mustached shopkeeper said, appar-ently unruffled to be waiting on a purple man, a badger in a waistcoat and jacket, and a knight with all the fashion sense of a novelist. "What can I do for you today?"

Aristophanes made a judgment call and decided that in a place of commerce, he could play it straight. "We're looking for the Ruby Helmet."

The shopkeeper tapped his fingers on his chin and pursed his lips. "I had an ebony helmet once, but that tall, pale fellow came back for it not long after he sold it to me. I traded two houses of secrets and mystery for it, and he bought it back for seven dreams. I also had Mercury's helmet—the one with the wings—but sold that one to a man called Garrett, or Garrick, or something like that."

"The one we seek," said Aristophanes, "is part of a larger set, called the Ruby Armor . . ."

"Of T'ai Shan!" the shopkeeper said, snapping his fingers. "I thought that sounded familiar."

He walked to a circular bookcase in the next room and pulled a copy of Machiavelli's *The Prince* out just far enough to release a catch hidden in the shelving. A panel slid back, revealing the Ruby Helmet, sitting on a pedestal.

"There have been inquiries over the years, of course," he said as he returned to the companions, holding the helmet, "but few willing to pay an acceptable price. Pieces this old are not easy to come by."

"How old is it?" asked Uncas.

"Nine, perhaps ten thousand years old," said the shopkeeper. "It was a little before my time, so I can't be certain."

"I thought you looked familiar," Aristophanes said cautiously. "What did you say your name was?"

"I didn't," came the reply, "but as you've asked, it's Trisheros."

The Zen Detective went pale—this apparently meant something significant to him. "Thrice Great?" he whispered.

"No," Trisheros said, shaking his head. "You're thinking of my father. He's considerably older and doesn't come into the shop much anymore. What did you say your name was?"

"His name is—," Uncas began.

"*Steve*," the detective interrupted. "It's just . . . Steve. A pleasure, I'm sure." He gestured at the helmet. "What would you like for it?"

"Hmm," the shopkeeper mused, rubbing his chin. "I don't really know that I need much of anything right now," he said apologetically. "Unless you happen to have a photograph of the *Painting That Ate Paris*."

"Uh, no," said Quixote. "I don't think we do. But pray tell, why would anyone?"

"Oh, no one wants the actual painting, to be sure," the shopkeeper said, "but the photograph can fetch a good price from collectors in the know. And it doesn't devour anything—just gives the viewer a vague sense of unease. Very avant-garde."

"Is there anything else you'd consider?" Aristophanes asked, feeling that the shopkeeper might be the bartering kind—especially considering his lineage. "We have access to a great many things."

"I assumed you were not the principal buyers," said Trisheros. "For whom are you working?"

The companions looked at one another. Finally Aristophanes chose to answer. "The Caretakers."

"Ah," the shopkeeper said, as if this answered more than one question. "Then the price is a simple one. I would like a copy of the *Imaginarium Geographica*. If you can do that for me, the helmet is yours."

"No problem!" Uncas said as Quixote grinned and Aristophanes slapped his head and groaned. "I gots twelve copies in—"

"In the back of the Duesenberg," the detective finished. "Of *course* you do."

"How many would you like?" asked Uncas.

"Er, ah . . . ," Trisheros stammered. "Just one will do, thank you."

The little mammal rushed out the door, then popped the lid of the trunk and jumped inside to get the book.

"Why would he—," the shopkeeper began.

"I've learned to stop asking," Aristophanes said as Uncas returned with a copy of the fifth edition of Mr. Tummeler's abridged, annotated *Imaginarium Geographica*. "Just smile and nod."

"It's even signed by King Artus," Uncas said proudly. "No extra charge."

"Thank you," said Trisheros.

"What was that 'Thrice Great' business about, anyway?" Uncas asked as they drove away from the Abraxas House. "You seemed t' know who he was f'r a minute there."

"Not him, actually," the detective answered pensively. "His father—Hermes Trismegistus. 'Thrice Great' is what the name means. He's one of the oldest beings alive—far older than I am—and some people think he was a god. And," he added, "he might have been."

"I've read about him," said Uncas. "In th' Little Whatsit. He's the one who communed with angels, right? Learned their language an' . . ." The little mammal stopped suddenly, whiskers twitching. "An' taught it all to . . . John Dee."

"Maybe," Aristophanes said, features darkening as he turned to look out the window. "I wouldn't know anything about that."

Trisheros knew just the place to shelve his newly acquired copy of the *Imaginarium Geographica*. There was space on a special shelf in the Rare Books Room, right next to the *Encyclopedia Mythica*, *The Journal of Ezekiel Higgins*, *The Book of All Stories*, and the copy of the Little Whatsit he had acquired some years earlier from an agent of the Caretakers who called himself a Messenger. His name had been Ransom, and he had been welcomed as both a seeker of knowledge and a customer.

Not so the one who was hovering around outside the door.

Trisheros murmured a few words ripe with ancient power, and the runes above the doorway—above every doorway—glowed with eldritch energies.

"I'm sorry," he said softly, not looking up from his work. "But this is one of the few places, anywhere, anywhen, that is barred to you. I know who and what you are. Once, I might have become as you are now myself. But I chose this, and I'm all the happier for having done so."

He paused and cocked his head, as if listening to an answer. "Nor do I wish you any harm," he said. "Quite the opposite. I wish you luck. And . . ." He paused again, listening.

Whoever it was that had been outside was gone now, and the old man sighed.

"And," he finished, more for himself than for the entity with whom he'd been speaking, "I wish you peace. But I fear that is not a card in the hand you were dealt. And I'm sorry, boy. Very sorry."

He filed the *Geographica* on the shelf with the other books and turned out the light.

"This will be most difficult," Aristophanes said when they'd arrived at their next destination. "Not many people ever come here. And those who do almost never return.

"It's called Tartarus," he explained, "although it's not the common one most people would think of."

"The Greek underworld," said Quixote. "I've read my mythology."

"Have you now?" said Aristophanes. "Your mythology won't have told you about this place—it's about as dank and foul a region as exists. The only reason I'm here is that I expect a great reward at the end. And I'd better get it."

"I'm sure Verne will take good care of you," Quixote said, peering through the gloom. "Access to the inner circle, and the like."

"Right," said the detective. "Verne. That's what I meant."

The wall ahead was foreboding and seemed impossibly high. From below, the companions could just make out the shape of heads set along the length of the uppermost stones.

"Brr," said Uncas. "Are those f'r reals?"

"Plaster," said Aristophanes. "Or so I've been told."

"There's no gate," said Quixote after a brief trot around the walls. "The road encircles it, but there's no way in."

"That's what I'm here for," said the Zen Detective. "One of these stones along the path is a catch that releases an opening in the wall."

"How do you know which one?"

"Because in a past life, I was a philosopher of unknown things," came the reply from the now-irritated detective, "and finding unfind-able things is what I do best."

Aristophanes walked slowly around the pathway, not even really examining the stones but more getting a feel for the atmo-sphere of the place. He had explained to Uncas that sometimes being a Zen Detective was nothing more than imagining oneself as the person or thing that was lost, and then going to the place that they would go. It was apparently a very successful tech-nique, because in less than ten minutes, he waved them over to where he stood.

Aristophanes pointed to a roundish, nondescript stone half-buried in the path and covered with scrubby grass. "There," he said. "That's the one."

Without waiting for a consensus, he stepped firmly on the stone, and immediately a section of the wall in front of them came crumbling down in a torrent of stones and dust. In moments they were looking through a broad hole into the interior of the wall.

"Oh my," said Uncas. "I thought a door would swing open, or the stones would magically rearrange themselves into an entrance, or something like that."

"Maybe in the entrance to an alley of shops in London, it would do that," Aristophanes said as he stepped over the pile of rubble and inside the wall, "but this isn't that kind of place. Don't worry about it, though," he added. "It's charmed—the wall will be back in place within the hour."

"Then how d' we get out again?" asked Uncas.

"We make sure we're already gone when it closes," Aristophanes said gruffly. "Come on. Follow me."

◆　◆　◆

Within the wall the companions found a thick, tangled wood of ancient dead trees. A black river flowed through the wood, and Aristophanes advised the others not to touch the water. Along the banks, someone had placed a variety of stuffed animals, perhaps to use as a lure for unsuspecting travelers. Up ahead, the trees gave way to a clearing, where there stood a crumbling Moravian church, ringed about with willows.

"That's what we want," Aristophanes said. "There should be a staircase inside that leads into the catacombs."

There was indeed a staircase, and the companions lit a torch to follow the steps down. Inside the catacombs, they followed a winding path, led only by the Zen Detective's innate sense of direction. Eventually they came to a large chamber lined with openings in the walls.

"Boy," said Uncas, "we could sure use some Lightening Bolts right about now."

Aristophanes looked at the badger like he was insane. "Are you insane?" he asked. "The last thing we need here is a thunderstorm."

"I didn't say 'thunderstorm,' I said we could use some Lightening Bolts," said Uncas. "You know, the kind that 'luminates stuff. We had a couple in the boot o' the Duesenberg."

The detective sighed and looked at Quixote. "Do you ever win an argument with him?"

"No," said the knight. "He's usually right."

In one of the openings they could see the skeleton of a man. It had been partially gilded—the ribs and thighs glistened with gold. In another was a glass bust of a beautiful maiden.

As they passed through the chamber, they found many more such talismans: a willow rod that Aristophanes said had been used to beat to death a forgiven penitent; a carved wooden toy that resembled a top, which he said would tell the day of one's death when spun; a collection of black paper hearts; and the skeleton of a dwarf, which he told them belonged to a son of the biblical Lilith.

In the last opening was the breastplate.

Aristophanes started to reach for it, but Quixote stopped him. "Wait," he explained, pointing to the far end of the chamber. "First we must make certain we have permission."

Another skeleton sat, watching them. It held an aeolian harp in its arms, and one hand was poised to play. As Aristophanes reached for the breastplate, the hand moved nearer to the strings.

"And if we don't?" asked the detective.

Quixote pointed up, to where a hundred more skeletal warriors sat in their own alcoves, waiting for the harp to summon them to life.

Aristophanes slowly pulled back his hand. "So what do we do?"

In response, Quixote strode over to face the skeleton and removed his hat, bowing as he did so.

"I am Don Quixote de la Mancha," he said, "and I am on a quest to retrieve the Ruby Breastplate there. I humbly seek your permission to remove it, if it be the good Lord's will that I do so, that I may succeed."

The skeleton nodded once, then lowered its hand and sat back in the alcove. Quixote walked back over to the others and removed the breastplate from the wall, handing it to an amazed Aristophanes.

"I can't believe it!" the detective exclaimed. "How in Hades's name did you know to do that?"

Quixote shrugged as they made their way back up the stairs. "It's something I learned long, long ago," he said, smiling. "You should always ask for what you want in life, because you might," he added, "just actually get it."

Standing at one of the tall windows of the house, the Chronographer of Lost Times waited, something he was very unaccustomed to doing. For the boy, the adept, it was worth it, though. His was a talent Dee had never seen, not even in Tesla or Blake. A talent that would change the nature of the game itself.

A talent that would ensure the Echthroi's victory, if it could only be channeled properly.

A voice from the door startled Dr. Dee—something else that very rarely ever happened. "You asked for me, Doctor?"

"Yes," Dee said without turning around. "What do you have to report?"

"Victory," the boy said. "I've been to all the prospective futures and see nothing but victory, complete and absolute."

Dee frowned. He was expecting a report on the Caretakers' activities, not this . . . rallying cry. "That's . . . good," he said at length, "but we need to be prepared. Our first battle is approaching quickly, and soon our agent will be bringing us everything we need for—"

"Victory," the boy interrupted. "It's all going as it's supposed to go, Dee." No "Doctor" this time.

"Fine," the Chronographer said, irritated. "Tell Tesla I'd like to see him."

The boy bowed slightly and left.

It was a full five minutes before Dee realized the boy had never actually said that it was the Cabal's victory he had seen in all the possible futures—and that realization left the Chronographer of Lost Times feeling uneasy for the rest of the night.

The regent rose to his full height,
which was greater than it had first appeared.

Chapter Twenty
The First King

◈

Rudyard Kipling ran down the street with as much speed as he could muster. He had anticipated some kind of surreptitious attack from the Cabal, perhaps on the Kilns, or even at Tamerlane House again, after the burglary. But an attack on the Hotel d'Ailleurs in Switzerland was a long way down on that preparedness list—in part because it had been kept secret even from most of the Caretakers, and in part because William Blake would have warned them.

Unless, Kipling worried, Blake didn't know. In which case, he might have been discovered as a covert operative of the Mystorians and the Caretakers.

Either way, he reasoned as he rounded the corner opposite the hotel and saw the flames shooting up into the night sky, he had a greater priority.

Stepping back into a doorway of the building next door, he pulled out his trump and summoned Jules Verne.

"All right," Verne said when Kipling had explained the circumstances. "It's time. Use the special trump we made to bring them—"

"Way ahead of you, old chap," said Kipling. "I left it with

young Joseph Merrick in case of just such an eventuality. The first of them ought to be arriving there now. I'll hold out here as long as I can, to make sure we can save everyone."

"All right," Verne said, rolling up his sleeves. "Let us see where this goes. I'm going to rouse the Caretakers. When you've finished in Switzerland, go join Houdini and Conan Doyle and see to it that they're also ready."

"I'll take care of it, Jules," Kipling said as he closed the trump. "Believing is seeing."

"Yes," Verne said. "And hope springs eternal."

Edmund, with Charles and Rose's help, was able to remove the shackles that bound Aristophanes in the Corinthian stalls. He was dressed simply, if a bit dirty—but his skin was also fully as pale as theirs was, and he had no horn.

"If this is our Zen Detective," Charles whispered, "then we've caught him at an early stage in his life, but not"—he sniffed the foul wine spilled around the hay—"at a better one."

A splash of cold water from the troughs helped Aristophanes regain a bit of sobriety, and he thanked the companions for freeing him.

"You didn't have to do that, you know," he said. "The queen will not be pleased."

"Let's say we owed you a kindness, and leave it at that," said Edmund. "Will you flee, as the shipbuilder did?"

He shook his head. "I can't. I'm bound by a blood oath to stay, until she releases me. And my chance just went running off down the beach. I'm still grateful you freed me," he added quickly, "but it doesn't help overmuch."

"If you're bound," asked Rose, "then why were you chained?"

"Too much wine," Aristophanes admitted sheepishly. "I got, ah, shall we say, a little too personal with some of the local maidens."

"Well," Edmund said, moving protectively in front of Rose, "you seem to be doing much better now."

From outside, a tremendous noise arose—trumpets, and drums, and the cheering of crowds.

"Ah," said Aristophanes. "That'll be the beginning of the coronation. The last regent of the Old World is coming to select the ruler of the Archipelago. Three guesses whom the queen expects it to be."

"Do you know where this is happening?" asked Bert.

"Yes."

"Let's go have a look, then," the Far Traveler said, beckoning to his companions. "This could get interesting."

"Is this really what we should be doing?" Charles asked as they walked into the city and toward the noise. "Shouldn't we be finding a way to get home?"

"Someone from the Old World, they said," Bert replied. "That means someone who was a ruler before the divide of the Summer Country and the Archipelago. And that someone," he finished, "may be able to lead us to the Architect."

Aristophanes led them to a broad avenue, lined with trees, fountains, and all manner of ornate, stately buildings. Crowds of people thronged the street on both sides, leaving only a narrow path for the arrival of the regent and the queen, a path that terminated at a great amphitheater built around the Silver Throne.

"Look, there," Aristophanes said, pointing, "and see how a queen makes her appearance."

To the west, the chariot that Edmund had mended dropped out of the sky in front of the setting sun. It was being pulled by a great, vivid green-gold Dragon.

"Azer," Rose breathed.

The Dragon-drawn chariot landed on the street amid the cheers of the Corinthians and sped toward the amphitheater. Most of the crowd moved out of the way as it passed, but one old man, walking with a stick, hunched and slow with age, could not move quickly enough and was thrown to the ground when the chariot wheel struck him a glancing blow. Medea did not even notice.

Edmund and Rose ran to the old man and helped him to his feet, then walked him slowly to sit by one of the trees. Charles brought him some water from a fountain, which he accepted gratefully and drank greedily, while Bert brought him the walking staff—which, he noted with surprise, was made of lapis lazuli, gold, and . . . *cavorite*.

"Thank you, my children," the old man said, "for taking note of this tired old regent."

"Regent?" Bert said, handing him the staff. "As in . . ."

The old man gave Rose a wink and nodded. "People see what they want to see, what they look for," he said. "The rest may as well be invisible."

Bert sat next to the old man. "What is your name?"

"I have been called many things in my long life," the old regent said, leaning heavily on his staff, "but of those names, the one I most value was Friend, and the one I most regret was Enemy. And often, it was by the same man. So I know of what I speak.

"I was called the first king, and Ancient of Days, although that is a worthless title, earned only by virtue of being old, and not yet having died, and in truth applies far more to another great king than it ever did to me.

"So all these titles I have had and more, but when I look at the sunset of my life, I find I am no more and no less than I was when I faced my first sunrise. I am Gilgamesh. And that is enough."

"Long after it was first created, I spent many years in the Archipelago seeking the great Lord of the Creatures and Master Maker Utnapishtim," said Gilgamesh, "and went on many quests for the lords of the lands that have been taken there. Some called me a hero. More, I fear, than did so here, in the Summer Country.

"But," he continued, "Immortality was not to be mine. I have already lived many, many thousands of years, since before the time of the Great Deluge, and I am all that is left of that world. So now," he said, gesturing at the amphitheater, where Medea was impatiently awaiting the arrival of the grand regent of old, "I am brought to this."

Aristophanes had been watching, curious, from some distance away. But now Gilgamesh noticed him.

"Do you serve the queen?" he asked.

"When I must," said Aristophanes.

Gilgamesh rose to his feet. "Then please give her this message. We will discuss the ruler of the Archipelago, but in the old manner. Not here. Tell her to meet me in the Giant's Circle in one hour, if she wishes to retain her kingdom."

Aristophanes was taken aback, both by the content of the

message and the likelihood that Medea might slay the person who delivered it. "Whom should I say it is from?"

The regent rose to his full height, which was greater than it had first appeared. "I am Gilgamesh, King of Uruk, King of Sumer, Slayer of the World-Serpent, grandson of Nimrod the Maker, Blood of the Firstborn, and the regent of the world that was."

Aristophanes blinked rapidly, then nodded and disappeared into the crowd.

Gilgamesh offered his arm to Rose, who took it. "Shall we take a walk to the beach, my dear?" he asked. "It is a beautiful night."

The companions and the old regent chatted companionably as they walked away from the city, and Bert chanced to ask him if he knew of the Keep of Time.

"The Eternal Tower?" Gilgamesh answered. "Yes—I know of it."

"Do you know who made it?" Rose asked.

To the companions' disappointment, he shook his head.

"As old as these bones are," he said, "it was there long before my time. Long before the Archipelago was formed, after the Great Deluge. Everything was closer then. Smaller. But the world has grown.

"I saw the tower in my youth, when I sought to find the Garden of the Gods and learn the secret of their immortality. Had I known then what I know now, I simply would have stayed in the First City."

"The First City?" asked Edmund. "Ever?"

Gilgamesh laughed. "If not, certainly among them," he said. "Would you like to hear about it?"

"I would," Edmund said as he quietly opened one of his books and grabbed a pencil. "Very much, please."

"What are you doing?" Charles whispered.

"Just a thought I had," Edmund whispered back. "Keep him talking and let me work."

"Some called it the Dragon Isle," said Gilgamesh, "and others, the City of Enoch."

"Atlantis?" Bert asked, barely able to draw a breath with the wonderment of all they were hearing. "Is it Atlantis?"

Gilgamesh considered this, then nodded. "Yes, I think I have heard some of the younger races calling it thus. But among those who have built it, and who lived among its gleaming towers, they had a different name.

"They called it the City of Jade. And there was no place like it anywhere else on Earth, nor shall there ever be again. It was destroyed during the Deluge—and on that day, the world was irrevocably changed. It was the end of the Earth's childhood. And those of us who remember the innocence still miss it."

Gilgamesh was still describing the wonders of the First City when they arrived at the Giant's Circle—a Ring of Power, to the companions—and found the Dragon Azer, Aristophanes, and a livid Medea already there.

"How dare you humiliate me in front of my people!" she shouted, not realizing she'd nearly run down the regent not an hour before. "What do you mean by this?"

"These circles were made for summonings and ordinations," said Gilgamesh. "And I asked you here to tell you that should he return, it is my intention to ordain your husband, Jason, as King of the Silver Throne of the Archipelago of Dreams. And only him."

"By what right?" said Medea. "Do you know what he's done?"

"He has made many mistakes," said Gilgamesh, "but he is also the first of the great heroes, and he is whom I have chosen."

Azer growled and circled around the outside of the ring as Medea considered her response.

"Is that your last word?" she asked.

"It is," said Gilgamesh.

"Then so mote it be," Medea replied, nodding not at the regent, but at Aristophanes.

The failed philosopher sighed heavily, then drew a blade from his tunic. Before the companions realized what was happening, he had leaped forward and plunged it into Gilgamesh's heart.

"If you will not choose me," Medea said coldly, "then you will choose no one."

"And any idiot can swing a hammer and chisel at a block of granite," Aristophanes was saying as Uncas bumped the Duesenberg across a poorly maintained road, "but only an artist with vision and experience can make the stone reveal a sculpture."

"So which do you have?" asked Quixote. "Vision, or experience?"

"Both," came the reply. "But not enough vision to do me any good, and much more experience than anyone can handle.

"There," the detective said, squinting out the windshield through the foggy haze outside. "That's the place we're after."

The structure that dominated the desert landscape was called the Tower of the Two Dragons. There were six distinct levels to the tower, and each represented whichever culture was dominant in the region at the time new portions were built. Going from the uppermost tier, which was built by the Moors sometime after the first millennium, Quixote could trace the history of the tower downward, citing each culture's contribution through the ages, until he came to the lowest, oldest tier, which stumped him completely.

Laughing, Aristophanes explained that it had been built by a race of giants prior to the Bronze Age, which was why Quixote couldn't identify it. He simply had no frame of reference for something architectural that was so old.

"Actually," Quixote harrumphed, "I have extensive experience with giants, and in the days of my prime, even tilted at two or three, to their eternal regret."

"Hardly giants like these," the detective said over his shoulder as they approached the base of the tower. "They're anthropophagous."

"I make no judgments about that," said Quixote. "That's for each living being to decide on their own."

Aristophanes slapped his hand to his face. "No, you idiot," he said. "That means they eat human flesh."

Uncas gasped. "Cannibobbles!" he squeaked. "Like that awful Burton. He's done that before." The little mammal shivered involuntarily and looked nervously from side to side. "I don't want t' be runnin' into no cannibobbles."

"Not to worry, little fellow," said the detective. "The giants hereabouts have been gone for many moons. And I don't think they'll be coming back during the short time we're going to be here retrieving the Ruby Gauntlets. Besides," he added reassuringly, "almost everyone else who even tries to get in is usually killed immediately, so we don't really have to worry about being bothered."

"Swell," said Uncas. "T'anks for sharing."

"Frenchmen in particular are forbidden to come here. When such have tried in the past, they first shed their skins like snakes before dying a horrible, horrible death," said Aristophanes. "That's why Verne would never set foot in this tower."

"Hmm," said Quixote skeptically. "I rather question the truth of that. I think you're having a bit of fun with us."

"It's true enough that he sent us here, rather than come himself," said Aristophanes, "and unless either of you is French, you're safe as long as you stay close to me."

"Well then," Quixote said, moving noticeably closer to the detective, "I am glad to be a Spaniard."

"So am I," said Uncas. "Not t' be French, that is."

"So would anyone be," said Aristophanes, "except the French themselves. And they're usually just grateful not to be Italian."

The desert sands gave way to smooth, flat stones, set in geometric patterns around the base of the tower. Aristophanes cautioned his companions to make sure to step only on the rectangular stones, and avoid the diamond-shaped ones altogether.

The doorway of the tower was made of stone and wooden beams, and consisted of two high arches set one within the other, which were then framed by larger rectangular patterns of delicately carved friezes.

"There are very old rituals involved in entering a place such as this," Aristophanes said, indicating the stained wood in the arches as they passed through. "There were wards set here to keep out unwelcome visitors under pain of a terrible death. And without an invitation, the only way to avoid the wards was to slay one's parents, and then anoint the symbols carved into the entryway with the sacrificial blood."

"Well," Quixote said jovially, "at least those particular wards no longer function as they're supposed to."

"No," Aristophanes said, turning around. "The wards are still up."

"But," Uncas said, looking back at the doorway, then at their guide, "we walked right through th' door, no fuss, no muss. And I certainly never kilt my parents."

"Nor did I," said Quixote as he also looked intensely at Aristophanes. "But if the wards are still up . . ." The sentence trailed off into the stillness of the tower.

The Zen Detective met their questioning look with a steady glare of his own—but said nothing. After a long moment, he turned and disappeared up the stairs.

Quixote and the badger both swallowed hard; then, after another moment, followed.

"I think," Uncas whispered to the knight, "that I might have preferred running into th' cannibobbles."

"I recognize the dragon on the right," said Quixote, indicating the design of one of the friezes.

"As do I," Uncas said, his tone one of reverence. "As would any animal from the Archipelago. He's the Lightbringer. The great red Dragon. Th' wisest and oldest of all the creatures, an' th' protector of all the lands that are."

"Do you know the other one?" asked Quixote. "The green-gold Dragon?"

"I don't know," said Uncas. "They seem to go together, judging by the carvings in this tower, but I have no idea who that is s'pposed t' be. An' I thought I knew all th' great Dragons."

"She does look familiar to me, though," Quixote said, scratching at his beard. "Something about the way the light falls on the sculpted features . . ."

Suddenly his eyes grew wide, and he moved closer to better examine the frieze. "Does she look like the Sphinx?" he asked Uncas. "The one we brought Master Verne last year?"

"Naw," Uncas said. "That'd be too unlikely t' believe."

"If you're done interpreting the art on the walls," said the detective, "I could use a little help here. I'm stuck. Stumped. Don't know what to do next."

"But," Quixote interjected, thinking about the blood at the entryway, "haven't you had business here before?"

"Yes," Aristophanes replied, disgruntled, "but on the fifth tier. I haven't had to open anything on the third tier before. I don't know how to resolve the cipher."

"Ahem-hem," Uncas said, clearing his throat. He removed a small parcel from his pocket. "This is, I believe," he said with a slightly puffed-out chest, "the very reason you brung me. Bringed me. The reason I'm here." He opened the Little Whatsit and, humming a little badger tune, began thumbing through its pages.

Aristophanes leaned in to ask a question, and the badger scowled. "Give me some room," he said without looking up from his task. "I'm *workin'* here."

The Zen Detective held up his hands in surrender and retreated to the far end of the room.

"It's some combination of pictographs and Aramaic,"

Aristophanes whispered to Quixote. "It's pretty unlikely that he'll find any reference to those languages in his little handbook, don't you think? Shouldn't we consider—"

"Oh ye of little faith," Uncas murmured, still absorbed in his task. "If only you had the faith of a mustard seed, oh, the mountains you could move."

Aristophanes snorted. "Now he's going to quote scripture at us? And badly at that."

Uncas turned and looked at the detective, one eyebrow raised. "Scripture?" he said. "Naw—I'm quoting Gran'ma Badger. Moved a mountain t' plant her mustard seeds. Made th' best mustard in th' whole of the Archipelago. Can't eat potatoes without it."

He turned back to the frieze and, with no hesitation, swiftly touched five spots on the pattern. A foot above his head, a heavy stone slab slid open to reveal a hidden chamber. Inside, pulsing with an unearthly red light, were the Ruby Gauntlets.

"Don't underestimate Gran'ma Badger's mustard," Uncas said, pointing a claw at Aristophanes, "and don't be disrespectin' th' Little Whatsit."

"Unbelievable," said the detective.

"That's my squire," Quixote said proudly.

At the Ring of Power on Corinth, the companions stood in stunned silence and disbelief at the terrible act Aristophanes had just committed.

He wiped the blade on the regent's cloak, then moved back to stand behind Medea.

"Why?" Rose cried.

"I made a deal," he said simply. "Medea meant to feed me to

the fishes, but she said that if I were to win your confidence and your trust, and discover what you were doing here, she would free me.

"Then he asked to come here, and she warned me what might happen—but said I could repay my blood-debt by slaying the regent. And so I have."

"I thought we could trust you," Charles said dully. "We did trust you—have trusted you, far more than you realize."

"Of course you can trust me," Aristophanes replied. "Right up until the point where you can't."

Of all the pieces of the Ruby Armor found thus far, the comb was the easiest to locate—a fact that both delighted and vexed the Zen Detective.

The sixth oracular parchment and the corresponding map pointed them to a place called Taprobane, which was a densely wooded island at the mouth of the Indus River. Aristophanes told Uncas and Quixote that he had often heard the island referred to as "Tanelorn," and that deep within the forest there was supposed to be an impossibly old city. Fortunately, they did not have to venture that deeply—the box containing the comb, a smooth black stone, and a human finger bone was buried underneath a stone marker on the edge of Taprobane's northern shore.

A marker that bore the sign of a Caretaker.

"Which one?" Aristophanes asked.

"My old friend, Cyrano de Bergerac," answered Quixote. "Interesting that he should have come here, but not recorded it in any of the Histories."

"Maybe he took the record with him," suggested Uncas, "before he got lost riding that comet."

"Before what?" Aristophanes asked as he pocketed the comb and closed the box.

"Long story," said Uncas. "Six down, one to go."

The final objects they needed to complete the Ruby Armor were the shoes. The last of the oracular parchments led them to a place that had no map, because no map was necessary. It was in London, in the secret subbasement of the Natural History Museum.

Unlike some of the other Soft Places, it could be gotten to without a slide, or a trump, or by other mystical means. But like Lower Oxford, the entrances to the secret level were all but impossible to see for most people, who weren't looking to begin with.

The lower levels of the museum were already a treasure trove of Egyptian artifacts and fossilized dinosaur bones, but the real worth of the collection was to be found farther down.

A docent called Trent, who appeared to be of Elven descent, met them at the reception desk and listened to their request for the shoes with a growing look of incredulity.

"I can't sell you the shoes," he said flatly. "The Board of Regents would simply never stand for such a thing. I'd be dismissed, and they'd be very, very vexed. As it is, they're still in a bad mood after someone managed to steal our Sphinx last year."

"That's a shame," Quixote said, reddening. "These things happen."

"I've dealt with regents before," Aristophanes muttered under his breath. "This could take a while."

Uncas, however, noticed that the docent had taken a keen interest in Don Quixote, and decided that they might have more leverage than they thought.

"How would the board feel about a trade?" Uncas offered. "The helmet of Don Quixote de la Mancha, in exchange for the Ruby Shoes of . . . uh . . ."

"Marie Antoinette," said the docent, who seemed to be considering the offer. "She apparently couldn't get them on in time and . . ." He made a chopping motion with his hand. "Well, you know."

"My helmet?" whispered Quixote. "I've had it for centuries—it's just now broken in."

"Shush," said Uncas. "We'll get you a new one, with a phoenix feather or something."

"Deal," said Quixote.

"Deal," said Trent. "I'll get the shoes. But," he warned, "be careful with them. You don't have to be wearing them to use them—just in contact with them. We've lost three janitors, a schoolboy from Surrey, and a beagle that way."

"I have to tell you," Aristophanes said as they opened the trunk of the Duesenberg, "you've been the most unusual, helpful, and irritating clients I've ever had. And despite my initial reservations, I've actually enjoyed working with you."

"Thanks," said Uncas. "I think."

"Here," the detective said to the others. "Gather up the ends of that tarpaulin, will you?"

Together the three of them made a makeshift sack out of the tarp, which held all the ruby objects, as well as the Infernal Machine.

Aristophanes lifted it out of the car and slung it over his shoulder.

"What are you doing?" asked Quixote. "Aren't we taking all this back to Tamerlane House?"

"We have one more little trip to take," said the detective. He unwrapped the Ruby Shoes and slipped them into his pockets—then took hold of Quixote's arm.

"Uncas," he said, "please take my arm."

"Okay," said the badger. "But . . ."

In a trice, the trio vanished, leaving the empty Duesenberg sitting outside the museum.

"... whyfor?" Uncas finished, as the three companions reappeared on the grassy slope of an island that was definitely not England.

"Well," said Quixote. "At least now we know the shoes work."

"Where have you brought us to?" Uncas said, looking around in wonder. In the distance, they could see the mist-shrouded statues, great elongated heads, that stood along the paths of the island as silent sentries.

"This is the only actual island of the Archipelago that stayed on this side of the Frontier," said Aristophanes. "Welcome to Easter Island."

"Fascinating!" said Quixote. "I've always wanted to come here. Although," he added, "all the giants are long gone."

"Yes," the detective said. "They are."

"Maybe we should come back on a different day," said Uncas. "After we've taken the Ruby Armor t' Scowler Verne."

Aristophanes sighed, deeply and long. He turned to the badger and the knight, his expression a mix of regret and resolve. "Have I ever told you that you shouldn't trust me?"

Quixote and Uncas looked at each other, puzzled, then back at the detective. "No," Quixote said slowly. "I don't think so. And we haven't felt the need to ask—not for quite a while, anyway."

A pained look crossed Aristophanes's features. "Well then," he said abruptly, "I'm sorry to tell you this—but you shouldn't have trusted me."

Uncas's face fell. "Are you going t' keep th' armor for yourself, then?"

"No," Aristophanes said as he drew the dagger from its sheath, "we're going to deliver it all to my client. My true client."

Uncas let out a strangled squeak when he saw the dagger. "We aren't taking this back to Jules Verne, are we?" he asked, whiskers drooping.

"No," said the detective. "We're going to take it all, every piece, to Dr. Dee."

PART SIX

Mysterious Islands

"If you want to surrender gracefully now, Dee . . .
no man will think the less of you . . ."

Chapter Twenty-One
The House on the Borderlands

Dr. Dee stood at his window in London, watching as Benjamin Franklin and the magistrate exchanged pleasantries outside before continuing on their respective paths. He wondered, not for the first time, whether Franklin would be worth recruiting into the ICS—and then, as before, pushed the thought out of his head. Something about the American gave him a terrible sense of déjà vu—and that was not just a feeling, but a caution. Especially for one who travels in time.

Since formally leaving his position with the Caretakers, he had accelerated his plans for the Imperial Cartological Society. And, as the Caretakers became more and more obsessed with imaginary geographies and protecting the past, Dee had concerned himself with the substance of the real world, and the possibilities of the future.

Working with William Blake, he had all but perfected the Anabasis Machines, incorporating spatial transportation abilities that none of the Caretakers had even begun to suspect were possible. That meant that his travel in the Summer Country was all but unrestricted, and his ability to leap back and forth in time, even more so.

It amused him to realize that it had been his younger self who last met with the Dragon Samaranth not far from this place, but a century in the future. To be older, and now standing in his own past, *was something that would have clouded the minds of lesser men—but he had never been that kind of a man, not even centuries earlier, when he first proposed the founding of the ICS to Queen Elizabeth.*

It had taken him many years to establish it as an organization separate and apart from that of the Caretakers—and those they rejected from their membership had made excellent candidates for his. Especially the learned barbarian, Burton. Yes, Dee thought. That one has potential. He could even be my successor—if, that is, I ever intend to step down from my position. So, Second in command, then. *Burton would have to be satisfied with that—as would Dee. None of the other recruits were even close to being in Burton's league.*

As if in response to Dee's unspoken thoughts, there was a knock at the door. He turned to see Daniel Defoe walk in, wearing a cunning smile.

Defoe approached his master and quickly whispered his report. Dee frowned at first, and then, slowly, began to smile as broadly as his protégé.

"At Franklin's, you say?" he said, mentally checking the box that said his intuition was sound. "And they carry the watches, as we do?"

"And the Imaginarium Geographica," *said Defoe. "The real one. They are Caretakers, I've no doubt."*

Dee turned and looked out the window again. He knew that the Caretakers had blundered badly in the future, and that the Archipelago was no longer connected to the Summer Country. More, he knew that the Keep of Time had fallen, and with it, their ability to use the Anabasis Machines.

He reached down and stroked the large, leather-bound book on his desk. It was only the maps he had recorded within, the maps of time, rather than space, that had preserved the ability of the ICS to travel in time—and the Caretakers had no Chronographer of their own. So if they were here, in Revolution-era London, he mused, then they must have found a way to begin to reweave the threads of time. And that could not be countenanced.

"I don't know who all the men are," Defoe was saying, "but they also have several animals with them—talking animals—and three children. Two girls, one of whom can fly, and a young boy."

"And why is this of interest to me?" asked Dee.

"The second girl," said Defoe, "has no shadow."

"Hmm," Dee said. "That is interesting."

There was another knock at the door, and Dee gestured for Defoe to leave, but not before giving him instructions. "Find out all that you can about them," he said firmly. "Do not come back until you have."

Defoe stepped out of one door as another of Dee's associates entered through the first. "Greetings, Doctor," Nikola Tesla said. "I couldn't help but overhear. You're right to wonder about the girl."

"Who is she?"

"Rose Dyson," Tesla answered. "The Grail Child."

Dee whirled on his colleague. "The Grail Child! Here? Then the Caretakers who are with her . . ."

Tesla nodded. "Two of the three Caretakers of prophecy," he said, "and several others—including Burton, and the End of Time."

The Chronographer frowned and put his hand to his chin, stroking it in thought.

"Burton . . . ," he said at last. "That . . . is an unexpected defection. We should keep a tighter rein on him. But he's not my immediate concern—it's the End of Time who could discern our true natures. Have him dealt with as quickly as possible. I'll brook no delay in this, Nikola."

"Fine," Tesla said, chagrined at the other's tone. "And the girl?"

"Defoe said she has no shadow," he said at last. "This is an opportunity, Nikola. One we should not miss. Do we have a spare we could use, back at the House? Lovecraft's, perhaps?"

Tesla shook his head. "We have assigned that one to Defoe. We do have Crowley's, though."

"Fine," Dee said, waving his hand. "They are at Dr. Franklin's—have the Lloigor fit her with the Shadow, as soon as possible. It will take time to corrupt her fully, if it can be done at all."

The other shrugged. "She lost her own shadow," he said blithely. "That is not coincidental. There is one other thing, Doctor. The boy—he is special."

"How so?"

"Here," Tesla said, holding out his ebony-colored watch. "Look for yourself."

Dee examined the display on the watch for a moment, and a look of astonishment suddenly blossomed on his face. He looked at Tesla in disbelief, then took out his own watch to verify the other's findings. They were correct.

"He has no zero points," Dee murmured, "no life-thread binding him to this time, or any other. How is this possible?"

"He's from a might-have-been," said Tesla. "A possible future. That's the only reason there are no zero points connected to him. They haven't happened yet. But that isn't the most significant thing about him."

Dee waited. "Well?"

"His aiua," Tesla said, smiling. "It's almost identical to the Grail Child's. His lineage is the same. So I thought he might be a candidate—"

Dee silenced him with a gesture. "Don't even say the word," he said sharply. "We put too much weight on Mordred as a candidate, and *now he is forever out of our reach. I won't make that mistake again."*

He turned back to the window. *"Keep an eye on Defoe. Have the cat deal with Burton's guide, the Time Lord. And learn all you can about this child."*

"And if he is what he appears to be?" asked Tesla. "Do we bring him here, or . . ." He paused. "Kill him?"

"No," said Dee. "They found him in a future, so we should hide him in the future . . . in a might-have-been. The Caretakers are far too enmeshed in the past—they will never think to look for him in a past that hasn't happened yet. Have Defoe do it—he's reliable, and expendable.

"And," Dee continued, more to himself than the other, "when the time is right . . .

". . . what is theirs will become ours. And this boy may be the key to winning it all."

The open secret that was Verne's Mystorians became much more open with the destruction of the Hotel d'Ailleurs, and the subsequent evacuation to the refuge that he had prepared for them.

It was a smaller place than the hotel, but it didn't need to be larger than it was. It was built on one of the smaller of the Nameless Isles, just to the east of Tamerlane House. The island was also ringed about with rune stones, but these were not merely protective. They were essential.

Evacuating the still-living members of the Mystorians was not a problem—but moving out those who were ghosts took much more preparation. Their new home had to be identically prepared with the markings that allowed the ghosts to manifest, and Verne's special trump had to be used to allow them to pass.

Kipling activated it just in time, and nearly didn't make it through himself before the hotel roof collapsed in flames.

At Verne's behest, the Caretakers Emeriti had gathered together to hear Kipling's report. The tulpa had survived the flames but was not unscathed—his jacket was terribly scorched, and his hair and mustache were singed badly.

"And everyone is now safely here?" Verne asked when Kipling had finished.

"Almost," he replied. "Young Joseph Merrick stayed the longest, to make certain everyone else was safe. But I didn't see him come through the trump, and he has not as of yet manifested again at Haven."

Verne dropped his head and sighed. "I see."

"Is it the principal duty of the Prime Caretaker to form secret organizations?" asked an angry Alexandre Dumas. "And to keep it from his colleagues?"

"The principal duty of the Prime Caretaker," Verne said slowly, "is that of finding, and training, the Imago—the one who will become the protector of this world."

"Pfah," Leonardo da Vinci snorted. "That is a myth."

"It is not," said Verne. "Rose may be such a being, but the lost prince may be also. That's why the Cabal wanted him—and why we have sought him."

"To use him for ourselves?" asked Dumas.

"No," said Geoffrey Chaucer, in a tone that said he would brook no dissent. "To prevent the Cabal from turning him into the Archimago—the destroyer of worlds."

"In the days before the Caretakers," said Verne, "there were those of wisdom and learning who were asked by the Dragons to perform the same function. The greatest of these whom you may know of was Chiron."

"The centaur?" Jack asked. "Achilles's teacher?"

Verne nodded. "And the teacher of many, many others—most of the great heroes, in fact. He was the great-umpty-great grand-sire to your friend Charys, I believe.

"He also taught those who were to become the protectors of the Archipelago, including Jason. But Medea's betrayal prevented that, and the Silver Throne sat empty for almost three thousand years. When John Dee became a renegade, his primary purpose—we thought—was to create and control a king of the Archipelago. But we now know it is much worse—he intends to create the Archimago and open our world to the Echthroi."

"How is it that a renegade Caretaker knows so much that he can cause us such great trouble over and over again?" John said, exasperated. "Not even Burton gave us as much grief as John Dee!"

"Burton never even became a full Caretaker," Twain said, answering before Verne could reply, "but Dee was. And more than that, for many years he was the most significant one."

"Oh, dear," said Jack. "You mean . . ."

"Yes," Twain said. "Before my apprentice, Jules Verne, was appointed to the position, the office of Prime Caretaker was filled by Dr. Dee."

"So what do we do now?" asked John. "I hope you have some sort of plan."

"I always do," Verne said as he removed a trump from his breast pocket. "Gather close, and listen in. The endgame is about to start."

✦　✦　✦

There was nothing Uncas and Quixote could do except follow Aristophanes up the hill on Easter Island. He was walking toward a massive, dark house, which was too Gothic to have belonged there. With a chill, Quixote realized that their detective was not lying—he had been working for another client the whole time, and this edifice they were approaching was the House of Dr. Dee.

"You'll serve Dee, and betray th' Caretakers?" Uncas asked. "Shame, Steve. Shame, shame on you."

"I have been in the service of the Caretakers for over two thousand years," Aristophanes said, his voice gone low and menacing, "and it was not by my own will, but out of necessity—just as it was a necessity to ask for your help to find the Ruby Armor. You needed my machine, but I needed your maps."

"And th' Little Whatsit," said Uncas. "We did a lot more than read maps. We were your gosh-darn partners, Steve!"

The unicorn detective took a deep breath. "Aye," he admitted. "You were. But now that time is done."

Several men were walking from the house to meet them on a broad field. Quixote only recognized John Dee, but Uncas knew the others from his son's enthusiastic descriptions of them, as Fred was a voracious reader of fantastic fiction. Many of his favorite writers—several of whom were dead—were standing before them now.

"Scowlers Lovecraft, Tesla, Cabell, and Chesterton," said Uncas, "John Dee, and Aleister Crowley. And," he added, frowning, "Daniel Defoe."

Defoe bowed and smiled at the badger. "I've met your offspring, I believe," he said with a smirk. "He looked like he'd make good eating. So do you."

"Try if you like, but you'd better do it quick," Uncas said, looking at his watch. "Your dinner bell is about to be rung, you self-righteous—"

Defoe scowled and turned to Dee. "What did we need to bring them here for? Couldn't the unicorn just kill them and be done with it?"

"I brought them," Aristophanes said as he showed them the tarpaulin containing the Ruby Armor, "so they wouldn't go running off to tell their Caretaker friends what I was really up to. And I didn't kill them, because that's not what you paid me for."

"That can be rectified," said Defoe.

"Bring it on," said Uncas.

Lovecraft laughed and walked forward. "Brave words, little badger, when you're surrounded by the enemy."

"Tell you what," said Uncas. "If you surrender now, I'll put in a good word for you with th' Caretakers."

"Surrender?" an astonished Lovecraft asked as he stopped in front of Uncas. "Are you *insane?*"

"You're a storyteller, ain'tcha, Mr. Lovecraft?" Uncas asked. "Well, this is that part of the story where th' heroes snap their fingers and th' cavalry rides to th' rescue."

"Except," said Lovecraft, "you are on an island in the middle of the greatest ocean on Earth, and there is no one who even knows where you are, much less how to ride to your rescue. Face the facts, little animal." He bowed low to look the badger in the eye. "We hold the upper hand. And you have no cards left to play."

"Oh, I gots one," Uncas said, stepping backward as he reached into his jacket. "But it'll do th' trick, I think."

It was a trump. Jules Verne's own trump to Tamerlane House.

"You get all that, boss?" Uncas said into the card.

"Perfectly well," said the voice of Jules Verne. "Bring us through, Uncas."

"It's one of Dee's cursed *cards!*" Crowley snarled. "And it's *open!*"

Before any of the Cabal could stop him, the badger had concentrated on the card, which began to grow. In seconds it was a full-size portal between Easter Island and the Nameless Isles, where, as Uncas had said, the cavalry was waiting to cross over.

"Greetings and salutations," Nathaniel Hawthorne said as he stepped across the boundary of the card. He was carrying a sledgehammer, and he hefted it with purpose. "I'm in the mood for popcorn and cracking skulls. And I didn't bring any popcorn."

Behind him were John, Jack, and Verne, followed closely by Dickens, Twain, Irving, the badger Fred, and Laura Glue, all bearing drawn weapons.

"Keep the portal open," Verne said to Uncas. "More will be coming through in a moment. The advantage is ours."

"It's still Dee's battlefield," said John.

"You have your warriors, and I have mine," said Dee. "I see that you have brought samurai swords. Shall we settle this in the old samurai way, then?"

"What is he talking about?" asked John.

"There's an old story," Verne said, not taking his eyes off Dee and the Cabal, "about two samurai who met on a bridge. Neither one would give way to the other, and so they drew their swords—and instead of attacking, froze. Every little while, one of them would change position, and the other would change his to match."

"A battle of perceived skills, not actual combat," said Hawthorne. "I remember the tale."

Verne nodded, still watching Dee, who seemed only too content to listen in with the rest. "Each was assessing the other's abilities, and they were each so skilled that a single pose revealed a lifetime of training. So each would pose, and the other would assess, and counterpose.

"Finally, after nearly a day and a night, one of the samurai finally realized that he would be beaten, and he bowed, sheathed his *katana,* and stood aside to let the other pass."

"So was it the good samurai or the bad samurai who won?" asked John. "We're dealing with a good-versus-evil matter here, and it would be nice if you'd clarify."

"I can't remember," said Verne. "That was not the point of the story."

"Which is?"

"That assessment of your opponent can also be a weapon," said Dee, "and may decide the battle, all on its own."

"That's the stupidest thing I ever heard," Jack said as he drew a second blade. "We can take them, Jules. That's my assessment."

"Ah," said Dee, "but all the pieces are not yet on the board." He raised a finger, and a door on the house behind him opened. Three William Blakes strode out and joined the members of the Cabal. "Your move."

Verne smiled and cleared his throat. Three more William Blakes appeared in the trump portal and stepped through to join the Caretakers.

Dee frowned. "Matching bishops, then."

"Not quite," said Verne. He waved at the Cabal's William

Blakes, and they walked across the field to join the Caretakers. "Sorry," they said in unison.

"I told you not to trust him!" hissed Tesla. "I mean, them. Him. Whatever it is."

"Six Blakes will not defeat us," said Dee. "What else do you have?"

"We have the resources of every Caretaker who has ever lived, as well as every worthy member of the Imperial Cartological Society who was wise enough to leave," said Verne.

"Point," said Crowley.

"Oh, shut up," said Tesla.

"I have the Ruby Armor of T'ai Shan," said Dee. "Every weapon in the world that can defend against or be used to attack an Echthros is *mine*."

"Actually," Aristophanes said, "in point of fact, it isn't."

Before any of the Cabal could react, the Zen Detective swung the tarpaulin full of armor over his shoulder and quickly crossed over to stand beside Verne.

"Well, I'll be dipped," Uncas said, squinting up at Quixote. "I though we wasn't supposed t' trust him."

"I still don't know that you can," Aristophanes said with a sigh. "I'm not a very trustworthy guy. But I'd like to think I've learned a few things in the last couple of millennia, and one thing I try to do is not be on the wrong side of a battle. They," he finished, gesturing at Dee, "are definitely the wrong side."

"You've always served us well," Verne said, "and I for one have always had faith in you, Steve."

It wasn't possible for the detective's skin to redden, but it was obvious he was uncomfortable with the compliment. "I made a bad choice a long time ago," he said brusquely, "and I've worn the punishment on my skin ever since. That's a difficult weight to carry without some kind of remorse."

"We have a contract, detective," Dee hissed.

"You never paid me," Aristophanes shot back, "and the Caretakers made me an offer you can't match. No deal."

"If you were on our side all along," said Uncas, "then why did you let them think you were on their side a'tall? And why bring us here?"

"Because," said Verne, "we really did need Steve to find the armor, and Dee would never have let that happen if Blake hadn't convinced them that he would do it for the benefit of the Cabal. And he brought *you* here, so you could bring *us* here."

"That's pretty smart," said Uncas.

"Thanks," Verne and Steve said together.

Verne turned back to Dee. "Your move."

In response, Dee raised his hand, and suddenly the doors of his house all opened at once. The fields behind the Cabal were flooded with every manner of foul creature who had ever haunted children's nightmares: the half-men Wendigo; the skull-headed Yoricks; and a dozen other kinds of monstrous beings who had been collected from the Archipelago years earlier. Now they were led by Dee's new lieutenant, William Hope Hodgson.

"I have an army," said Dee, "and I have your people to thank for it. Burton gathered them, and Kipling led them. They may have defected to your side, but the army is still mine."

"And I," Verne said, "have *goats*. If you want to surrender gracefully now, Dee, I'm sure no man here will think the less of you for it."

Without waiting for a response, Verne opened a second

trump—this one to Lake Baikal, where three of the Caretakers were waiting to step through.

Kipling, Houdini, and Conan Doyle came through the portal, then clambered for safety atop the rocky ledge as a wave of armor-clad battle goats swept past, heading straight for the enemy.

"Hello, Hodgson," called out Houdini. "I see you've finally found your proper position in life."

"Hello, you *hack*," Hodgson replied. "You still cheating people with the milk can trick?"

"I never . . . !" Houdini began.

"Save it for another time," said Conan Doyle.

"He can't be serious!" Crowley exclaimed. "*Goats?* He actually thinks we're going to be afraid of goats?"

"I don't know," Defoe said, hesitant to voice his skepticism. "Those badgers don't look like much either, but give them some stale baked goods and they can take you out at a hundred paces."

"And we hear pretty good too," Fred called out, gesturing for Defoe to cross the field. "C'mon, you dragon turd," he said defiantly. "I'll be your blueberry."

The goats lined up across the battlefield in front of the Caretakers in one long column, three rows deep.

"Help me, help me, Dr. Dee!" Crowley cried in mock terror. "Jules Verne is here, and—and—he's pointing a bunch of *goats* at me!"

Verne's response to the mockery was to raise a finger and gesture to one of the goats. A shaggy, potato-colored goat in heavy armor clanked her way over to the Prime Caretaker.

"My war leader, Elly Mae," he said to the others by way of introduction. He scratched the goat behind the ears and pointed at one of the smaller iconic statues, which stood only twenty yards off to the left.

"Elly Mae!" he commanded the war leader. "Bonk! Bonk the noggin!"

Elly Mae bleated an acknowledgment and darted off toward the statue, picking up far more speed than any of them would have expected in a goat.

She lowered her armored head and struck the statue with a tremendous bonk that threw her back on her haunches.

"Hah," said Crowley. "That's just—"

"Wait," said Verne.

With a great noise that sounded like an enormous tree splitting, a crack ran up the height of the statue, and it shattered into a dozen pieces.

"Shades," hissed Tesla.

"I'm in awe," said Jack.

"Meh," said Elly Mae, and ambled her way back to rejoin the ranks of the battle goats.

"Cavorite armor, laced with runic silver," Verne said, smiling broadly. "We've been working on it for years, and the goats know how to use it. Nothing your creatures of Shadow have can penetrate it. And now the goats are angry. You shouldn't have made them angry, Dee."

"You can still rejoin us, Kipling," Dee said, moving his attention to a different kind of attack. "What Burton once offered you is still there to be taken. Your son can still be returned to you."

For the briefest of instants, Kipling seemed to hesitate before steeling himself and shaking his head.

"Why not?" Dee exclaimed, the slightest tinge of frustration starting to creep onto his voice. "Isn't it what you want? To have your son again, living and whole?"

"My son died honorably," said Kipling, "and my time with him is cherished—but past. To try to reclaim it would be to mock those memories. And while you are right, that I do long to be reunited with him, I have learned something from these men." He looked at John and smiled. "Sometimes there are things that are more important to the world than what I want."

Across the field, Crowley slapped his head. "Idiot," he grumbled. "I told you not to even try to tempt him, Dee."

"Shut up!" Dee said, striking Crowley a blow across the face. The game was not going as he had planned.

"I gave you a chance," Dee said to Kipling. "My army is going to tear you all to pieces."

"Oh, I really don't think that's going to happen," Kipling replied. He walked to the front of the battle lines and began to recite a verse:

From ghoulies and ghosties and long-leggedy beasties and all creatures which go bump in the night may the good Lord pre-serve us, amen.

"Hah!" Lovecraft barked. "What, is that supposed to be some kind of a prayer?"

"Not a prayer," Kipling said, smiling slyly. "A *Binding*."

There was a low vibration in the air as the invocation Kipling spoke triggered the Binding, which swept through the ranks of Dee's army like a plague in London. As one, all the Wendigo, Yoricks, and the rest of the creatures that had been in the thrall of the Lloigor crossed the field, where they formed ranks behind Kipling, who bowed gracefully at his opponent.

"My bishop takes your pawns, Dee," said Verne. "All your pawns. Your move."

"I have just one left," said Dee.

To John's right, next to Verne, Dr. Raven suddenly appeared out of nowhere. Verne was startled, and slightly puzzled, by the Messenger's appearance.

"Dr. Raven!" John exclaimed. "What are you . . . ?"

"All good things happen, Caveo Principia," Dr. Raven said to John, "in time."

Dr. Raven strode away from the Caretakers and across the field to stand next to Dr. Dee. He turned to face his friends from Tamerlane House, and as he did so, his form shimmered and changed. He youthened, and where Dr. Raven had been standing there was now a younger version, not much older than Edmund McGee.

Only this younger version wore two watches: the silver watch of Verne's Messengers and the Caretakers, and the ebony watch of the Cabal. He also wore one of the silver rings, but none of that was what struck fear into those on the Caretakers' side of the battle-field.

As he walked, the Ruby Armor of T'ai Shan vanished from the bag Aristophanes had carried it in and reappeared—on the young Dr. Raven.

He was now wearing the armor Jules Verne had told the Caretakers would give the bearer near-infinite control over time and space—and he was standing with the Lloigor Dee.

"That," said Dr. Dee, "is checkmate, my dear Verne."

. . . in all three faces, the eyes blazed with the flames of vengeance.

Chapter Twenty-Two
The Furies

✦

The skies over the beach at Corinth suddenly grew dark. As Rose cradled the body of Gilgamesh in her arms and tried to understand what had happened, the others formed a protective triangle around them.

"That was not worthy of a queen," Bert said, "and not worthy of a Dragon."

Azer seemed to take pause at the Caretaker's admonition. "This world was meant to be ruled," the Dragon hissed, "not cultivated and given over to *children*—even one who calls himself a king."

"That decision," said a voice that echoed across the sky, "was not yours to make."

Above their heads, where the clouds were swirling together, a terrible apparition appeared.

The woman was ten feet tall, with flowing robes, and appeared at times to have three faces, or perhaps even three bodies. The lines were indistinct and flowed into one another so that it was never entirely clear if this was one woman, or three. One of them carried a hammer, and another carried a torch. But in all three faces, the eyes blazed with the flames of vengeance.

"Hecatae!" Aristophanes breathed. "The goddess of the cross-roads!"

Rose was equally taken aback by the extraordinary apparition before them. The goddess was, after all, of the pantheon Rose had been raised to believe in. She gently set Gilgamesh's body aside, then knelt and bowed her head. Following her example, Bert and Charles did the same.

"The Furies," Rose said under her breath. "The first Morgaine."

"He was of the blood of the firstborn," the Hecatae said, voices ringing out in a terrible harmony. "It is forbidden to harm those of his line. Forbidden to spill their blood. Forbidden to kill."

Aristophanes cowered. "I had to do it!" he cried. "I had no choice!"

"You have not acted as a man should," said the Hecatae. "You have acted ignobly, in haste, and for the weakest of reasons, little philosopher. And henceforth, you shall be marked, so that those around you in this world will know of your crime, and of your shame."

The Hecatae pointed a finger at Aristophanes, who was looking to Medea, hoping for some kind of intervention or protection—but the sorceress ignored him. He had done what she wanted, and now she had no further use for him.

"Wait!" he called out to the goddess. "Wait! I can serve you instead! Please!"

"You wished the freedom from responsibility to your fellows," one face of the goddess said. "Now you shall stand forever apart from them, cloaked in the colors of a king, that all shall know your coward's heart."

As she spoke, Aristophanes clutched at his arms, which had

begun to turn crimson, as if he were covered in blood, then a rich shade of purple, which began to spread up his arms and over his entire body.

"You wished the attentions of the crowd," the second face of the Hecatae said, "now be among the most sought-after of creatures, desired and pursued, so that your only refuge will be in the shadows you served this day."

The philosopher screamed, as a bright red whorl appeared on his forehead. In moments it had grown into a bump, which burst with a spray of blood and skin as a horn sprouted out of his skull.

"And you, who spoke truths, and betrayed those truths with the sting of a blade, now be in the flesh what you summoned with your actions, and never know another's touch, lest they be poisoned by your own.

"All these things you now are, and forevermore shall be, until the end of time. So mote it be."

With a scream, Aristophanes fled, running across the top of the dunes. In seconds he had disappeared from sight, but the companions could still hear the echoes of his scream.

The Hecatae turned their attention to Medea.

"It is forbidden," they said again. Medea scowled. She had hoped—no, expected—that using the philosopher as the hand that killed Gilgamesh would spare her the vengeance of the Furies. Apparently that was not true.

Medea stood facing them, defiant. "It was my right, as queen," she said, all but spitting out the words in anger. "My right to rule. He should have chosen me, not my husband!"

"Jason will pay the price for his choices, as you will pay the price for yours," the goddess said. And Medea's stolid composure finally cracked, and she fell to her knees, trembling. "But it's not fair!" she cried. "Before his betrayal, I believed I was to rule with him, on the Silver Throne! And after, if not with him, then in his stead! And this old fool," she continued, gesturing at the body of Gilgamesh, "would not grant me his blessing, even though he knew I would kill him if he did not!"

"Your words have caused great pain, great misery," they said to the cowering Sorceress, "and so has your vanity. Thus, forevermore, these shall be all that you have."

"Daughter," the Hecatae said to Rose. "You are our heir. You are the Moonchild. And you have served us honorably and well. The punishment must come from your hand."

Rose gasped. "Me?" she exclaimed. "How—how could I possibly punish her?"

"It is your responsibility," the Hecatae said. "None other has the right. And we have already given you the means, in your past, which is still our time to come."

Rose nodded slowly, finally realizing what the goddess meant. She reached into her pocket and removed the multifaceted mirror, which, on impulse, she threw into the air. It began to spin and expand—and then it began to draw the queen of Corinth toward itself.

Medea screeched in protest, but the sound was drowned out by a thunderclap. Lightning flashed, blinding the companions for a few seconds, and when their vision cleared, Medea was gone.

Where she had crouched was the mirror, larger now, which reflected nothing of its surroundings, but which bore the image of the sorceress. She was weeping and pounding her fists against her transparent prison.

"So mote it be," said the Hecatae. "Forevermore you will dwell as an image in a cave of images, until such time as your children have redeemed you."

The mirror vanished from the sand. In that instant, Azer, who had witnessed all that had transpired, stroked her wings into the air and took flight.

Rose and her companions saw, for the first time, something that was rarely if ever seen in the face of a Dragon—*fear*.

"Stop," said the Hecatae, and in midair the Dragon froze, suspended above them.

"You have betrayed your calling," the Hecatae said, their voices reverberating in the air, "and a price must be paid."

"I did not choose this!" Azer hissed through gritted teeth. "I did not choose to descend! He did this, he chose—"

"The choice was yours, as it always was," asserted the Hecatae. "And the price you pay is yours also, until such a day when you choose to serve someone other than yourself once more."

As they watched, Azer transformed from a Dragon to a terrible, beautiful woman, then back to a Dragon again, before finally falling to the sand as a half-formed Dragon with the woman's head and torso. Azer had also been transformed to stone—to *cavorite*.

"This is why she brought us here, to her home on Autunno," Burt murmured to the others. "This was the day she became the Sphinx."

Rose looked up at the goddess. "What of Gilgamesh?"

"We shall bear his body to the Elysian Fields," the Hecatae said, dropping closer to gather up the old regent's body, "where he shall rest until such a time as he may be called upon to rise, as great heroes are needed to do."

"I'm sorry," Rose said. "I'm sorry we couldn't stop them from killing him."

"Daughter," the Hecatae said as they bore the body of Gilgamesh up into the clouds, "you have ever pleased us with your choices, and you please us still. Go now, and do the work you have set to do, and be not troubled. For your path is just."

With that, the Hecatae disappeared. The clouds cleared, and the moon was rising. And once more, the companions were alone.

They spent the night on the beach, if for no other reason than that the Ring of Power was familiar and gave them a measure of security. Although after what had happened with Azer, none of them was quite so sure summoning Dragons would ever be such a good idea again.

"Samaranth always did mention," Charles said, "that he wasn't a tame Dragon. The same apparently went for his wife."

"What are you doing?" Rose asked Edmund, who had been busying himself with his drawings all night.

"I've tried using the old trump to Tamerlane House," he replied, "but we're simply too far away from any other recorded zero points for it to work across space and time. It still isn't working well enough. And anyway, if we try to go back, whether by trump or by trying to find the keep, we'll be going in the wrong direction."

"Wrong direction?" Charles exclaimed. "Don't you want to go home?"

"What I want," Edmund replied, "is to put an end to all this and restore what's been broken. But it's not my choice—it's yours." This last he said not to the Caretaker, but to Rose.

"Mine?" she exclaimed, blushing slightly. "We're all making these decisions together, I thought."

"Yes," Bert said, "but it's been obvious all along who is the true factotum. Rose, you are the true fulcrum of history, and we will do as you feel best. It's your choice. Decide, and we will follow."

"Then I say yes," Rose answered. "We should keep pressing into the past. What are you thinking, Edmund?"

"While Gilgamesh told us about the First City," he explained, "I was making a drawing on one of the trump sheets in the *Geographica*. I think we can use it to go there and learn more about the Architect."

"And this one?" Rose asked, picking up a copy he had made on a sheet of bronze. "What is it for?"

"The Caretakers."

"So they can try to rescue us somehow?"

"No," said Edmund. "Not to rescue us. We can't risk anyone else interfering with the course of Chronos time. We've done too much already."

"What's happened had to happen, because it did happen," Bert said, "and it could not have happened any other way."

"So if we aren't going to ask someone at Tamerlane House to attempt a rescue," said Charles, "what is it you're thinking of, Edmund?"

"He's thinking of a legacy," said a voice behind them. "That's the only reason to craft something in metal."

It was the shipbuilder, Argus.

"I heard rumors that the queen had disappeared," he said,

"along with her Dragon. And in their place, the Corinthians have found a Sphinx. They have asked me to stay and help them create a temple around it, as a tribute to the gods."

"If you want," Charles said, "there's a nice, sturdy little building about a mile that way that would be perfect for the Sphinx."

Argus nodded. "And what of Medea?" he asked.

Rose looked at her friends. "She got the immortality she was looking for."

The shipbuilder smiled and sat, leaning back against the rock to soak in the sun. "No one lives forever, my young friend."

"Maybe not forever," said Rose, "but long enough for all practical porpoises."

"Hmm?" Argus raised his head. "What do you mean?"

"It's a badger joke," Rose replied, grinning. "It means you will live long enough to do what we want to ask of you."

"Ah," Argus said, bemused.

"The Corinthians asked you to construct the temple of the Sphinx?" Edmund asked.

Argus inclined his head in answer.

"Would you do something for me?" Edmund asked. "Just a small, simple request?"

"What is it?"

Edmund handed him the drawing on the sheet of bronze. "When you're done," he said, "simply place this inside the base of the Sphinx."

Argus frowned. "When the structure is finished, it will be considered sacred," he said. "It isn't meant to be used. No one will ever go inside, not without some extreme compulsion to do so."

Now it was Edmund's turn to smile. "That's what we're counting on. Will you do it?"

Argus smiled. "I am here in the sun today because of your good will," he said. "I will do as you ask."

After breakfasting together, the companions bid Argus good-bye and began to gather their things together. All except Bert, who had rolled up his trousers and waded out into the ocean.

Rose waded out of the surf and toward Bert. The Far Traveler had been consulting his watch, with a grim expression on his face. As she approached, Bert hurriedly snapped the watch closed and adopted a halfhearted smile that failed miserably to conceal his turmoil.

"What is it, old teacher?" Rose asked him. "That's the third time this morning you've checked your watch and not been pleased with what you saw there."

Bert sighed. "I didn't realize that anyone had noticed."

"I think we've all noticed," she said, looking over to where the others were, near the rocks. "I'm just the one who lost the draw about which one of us would mention it to you."

"As Argus said," Bert remarked with tears in his eyes, "no one lives forever."

"Your time isn't up yet," said Rose. "Come and see—our young Cartographer has a plan."

"Verne sent us the only object he knew would survive eight thousand centuries," Edmund was saying to the others, "namely, the Sphinx. So at some point in the future, he is going to have to open it, and when he does, he'll find the bronze I made of the drawing and know where we're going to go—because I've tested it, just a little, and I think we can use the drawing I made as a chronal map."

"That's a tall order," said Rose. "According to Gilgamesh, it was thousands of years ago."

"We're going to have to try it," Edmund said. "I believe in you, Rose. And I think that I've drawn it accurately enough. We can see this through. We just have to believe."

She took his hand, and the others stood next to them inside the Ring of Power as Edmund concentrated on the drawing he held.

The young Cartographer's hand trembled, and he bit his lip, hoping the pain would steady his hand before the others noticed. In response, Rose squeezed his arm supportively, then added her own concentration to the drawing. But still, nothing happened.

And then, deep inside the drawing . . .

. . . a leaf fell from a tree and floated gently on a breeze in the faraway place, coming closer and closer until it brushed past Edmund's fingers before drifting out of the frame.

The trump shuddered, and then, much to the companions' relief, it began to grow and expand, until it was more than a dozen feet across, and nearly as high.

"Well done!" Charles exclaimed, applauding respectfully. "I doubt the original Cartographer could have done any better."

"Well," Bert began.

"Hush that," Charles admonished. "He did very well."

"Shall we?" Edmund said, beaming at the others.

"Absolutely," said Rose.

On the broad field in front of the house on Easter Island, the two armies faced each other, waiting, each wondering what this new defection meant to the Great Game.

"I am the true heir of this armor," said Dr. Raven, "and I always have been."

"Dee's plans do not serve reality," Verne said cautiously. "They serve the Echthroi."

"This is not the only reality there is," Dr. Raven said, his voice even and clear. "There are other places and times where a man may reinvent himself, even if that reinvention is a fiction."

"Is that what he is?" John said to Verne. "Is he a fiction, like Henry Morgan?"

"No," Raven said, answering John's question. "Not like that. I am as real as you are, Caveo Principia. But sometimes, reality gets in the way of what's really important. And the only way you can learn what you need to learn is to practice being fictional for a while."

"There is no time for this, boy!" hissed Dr. Dee. "We must—"

Dr. Raven cut him off with a glare. "There is time enough for everything, Dr. Dee," he said, as if it was a command. Dee opened his mouth to respond, but Dr. Raven had already turned back to face the Caretakers.

A thought passed among several of the Caretakers, which John and Twain confirmed with a glance—that exchange with Dee was significant. Not only was Raven not cowering before Dee, as the other members of the Cabal did, but he had in fact put him firmly in his place—which seemed to be subservient to Raven.

Was it possible? John wondered in amazement. Was Raven the true leader of the Cabal, or had Dee actually created a paladin he couldn't control?

"Even now," Raven continued, "we're creating new fictions

where we all play our parts. But it's all just a continuation of an old tale, already begun."

He nodded to the members of the Cabal, who scrambled up the hillside and into the House, where they closed the doors behind them. After a moment, and a last glance at Verne, Dee followed.

Verne took a few steps toward the armor-clad Messenger, hoping that with Dee gone, the younger man might be more open to reason, but Raven held up a hand, stopping him.

"This part of the story is ended. It's time for us to go away, to lick our wounds and rewrite the fiction that is to come." He turned to John. "We will meet again, Caveo Principia, on a different battle-field."

Something clicked in John's mind, and he moved in front of Verne, who was at a complete loss for words.

"You know me, don't you?" John asked Raven. "Somehow we know each other, from before Jules introduced us."

For the first time since he had donned the armor, Raven smiled—and it was a brilliant, charismatic smile.

"We do, Caveo Principia," the young man replied. "Long ago, and also, not so long ago.

"I am the age you see now because I choose to be. It was the age when I was brought back into this story by Dr. Dee and his Cabal. It was when I had lived through another fiction, in another time, and I had leaned to make my own way in the world.

"In that fiction, I chose my own names. There were times I was known as Jude, and others as Obscuro, the Zen Illusionist. At one point I thought I might be Saturn, but it turned out I was mis-taken. At some other point in my future, I become Dr. Syntax, and then Dr. Raven, and it was as Dr. Raven that I made myself known to the Caretakers and began my work as one of the Messengers for Jules Verne. But," he continued, "before that, you and I met, and I was known by a different name."

With a thrill of fear, John suddenly realized what that name might have been, but he wasn't sure he should ask it, for fear the young man would vanish altogether.

"If you're serving the Cabal," he said carefully, "then why become Dr. Raven at all? Was it merely to spy on us?"

"Not spy, observe," said Raven. "I had been left entirely alone, and I found out, also on my own, who had created the life they thought I should lead, and why. In learning about the Cabal, I came to learn of the Caretakers—and I wanted to know you better."

"It hasn't helped you to choose more wisely," said John, "or else you just hadn't learned enough about the difference between right and wrong."

"You may be correct on the latter point," Raven ceded, "but as to the former, I haven't chosen anything yet. I'm simply assessing the rest of the pieces on the board."

As he spoke, the entire structure of the House on the Borderlands began to shimmer, as if it had been immersed in a wave of hot air. A moment later Raven himself began to shimmer and grow transparent.

"We always seem to be seeking what we already have," Raven said as he grew less and less visible, "like Jason of old, searching for his lost sons. Even when he found them, he couldn't see them. And so even with a father within their reach, they were still orphans."

He stopped and considered what he'd just been saying. "That's a terrible story," he said, frowning. "I don't much like it. The tale of Odysseus and Telemachus is a better one, I think."

"Odysseus missed his son's entire childhood," said John. "Telemachus never knew his father when he was growing up."

"Ah, but Odysseus did return to Ithaca," said Raven, "and Telemachus never, ever, believed that he had been abandoned. His father was simply delayed—and when he finally returned, Telemachus helped him to reclaim his kingdom. Yes," he said, nodding in satisfaction. "That's a much better story."

"Telemachus was Rose's uncle," Verne said cautiously, having found his voice, "and John Dee is no Odysseus."

"No, he isn't," the young man said, keeping his eyes focused on John, "but perhaps I might become a Telemachus."

Behind him, the House had begin to shudder and rise. Stones were dropping from the foundation, and strange lights were beginning to appear all around it.

"Telemachus," John said, realizing that only moments might be left, "what was your *first* name?"

"I don't remember the name I was given at birth," the newly self-christened Telemachus said, "but when I was a child, I chose my own name, as I have done before, from the books I was reading, from the stories I liked. And although I couldn't read, the animals who cared for me could, and I loved being read nursery rhymes as I fell asleep each night there in my room on Paralon."

Hearing that word, Jack sat up in shock, staring at the nearly vanished Telemachus, as did all the other Caretakers. Verne gave a quiet moan and dropped to his knees, and John barely managed to remain standing himself.

"Oh, my dear Lord," John said under his breath.

"Yes," Telemachus said, his smile now showing as much sadness as goodwill, "we met in a place that was once in the future but is now long in the past, and my name . . .

". . . was *Coal.*"

And in that instant, Telemachus, once called Coal, the missing boy prince of Paralon, vanished, and with him, the entire Nightmare Abbey.

The young man, John Dee, the Cabal, and the House on the Borderlands were gone.

. . . *hanging next to his own . . . was a full-size portrait of a woman.*

CHAPTER TWENTY-THREE
Choices

❖

Bert and Edmund had no idea where they'd suddenly appeared, but Charles and Rose recognized where they were immediately—not because there were familiar landmarks with which they could orient themselves, but because there were no landmarks at all. There was literally nothing but an expanse of whiteness in every direction. There was no shadow or context to even indicate whether they were in a small white space or standing on an infinite expanse of nothingness. There was, simply, nothing. And then he appeared.

The old man was just as Charles and Rose remembered him. Thin, impossibly old, and hunched more with responsibility than with age. He was dressed simply in a white embroidered tunic, and he was holding a watch—one of the silver pocket watches that belonged to the Caretakers. And he was smiling—at *them*.

"Excellent, excellent," he said, the smile never faltering. "You are right on time. This pleases me. It pleases me very much. How are you, Rose?"

"You remembered this time," Rose said. "I'm well, thank you."

"And you?" he said, turning to Charles. "You've been youthened. I don't know that the hair suits you, though."

"Oh, ah, thanks," said Charles. "I think."

"And you," the old man said to Bert. "You have traveled often in time, I think."

Bert drew himself up to his full height and answered with as much dignity as he could muster. "I have. They call me the Far Traveler."

The old man nodded as if Bert had just recited a grocery list. "Oh, do they now? Yes, yes," he said, waving his hand and smiling—condescendingly, Bert thought—"that's very nice for you. Now, Rose," he continued, "what is it that you're trying to do, that brings you back to Platonia?"

'We're trying to discover the identity," she said, "of the Architect of the Keep of Time."

"The Architect?" the old man said. "That's what you've gone flitting about searching for? Why would you need to know that?"

"Because, ah," Charles stammered, "we broke it. That is, I did. I broke time."

"You broke time, you say?" the old man answered. "Not possible. Time is eternal. Only we ever change."

"We broke the keep," said Bert, "and now we're just trying to find a way to repair it."

"But," the old man said gently, "that was not the reason you wanted to go into the future, was it?"

Bert took a breath as if he meant to respond, then slumped inward and pursed his lips, thinking. "No," he finally said, looking not at the old man, but at his companions. "No, it really wasn't. Not the entire reason, anyway."

"I understand," the old man said, resting a hand on Bert's shoulder. "But it is the others who must go on." He checked his watch. "Your time is nearly done, Far Traveler."

"There's still a task to be done, still work—," Bert began, but he stopped and looked mournfully at Rose. "It is time, isn't it?"

"In more ways than one," Charles admonished. "You've done all you needed to do, Bert. Now it's up to us."

The old man turned to Edmund. "It was a very good drawing you made. If you had been using it in conjunction with an actual time machine, instead of just as a trump, you'd have made it through easily."

"Oh," Edmund said, crestfallen.

"Don't worry, young Cartographer," the old man said. "You get better. Much better."

He turned to Rose. "And you, Rose. All I can tell you now is to trust in yourself, and to not be afraid of your shadow."

She blinked at that. "Why would I be?"

"You shouldn't," he repeated. "It's the only way you will find it again."

The old man bowed his head and spun the dials on his watch. "Close your eyes," he instructed them, "and do not be afraid. Remember . . . ," he finished as his voice began to fade, "all good things happen . . .

". . . in *time*."

John Dee's house on Easter Island was gone—but not all the members of the Cabal had vanished with it. Standing there in the expanse of grass where the house had been was Daniel Defoe.

"No!" Defoe howled with rage. "You promised! You promised me, Dee! I want my amnesty!"

"Amnesty?" asked Jack. "What is he talking about?"

"His time is nearly up," said John. "If he doesn't go back to Tamerlane House right now, he'll vanish forever."

"This," said Jack, "does not sound like a problem to me."

The former Caretaker had no choice but to approach his former colleagues and appeal for mercy. He had been abandoned by his masters and had no way to even begin to fight against the army of creatures that he faced.

"Defoe has a watch," said Verne. "Why doesn't he use it to escape?"

"And go where?" asked Jack. "There are wards around Tamerlane House. And without one of these," he said, holding up his ring, "he's not getting in."

"Well, we can't just leave him here to die in a puff of smoke," said John. "I say we take him back to Tamerlane and then decide what's to be done with him."

"Shame, shame," Uncas said to Defoe. "You could have come with us and been a part of everything. But now you belong to no one at all."

"All I need," Defoe said, "is one of those rings, and I can hide forever in Tamerlane House. And you, little rodent, are going to give it to me!"

Suddenly Defoe pulled a wicked-looking dagger out of his boot and launched himself at Uncas.

None of the other Caretakers was close enough to rush to Uncas's defense—but someone else was.

Aristophanes threw himself against the little badger just as Defoe thrust out the dagger. Uncas tumbled to the grass unharmed, but the former Caretaker had delivered a terrible wound to the detective—a wound that Aristophanes had returned in kind. Defoe had plunged the dagger deep into Aristophanes's stomach, but he had forgotten that the detective was not unarmed.

The Zen Detective had removed his hat—and for the first time, the Caretakers saw that his horn had not been filed down, as he claimed. It was stout and sharp and protruded from his brow very much like the thorn on a rose stem—and it was lodged deep in Defoe's shoulder.

Defoe pulled back and screamed in pain as the horn stabbing into his shoulder broke off, dissolving into poison.

"I'm sorry," Aristophanes gasped, clutching at his wound. "So, so sorry."

"It's only a flesh wound," Defoe spat. "You'll die long before I do."

"You're wrong, Daniel," Verne said sadly. "Steve has all the time in the world, and you don't."

The Prime Caretaker turned to the others. "You've noticed no one ever touches Aristophanes. That's because he was cursed, thousands of years ago. His skin is toxic enough to make a man seriously ill. But the poison in his horn is potent enough to kill any living thing. Even," he said, looking at Defoe, "those who reside in magic portraits. I'm sorry, Daniel—but you brought this on yourself."

The alarm on Defoe's watch suddenly rang, but was drowned out by his frustrated howl. He pushed away from the Caretakers and fell to the grassy field just as the last rays of the setting sun streamed across the top of Easter Island.

"May God have mercy on you," said John, "if it be right that he do so." And with one last cry of anguish, Daniel Defoe evaporated into the sunlight.

✦   ✦   ✦

John turned and looked at where the other Caretakers were standing protectively around Aristophanes, who had gone pale from the wound, which was bleeding profusely.

"That's Defoe taken care of," said Hawthorne, "but what's to be done with the unicorn here?"

"We're taking him back to Tamerlane House," Verne said. "I owe him a payment, and I think he's more than earned it."

"But the armor is gone!" the detective exclaimed. "I didn't fulfill—"

"Earned it," Verne said again, looking at Uncas. "Armor or no, you've earned it."

"Let's go," John said, suddenly weary. "There's nothing more to battle over here now."

"No," a voice said from somewhere behind them. "Not here. And not now. But soon, Caretaker."

It was Defoe's shadow speaking—with the voice of someone else they thought was a friend.

The shadow twisted and spun on the ground, assuming first Lovecraft's silhouette, then Dee's, and Defoe's, and finally it coalesced into the shape . . .

. . . of a cat. A Cheshire cat.

"Grimalkin?" John said in disbelief. "Surely you haven't betrayed us too?"

"Not betrayed, boy," the cat answered, licking at its fur as if entirely unconcerned that it had just revealed itself as an enemy agent. "I am simply doing what I must, what the Binding compels me to do."

"The collar," said Verne. "I never realized it, but it must be the collar. Dee has had a spy with us all along."

"There are greater Shadows than I in the House of Tamerlane," Grimalkin said as he began to fade in the twilight, "and they are no less prisoners of fate, for as surely as this ring around my neck binds me, so are they also bound."

"But why reveal yourself to us now?" Blake asked, suspicious. "We would never have known."

"There are Bindings, and there are covenants," Grimalkin replied. "I was bound to serve Dee, but I did not choose it. Long ago I made a covenant, which I am only now able to fulfill by giving you a warning."

"What warning?" said John.

"The girl," said Grimalkin, as he continued to vanish. "The Grail Child. Her shadow is not her own, but an Echthros, and everywhere she has gone, or will go, the Cabal can also go. She carries with her the seed of your destruction. Do with this what you will.

"Farewell, little Caretaker," the Cheshire cat's grin said as it vanished into the rising light. "And fear not. We will meet again—and sooner than you think."

And then the cat was gone.

"All right," John said to the other Caretakers. "Let's get Aristophanes home and tended to. I'm done with all this business today."

It took some time for the Caretakers to sort out who would be responsible for dispersing or attending to what parts of the Wendigo-Yorick-goat army, so it was late in the evening when John finally pushed open the doors of the great hall at Tamerlane House to collapse into a chair with a tall, tall ale. However, he had one more shock to experience before the day was over.

"We tried to summon you sooner," said Jack. "Someone is here to see you."

The other Caretakers, who were crowded around the table, parted, and John saw who was sitting in the chair opposite Jack.

"Hello, my boy," said Bert. "It's . . . good to see you again."

Joyfully, John rushed forward and embraced his mentor. "Bert! You're back!" he exclaimed, looking around. "Where are the others?"

"It's just him, John," said Jack. "But the others are fine, as far as we know. Bert's just been telling us about it all now."

Bert clapped John on the shoulder, then took Jack by the hand. "I wish Charles were here," he said. "Otherwise, it's just how I had hoped it would happen."

"How you hoped what would happen?" asked John.

Almost as if answering his question, Bert's watch began to ring with a strange chiming—a noise John had never heard it make before.

Bert's eyes grew wide, and he looked up at the other Caretakers, several of whom had moved closer to him. "Oh dear," he stammered. "I've forgotten. I needed one more sitting with Basil. . . ."

His eyelids fluttered, and he grew pale. Twain and Dickens moved around the table and gently helped the Far Traveler sit back down into his chair, where he immediately slumped into the cushions.

"What is it?" John whispered to Verne. "What's happening to him, Jules?"

"Not him," Verne replied quietly. "Well, not just him, I should say." He checked his own watch and nodded as if in confirmation. "That's it, then," he said to the others. "H. G. Wells has died."

The house at 13 Hanover Terrace, in Regent's Park in London, had no runes carved in its doors, nor along its hallways, or in the room where the aged author took his last breath. But even though those attending to the body could not see those who had come to pay their respects, he was not without friends.

"It was a good death," said Baum.

Franklin nodded. "Agreed."

"Do you think he'll join us?" Lewis Carroll asked. "I mean, join us as, you know, a spirit?"

"No, I think not," said Macdonald, looking around the room. "I think he did the things he needed to do, and that was enough."

"He also knows," Franklin added, "that he has a brother elsewhere to continue the work. So there's no need for him to stay the way that . . ."

He couldn't quite bring himself to finish the sentence, nor did he need to. And for a brief moment, the thirteen ghosts gathered around the bedside of H. G. Wells felt a twinge of regret, and the slightest envy.

Then, murmuring words of blessing and personal prayer, the members of the Mystorians took their leave of London.

In the portrait gallery of Tamerlane House, the Caretakers Emeriti gathered closely around the new portrait that had just been hung at a place of honor in the center of the west wall, among the portraits of the greatest and most distinguished members of their group.

"That really should have been my spot, you know," grumbled da Vinci, "instead of over in the corner, next to George Gordon."

"Oh, shut up, Leo," said Irving. "Someone had to be next to him."

"I resent that," said Byron.

"Hush, all of you," said Twain. "He's waking up."

It was a slow rise back to consciousness. The light around him came up gradually, but when his vision finally cleared, Bert could see the gathered Caretakers all beaming up at him.

"Let me," Verne said, placing his watch into the frame just out of Bert's field of vision. "Here," he said, extending his hand as the frame blazed with light. "Come join us, Far Traveler."

Bert stepped out from the portrait on the wall and into the midst of his colleagues, who burst into spontaneous applause.

"Basil finished," Bert said, a bit dazed by all the attention. "He finished my portrait."

He wheeled around to Verne. "What if I'd changed my mind and decided I wanted to be a tulpa instead?" he said. "I thought there'd be more time to choose."

"Bert, my old friend, my old sparring partner," Verne said, clapping a large hand on the smaller man's shoulder. "You chose long ago, and we both know it. This was the path you preferred. And so we'd had it prepared for some time."

"Humph," Bert snorted indignantly. "You could have prepared a tulpa, too, if you'd wanted."

Twain puffed on a cigar and blew a plume of smoke into the air. "Certainly we could have," he said, "but then if you'd chosen not to take it, someone would have had to spend a lot of time dispersing it. They don't just go away on their own—not right away, that is. And it wouldn't have done to have another you wandering around where just anyone's will could step in and mess with his—your—head."

"Ah," Bert said. "So you figured it out. The Cabal did steal the wisp of a shadow of—"

"We'll deal with that later," Verne said quickly, glancing at Jack.

"It also means," Bert said with a heavy sigh, "that I'm restricted to Tamerlane House. Forever."

"Forever may be just long enough," Dickens said with a wink at Twain, "and I think staying at Tamerlane House will be your preference from now on. Turn around."

"What the blazes are you talking about, Charles?" Said Bert. "I'm not—"

"Bert," John said, grasping his mentor by the shoulders. "Trust us. Just turn around."

Still complaining under his breath, the Far Traveler did as he was told—and what he saw left him without words or breath.

There, hanging next to his own portrait, was a full-size portrait of a woman. She was lithe, and simply dressed, and had the innocent beauty of one who had only known trust and love in her world.

Bert reached a trembling hand out to touch the portrait, but he stopped an inch short of it, as if it were a gossamer dream that might disappear if it were disturbed. "Jules," he whispered softly. "How . . . ? How did you . . . ?"

"Using young Asimov's psychohistory, the Mystorians had calculated a high probability of the might-have-been future you and the others traveled to," Verne replied, "and with each passing day, the percentage grew higher. So I took a risk and took your machine into your future. Into *her* future. I knew that someday you would try to return, if you found the means to do so. But my messengers found more and more future timelines were *changing*. And I didn't want to risk that this future would change, and take with it any hope of finding Weena again.

"Because you'd been there, you had already made it a zero point, so I knew I could get there. I was a little more concerned about having the same trouble you did in getting back."

Something clicked together. "Your missing year," Bert said. "The year we thought you'd been lost, right after John, Jack, and Charles became the Caretakers."

"Yes," Verne answered, nodding, "and just as I founded the Mystorians. I didn't want to risk making an anomaly out of myself—being a tulpa, I had no clue what that might do to the timestream—so I pulled back and returned a year after I'd started. But I accomplished what I went there to do."

"I explained to her why you hadn't been able to return, and I got her permission to take this." He pulled a small cube out of his pocket. "I took along one of my optical devices and took a remarkable image of her that I could bring back."

Bert reached out again but still didn't dare touch the picture. "So . . . this is a photo, then?"

"Not at all," Verne said, smiling broadly. "A portrait. One of Basil's best."

"There was a concern," said Twain, "that you wouldn't be able to bring her back, the way you had Aven. But only the one machine had ever gone that far into the future, and having used it once, you had no way of going back—until young Rose and Edmund came to us."

"But Jules could go, using my machine," Bert said. He spun

and looked at Verne, then the other Caretakers, all of whom were beaming. "You were all in on this?"

"Some of us knew," said Dickens, "but you know Jules—he likes to keep his own counsel. This is the first time we've invited a non-Caretaker to have their portrait done, and so this was hung only a few moments before yours was."

"So she's never come out of the portrait?"

Twain stepped forward and gave Bert a push. "No," he said with a grin, "we figured that'd be your job, young fellow. So," he added, "what are you waiting for? Bring her out!"

He paused. "Will it—will she still be . . . my Weena?"

For the first time, Poe spoke. "She will. She chose this, freely, and as with your own portrait, she lives because her aiua is the same. Only the form is different."

"As you are still our Bert, she'll be your Weena," said Twain. "Do it, son."

Trembling, Bert removed his watch from his pocket and placed it into the indentation at the base of the frame. The light from the portrait washed over him as tears streamed down his face.

Almost hesitantly, a hand reached out from the portrait. Bert took it, and gently pulled her forward into the room, before losing his composure and embracing her amid the cheers and claps of his colleagues.

"Hello, my sweet Weena," he said into her hair as they embraced. "Welcome home."

Somewhen, far in a future that may yet come to pass, the Barbarian who had become a Dragon prepared to tell his stories, as he had once done long ago, in another life, another time.

It had taken nearly a year of hard labor to create a new amphitheater where the stories were told, to re-create a stage and carve rows of terraced seating out of the earth and stone that formed this small, natural canyon.

Above, the Dragonships watched, silent sentries and testaments to a long-vanished past—a past from which the storyteller had come, and to which he could never return. Not without a price that was too costly to pay, and risking all the good work that had brought him here, to this place, and this time.

Sometimes, at night, he could feel the waves of time shimmering off the stones of the amphitheater, and in those moments, he felt regret—but as always it passed quickly, for he knew that being in this place was his destiny. It was his great work.

"All the best stories are written in books," he said, smiling at the children clustering around him, "as they once were, and as they will be again."

The grown-ups who came to listen sat to either side of him, as the smaller children clambered on top of them, eager, waiting to hear the story he would tell them tonight.

"It has been one thousand nights, and I have told you one thousand stories," the storyteller said, "and tonight will be the one thousand and first.

"How?" the children asked. "How does it begin, Sir Richard?"

"It begins," he said, "as all the best stories do. Once upon a time . . ."

Chapter Twenty-Four
The Ancient of Days

❖

"Praise the Lord and bless Basil's sainted head," said Bert as he took a seat alongside John in the banquet hall. "He was prepared, or I ought to say, Jules was. They had a portrait waiting to be finished in the event of my eventual demise. I was rather hoping it would be later in coming—but their second surprise more than made up for it."

Weena sat alongside Bert and was being patiently cheerful as she tried to take in everything her husband was explaining to her. It would be a very long process, but in the meantime, Bert was happy—and still among the Caretakers. And to John and Jack, that was all that mattered.

Bert had told most of his story when he reappeared at Tamerlane House, and the rest after he died and then reemerged from his portrait. And while the Caretakers were happy to know that Charles, Rose, and Edmund were safe, the rest of what he'd had to say about the city of Dys, and Lord Winter, and the Last Redoubt created more questions than answers.

Almost as much attention was being paid to the newest resident of Tamerlane House: the Zen Detective, who took a seat next to

There, in the near distance, was the City of Jade.

Uncas, and who, to everyone's surprise, was not only fully recovered from his wound, but was noticeably lighter skinned than when he'd arrived.

"That's not all that's changed," Aristophanes said. He reached across the table and offered Verne his hand—which the Prime Caretaker took and shook, once, then again.

"Uh, isn't he supposed to be poisonous to the touch?" asked Quixote. "No offense, Steve."

"None taken," the detective replied, "and no longer."

"That was the deal we made," said Verne, nodding at another guest who was just joining them at the table—the Messenger Beatrice.

"His horn is still quite deadly," Verne said, "but the Lady Beatrice is just as adept at removing toxins as she is at creating them."

While everyone commented on Bert's account of the future, no one was quite bold enough to address the matter of Lord Winter, which was just fine with Jack. He was less concerned about the ancient future and the possibilities that a shadow-version of himself might become a tyrant and a servant of the Echthroi, than he was about the still-missing boy prince, who Blake confirmed had been Dr. Raven all along.

"Raven—or Telemachus, I guess—is, in fact, the boy Coal," he told the Caretakers. "When I discovered it for certain, I was not in a position to leave Dee's House, and the Cabal were watching me too closely to send a message out. But there is no doubt—he is the missing prince."

"But Dr. Raven was looking for the boy too, wasn't he?" asked Jack. "How is it he kept his true identity so well hidden?"

"He's a true adept, like Rose," said Blake, "maybe even better than she is."

"But why couldn't we find him?"

"He was in a might-have-been in the future," said Verne. "That's the only place where Defoe could have hidden him where we'd have little hope of ever finding him."

"Why?" asked John. "You find things lost in time all of the, ah, time."

"In the past, yes," said Verne, "but the future is a different matter. The past already exists, and thus can be treated as archaeology. What we want is there, it just needs to be looked for patiently enough. But the future is all possibility, and must be treated as psychohistory. And even Isaac's best techniques can do little to find one lost child amid a myriad of possible futures."

"It was Crowley who figured out that the Sphinx could travel not just in time and space, but also between real time and might-have-beens," said Blake. "That's how we knew that it could be used to give a lifeline to Bert and the others when we realized they'd gotten lost in their own might-have-been."

"But shouldn't they have gone to the same time, uh, place, that Bert had?" Jack asked. "Isn't it a zero point?"

"That may be my fault," said Shakespeare. "We think, but can't be certain, that the cavorite platform is what threw them askew. I'm working on it."

"Wait a moment," John said, thinking about everything they'd discussed. "Blake, you said that Defoe couldn't go retrieve Coal because they didn't have the Sphinx—because we had it here. Why couldn't we use it to go after him ourselves once you knew how to track him?"

"Because of how the Sphinx works," Poe said from his alcove above. "The payment she has always required has been a human life—a price Defoe and the Cabal would willingly pay, which we would not."

"But a life wasn't required for Bert and Rose and the others to use in the future," said John.

"Because Rose had the only other thing Azer would accept," said Verne. "The ability for Azer to choose her own redemption, and the promise of being a full Dragon again. Despite the sum of those efforts as they stand, I still believe it was all worth the risks we've taken."

"Worth the . . . ," John began, astonishment choking his words. "But Jules, we lost the armor! To a possible enemy who can now do almost anything!"

"Yes, but you heard the boy," Verne replied. "He's still deciding what to do, and how he'll choose. For all we know, he's already on our side, and working against the Cabal from within."

John blinked a few times, then looked over at Jack, who was sitting with an inscrutable expression on his face. Wordlessly, John rose from his chair and walked to the head of the table, where he delivered a devastating right cross directly to Jules Verne's jaw.

The Prime Caretaker went sprawling across the floor as blood splattered across his shirt and coat. He rolled over, his eyes flashing with anger, preparing to lash out over the unfair blow. . . .

And then he realized that not a one of the Caretakers Emeriti had risen to his defense. John stood next to his chair, panting with anger and effort, and Jack sat where he was, with a slightly stunned look. But all the other Caretakers had remained in their seats, and only a few even dared to meet his eyes.

"Well," Verne said heavily as he pulled himself to his feet and straightened his waistcoat, "I see that your opinion of me is in the majority, young John."

"No more secrets, Jules," John said, his voice firm and steady. "The warning about the Echthroi that was given to Rose last year, when she was told to seek out the Dragon's apprentice, the whole key to the restoration of the Archipelago—it's all there in that one simple phrase. *No more secrets.* And keeping secrets seems to have been all that you've done, since even before we met.

"Even nearly losing our friends to that might-have-been," John continued. "You even planned for *that*, didn't you?"

"Now, John," Twain started to say, "how could he possibly—"

"If he didn't know," said John, "then why did he have Quixote and Uncas steal the Sphinx a *year* ago, when we were in eighteenth-century London?"

"I know he hasn't always planned for the big picture," Bert said, trying to steer the discussion into more pleasant waters, "or else he'd have made other plans for Richard Burton instead of letting him defect to the ICS."

"It's too bad you didn't think of that earlier in your career as Prime Caretaker," John said to Verne. "Burton would have made an excellent candidate for a new Mystorian."

Jack chuckled at this, as did one or two of the Caretakers Emeriti—but Verne didn't even smile, or acknowledge the comment except to keep a level gaze at John. At first John thought Verne simply misunderstood what he'd suggested—and then he realized, Verne did understand. Far too clearly.

John rose slowly from his seat. "How long?" he asked, his voice low and vibrant with restrained anger. "How long has Burton been working for you, Jules?"

At this, several of the other Caretakers gasped in dismay, and Bert simply put his head in his hands. Chaucer, Spenser, and Cervantes clucked disapprovingly, while da Vinci gave a small smile of smug satisfaction. Poe, for his part, simply continued to observe impassively from above.

"Since just after the Dyson incident," Verne said, still looking steadily at John.

"Chaos," John muttered, shaking his head. "It's all chaos, Jules."

"Entropy is life," said Poe. "Chaos is life. Perfect order is stagnation, is death. Only in disorder is there the possibility of change."

"So what do we do now?" John asked. "Of what are we still Caretakers?"

"We continue the work that we are doing," said Verne. "We monitor the events of the world and ensure that Dee and his cohorts don't manage to cause any trouble. We keep our eyes and ears open for young Telemachus, so that when the time comes, we might help him choose our side instead of theirs. We continue to develop the new mandate of the Imperial Cartological Society to seek out new apprentice Caretakers to further the spread of knowledge about the Archipelago with those who would help us protect it. And . . ."

"And," said Twain, "we wait."

"Yes," Verne said, nodding. "We wait. And see if Rose manages to do the task she has been set to do since the moment she was born."

"And how long do we wait?" asked John. The frustration he felt was evident in his voice, if not his expression, which remained steadfast and calm. "Do we wait a year? Five? Ten? Twenty? How long a time do we wait for some sign of them before we make some sort of effort to find them and help them?"

"Our part in Rose's quest is done . . . at least for now," Verne added quickly. "They will either find the Architect and the secret of the keep, or they will not. It's now entirely out of our hands."

"Well," John said, "I hope the angels are watching, and send them whatever help they need."

"I'll drink to that," Shakespeare said, lifting his glass and winking at Jack. "I was just thinking the exact same thing."

Rose opened her eyes to find she was no longer in the white space of Platonia. Instead she was standing on a gentle slope that overlooked a magnificent city.

Gilgamesh had remembered the details of the First City far better than he believed he had, and Edmund had transcribed them as an illustration on the parchment with remarkable fidelity.

There, in the near distance, was the City of Jade. It would have been impossible to mistake in any landscape, but here, in this time, it was all-dominating.

"By Jove," Charles said, hugging Edmund. "Well done, my boy. Well done!"

"Take a deep breath, breathe it in," Rose said. "That's the air of a new world, a world that is whole and unbroken. A world," she added with a note of relief, "that knows nothing of Shadows."

"It doesn't really feel any different . . . ," Edmund began to say, but then, as he spoke, he realized that wasn't quite true. It was different, in the same way that the Night Land of Dys in the ancient future was different from 1946.

Just ahead of them was a paved footpath. A boy was approaching, carrying a large, flat marble tablet. He looked like a normal child, except for two things: The expression on his face was one of someone far older than he appeared, and he bore markings on his forehead identical to those of the Winter Dragons.

Involuntarily, Edmund took a step back. "More Lloigor?" he said, swallowing hard. "Are we back in the Night Land?"

Charles shook his head. "Look around," he said, sweeping about with his hands. "There is nothing of the Echthroi here. No darkness that isn't natural, and no chains cover the sky. And the boy may appear strange, but he's not a Lloigor. I'd stake my right arm on it."

The boy stopped when he saw the companions looking at him. He scrutinized them, puzzled. "You really are unusual creatures, aren't you?" he said with unabashed curiosity. "You must be in the Book—but I can't seem to remember you. What was it you were called again?"

"I'm Rose, and this is Edmund," she said, gesturing at the others, "and this is Charles."

"I am Nix," the boy replied, frowning. "You should know me by my countenance."

Rose laughed. "By my body and blood," she said, hands on her hips. "I don't think I've ever seen such a mirthless child as you. Not in my whole long life. If she were here, Laura Glue would give you *such* a beating."

"I am not a 'child,'" said Nix, "I am the second assistant Maker of the thirty-fifth Guild of Makers, of the nineteenth Host of

Angels of the City of Jade." He punctuated the statement with a huff. "And now, having conversed with you, I am thusly behind schedule, and with little regret, I must repair."

"Pardon me," Edmund said pensively. "But did you say you were an *angel?*"

"Of course I am an angel," Nix said, so irritated he spat as he spoke. "How did you get Named if you aren't even complete enough to know that?"

It was only then that Nix really noticed Charles—in particular, his height.

"Oh!" the angel said. "I beg forgiveness. I did not realize . . ." His eyes narrowed, and he looked Charles over from top to bottom, seeming to note the pale color of his skin and his burgundy hair as much as his features. "You carry no sigil," he said at length. "Are you Nephilim?"

Charles had been observing the angel's reactions and sensed the loaded nature of this question. "No," he said quickly. "Seraphim."

Nix visibly relaxed. "Ah," he said, consulting his tablet. "I apologize. There are many powers and principalities whom I do not know arriving for the summit."

"Yes, the summit," Charles said. "Can you tell us where it is? We've only just arrived and have not yet gotten our bearings."

Again Nix looked at them suspiciously, as if there were something amiss. But he couldn't quite put his finger on it, and still, they were in the company of a Seraphim. . . .

For emphasis on Charles's request, Rose reached into her bag and withdrew the hilt of Caliburn, just enough to show that she carried a weapon. Nix nearly dropped the tablet.

"I am already late," the angel said, glancing down at whatever list was scrolling across the stone tablet, "and I would be later still were I to tarry any longer with you. But I can tell you how to find someone who can. He's likely got nothing better to do."

"That should do nicely," Charles said. "Thank you. Who is he?"

"He is a minor Namer from a minor guild," Nix continued as he began to immerse himself in his tablet once more, "but as I said, he is more likely to be able to help you than I. He is the eldest of us all, save for perhaps one or two of the original masters of the upper guilds, and therefore quite useless."

"And is he an angel as well?" asked Edmund.

Nix snorted his disdain but didn't bother even turning around to answer the question. "Of course he is," the angel called back over his shoulder. "What kind of question is that for minions of a Seraphim? There are none here in the City of Jade save for the Creators and the Created, and even those who add little value to the work may still contribute. You will find him in the lower rooms of the tower just ahead."

"How will we know him?" Rose called out.

"Ask for him," Nix answered as he disappeared over the crest of the hill. "His name . . .

". . . is Samaranth."

"The rest of the household is sleeping, I take it?" John said to Jack as he entered the gallery at Tamerlane House and took a seat next to his colleague.

"Yes," Jack said, offering his friend a cup of Earl Grey. "It's been a very, very long season, but it's an old habit, I'm afraid, this working till the wee hours. I've just been working on some notes for integrating more of the Little Whatsit into the curriculum for the ICS."

"That was an inspired choice," John said, "renaming it as the International Cartological Society."

"All Warnie's idea," said Jack. "He never really approved of it being called 'Imperial.'"

The Caretaker lowered his head and sipped at his tea. "They haven't failed, you know," he said softly. "It isn't over, John."

"How?" John murmured. "How do we know they haven't failed? We've had no word at all, and it's been months!"

Jack gripped his friend's arm in reassurance. "Because," he said steadily, "we are still here. The world continues to turn. And the Echthroi have not defeated us."

"Will it all be worth it, in the end?" John asked. "All this effort, and all that we've had to endure?"

"It's worth protecting the stories," Jack said simply, "when the stories are all we have left to protect."

"I miss him," John said suddenly. "I miss Charles."

"So do I."

"Ah, well," John said, rising. "It's getting late. Thank you for the tea."

"Gentlemen," a voice said from the far end of the gallery. "Before you retire for the evening, may we show you something?"

The speaker stepped forward into the light. It was William Shakespeare. Laura Glue and the badger Fred were with him. "With your permission." He said mildly, "I think we should move this discussion outside. I may have discovered a way to help our friends."

◆   ◆   ◆

John and Jack followed the trio outside Tamerlane House, to see what it was that Shakespeare had built.

"This hasn't exactly been authorized," Shakespeare explained, "so we've been working on it on the sly, just Laura Glue, Fred, and I. We wanted to make certain it would function before we showed anyone, and you two gents are the first."

The group traipsed across a rickety, fragile-looking bridge that had been hastily constructed to make Shakespeare's latest creation, which he called the Zanzibar Gate, easier to reach. To build it, he had commandeered one of the smaller border islands to the west of the main island where the house stood, and had constructed it there, just past where the wooden bridge ended.

The Zanzibar Gate was shaped like a Mayan pyramid and was about twenty feet high and half again as wide, with a fifteen-foot aperture in the center. It stood at one end of the small island, looming like an old monolith that had existed for ages—giving that impression in part because of the ancient stone of which it was constructed. There were symbols carved into the settings at several points along its radius, and on the right, a pedestal lined with colored crystals that could be used to activate the gate.

"It is, I have reason to believe, truly representative of the best of both worlds," Shakespeare said, beaming. "The technology I have integrated into it will allow us to travel into the future, and then it can be used in the same way as the keep to travel into the past. The design is, if I do say so myself, flawless."

Laura Glue suppressed a giggle, remembering how difficult it had been to get him to admit that he had any kind of proficiency at all, much less claim credit for his work. And now the opposite was true—he was good at what he did. And more, he reveled in it.

"I don't believe it!" John said, marveling. "You've repurposed the stone from the actual keep! Brilliant!"

"The doors are gone, as Sir Richard had noted, as is the original bracing," Shakespeare explained, "but the bracing was merely for support, and the doors were to create focal points. The power itself is located in the stones."

"How did you get these?" Jack said in amazement as he examined the flame-scorched stones of the gate. "When we set fire to the second keep, I assumed the remains were left in Abaton. And after the Archipelago fell . . ."

"Abaton isn't in the Archipelago," said Fred. "It exists in one of the Soft Places, which abut this dimension. We had access to them the entire time—but, like you, we believed the power was in the doors. It wasn't. Only Will figured that out."

"So the trip into the deep past you've proposed is possible?" asked Jack.

"Yes, well," Shakespeare said hesitantly. "In theory. There's only one slight glitch to the gate I haven't yet been able to overcome."

"Uh-oh," John said, frowning. "Here it comes."

"It operates on the same principle as the doors within the original keep," Shakespeare said with obvious melancholy. "Through the work I had been doing with Rose and Edmund, we can basically calibrate it, and point it at the time and place we need to go. . . . But we still can't activate it, not without a power source—and the keep operated on a very . . . ah, *unique* source of power."

"How unique?" asked John.

"The Dragons," Shakespeare said. "Without a Dragon on one side or the other, there's no way to activate the portal. The stones simply won't work. And we've tried everything we can think of— but in truth, we really just need a Dragon. And unfortunately for us, there are no Dragons left."

Epilogue

❖

Somewhere beyond Elsewhere and Elsewhen, the last of the Dragonships waited.

It had carried out the duties for which it had been created, including this, the last voyage into the Archipelago of Dreams. It had been many years since its creation, and it had grown accustomed to waiting, and serving. This was its purpose, its function.

Those who had sailed the ship here to what was once a great island had not returned. So the ship waited on the long, lonely expanse of sand where it had landed, but no one came.

Then there was an explosion of darkness at the center of the island, followed by a spreading shadow that covered land and seas alike. The island was slowly consumed, but still, no one came to take the ship away, to find safer waters or another sheltering harbor. The ship vibrated with restless energy, anxious for action, but it held its place and waited. Then, finally, when the darkness had nearly devoured the island and rose up to blot out the sun itself, the Dragonship decided to act.

Gradually, almost painfully, it slid itself back into the waters from where the beach had begun to make a claim on the ship. Farther down, another of the ship's siblings had not been as fortunate—but *then, that ship no longer had a living Dragon on its prow.*

Somewhere within, the Dragonship felt a pang of shame and regret, then steeled itself against the distraction of the emotions to better focus on the task at hand as it turned from the island and headed for more open waters. The darkness sweeping across the horizon behind it was almost as foreboding as the darkness ahead.

The Frontier was a living storm front, and the very air reverberated with the constant sound of thunder. From ocean to the limits of the sky, lightning flashed and exploded with violent energies, and the sea itself rose up into crushing waves that battered the ship as it crossed the threshold.

The journey across the expanse of the Frontier seemed to take an eternity. In reality, it was only a thousand years. In times past, the transition was between worlds, from the Summer Country to the Archipelago of Dreams, and back again. But the Archipelago was no more, having been swallowed up by an evil from outside space and time—and what was hours or days on one side was centuries on the other. The ship was crossing the boundary between entropy and order, and it was not an easy passage.

The stresses of the transition nearly ripped the ship apart—stresses that it bore because it was built by a Maker; and because it had will. Will to endure. Will to return. Will, because something greater had reached across the vast distances and spread of years and called to the Dragon within—and it was a call it could not deny, from someone it could not abandon.

Someone to whom the Dragon had given its heart.

Someone to whom the Dragonship it had become was determined to return.

Someone who needed the help that only it could provide. And so it would not brook failure in this—it would, somehow, cross the uncrossable barrier.

And then, it was through.

The ship slid roughly onto another beach, on an island that was of both the Archipelago and the Summer Country. In the distance were the familiar towers and minarets of the place that was its home—the one place the ship had sought to find.

The last of the Dragonships had returned to Tamerlane House at last.

The Black Dragon *had come home.*

Author's Note

❖

This is not the book I intended to write.

In point of fact, it isn't even the book I *wrote*—not at first. Between the initial draft of a book and the final revision there are often a lot of changes made, but I don't think I've revised anything as dramatically as I did between the first two passes of *The Dragons of Winter*.

There are challenges that are unique to writing series fiction, the biggest of which (for me) is making sure that each book is a standalone read while keeping the momentum of the overarching storylines going. It was difficult with Book Four, harder with Book Five, and darn near impossible to do with Book Six. I think the realization that the final volume was quickly approaching only added to the difficulty. I'd known for a few years now that Book Seven would be the conclusion of the story I began with *Here, There Be Dragons*, and so it was tempting to leave a lot of threads unresolved in Book Six. By now readers have become accustomed to my unusual mix of literature, history, mythology, and pop culture, and fully expect that the details (of which there are many) really matter, that story bits planted in one volume may not fully spring into bloom until a later book. But that wasn't the reason for the change.

I rewrote the book in its entirety to make certain that it fulfilled the primary goals—being a satisfying read while advancing the series storyline—while also augmenting the one thing I felt was lacking in the first go: *hope*.

I rewrote the entire book in order to point everything toward these final pages of the epilogue, to those final lines, to the *last* line. Because to me, that last line is what ties together the entire series. It is what matters most to me, in both fiction and in waking life—the knowledge that when it seems everything is on the verge of utter disaster, someone will still step forward, extend a hand, and say, "Don't sweat it. I've got this," and be believed, and in doing so restore hope where before there was none.

I love the idea of someone being capable of saving the day—that's part of what makes all heroic fiction so thrilling, I think. I've tried to instill that in my own work, and I knew that I was going to be bringing everything together in the final volume in a (hopefully) exciting and satisfying way. But while this book had all of the necessary dramatic elements, and all of the really fun things I enjoy writing, it was lacking in hope. And that, to me, is too necessary an ingredient to exclude. The first draft, as it stood, was already a good book—but I needed what I'd written to be questioned aloud. And once that was done by my editors, the path was absolutely clear to me.

The story was a huge amount of fun to write. I'd been waiting a while to use some of the new characters, like Aristophanes; the same goes for the collected Mystorians. Uncas and Quixote all but write themselves; young Telemachus opens up the backstory to include some of my other works; and the chance to include battle goats made me a hero to my children. But all of that whimsy and spectacle and drama was to get to the last pages of doom and despair, so that I could end with the epilogue that I wrote.

The conclusion is coming, but no story—not even that of John, Jack, and Charles—is ever truly over (this is a series involving lots of time travel, after all) and there is one more chapter to go for the most unlikely hero of them all, who chose redemption, and in doing so, restored hope. I can't ask any more of a character, or a book.

James A. Owen
Silvertown, USA